BLOODY TRAIL
OF THE
MOUNTAIN MAN

D1015972

Look for these exciting Western series from bestselling authors
WILLIAM W. JOHNSTONE
and **J. A. JOHNSTONE**

The Mountain Man

Preacher: The First Mountain Man

Luke Jensen, Bounty Hunter

Those Jensen Boys!

The Jensen Brand

Matt Jensen

MacCallister

The Red Ryan Westerns

Perley Gates

Have Brides, Will Travel

The Hank Fallon Westerns

Will Tanner, Deputy U.S. Marshal

Shotgun Johnny

The Chuckwagon Trail

The Jackals

The Slash and Pecos Westerns

The Texas Moonshiners

AVAILABLE FROM PINNACLE BOOKS

BLOODY TRAIL
OF THE
MOUNTAIN MAN

WILLIAM W.
JOHNSTONE
and J. A. Johnstone

PINNACLE BOOKS
Kensington Publishing Corp.
www.kensingtonbooks.com

PINNACLE BOOKS are published by

Kensington Publishing Corp.
119 West 40th Street
New York, NY 10018

Copyright © 2019 J. A. Johnstone

All rights reserved. No part of this book may be reproduced in any form or by any means without the prior written consent of the publisher, excepting brief quotes used in reviews.

This book is a work of fiction. Names, characters, businesses, organizations, places, events, and incidents either are the product of the author's imagination or are used fictitiously. Any resemblance to actual persons, living or dead, events, or locales is entirely coincidental. To the extent that the image or images on the cover of this book depict a person or persons, such person or persons are merely models, and are not intended to portray any character or characters featured in the book.

PUBLISHER'S NOTE
Following the death of William W. Johnstone, the Johnstone family is working with a carefully selected writer to organize and complete Mr. Johnstone's outlines and many unfinished manuscripts to create additional novels in all of his series like The Last Gunfighter, Mountain Man, and Eagles, among others. This novel was inspired by Mr. Johnstone's superb storytelling.

If you purchased this book without a cover, you should be aware that this book is stolen property. It was reported as "unsold and destroyed" to the publisher, and neither the author nor the publisher has received any payment for this "stripped book."

All Kensington titles, imprints, and distributed lines are available at special quantity discounts for bulk purchases for sales promotions, premiums, fund-raising, educational, or institutional use. Special book excerpts or customized printings can also be created to fit specific needs. For details, write or phone the office of the Kensington sales manager: Kensington Publishing Corp., 119 West 40th Street, New York, NY 10018, attn: Sales Department; phone 1-800-221-2647.

PINNACLE BOOKS, the Pinnacle logo, and the WWJ steer head logo are Reg. U.S. Pat. & TM Off.

ISBN-13: 978-0-7860-4354-5
ISBN-10: 0-7860-4354-7

First printing: December 2019

10 9 8 7 6 5 4 3 2 1

Printed in the United States of America

Electronic edition:

ISBN-13: 978-0-7860-4355-2 (e-book)
ISBN-10: 0-7860-4355-5 (e-book)

THE JENSEN FAMILY
FIRST FAMILY OF THE AMERICAN FRONTIER

Smoke Jensen—*The Mountain Man*
The youngest of three children and orphaned as a young boy, Smoke Jensen is considered one of the fastest draws in the West. His quest to tame the lawless West has become the stuff of legend. Smoke owns the Sugarloaf Ranch in Colorado. Married to Sally Jensen, father to Denise ("Denny") and Louis.

Preacher—*The First Mountain Man*
Though not a blood relative, grizzled frontiersman Preacher became a father figure to the young Smoke Jensen, teaching him how to survive in the brutal, often deadly Rocky Mountains. Fought the battles that forged his destiny. Armed with a long gun, Preacher is as fierce as the land itself.

Matt Jensen—*The Last Mountain Man*
Orphaned but taken in by Smoke Jensen, Matt Jensen has become like a younger brother to Smoke and even took the Jensen name. And like Smoke, Matt has carved out his destiny on the American frontier. He lives by the gun and surrenders to no man.

Luke Jensen—*Bounty Hunter*
Mountain Man Smoke Jensen's long-lost brother Luke Jensen is scarred by war and a dead shot—the

right qualities to be a bounty hunter. And he's cunning, and fierce enough, to bring down the deadliest outlaws of his day.

Ace Jensen and Chance Jensen—*Those Jensen Boys!*
Smoke Jensen's long-lost nephews, Ace and Chance, are a pair of young-gun twins as reckless and wild as the frontier itself . . . Their father is Luke Jensen, thought killed in the Civil War. Their uncle Smoke Jensen is one of the fiercest gunfighters the West has ever known. It's no surprise that the inseparable Ace and Chance Jensen have a knack for taking risks— even if they have to blast their way out of them.

CHAPTER ONE

Big Rock, Colorado

It had rained earlier in the day, and though the rain had stopped, the sky still hung heavy with clouds, as if heaven itself was in mourning. Phil Clinton, editor of the *Big Rock Journal,* made the observation that this was the largest number of citizens ever to turn out for a funeral in Big Rock, Colorado. The Garden of Memories cemetery was so full that the mourners spilled out of the grounds and onto Center and Ranney streets. The service had been held in the First Baptist Church, which shared the cemetery with St. Paul's Episcopal. And because of Sheriff Monte Carson's popularity, memorial rites were held in St. Paul's even as the funeral was being conducted in the Big Rock Baptist Church.

Father Pyron stood with the mourners, but it was the Reverend E. D. Owen who was conducting the burial service. Monte Carson, dressed in black, and with his head bowed, stood alongside the coffin of Ina Claire, his wife of the last fifteen years.

Sheriff Carson had invited Smoke and Sally Jensen, Pearlie Fontaine, and Cal Wood, all of whom were also wearing black, to stand with him next to the open grave. That was because the four represented the closest thing Monte had to a family.

It was quiet and still and Reverend Owen stood there for just a moment as if gathering his thoughts. In the distance a crow cawed, and closer yet, a mockingbird trilled.

The pastor began to speak.

"We have gathered here to praise God and to bear witness to our faith as we celebrate the life of Ina Claire Carson. We come together in grief, acknowledging our human loss. May God grant us grace, that in pain we may find comfort, in sorrow, hope, and in death, resurrection.

"Monte, we say to you in the midst of your sorrow and loss that we are grateful that your love for Ina Claire was such that we are all able to share in her quiet gentleness and firm resolve to live her life for you, and others. We take joy and relief in knowing that her suffering has ended, and now into the everlasting arms of an all-merciful God, we commit the soul of our beloved Ina Claire. Amen."

Reverend Owen nodded, and six of the leading citizens of Big Rock: Louis Longmont, Tim Murchison, Ed McKnight, Elmer Keaton, Mike Kennedy, and Joel Montgomery, using ropes, lowered Ina Claire into the grave. When the coffin reached the bottom, the ropes were withdrawn, then the six men stepped away. Reverend Owen nodded toward Monte, who stepped up to the open grave and dropped a handful of dirt, which, in the silence, could be heard falling upon the coffin.

"Ashes to ashes, dust to dust, in the sure and certain hope of eternal life," Reverend Owen said.

When Reverend Owen turned and walked away from the graveside, Sally stepped up to embrace Monte.

"We will miss her so," Sally said.

"Thank you, Sally," Monte replied, his voice thick with sorrow.

The funeral reception was held in the ballroom of the Dunn Hotel. Ina Claire had been an orphan and was without any family. She had been married and divorced before she met Monte, but her former husband had died several years ago. The funeral reception was organized by Sally and some of the other ladies in town.

"It's too bad none of Sheriff Carson's family could have been here," Mrs. Carmichael said.

"He doesn't have any family," Mrs. Owen said. "That's why Ina Claire's death is so sad. It has left him all alone."

"But I hear she was suffering terribly with something they call the cancer over the last month," Mrs. Carmichael said.

"Yes, she was. And now, mercifully, her suffering is over. In a way, Monte's suffering is over as well, as he suffered with her."

Smoke and Pearlie had been standing with Monte, but because Smoke thought that their standing together might prevent others from coming up to offer the sheriff their condolences, he put his hand on Monte's shoulder and squeezed.

"In case you need us for anything, Monte, we'll be right over here," Smoke said.

Monte nodded as Smoke and Pearlie walked away.

Smoke had poured himself a cup of coffee and was perusing a table strewn with various pastries when Phil Clinton, the editor of the local paper, stepped over to speak to him.

"You and the sheriff seem to be close friends," Clinton said.

"We are."

"You two have been friends for as long as I have been here. I'm curious. How did you two meet?"

Smoke chuckled as he chose a cinnamon bun. "He was hired to kill me," Smoke said, easily.

"What?" Clinton gasped.

"Once, there was a fella in these parts by the name of Tilden Franklin. He was a man of some importance who had plans to take over the county and he planned on using Pearlie and Monte Carson to help him.

"Then, when I came along and started my ranch, Franklin figured I was in the way. He told Monte and Pearlie that he wanted me killed. Neither one of them would go along with that, and the result was a battle between a lot of Franklin's men, Monte, Pearlie, and me.

"When it was over I offered Monte the job of sheriff here in Big Rock, hired Pearlie on as foreman of Sugarloaf, and those two, onetime enemies, have been my best friends ever since."

Smoke waited until he saw Monte and Sally standing together, then he walked over to join them.

"How are you holding up?"

"I've already been through this once before, Smoke, when I lost my first wife. It isn't fair that I would have to go through it again."

"I can't argue with that, Monte."

"I know everyone is saying that Ina Claire is in a better place," Monte said. "And I know that she is, especially since she was in so much pain toward the end. The laudanum helped with the pain, but to be honest, it sort of took her away from me even before she died, if you know what I mean."

"I know," Smoke said. "And, Monte, I can fully relate to the pain you're going through now."

"Yes, you lost a wife and a child."

Smoke nodded. "Nicole and Arthur. Murdered." For just a moment the hurt Smoke was sharing with Monte became his own, as he recalled returning home to find his family dead. Smoke went on the blood trail, tracking down and killing the men who had so destroyed his life.

After that, Smoke didn't think he would ever be able to love again. But he met a beautiful and spirited young schoolteacher who changed his mind.

"I got over it once before," Monte said. "I can get over it this time as well."

"You will get over it, but don't force the memories of Ina Claire away too quickly," Sally said. Sally had been standing with the two men, listening to their conversation. "I know that there is a place in Smoke's heart where Nicole still lives. I'm not jealous of that, I love him for it, because it tells me how deeply Smoke can love. In fact, even though I never met Nicole, I can't help but think of her as my sister."

"It's funny you would say that, because Ina Claire once said that she thought of Rosemary as a sister. But you don't have to worry that I'll ever forget her," Monte said. He smiled. "I believe, with all my heart, that the thunderstorm we had earlier this morning was just her talking to me. Lord, that woman did love thunderstorms for some ungodly reason."

Sally laughed. "I remember that a thunderstorm came up during yours and Ina Claire's wedding reception. We had it out at Sugarloaf and I told her I was sorry that the reception might be spoiled by the storm, but she said, *'No, I love it! It's just God applauding the fact that Monte and I were married.'* For a long time I thought she had just said that so I wouldn't feel bad about the storm."

Monte chuckled as well. "No, she actually believed that. She told me the same thing."

Sally embraced Monte. "Anytime you feel the need for company, you are always welcome at Sugarloaf."

"Thank you, Sally. With friends like Smoke, you, Pearlie, and Cal, I'll get through this."

The obituary in *the Big Rock Journal* the next day was accorded the honor of appearing on the front page of the paper.

Ina Claire Carson

Ina Claire Carson, 36, wife of Sheriff Monte J. Carson, died yesterday after a long battle with the terrible disease of cancer.

Mrs. Carson was raised in the Baptist Orphanage in Jackson, Mississippi. Because she was left there as an infant by persons unknown, she was without family, save her husband, Sheriff Carson.

Although Mrs. Carson was without

family, she certainly wasn't without friends. Kirby Jensen, better known to his friends as Smoke Jensen, was there with his lovely wife, Sally. Smoke, Sally, and Smoke's two longtime friends and employees, Wes (Pearlie) Fontaine and Cal Wood, were accorded family positions at both the church and graveside funeral services.

Mrs. Carson was well known and well loved by all the citizens of Big Rock. She was especially renowned for her oatmeal cookies, which she graciously baked for all the prisoners in the Big Rock jail.

Although the atmosphere in Longmont's Saloon was never boisterous, it was generally happy and upbeat. Not so today, as even the patrons who had not attended the funeral on the day before, were quiet and respectful. That was because Monte was in the saloon, as were Smoke and Pearlie. Louis Longmont, who owned the saloon, had just read the obituary.

"This is a very nice article about Ina Claire," Louis said. "You and she have been such a wonderful part of our community. I know it will be hard for you, but I also know that you will carry on, providing the steadying influence that will keep Big Rock the fine town it is."

"I have no doubt about it," Mark Worley said. For some time Worley had been Monte's deputy, but six months ago the town of Wheeler was in need of a city marshal, and they sent a delegation to talk to Monte about Mark. Monte gave him the glowing recommendation that got him hired. So far, Monte had not taken on a new deputy. Mark had come to town for the funeral and had stayed an extra day.

"How are you liking it over in Wheeler?" Pearlie asked.

"It's been great," Mark replied. "Oh, I miss all my friends over here, but I've made new friends, and I really like being in charge. Not that I minded deputing for Monte, you understand, but it is good to be the top dog."

Pearlie laughed. "Yeah, well, just don't let it go to your head. You always did think a lot of yourself."

Pearlie was teasing. Actually, he and Mark were good friends.

"I should get another deputy, I suppose," Monte said. "But to be honest, searching for another deputy hasn't been the most important thing in my mind for the last few months."

"Take your time in looking for one," Smoke said. "It isn't like you can't make an instant deputy if there is a sudden need for one."

Monte nodded. "Yeah, that's the way I see it. You, Pearlie, and Cal have helped me out more than once. And I appreciate that, because it means I can afford to be choosy."

"Speaking of deputies, and sheriffs, and all that, I'd better get back to Wheeler and my never-ending battle of fighting crime and/or evil," Mark said with a laugh.

"Thanks for coming over, Mark. I appreciate that," Monte said.

"Smoke, we should get going, too," Pearlie said. "We've got a lot of calves we have to gather."

For a while Sugarloaf had abandoned cattle and raised horses only. But when Smoke's friend Duff

MacCallister introduced him to Black Angus cattle, Smoke had gone back into the cattle business. Angus were a little more difficult to raise than longhorns, but they were many times more profitable.

"What did you say?" Smoke asked.

"I said we needed to get back to the ranch. We have work to do."

Smoke looked at the others and smiled. "Would you listen to this man, telling me *we* have work to do?"

"Pearlie, maybe you don't understand, you are the foreman of Sugarloaf, but I am the owner. Do I need to tell you who is in charge?"

Although Smoke spoke the words harshly, he ended his sentence with a laugh to show that he was teasing.

"We need to get back to the ranch, we have work to do," Smoke added.

"The boss man is right," Pearlie said to the others. "We need to go."

Shortly after Mark, Smoke, and Pearlie left, Monte told Louis good-bye, and walked down to his office. There was nobody in jail at the moment, and because he was without a deputy, he was all alone.

He was unable to hold back the tears.

CHAPTER TWO

Capitol Hill, Denver, Colorado

State Senator Rex Underhill's house sat but a few blocks from where the new capitol building was to be built. His Victorian house was large with wings and bay windows and gingerbread decorating features. He built the eight-bedroom house in the most elegant part of Denver merely for show. It was a gaudy display of ostentation, especially since, except for his servants, he lived alone in the house.

After Senator Underhill finished reading the obituary of Ina Claire Carson in the Denver newspaper, he laid it beside his now-empty breakfast plate.

He thought of the names he had just read; Monte Carson, Smoke Jensen, Pearlie Fontaine, Cal Woods. It was too bad that the obituary was not for one of them. It would be even better, if it could be for all of them.

"Another cup of coffee, Señor Underhill?" The question snapped Underhill out of his reverie.

"Frederica, I have told you to call me *Senator* Underhill."

"*Sí, señor*, uh, *sí*, Senator. Sometimes I forget," Frederica said.

"You are forgetting too many times, and if you don't start remembering, I'll let you and Ramon go and hire some new domestics, perhaps Americans who understand the language so I won't have to keep repeating things."

"I will not forget again, Señor Senator."

Frederica was a plump woman whose dark hair was now liberally laced with gray. Her husband, Ramon, took care of the lawn, and his hair was all white.

"Are you going to stand there gabbing, or are you going to pour me another cup of coffee?" Underhill asked.

"Coffee, *sí*," Frederica said as she poured a dark, aromatic stream of liquid into the cup.

Senator Underhill eased his harsh admonition with a smile. "What would I do if I let you go, Frederica? Where else would I find someone who could make coffee as good as yours?"

"*Sí*, Señor Senator, nowhere else will you find coffee this good," Frederica said with a relieved smile.

Underhill took his coffee out onto the front porch and sat in a rocking chair to watch the vehicles roll by. Here, in Capitol Hill, nearly all the vehicles were elegant coaches, fine carriages, or attractive surreys, for only the wealthy lived in this part of town.

Rex Underhill hadn't always been wealthy. His father had been a sharecropper barely scratching out a living in Arkansas, and even that was gone after the war. When Underhill left home nobody tried to talk him into staying, because his departure just meant one less mouth to feed.

Underhill survived by a few nighttime burglaries here and there, then he graduated to armed robberies. He robbed a stagecoach in Kansas, killing the driver, shotgun guard, and single passenger. Because he left not a single witness, he was never regarded as a suspect for the crime. He got twelve thousand dollars from that holdup, and he moved on to Colorado, where he became the secret partner of a couple of men—Deekus Templeton and Lucien Garneau—in a scheme to take over most of the ranch land in Eagle County. It was a plan that, on the surface, had failed, miserably.

Underhill glanced at the paper again. He had read the obituary because it was about the wife of Monte Carson. Carson was the sheriff of Eagle County. Eagle County was also the locale of the Sugarloaf Ranch and Smoke Jensen. Smoke Jensen was the biggest reason for the failure of the grand plan to own all of Eagle County.

Underhill was fortunate, however. The principals in the attempt to take over Eagle County were all killed. Underhill survived the plan because nobody knew that he had been involved. Also, he had not only been Deekus Templeton's and Lucien Garneau's secret partner, he had also been their banker, providing some operating funds in the beginning, but holding on to the money from a couple of bank robberies that neither Templeton nor Garneau could afford to deposit in a bank. When the two men died, Underhill profited from their deaths, immediately becoming over forty thousand dollars richer.

That was the money he had used to begin his political campaign. He was a state senator now, an office that put him in a position to take advantage of the many opportunities for enrichment that came his way.

Lately, Rex Underhill had been contemplating another political move, one that would greatly increase his chances to capitalize on his political position. He sold influence now as a state solon. How much more valuable would be the influence of a United States senator?

Rock Creek, near Big Rock

Just under one hundred miles west of where Rex Underhill was having his breakfast, six men were staring into a campfire, having just finished their own. They were camped on Rock Creek at the foot of Red and White Butte, about five miles north of Big Rock.

A little earlier that morning the leader of the group, Myron Petro, had proposed a job he thought they should do.

"It'll be like takin' money from a baby," Myron said. The men to whom he was pitching his idea were his brother Frank, Muley Dobbs, Ethan Reese, Wally Peach, and Leo Beajuex. All of the men were experienced outlaws except for Beajuex, who was the youngest of the lot.

"I don't know how you ever got the idea that robbin' a bank in Big Rock is goin' to be easy," Wally Peach said. "There ain't no way it's goin' to be easy on account of Monte Carson is the sheriff there, 'n he sure ain't easy. Hell, he's one of the toughest sheriffs there is anywhere."

Myron grinned. "Sheriff Carson ain't goin' to be no problem at all 'cause, case you don't known nothin' about it, his wife just died. That means he's so all broke up about it that he can't hardly do his job no more."

"I ain't never seen this Sheriff Carson feller but I've sure heard of 'im," Muley Dobbs said. "'N what I've heard is the same thing what Wally just said. Sheriff Carson's s'posed to be one tough son of a bitch. So, how is it that you know his wife died?"

"I heard talk of it yesterday when I was in Red Cliff."

"Yeah, well, I wish they was some way we could be sure," Muley said.

"All right, s'pose you 'n Beajuex go into town 'n have a look around?" Myron suggested. "You could maybe scout the bank whilst you was there, too."

"Nah, don't send the kid," Frank said. "He wouldn't have no idea what the hell he would be lookin' for. I'll go."

"All right, tomorrow you 'n Muley go into Big Rock, have a look around town, then come back 'n tell me what you've found out. We'll hit the bank day after tomorrow."

That night, as the six men bedded down around the dying campfire that had cooked their supper, they talked excitedly about the money they would soon have.

Leo Beajuex listened, but didn't join the conversation. He had never done anything like this before and he was very apprehensive about it. He wasn't going to run out on them—these men were the closest thing to a family he had. He had met them six months earlier, when he was supporting himself as a cowboy on the Bar S Ranch down in Bexar County, Texas.

Actually, saying that he was a cowboy would be a considerable overstatement of his real position. Ron Stacy, owner of the Bar S was a tyrannical boss, especially to someone who was a menial laborer, as Leo was. Whereas the cowboys got thirty dollars a month and found, Leo was paid fifteen dollars. He got the worst jobs on the ranch, and Stacy wasn't averse to physical abuse.

It all came to a head one day when Stacy took a leather strap to Leo because he hadn't cleaned a stall. As it turned out, he had cleaned it, the mess was from a horse that had just been moved into the stall.

Deciding that he had had enough, it was Leo's plan to steal a couple of cows and sell them for just enough money to help him get away. However, while he was in the act of cutting them out, he saw the Petro brothers and the other three men doing the same thing but on a larger scale.

"Boy, if you got 'ny idea of tellin' anyone what we're a-doin' here, we'll shoot you dead," Myron Petro warned.

"Why would I want to tell anyone?" Leo replied. "I'd rather join you."

They rustled forty-nine cows and sold them for twenty-five dollars apiece. That gave them a little over two hundred dollars each, which, for Leo, was more than a year's wages.

There had been a few other, small jobs. They got

a hundred and fifty dollars from a stagecoach holdup, and eight hundred dollars from some stolen mules.

So far, at least since Leo had been with them, there had been no shooting. But when the subject came up this afternoon, Frank said that if they had to, they would kill anyone in the bank, as well as anyone on the street who tried to stop them.

Although Leo had come close, he had never killed anyone, and he hoped that nobody would be killed as a result of the job they were planning now.

As the campfire burned down, a little bubble of gas, trapped in one of the burning pieces of wood, made a loud pop and emitted a little flurry of sparks. Leo watched the golden specks as they rode the rising shaft of heated air into the night sky, there to join with the wide spread of stars.

He wondered what would happen in two more days.

Big Rock

The next day Frank Petro and Muley Dobbs rode into town. Even at an easy pace, the ride into town took less than an hour.

"Lookee there," Frank said, pointing to some of the shops and businesses they were passing. "All them buildings has black ribbons on 'em, so that means for sure that somebody died."

"Yeah, but it don't mean for sure that it was the sheriff's wife what died, without we hear someone say it," Muley said. "'N the best place to hear it said is in a saloon, just like this one."

They were just passing the saloon as Muley pointed it out.

"Longmont's," Frank said, reading the sign. "I don't know, it looks a bit fancy for the likes of us."

"The fancier it is, the easier it is to find out information. Besides I'm a mite thirsty, aren't you?"

"A beer would be good," Frank agreed.

"And maybe a couple hands of poker," Muley added.

"No, I don't know, Muley, I've seen you play poker before. More times than not, somethin' gets your dander up, then you go off half-cocked 'n wind up in trouble. We most especial don't want no trouble today, that's for damn sure."

"You don't worry none 'bout me playin' poker. That's a good place to find things out. You just stand up there at the bar, drink your beer, 'n keep your eyes 'n ears open," Muley said. "If you hear somethin' that don't sound right, let me know."

The two men stepped inside, then looked around.

"Whooee, I sure ain't never seen no saloon this fancy before," Frank said.

The long bar that ran down the left side of the saloon was more than just gleaming mahogany. The front of the bar was intricately carved to show a bas-relief of cowboys herding cattle. The hanging overhead lights weren't wagon wheels and coal oil lanterns as was often the case, but cut crystal chandeliers.

"There's a card game," Muley said, pointing to a table where a game was in progress.

"Muley, be careful. Don't go gettin' yourself into no trouble," Frank cautioned.

With a nod as his only response, Muley walked

over to the table. "You fellers willin' to take on a fifth player?"

"No need for five players, you can have my seat," one of the players said. "I need to be gettin' along anyhow."

"The name is Muley," the big scruffy-looking man said as he took the chair just vacated.

A short while after Frank and Muley rode into Big Rock, Smoke and Sally came into town. Sally could ride as well as any man, but they came in a buckboard because Sally wanted to do some shopping and it would be easier to take the purchases back in a buckboard than on horseback. They drove in from the west, following Sugarloaf Road until they passed the depot and Western Union, at which place Sugarloaf Road turned into Front Street. As had Frank and Muley before them, Smoke and Sally noticed that many of the buildings on Front Street had a black ribbon on the door.

"That's nice of them to honor Monte in such a way," Sally said.

"You aren't surprised, are you, Sally? Monte is a popular sheriff and Ina Claire was well liked," Smoke said.

"*Well loved* is a better description."

"I'll go along with that," Smoke said as he parked the buckboard in front of the Big Rock Mercantile.

"I'll be in Longmont's when you're ready to go back home," Smoke said as he tied off the team.

"Really? And here I thought I might find you in the library," Sally teased.

"Sally, has anyone ever told you that sarcasm doesn't become you?" Smoke asked with a little chuckle.

"You mean besides my mother and father and all four of my grandparents? Oh yes, you have as well."

Sally kissed Smoke on the cheek, then started toward the store, as Smoke crossed the street to get to the saloon.

Owner and proprietor of the saloon was Louis Longmont, a Frenchman from New Orleans, who was quick to point out that he was truly French and not Cajun. The difference, he explained to those who questioned him, was that his parents moved to Louisiana directly from France, and not from Arcadia.

Longmont's was one of two saloons in Big Rock, the other saloon being the Brown Dirt Cowboy Saloon.

The Brown Dirt Cowboy tended to cater more to cowboys and workingmen than it did to professional men, storekeepers, and ranch owners. The Brown Dirt Cowboy provided not only alcoholic beverages and a limited menu, but also bar girls who did more than just provide friendly conversational company for the drinking man.

Longmont's, on the other hand, was more like a club in which ladies were not only allowed, they were made to feel welcome, and assured there would be no stigma to their frequenting the establishment. It also had a menu that could compete with the menu offered by Delmonico's Restaurant, which was just down the street from Longmont's.

Like the other business establishments along Front Street, Longmont's had a black ribbon on the door.

Stepping into the saloon Smoke stood just inside the door for a moment to peruse the patrons.

There were seven men standing at the bar, only one of whom he had never seen before. Three of the tables had customers, and two of the girls were standing near two of the tables, having a smiling conversation with the drinkers. Smoke knew both Becky and Julie and he exchanged a nod with them. He also knew the seated drinkers. There was a poker game going on at the third table, and here Smoke recognized three of the men. Two were cowboys from a nearby ranch and the third was Mike Kennedy. He didn't know who the fourth man was, but there was something about him that gave Smoke a sense of unease.

In addition to those three tables, there was a fourth table. This was Louis Longmont's special table, so designated because nobody but Louis ever sat there unless they were personally invited by Louis.

The pianist was playing, not one of the typical saloon ballads, but a piece by the Polish composer Frédéric Chopin. This kind of music would never be allowed in most other saloons, but it had become a signature for Longmont's.

Tim Murchison, owner of Murchison's Leather Goods, was sitting at the table with Louis, and Smoke, without being invited because Louis had once told him that his invitation was permanent, joined them.

CHAPTER THREE

"I saw you and Sally coming into town in the buckboard," Louis said after Smoke sat down. "Spending your money, is she?"

"What else would you do with money?" Smoke asked.

Louis laughed. "Indeed, and what would be better than to spend the money on a lady as beautiful and delightful as Madame Sally?"

Smoke had taken a seat on the far side of the table, with his back to the wall. Although this would normally be Louis's position he gave it up to Smoke because he knew that over the years Smoke had made many enemies; enemies who wanted him dead so badly that they were more than willing to shoot him in the back. And that wasn't something Louis ever intended to let happen in his saloon.

Smoke kept an eye on the swinging batwing doors at the entrance, but he also studied the stranger at the bar, as well as the poker player that he didn't know.

"Who are the two strangers, Louis? Do you know them?" he asked.

"They came in together," Louis said. "I don't know either one of them, but I heard the poker player introduce himself to the others as Muley. I doubt that's his given name. I can't imagine a mother looking down at her newborn for the first time and saying, *I think I'll call you Muley.*"

"It could have been worse. She could have called him Jackass," Tim suggested.

Smoke and Louis laughed.

"Have you seen Monte today?"

"He's been in here a couple of times," Louis said.

"How does he seem to be doing?"

"He's holding it together pretty well. I think he's going to come through this all right," Tim said.

"I do, too," Louis said. "Ina Claire was sick for quite a long time, so it isn't like her dying came as a sudden surprise to him."

"Yes, at least he has had time to adjust to it," Smoke said. Again he couldn't help but think of Nicole.

"You son of a bitch, you're cheatin'!" one of the cowboys playing poker shouted at Muley. "I seen what you done!"

Muley stood up so quickly that the chair he was sitting in fell over with a loud bang. He drew his gun and pointed across the table at the cowboy who had called him out.

"Nobody calls me a cheat and gets away with it!" He cocked the pistol.

"Put away that gun, mister, none of those men are armed!" Smoke called to him.

With a loud angry shout, Muley swung his gun toward the table where Smoke was sitting. Louis and Tim dived for the floor.

"No!" Smoke shouted.

Muley pulled the trigger, and Smoke felt the compression of the air as the bullet whizzed by his ear. Smoke drew and fired before the stranger could shoot again.

Muley got a shocked look on his face, dropped his pistol, and slapped his hand over the entry wound. The blood streamed through his fingers.

"Son of a bitch! You've, you've kilt me," Muley said in disbelief.

Slowly, he collapsed to the floor.

Mike Kennedy was the first of the other three players to get over the shock of the sudden gunplay, and he bent down to examine Muley.

"He's dead," Kennedy said. Kennedy looked up toward the other players. "Cecil, are you sure he was cheating?"

"Look up the sleeve of his left arm," the cowboy who had challenged Muley said.

Mike pulled out two cards, a five of hearts and a seven of clubs.

"What good would these cards do him?" Mike said.

"Those are the cards he was dealt," Cecil said. "He replaced them with the cards he needed. Now turn over his hand to see what he wound up with."

Mike did so, and showed a hand of three aces and two fours.

"Damn, look at that, will you? That son of a bitch just improved his hand to a full house," the cowboy said.

"I'll get the sheriff," Tim offered.

Nobody noticed when the man who had ridden in with the stranger left the saloon.

It took only a few minutes for Sheriff Carson to arrive and he looked down at the body.

"Someone want to tell me what happened?"

Three or four people began to speak at the same time and Monte held up his hand. "Don't all of you talk at once. Smoke, you tell me what happened."

"Since I'm the one who killed him, Monte, you should probably hear the story from someone else."

"Good idea."

"Since the bullet this . . . gentleman," Louis said, setting the word apart to indicate the deceased was anything but a gentleman, "fired came so close to me that I could literally feel it passing, I believe I am qualified to give you the facts."

Monte listened to the story, then nodded. Again, he looked down at the body. "Does anyone know who this is?"

"He said his name was Muley," Mike Kennedy said. "He didn't give his full name."

"That fella standing over at the bar came in with him, maybe he'll know," Tim Murchison pointed out.

"Which one?" Monte asked, looking toward the bar.

"He's gone," Tim said.

Frank Petro couldn't believe the sudden and unexpected turn of events. He wasn't that surprised to see Muley get into an argument. Muley was the kind of person who was easily pissed off, he had even had spats with the others in their own little group. But to see the argument progress as rapidly as it did to an actual shooting was as big a shock to him as it was to everyone else in the saloon.

For just a second he was too stunned to react. Then he watched one of the men kneel down by Muley's prostrate form.

"He's dead," Kennedy said. Kennedy looked up toward the other players. "Cecil, are you sure he was cheating?"

"Look up the sleeve of his left arm," the cowboy who had challenged Muley said.

Mike pulled out two cards, a five of hearts and seven of clubs.

"What good would these cards do him?" Mike said.

"Those are the cards he was dealt," Cecil said. "He replaced them with the cards he needed. Now turn over his hand to see what he wound up with."

It had been the mention of the sheriff that jarred Frank out of his complacency. He couldn't wait around for the sheriff. He knew that the others had seen him come in with Muley, and the sheriff would be asking him a lot of questions, questions he didn't want to answer.

While everyone was still staring at the body, Frank took that opportunity to slip out. As soon as he left the saloon he mounted his horse and was about to ride away, when he noticed Muley's horse. There was no sense in just leaving it here; besides, the horse could lead the others back to the gang's hideout. He decided to take it with him.

Frank untied the reins of Muley's horse and rode away, moving slowly so as not to attract attention. Then, as soon as he was out of town he began to gallop, switching horses halfway. Doing so allowed him to make the five-mile ride in less than fifteen minutes.

"Here, what's going on here?" Myron asked. "Why are you leading Muley's horse? Where is Muley?"

"He's dead," Frank said. "The damn fool got caught cheatin' at cards and he pulled his gun."

"You're saying that Muley is the one that pulled his gun, but he's the one that's dead?"

"Yeah, there was another feller in there that shot 'im."

"Damn it, Frank, why did you let that happen?"

"What was I goin' to do, hit 'im on the head?"

"There ain't no sense in gettin' down none on Frank," Wally said. "Muley was a hothead. Hell, we all of us knowed that."

"'N he was also a card cheat, we knowed that, too," Ethan added. "'N card cheats most always wind up gettin' theirselves kilt."

"Well, let me ask you this. Did you find out what you was s'posed to find out when you was in town? Did the sheriff's wife die?"

"Oh yeah, she's dead, all right. 'N here's another thing, it ain't only the sheriff that's all sad about it, 'cause it turns out that near 'bout ever' business in town has got one o' them black ribbon bows on the door or in the winder light."

Myron nodded, with a satisfied grin. "That's good, that's real good. But with Muley dead that means we'll be short one man, 'n that'll leave you to be standin' lookout on your own when we hit the bank," Myron said.

"Why don't we let the boy stand lookout?" Wally Peach asked.

Myron shook his head. "No, I'd feel better if my brother did it. Leo can stay out front and hold the horses for us when we go in."

"I'm not going in?" Leo asked.

"It's better you stay outside," Wally said. "That way you won't actual be robbin' the bank. You'll just be holdin' the horses."

Leo nodded and felt a sense of relief. He was thankful that he wouldn't be exposed to any danger, but he was even more relieved that he wouldn't actually be robbing a bank. He knew that it was splitting hairs, because even if he did nothing but just hold the horses out front, he would still be a participant in the robbery.

"You ain't goin' to cut 'n run out on us, are you, kid?" Ethan asked.

"No, I would never do that!" Leo swore.

"When are we goin' to do it?" Peach asked.

"I was thinkin' about doin' it tomorrow," Myron said. "But it could be that Muley gettin' hisself kilt 'n all might be a good thing for us."

"How is Muley gettin' kilt good for us?" Ethan asked. "Like you said, that means there's one less of us to do the job."

"Yeah, 'n one less in on the split. Plus, you know how people is. There ain't no doubt but what ever'body's more'n likely tellin' each other stories 'bout how it happened 'n all." Myron chuckled. "By now, half the folks in town will be tellin' how they was dodgin' bullets 'n such. 'N with all of 'em bein' sad about the sheriff's wife dyin', and discombobulated because of the killin', that will make it harder to form up a posse, 'n by the time they get one put together, we'll be long gone from the place. Yes, sir, 'stead of doin' it tomorrow, now I'm thinkin' that the best time to do the job would be right now."

"Myron, I'm goin' to need to give my horse a breather," Frank said. "I rode him pretty hard comin' out here."

"That ain't goin' to be no problem," Myron said. "We'll be ridin' in real slow, 'n you won't be goin' all the way into town, anyway, seein' as you'll be standin' watch to make sure the way is clear when we leave after we've got the money."

"Hey, Myron, how much money do you think there'll be?" Wally asked.

"I don't know, twenty, maybe thirty thousand dollars. It's a bank, so there'll be a lot of money."

Wally smiled. "Soon's I get all that money I'll be goin' back to Memphis 'n lordin' it over all them that never thought I'd amount to anythin'."

"That wouldn't be very smart," Frank said.

"What do you mean? Why not?"

"Well, 'cause for one thing ever'one there would know you. 'N in our business it's best to go where people don't know you. Besides which, if you was to go back to Memphis with all that money, seein' as you never had nothin' before, don't you think that'd make folks suspicious? Now me, I'm goin' to San Francisco. I hear they got whores there that's so purty that you have to pay money just to look at 'em."

"Hah!" Ethan said. "Ugly as you are, Frank, most any woman would make you pay just to look at 'em."

"In Frank's case, a woman would have to be paid to look at him," Peach added.

The others, including Frank, laughed.

"Yeah, well, we ain't got the money yet, 'n we ain't goin' to get it till we get the job done. So let's quit jawbonin' 'n go rob us a bank," Myron said.

CHAPTER FOUR

Big Rock

Leo had not been able to sleep the night before, so worried was he about what lay ahead. He had passed on breakfast and lunch, but was still more nervous than hungry. And now, as the five men rode into town, Leo rode behind the others, thinking about what they were about to do. He had never done anything like this, and even though he was only seventeen years old, he knew this would change his life forever. Once he took part in a bank robbery, especially if someone in the bank were to be killed, he would never be able to leave the life of an outlaw.

Leo's initial entry into outlawry had been by happenstance. But if he went through with this today, he would be making a permanent commitment to a life that he wished he had never gotten into in the first place.

"Leo, what are you doin' back there, boy?" Myron called to him. "Keep up with us, we can't be stragglin' into town. We have to do ever'thin' just right in order for this to work."

Leo gave a quick thought to turning around and galloping away from the rest of them. But he knew about the planned bank robbery, and he knew if he tried to run away now, they would kill him.

They reached the edge of town and Leo sat in his saddle and looked out at the peaceful little community. How he wished he could have a life that would fit into such a tranquil setting. *Oh Lord, how did I get myself into this situation?* he wondered.

"Frank, you stop here," Myron ordered. "The rest of us will take a ride right down through the middle of town just to look it over. Ethan, you look to the left side of the street, Wally, you look to the right. See if you see anyone packin' a gun that could give us any trouble. Leo, you stay close now."

Big Rock

At that exact moment, Monte was in the mortuary talking to Tom Nunnley, the undertaker.

"Nobody has come to identify him?" Monte asked.

Tom shook his head. "We still only know him as Muley."

"Well, there can't be that many people known as Muley. Maybe someone will come along later who will be able to tell us who it is. In the meantime, here's the payment."

Tom nodded as he accepted the city money.

"Let me know when you're going to plant him. Nobody should have to be dropped in a hole with nobody there."

"It'll probably be tomorrow or the next day," Tom

said. "My normal gravedigger is out of town right now, but he should be back today or tomorrow."

"Thanks."

Leaving the mortuary, Monte started back up Lanning Street to return to his office. Just before he reached his office he saw four men riding down Front Street, and there was something about them that caught his attention. There was a familiarity about them, not that he had seen any of them before, but he had certainly seen their type before.

They rode slowly from Earl's Blacksmith Shop at the east end of Front Street, all the way down to the west end of the street. Had they crossed Tanner Street and stopped at the depot or even gone on through the town, Monte wouldn't have given them a second thought. But they stopped in front of White's Apothecary and remained mounted.

Monte noticed also, that Smoke's buckboard was still in town, which meant that Sally was shopping. And if she was still shopping, Smoke was still in Longmont's Saloon. Stepping into the saloon he stood just inside the door and held up his hand to get Smoke's attention.

"Monte," Louis called. "Come join us."

"Not just now," Monte said. "Smoke, I need you."

Smoke excused himself then left the table and started toward Monte, who had come only a few feet into the room. "Do you need to talk to me about the shooting?" Smoke asked as he joined his friend.

"No, something else. Let's step across the street to the bank," Monte said. "It may be nothing but . . ."

"Let's go," Smoke said, indicating by his quick response that Monte didn't need any further explanation.

As the two crossed Front Street Smoke caught, out of the corner of his eye, the four mounted men down at the far end of the street.

"The men in front of the drugstore?" he asked, without looking or pointing toward them.

"Yes."

"Yeah, you're right to be a little suspicious. It won't hurt to spend a few minutes in the bank."

By now all the members of Myron Petro's gang had regrouped after their scouting ride through the town.

"Did either of you see anything that we need to worry about?" Myron asked.

"Nobody on my side of the street," Ethan said.

"One young guy, looked like a cowboy, on my side," Wally replied. He chuckled. "He was wearin' a gun, but he don't much look like he even knows which end of the gun a bullet comes out of."

Myron reached down to loosen his pistol in the holster. Then he grinned at the others.

"All right, boys, what do you say we go make ourselves rich?"

"Can you just think about what it's goin' to feel like to hold all that money in your hand?" Ethan asked excitedly.

When Leo was a boy back in New Orleans, he and some others went swimming in a creek. There was a high bridge across the creek, and the others dared Leo to jump from it. As soon as he jumped, he had second thoughts about it, but he knew he couldn't "un-jump." He felt that same way now. It was not possible for him to turn around and ride away.

Neither Leo, nor any of the others, had seen the two men step into the bank just a moment earlier.

"Hello, Sheriff, Smoke, what can I do for you?" Joel Montgomery asked, greeting the two men as they entered. Joel was president of the bank. "Wait, Monte, don't tell me you were foolish enough to play cards with Smoke and you have to make a withdrawal to pay what you lost," he added with a laugh.

"Joel, I need for you and Carl to step back into your office for a few minutes," Monte said.

"What? Why?"

"Because we don't want you in the line of fire," Smoke said.

"Heavens, do you mean . . . ?"

"I hope not, and if nothing comes of it you can come out again in a few minutes. But for now Smoke is going to be sitting behind your desk, and I'm going to be the teller."

Joel nodded, then called over to his teller.

"Come, Carl, quickly," Joel ordered, realizing that no further discussion was needed.

Not until after Joel and Carl were gone, did Smoke take his seat behind the president's desk. Once in position, he pulled his pistol and held it in his lap. Monte got behind the teller's cage and laid his pistol under a piece of paper just beside him.

"All right, hand the reins to Leo. Leo, no matter what happens, don't you leave here until we come out," Myron ordered. "You got that?"

"I'll be here," Leo said as he took the reins from the other three men.

"Ethan, Wally, pull your bandannas up over your mouth and nose," Myron said, demonstrating to the others what he meant.

When the three men had the bottom half of their face covered, Myron nodded, pulled his pistol, and started for the door. Ethan and Wally, with their own guns drawn, followed him in.

It had been less than a minute after Smoke and Monte had assumed their position behind the president's desk and the teller cage, when three masked men came in. All three were holding pistols.

"This is a holdup!" one of the three men shouted.

"I don't think so!" Smoke said, standing then with a gun in his hand.

"What the hell? Shoot him! Shoot the son of a bitch!" one of the three would-be bank robbers shouted.

"No, drop your guns, you're covered!" Monte called out from behind the cage.

"Two of 'em?" one of the outlaws called out in alarm.

All three outlaws opened fire, one of them shot at Monte, and his bullet crashed through the glass just to the left of the teller's window. The other two shot at Smoke, one bullet hitting the inkwell, sending ink splashing out onto the desk. The second gunman's round plunged into the wall behind Smoke. Not one of the three men got off a second shot as they were cut down by Smoke and Monte.

The shooting was loud, short, and furious, and it left a heavy, acrid smell of gun smoke in the air.

Leo heard the gunfire from inside the bank, and he cringed.

"Oh no, they've killed the people in the bank," he mumbled with a sinking feeling in his body. It was all he could do to keep from dropping the reins and galloping away. But he had given his word that he would stay, and while it might be misplaced loyalty, he felt bound to honor his word.

An armed man suddenly darted out through the front door of the bank, but it wasn't Myron or either of the other two who had gone in but a moment earlier. He thrust the gun up toward Leo and pulled the hammer back. In the quiet after the earlier shooting, the sound of the gun being cocked was very loud. Leo well understood the meaning of the sound.

"Climb down from that horse, mister!" the armed man called.

Leo, with his hands in the air, dismounted, meekly.

"I ain't goin' to do nothin', mister. I ain't goin' to do nothin' at all."

From the west end of the street Frank had heard the shooting and, expecting his brother and the other three men to be coming at a gallop, he looked around to make certain there was no one there to impede the escape.

To his surprise, nobody came, and curious, he rode into town a little ways to see if he could find out what was going on. That was when he saw Leo Beajuex being led up the street with his hands in the air.

Frank waited to see if the others would come out with their hands up, and when they didn't, he knew that something had gone wrong, very badly wrong. Myron and the others were dead, he knew that with an absolute certainty. He thought about riding on farther into town, but remembered that he had been seen by many earlier this morning when Muley had been shot. That, alone, wouldn't necessarily connect him to the bank robbery, but it could cause some to be curious enough to want to ask a few questions.

Frank turned his horse and rode away. He was glad Myron had picked him to stand watch because now there was no way he could be connected with the bank robbery. Also, if not for standing watch, he would be dead, like the rest of them.

No, not all of them were dead. Leo Beajuex was still alive.

"Why won't you give your name?" Monte asked his prisoner.

"I . . . I'd rather not give you my name," Leo said.

"Why not?"

"You've caught me, why do you need my name?"

"Son, I want you to consider your situation," Monte said. "You're in a lot of trouble, and right now about the only thing you can claim as your own is your name. Are you going to give that up?"

The prisoner, who was considerably younger than Monte had first believed, thought for a moment about Monte's comment.

"Leo," he finally said. "My name is Leo Beajuex."

"How old are you, Leo?"

"I'm nineteen."

"How old?"

"Nineteen."

"Why are you lying to me, son?"

It was the way the sheriff had asked the question, not aggressively, but in a quiet and compassionate voice, that caused Leo to respond.

"All right, I'm seventeen," Leo said, and with that confession his tough-guy façade failed him and his eyes brimmed with tears.

Monte wet a cloth and handed it to him. "Here, wash your face, you'll feel better," he said. He made no mention of the tears.

"Thanks," Leo said as he dabbed first at his eyes, then he swabbed his whole face.

"Leo, I think you'll have to admit that seventeen is a little young to be holding up a bank, don't you think?"

"I didn't hold up the bank, Sheriff, all I done was wait out front 'n keep a-holt of the horses."

"By the law, that makes you just as guilty," Monte pointed out.

"It does? Myron said that if we was to get caught, me a-hangin' on to the horses wouldn't be the same."

"Is Myron one of the three who went inside?"

"Yes, sir, Myron Petro. He was our leader. The other two was Ethan Reese and Wally Peach. Wally, now he was the one closest to me in age, him bein' actual nineteen."

"Leo, would you be willing to come down to the undertaker's place and identify them?"

"I just told you who they are. Do I have to look at them?"

"It would help your case by showing a degree of cooperation," Monte said.

"But they were my friends, and now they're dead. I don't want to look at dead friends."

"Son, you sure chose the wrong friends if you didn't expect to ever see any of them dead. Lots of folks wind up gettin' killed in your line of work."

Leo shook his head. "Yes, sir, I suppose that is so, but I haven't had to see any of them before."

"Then you have been damn lucky. But now you are about to," Monte insisted. "Come along, maybe it will be a good lesson for you."

Reluctantly, Leo let himself be led the block and a half between the jail and the undertaker's office, which shared a building with Sikes' Hardware Store. Leo was wearing handcuffs, but Lanning was not one of the busier streets, so nobody noticed him.

"In here," Monte invited, opening the door.

Leo looked aside and closed his eyes.

"Open your eyes, Leo."

With his eyes tightly shut, Leo shook his head. "No."

"Leo? You can't identify the bodies if you don't look at them."

Reluctantly, Leo opened his eyes then looked at the nearest body. "This is Muley Dobbs," he said.

"Wait a minute," Monte said. "You know this man? He wasn't one of the robbers."

"I know, he come into town to look around for us, only he got hisself kilt while he was in town."

"Well, thanks, that solves the mystery of who he is. Now, how about identifying the rest of them?"

After a moment, Leo attached a name to each of the other three bodies. "Can we go back to jail now? This is giving me the chills. I mean, they was all alive this mornin'."

"All right, son, you've done what I asked you to do. We can go back to the jail now."

CHAPTER FIVE

"Leo, I tell you the truth, boy, you don't seem like the kind of person who would try and rob a bank. How did you get involved with such men?" Monte asked when they got back to his office. Monte had not yet put Leo in a cell, and, though still handcuffed, the boy was sitting in a chair near Monte's desk.

"It was Wally. Like I told you, he was most near my age, 'n he's the first one of 'em that I met, 'n he introduced me to the others. Myron didn't want to have nothin' to do with me, but Wally talked 'im into bringin' me along with 'em. We stole some cows 'n a few horses 'n was sellin' 'em for a little money, then Myron figured we maybe ought to leave Texas, which is where we was. Then, not long after we come here, he decided we should rob the bank. I wasn't that keen on it, but Myron said if we did that, we could make enough money to go somewhere 'n maybe all of us go together 'n start our own ranch.

"I wasn't that sure I wanted to stay with the rest of 'em. I figured if they robbed one bank they'd more'n likely want to rob another 'un. If you want to know the truth, what finally made me decide to go along with it is because I figured maybe I'd have me enough money so's I wouldn't never be hungry no more."

"You've had to go without food before?"

"Yes, sir, lots of times," Leo said.

"Speaking of that, it's after lunchtime," Monte said. "Are you hungry now?"

"Yes, sir, I got a real powerful hungry on me, seein' as how I ain't et nothin' a-tall since early this mornin' and I didn't even eat nothin' then on account of I was a-scairt of what we was plannin' on doin'. But I did have me some beans and a biscuit yesterday."

Monte studied him for a moment. "My wife would have just loved to make cookies for you."

Leo recalled the cookies his mother and some of her friends had made for him when he was a boy back in New Orleans.

Leo smiled. "Yes, sir, tell 'er to go ahead 'n make me some. I love cookies more'n just about anythin', 'n I ain't had me none in a coon's age. Oh, wait, I thought your wife was dead."

Monte shook his head sadly. "She is." He looked up sharply. "How did you know?"

"Myron heard about it 'n that was one of the things he sent Muley 'n . . ." Leo paused in midsentence. He was about to say *Muley and Frank*, but he decided to leave Frank's name out of it. "He sent Muley in to scout the bank 'n find out for sure whether or not your wife was dead."

"Why did he want to know whether or not my wife had died?"

"I think it's 'cause he figured if she was dead,

you'd be feelin' too bad to be able to do anything to stop us. I didn't like that idea, by the way. I thought it was real mean of him to want to use somethin' that's real sad so's we could hold up the bank."

"As you can see, it didn't work."

"No, sir, it sure didn't." Leo was quiet for a moment before he spoke again. "Sheriff, I'm real sorry 'bout your wife," Leo said. "I mean, bein' that she's dead 'n all. That's a real sad thing."

"It's a part of life, son. We're all going to die, some-time. Suppose I go get you something to eat?"

"Yes, sir, thank you, I'd pure dee appreciate that."

"I'll have to put you in a cell while I'm gone."

"Yes, sir, I figured you would."

Leo watched the sheriff close and lock the cell door. After the sheriff left, Leo sat on the bunk and studied his surroundings. There were three cells, side by side along the back. Leo, who was the only prisoner, was in the middle cell.

The three cells were separated from the sheriff's office by a wall, on which hung a pendulum clock, the clock giving the time as lacking fifteen minutes of three. It was very quiet in the jail, the silence inter-rupted only by the ticktock of the clock, the sound in perfect rhythm with the arc of the pendulum.

Leo felt his stomach growl, and he was glad that sheriff had said he would be bringing him some food.

He lay down on the bunk and laced his hands behind his head, as he stared at the bottom of the top bunk.

"Hey, kid!" someone called. "Leo!"

Leo recognized Frank's voice, and he stood on his

bunk so he could look out the back window. He saw Frank standing in the back alley.

"How are you makin' out?" Frank asked.

"I'm doin' all right. The sheriff went to get me some food. What are you doin' back there, Frank? I thought you would be way gone from here, by now."

"What? You mean run away 'n leave my little friend behind?"

"Frank, you don't have to worry none, I ain't spoke your name or nothin'. There don't nobody even know you was a part of it."

"Good for you, kid."

"Look, you'd better go now. If the sheriff comes back 'n sees me 'n you talkin', he's liable to start askin' questions."

"All right, I'm goin'. I was just wonderin' how you was gettin' along. I hate leavin' you in jail like this, you bein' my friend 'n all."

"Don't worry none about me, I'll be just fine."

"I'll be seein' you," Frank said, and Leo watched him walk on down the alley until the angle of the cell window took him out of sight.

"*I'll be seeing you*," Frank had said. Leo hoped that he would never see Frank again.

After Frank left, Leo lay back down. This was the first time in quite a while that he had had any time for reflection, and at the moment, the memories were coming strong.

He remembered the last time he had ever seen his mother, and he felt a lump in his throat and a burning in his eyes.

"Ma, I've made a real mess of things," Leo said aloud, though speaking just above a whisper.

It had been over a year since he left New Orleans,

and while, in one way it seemed half a lifetime ago, in another way it seemed as if it had been just yesterday.

Scenes of those last few days were replayed in his mind.

New Orleans, Louisiana, two years earlier

"Oh, honey, I had four of them last night, and each one was worse than the one before."

Annabelle, the woman who was talking, was sitting at the breakfast table. In her late thirties, Annabelle, whose makeup from the night before was now fading, wore a thin housecoat which gapped in front to offer a good view of her bare breasts. There were six women at the table, in various degrees of dress, and Annabelle wasn't the only one whose breasts Leo could see.

The women felt no sense of embarrassment at having a fifteen-year-old boy in their presence. It wasn't unusual for Leo to see any of them totally naked, for often at night the women would make brief appearances in the upstairs hallway where Leo lived. Leo lived in the de Plaisir Maison, a whore-house in the French Quarter of New Orleans.

"Sweetheart, would you bring Lila that carafe of cream?" one of the women at the breakfast table asked Leo.

"Yes, ma'am," Leo said, walking over to the sideboard to get the creamer.

"Isn't he just the best-looking thing, though?" Lila said. "When he comes of age, I'll be glad to break him in."

"Lila, you keep your hands off my son," Chantal said.

"You're the one that's raising him in a place like this," Lila said. "He's not going to be a virgin forever. Someone is going to be first, why not me?"

"Believe me, if I had any other choice in the matter, I wouldn't keep him here."

"You could always put him in an orphanage," Annabelle suggested.

"Why would I want to do that?" Chantal replied. "He isn't an orphan. Besides, he's all I have and I'm all he has. I've raised him here since he was a baby, I'm not going to kick him out now."

"Ma, it's time for me to go to school," Leo said, uncomfortable with the discussion. His mother and the others often talked about him as if he weren't present, and he didn't like that.

"Kiss your ma good-bye," Chantal said, turning her face toward her son. Like the five women at the table, Chantal was not fully dressed.

Leo never walked directly to the school; he always went several blocks out of his way so he could approach the school from a different direction. He did that because he didn't want anyone to know that he was coming from a whorehouse. He was ashamed of his mother, and he was ashamed of where he lived.

Big Rock

The sound of a train whistle jarred Leo back to the present, and it took him a few seconds to realize where he was. Now, in the jail cell as he recalled those days, he was ashamed of himself for having been ashamed of his mother. He had learned that most of the women who followed "the trade" either terminated their pregnancies with abortion or gave away the baby as soon as it was born, often without ever seeing it. The fact that his mother carried him to term, and kept him, was extremely unusual. He knew, also, that she had taken a lot of heat for it.

Up until he was twelve years old he had lived in the same room with his mother, but would stay in the kitchen when she had a client. He had blankets and quilts in the kitchen and would spend the night there more times than not. Then, when he was thirteen he began working for the house, mopping the floors, cleaning the rooms, and doing the laundry. He wasn't paid directly, but his food was supplied and he was given his own private room next door to his mother's. Also, from time to time, he was able to do a few chores for the other women and that allowed him to earn a little money.

"Ma, I'm sorry I was ever ashamed of you," he said quietly. "I know you're up in heaven, 'cause even if you was a whore you was a good woman, 'n I just don't think the Lord would say you can't come in. I love you, and I miss you."

Leo felt his eyes burning with tears and he wiped them with his hands, then willed the memories away.

The Denver and Pacific Railroad tracks passed right behind the jail, and Leo looked through the cell window as the train passed by, slowing now as it came closer to the depot. He could see people in the cars and he wondered about them. Where had they come from? And where were they going? He had never ridden on a train, but he would like to do so, someday.

"Paper! Get your paper here! Sheriff stops bank robbers! Get your paper here!"

Leo could hear the paper boy hawking the news of

today, and it made him feel a little strange to know that he was actually a part of the news. Some, he had known, would be flattered by the notoriety. He was not.

From the *Big Rock Journal:*

BANK ROBBERY THWARTED

"I just had a feeling," Sheriff Carson said. "When I saw those four men riding into town, I just had a feeling."

Sheriff Carson then shared his feeling with Smoke Jensen and the two men hurried over to the bank to play to its conclusion, the sheriff's intuitive grasp of potential trouble.

"When the sheriff and Smoke asked Carl and me to step into the back of the bank, we didn't question them," Joel Montgomery told this newspaper. "We knew they wouldn't ask such a thing unless they had a real good reason to do so."

As it turned out, Sheriff Carson's feeling, regardless of what mysterious thing brought it on, was accurate. Shortly after the sheriff and Smoke took up positions in the bank, three masked men, carrying guns, stepped inside with the bold pronouncement that "This is a holdup!"

Stating their intended purpose was as far as they got in their nefarious plan, for rather than dropping their guns as ordered, the bank robbers made the error in judgment of trying to engage two of the most skilled pistoleers in the entire West in gunplay. Their ill-advised act of exchanging gunfire with Sheriff Monte Carson and his temporarily deputized Smoke Jensen was a fatal mistake, as all three of the desperadoes were killed.

The fourth outlaw, who had remained outside the bank to hold the horses for the other three, was placed under arrest and is currently in jail, has identified the three slain men as Myron Petro, Ethan Reese, and Wally Peach. In an earlier, and as it has developed, a related incident, the man shot in the Longmont's Saloon has been identified as Muley Dobbs. We have since learned that Muley Dobbs was a part of the bank robbery scheme, having been sent into town to scout out the bank for the nefarious activity the outlaws had planned.

With the demise of four of the outlaws and the capture of the fifth, no one remains of the group of desperadoes. The name of the captured fugitive is being withheld due to the fact that he is quite young.

This latest event where, by Sheriff Carson's keen analytical eye in anticipating potential trouble and spotting those most likely to perpetrate the crime, is but one in a long line of heroic incidents in service to our fair city. This paper cannot hold our sheriff in high enough esteem.

CHAPTER SIX

"*Triumphus Roma!*" Sally said as she greeted Smoke when he, Pearlie, and Cal came in from the barn.

"What?"

"It's the way Romans used to hail their conquering heroes."

Smoke smiled. "Oh, so I am your conquering hero now, am I?"

"You've always been my hero, Smoke. But now the whole world knows of it." Sally held out the copy of the *Journal* that carried the story of the attempted bank robbery. "Or at least those in the world who have read the latest issue of the *Big Rock Journal.*"

"It was Monte, really," Smoke said. "He's the one who spotted them, and he's the one who set up the reception. We didn't intend to kill them. I was certain they would give up when they saw that we had the drop on them, but they started shooting, and we had no choice."

"You don't have to explain anything to me, Smoke. I've never known you to shoot anyone without just cause."

"Miss Sally is sure right about that," Pearlie said. "I've been in enough scrapes with you to know that you'll always do the right thing, even if it isn't the safest thing."

"What's for lunch?" Cal asked.

"What's for lunch?" Sally laughed. "Here we are lauding *ex heroibus* and Cal wants to know what's for lunch. Leave it to Cal to keep things in perspective."

"'Lauding *ex heroibus*.' What does that mean?" Cal asked.

"I think it means 'roast beef,'" Pearlie said. "At least that's what it smells like."

"Pearlie, you have an excellent grasp of Latin," Smoke said as he leaned over to kiss a smiling Sally on the cheek.

"*Amor vincit omnia. Per aspera ad astra,*" Sally said with the hint of a grin

"She was talking about roast beef before, but I don't have any idea what she said that time," Pearlie said.

"What I said, Pearlie, was 'Do not despair, to err is human.'"

"Whoo wee, Smoke, I do believe you married the smartest woman in the world," Pearlie said.

Smoke laughed. "Pearlie, there's no way I would argue with you about that."

"You were in town when all the shooting and everything happened, Miss Sally, what did you think about it?" Cal asked.

"Oh, heavens, I was all the way down at the other end of the street in Murchison's Leather Goods. I heard the shooting but I didn't see anything at first. Then, when I stepped outside, I saw Smoke leading one of the bank robbers away."

"A young boy, as it turns out," Smoke added.

"How young?" Pearlie asked.

"I think he told Monte that he was seventeen."

"Seventeen? I didn't even start when I was that young," Pearlie said.

"I was," Cal said without further comment.

"What's going to happen to him?" Sally asked.

"Your guess is as good as mine," Smoke said as he helped himself to another serving of mashed potatoes.

Big Rock

"I'd like to do something for the boy, Smoke," Monte said the next day when Smoke was in town. He held up his hand. "Now, before you say somethin' about him bein' a bank robber 'n all, you have to know that I'm not all that proud of my past, either. Truth to tell, there's no telling where I was going, or what was going to happen to me until I run into you. And, you can say the same thing about Pearlie and Cal, for that matter. I mean, you rescued both of them, didn't you?"

"Actually, it would be more accurate to say that Sally rescued Cal," Smoke replied. "When he was about the same age as your prisoner, as a matter of fact."

"Yes, I know that, and that's what gave me an idea as to how you can help."

"All right, what can I do to help?"

"Well, it would be Cal, actually. Do you think he would be willing to come into town and talk to the boy? I mean, like you said, when Miss Sally took him on, he was scarcely older than Leo is now."

"Yes, I think he would. He's in town now, as a matter of fact, down at Nancy's Sweet Shop. I'll go talk to him."

"Thanks, I appreciate that."

Cal was still trying to make up his mind what kind of pastry he wanted when Smoke's entry into the shop was announced by the tinkling of a bell as the door opened.

"Made up your mind yet?" Smoke asked, causing Cal to turn toward him.

"Yeah, I think I'm going to get a couple of those apple tarts," Cal said with a smile of anticipation.

"No, get a dozen of those cookies instead. I'll pay for them," Smoke offered.

"A dozen cookies? No need to get that many. Pearlie already got what he wanted."

"They aren't for Pearlie. Get a dozen of those oatmeal cookies, drop them in a sack, then come with me."

"All right," Cal agreed. He had no idea what Smoke had in mind, but he trusted him enough that it didn't really matter. "Miss Nonnie, I guess you'd better gather up a dozen of the cookies for me."

"Yes, sir, Mr. Wood," Nonnie, the seventeen-year-old daughter of Nancy Kinder, said. Nancy was the owner of Nancy's Sweet Shop. Five minutes later, with Smoke having explained what he wanted as they walked back toward the jail, Cal and Smoke stepped into the sheriff's office.

"Cal, thanks for coming," Monte said. "I wonder if I could ask you to have a few words with . . ."

"Yes, Smoke told me what you wanted, and I'd be glad to. Why don't you go in the back, open the cell, and let me talk to him?" Cal said to Monte.

"Thanks, Cal, I appreciate that. But before you go back there, you'd probably better take off your gun belt."

"You'll need coffee with those cookies," Smoke said, stepping over to the small stove upon which sat a coffeepot emitting a rich, coffee aroma. I'll carry the cups."

Leo was sitting on the bunk in the cell with his arms wrapped around his legs, which were drawn up in front of him. Because the back of the jail was separated from the front by a wall, the prisoners in back had no idea who was arriving or leaving the building.

He looked up in curiosity when he saw three men coming back into the cellblock area. He recognized the sheriff and Smoke Jensen, but he didn't know the third man and assumed that he was a new prisoner.

Leo was surprised to see the sheriff open his cell and wondered why he wasn't putting the new prisoner in one of the other cells. Smoke handed the new prisoner two cups of coffee.

"Give me a shout when you're ready to come out," the sheriff said as he closed the cell door and then, with Smoke Jensen, went back to the front of the office.

Leo chuckled. "You must be some special kind of

a prisoner if all you have to do to get out is give the sheriff a shout."

"The name's Cal," Cal said, passing one of the cups of coffee to Leo. "And yeah, you might say I'm a special prisoner."

Cal pulled the little table up to the bunk, then a chair up to the opposite side of the table. He reached down and took out a handful of cookies, gave them to Leo, then took out a handful for himself.

"Wow! I almost can't remember the last time I had any cookies. Thanks, Cal, for sharing them with me."

"I bought them for you," Cal said.

"You bought them for me? Why?"

"I want to tell you a little story," Cal said.

"A story? What kind of story?"

"What difference does it make what kind of story? What else have you got to do besides sit here and listen?"

Leo laughed. "You've got that right. All right, tell your story."

"It happened when I was just about your age. I had run away from home, figuring I was enough of a man to be on my own. The only problem is, it didn't work out all that well. Oh, I had a few jobs here and there, mucking out stalls, mopping floors." Cal paused for a moment and shook his head. "Once I even had a job emptying shit barrels from the outhouses of a boardinghouse."

"Whoa, I'll bet you didn't like that, much."

Cal laughed. "No, I didn't. Well, as you can tell from the way my story is starting out, things weren't going all that well for me, so I held up a couple of stores. I think I managed to get about ten dollars from one of them, maybe twelve at another. My crime spree wasn't paying off all that well, and there was always the chance that I would get my fool head blown off.

"Then I found myself here in Big Rock, and I saw this beautiful lady comin' out of a store with her arms full of packages. I figured she must have money, else how was she able to buy so many things? And she was a woman, so I knew she'd be so scared that she wouldn't give me any trouble. I pulled a gun on her and told her to give me all her money."

"You mean, you actually robbed a woman?" Leo asked.

Cal laughed. "Don't be getting ahead of the story, Leo. Are you going to let me tell it, or not?"

"Oh, I'm sorry, no, go ahead 'n tell it, I ain't a-goin' to interrupt you no more."

"Whooee, Sally is goin' to have a good time teaching you."

"Teaching me what?" Having finished the first cookie, Cal reached for another one.

"You'll find out soon enough. Anyway, like I said, I pulled my gun and demanded all her money, then the next thing I knew she was pointing a pistol at me, and she got it out so fast that I knew damn well she knew how to use it. She made me turn my pistol over to her."

"So, you wound up here in jail just like me," Leo said.

"No, sir. What she did was, she took me home with her, fed me one of the best suppers I ever had in my life, gave me some clean clothes, and told me to take a bath. Then after I was fed, and cleaned up, she gave me a job."

"Wow, that's a real good story," Leo said.

"You know the two men that broke up the bank robbery? One was Sheriff Carson and the other was Smoke Jensen."

"Yeah, he's the one that came out of the bank and caught me, the one that was just in here."

"Miss Sally, the woman that gave me the job, is married to Smoke Jensen, and they're two of the best people I've ever known in my life. And you want to know someone who is just about as good as they are?"

"Are you goin' to say Sheriff Carson? Because if you are, I can almost believe it. I know that he has been really good to me since I've been here."

"Who are you, Leo?"

"I'm Leo Beaujuex, you already know that," Leo said.

"No, I mean, who are you really? Tell me about yourself. Where did you come from? How come you aren't living with your family and going to school? How did somebody no older than you, wind up robbin' a bank?"

Leo looked at Cal, then took a bite of his cookie and a swallow of coffee before he spoke.

"I don't have a family. I never did have a family, leastwise, I never had a family like other people. My ma was . . ." He paused as if having a difficult time getting it out. "I never saw my pa, and truth is, my ma never even knew who it was. You see, my ma was a whore in a New Orleans whorehouse, 'n that's where I grew up. When I was old enough, Madame Thibodeau, she was the *madame de la maison*, gave me some work to do so I could earn my own room. That way, my ma could have some privacy when she entertained her gentleman callers."

Leo gave a scoffing laugh. "That's what she 'n the other women called them, their 'gentlemen callers.' But, believe me, they weren't gentlemen.

"Ma had what the others called a *touch of the brush* 'n that made her some particular popular with some men."

"A touch of the brush?" Cal asked, confused by the term.

"She was a quadroon, one-fourth black. One of her grandmas was a black woman. And while some of the men liked that, there was one who didn't find that out about her until after . . . after he had been with her.

"He got really mad at her, told her she should have told him she was a nig . . . well, you know the word. That was bad enough, but then he started beating her.

"My room was next door 'n I heard Ma screamin' 'n even though she had told me never to come into her room while there was a man with her, I ran into the room and saw him beating her. I grabbed the water pitcher and smashed it over his head. That stopped him from beating on my ma, then he hit me and left.

"My ma died the next day. The doctor said she had so many broken ribs that some of them punched into all her innards, 'n that's what killed her."

Leo was quiet for another long moment.

"Oh, damn, Leo, that's really rough," Cal said.

"Cal, I didn't tell the sheriff this, truth to tell, I

ain't never told nobody this but, I feel like I need to get it off my chest. What I did was, I waited about a week, then I found the man that beat Ma to death. His name was Marcus Doyle, and he owned a fancy clothing store for men. I waited until I was sure there was nobody in the store but him, then I went inside."

As Leo continued to tell the story, he told it with such intensity of memory, that it was as if Cal were an actual witness to the scene.

"Kid, this is a store that caters to a higher class of gentlemen," Doyle said when Leo stepped inside. Doyle chuckled, a mean-spirited, mocking laugh. "I don't know who you are, but I'm certain you don't have enough money to be able to make a purchase in here, and I know you aren't a gentleman."

"You mean you don't recognize me, Mr. Doyle?"

"Recognize you? No, why should I recognize you?"

"For what I have to do, it is important that you know who I am. I want you to know why I'm doing it."

"Why you are doing what?"

"Why I'm going to beat you up."

"Now, why would you want to beat me up?" Doyle asked with a mocking laugh.

"Because you beat my ma to death."

"You! You're the whore's brat!"

"Yes."

"And you're going to beat me up, are you?"

"Yes."

An evil smile spread across Doyle's face. "What makes you think a young punk like you could beat me up?" Doyle put his fists up. "You little bastard, I'm going to rip your head off."

Leo had brought a hammer with him which, so far, Doyle hadn't seen. Leo stood there, holding the hammer behind his leg when Doyle lunged toward him.

Leo ducked under Doyle's rush and, as he did so, he swung the hammer, connecting with Doyle's knee.

Doyle let out a shout and went down, holding on to his knee.

Leo hit his other knee, and Doyle screamed again.

Leo stood there watching Doyle writhe in agony, and he was about to leave when Doyle managed to pull himself over to a nearby counter, where he grabbed a gun.

Doyle tried to turn toward Leo but his busted knees wouldn't allow him to do so. Again, Leo hit him with the hammer, this time in the hand that was holding the gun. Another scream of pain as the gun clattered to the floor.

Now Doyle was hopeless before him, and Leo drew back the hammer, intending to hit him in the head.

"No! No! If you hit me in the head with that thing it'll kill me!" Doyle begged.

"Yeah, that's what I plan to do."

"No, please, don't!"

"Why shouldn't I kill you? You killed my ma."

"It was an accident, boy, you know I didn't mean to kill her."

"It wasn't an accident that you beat her up."

"I was wrong about that. And I'm awful sorry. Look, I tell you what. I've got over two hundred dollars in my cash box. That's a lot of money. Take it.

Take it. Take it with my blessing, just don't kill me. Please, don't kill me."

"Where's the cash box?" Leo asked.

"There, under that counter." Doyle pointed.

Leo took the box from under the counter.

"You're going to regret this, boy. Someday you're going to regret this," Doyle said.

CHAPTER SEVEN

Big Rock

"I took all the money he had in his money box," Leo said, continuing his story. "Then I stole his horse 'n left New Orleans. I'm sure the police are countin' it as a robbery, 'n I suppose it was. But even though I told him I had come to kill 'im, I didn't really go there to kill 'im, I just wanted to hurt him a little. I didn't go there to rob 'im, either. Fact is, I didn't even think about robbin' 'im till he brought it up, and I knew I would need some money to make my escape."

Leo stopped talking and took a drink of his coffee.

"My name was Leo Boudreaux then, leastwise, that was the name my ma used. I don't think she knew for sure whether that was even really her name or not. I took the name Beajuex on account of I seen it writ out on a store when I was leavin' town."

"Leo, you say that I'm the only one you've ever told this story to?" Cal asked.

"Yeah. I . . . I needed to tell someone. I mean, it has just been weighin' down on me. Can you understand that?"

"Yes, I can understand it."

"Are you goin' to tell the sheriff? If you do, I'm pretty sure he'll send me back to New Orleans, and Doyle, bein' a big businessman 'n all, well, he could more'n likely get me hung by sayin' I tried to kill 'im. I didn't really try to kill 'im but, I'll be truthful to you, there was a moment there, especially when he took out that gun to shoot me, that I pure dee wanted to do it. 'N I coulda done it, too."

"I'm not going to tell Monte, and I don't think you should tell the story to anyone else. Listen, Leo, I believe Sheriff Carson wants to give you a second chance, just like Miss Sally gave me. So I'm asking you now, if you want that."

"Yes, sir, I would love a second chance!" Leo said.

"I need to believe you are serious. I mean, I don't want you saying this just to get some kind of a good deal, then turn it against him."

Leo shook his head. "No, Cal, I would never do anything like that. If he gives me a chance to get out of here, I'd be thankful to him for the rest of my life and he would never wind up regretting it."

"There's one more thing. You were part of a bank holdup, so it's not all up to the sheriff, and it's not going to be easy. The judge is the one who's going to be the one that actually makes the decision, but if you are honest with the sheriff, the judge will maybe go light on you, and then after you get out, Sheriff Carson can help you start a new life."

"Cal, I would swear on a stack of Bibles so high I'd have to climb a ladder to put my hand on 'em, that if I get another chance, I'll make ever'one proud."

"Leo, if you go back on that, I'll be coming after you myself."

"I swear, I won't go back on my word."

Cal nodded, then turned his head toward the front. "Sheriff?" he called.

Monte and Smoke both reappeared.

"The boy and I have had a nice talk. You can let me out," Cal said with a smile.

"Cal, you're goin' to talk to 'em for me?" Leo asked.

"I'm going to talk to them."

"Oh, don't forget your cookies," Leo said.

"They're your cookies."

"What do you think, Cal?" Monte asked when Cal stepped back into the sheriff's front office. "Is the kid worth a second chance?"

"Yes, sir, I think he is," Cal said.

Monte nodded. "Then I intend to do what I can for him."

Later, as Cal and Smoke rode back to the ranch, Smoke interrupted the silence.

"You were right when you told Leo not to tell his story to anyone else."

"You heard?"

"Yes, I didn't intend to hear it, but I had just stepped back to see how you two were doing when I heard Leo telling it."

"Then you know that Leo and I are a lot alike. Especially with our mamas and all."

"Yes."

"Did Monte hear it?"

"No, and I don't think he needs to."

* * *

"How was your visit into town?" Sally asked when Smoke and Cal returned.

"It was very good," Smoke said. He shared with Sally, Monte's intention of giving Leo Beajuex another chance.

"Just like you gave me, Miss Sally," Cal added.

"Have you had an opportunity to visit with him, to make a judgment?" Sally asked.

"Yes, ma'am, I talked to him for quite a while," Cal said. "I think Sheriff Carson is doing the right thing by giving him another chance."

"Are you sure you're not being a little hasty?" Sally asked. "I mean, does one conversation really give you enough information about him to make up your mind?"

Cal laughed.

"What is it? Why are you laughing?"

"How many conversations did you and I have before you brought me back here, fed me, and gave me a job?"

Now it was Sally's turn to laugh. "Touché," she said.

"What does *touchy* mean?"

"It means that, so far, you haven't been that much of a pain in the ass," Pearlie teased.

"No, it doesn't. What does it really mean?"

Sally laughed again. "Loath as I am to accept Pearlie's definition, I think I might just go along with him on this one."

Big Rock

Back in the jail, Leo had been thinking about his conversation with Cal. Was he really going to be given another chance? It seemed almost too good to be true, but if he did get another chance he would not make the same mistake twice.

He wished now, with all his heart, that he had not joined up with Myron and the others when they stole cattle from the Bar S Ranch. And though he could almost convince himself that Ron Stacy actually owed him for the few cows he took from his former employer, there was no way he could justify holding up the stagecoach or stealing those mules.

All that was behind him now and with Myron and the others dead there was nothing to prevent from making a new start in life.

Suddenly he felt a chill pass over him. How would he deal with the fact that Frank was still alive?

Red Cliff, Colorado

Inside the Turkey Neck Saloon, Frank Petro stood nursing a beer at the bar. He had come in with just enough money for a beer and a plate of beans. There were three women working the bar, talking to any of the men who would buy them a drink. In addition to sharing drinks with the customers, the women would also go upstairs with anyone who was willing to pay the price.

Frank wished he had enough money to go upstairs with one of them, but he didn't. He didn't even have enough money to buy their company for a few minutes, or even for a second beer.

It wasn't supposed to have been like this. By now he was supposed to have five or six thousand dollars in his pocket and maybe be halfway to San Francisco, riding first class on a train. Leastwise, that's what Myron told him.

Now Myron was dead and though Myron was his brother, the only remorse Frank felt over his death was that it had left him with no money.

If everything worked out, though, that would soon change. Earlier today, Frank had met a man who promised to let him in on a job. After that his pockets would be full again. Well, not as full as they would have been if the bank robbery had gone through, but at least there would be enough money to get something to drink and eat. He looked down at one of the girls standing at the far end of the bar, and she smiled a provocative invitation.

"Hello, honey," she said. "How would you like to buy me a drink?"

"I don't have enough money."

"Well, you be sure and come back when you do have enough," she said as she turned away from him and started toward one of the other patrons.

After this job, maybe he would have enough money to act upon her invitation.

He looked over at the wall clock.

"Is your clock right?" he asked the bartender.

The bartender, who was busy polishing glasses, set the towel down and pulled out his watch. He flipped open the case and looked at it, then glanced back at the clock.

"Yes, sir," he said. "It is lacking five minutes of nine o'clock."

"Thanks," Frank replied.

"Would you like another beer, sir?"

"No, thank you. Not just yet," Frank answered.

"Very good, sir."

The bartender went back to wiping glasses. Frank

raised his nearly empty beer mug, just enough to wet his lips.

According to the instructions, Frank was to go outside and stand under the lamppost in front of the livery at exactly nine o'clock and examine his pocket watch. He didn't actually have a pocket watch, he had sold it long ago. But he figured if he pretended to be examining one it would amount to the same thing.

He took another swallow of beer, then made a face. He had been nursing the beer so long that it had gone flat on him. It was pure hell to be in this world without money. He looked back toward the regulator clock and saw the minute hand move to one minute until nine. He finished his beer, slapped the mug down, wiped the back of his hand across his mouth, and started for the door.

"Come again," the bartender called to him.

"When you've got more money," the bar girl who issued the invitation added. She followed her chiding with a high-pitched laugh. The man standing closest to her guffawed in a rich, bass tone.

"I will," Frank replied.

Leaving the bar, Frank walked down to the corner street lamp and stood beneath it in the wavering yellow light.

"I wasn't sure you would show up," a voice said from behind him.

Frank turned toward the voice. The speaker was a tall, thin man with a full, dark mustache under a hooked nose.

"You said you had a way for us to make some money," Frank said.

"Not us, I won't be a part of it. Actually, it's a way for

you to make money," the man replied. "Five hundred dollars," he added.

Frank chuckled. "You know where I can steal exactly five hundred dollars? Wait, you're talking about robbing a person, aren't you, a person with exactly five hundred dollars."

"You don't have to steal the money, I'll give it to you as payment for a job I want you to do."

"What kind of job?"

"I want someone killed."

Frank hesitated for a moment. "I'm not exactly a fast gun. If you're talking about me prodding someone into a gunfight, you're going to have to get someone else."

Frank started to walk away.

"No, wait, don't go away," the hooked-nose man called out, to stop him. "You don't understand. There won't be any fight to it. I just want you to kill someone, and I'll pay five hundred dollars to have the job done."

"Who do you want me to kill?"

"Abe Harris, my brother."

"What?"

"Do you know the term *primogeniture*?"

"Prima what?"

"Primogeniture. It is an old English custom whereby the firstborn son inherits the parent's entire estate, leaving all his siblings out. My father was born in England and has let it be known that he intends to follow that custom. He's dying, and that means my brother will inherit the ranch, and I'll be left out in the cold."

"But if I kill him, won't you be suspected?" Frank

asked. "I mean, seein' as you're goin' to miss out on the inheritin' 'n all?"

"I will have the perfect alibi," Harris replied. "You'll do it tomorrow while I will be with my father. He and I are meeting with the cattle broker. Abe will be on the road to Mitchell at that time. There will be nobody around to see you."

"Where will you be after I do the job? Where do I go to get paid?"

"That's going to be the easy part. Abe will be carrying five hundred dollars with him. The reason he is going to Mitchell is to pay for some feeder bulls that we bought." Harris smiled. "You'll take the money from him, and everyone will think he was killed and robbed."

"You're sure he'll have the money?"

"Yes, as I said, he's taking a payment to Mitchell. Actually, he will have a little more than five hundred dollars since he always carries from twenty to fifty dollars anyway. You can take that as well, and consider it a bonus."

"If he doesn't have the money, just know that I'll be coming back for you," Frank said.

"He'll have the money."

CHAPTER EIGHT

Denver

State Senator Rex Underhill occupied a table near the now-cold, great stone fireplace of the Gentleman's Club of Denver. The Gentleman's Club was a very exclusive club, its membership not only controlled by the rather substantial dues the members were required to pay, but also because applicants for membership in the club had to receive unanimous approval from the existing members.

Membership in the club was eagerly sought, because it provided access to the most powerful men in city and state, both politically and economically.

Underhill wasn't the only person at the table. Also present was Albert Jaco, owner of AJ Mining. Jaco was a big man with a bald head that seemed to sit directly on his shoulders without the benefit of a neck.

"I have a problem," Jaco said. "The state of Colorado has put a restriction in place that prevents me from extending my operation into Mount St. John."

"Well, I'm always willing to help my constituents," Underhill said. He chuckled. "Even when they aren't my constituents," he added.

"It doesn't matter whether you represent me or not, I've been told that you can get things done. I wasn't told wrong, was I? You can get things done?"

"Mr. Jaco, it isn't a matter for whether I can get things done, you understand. Almost anyone in the general assembly can get things done. The question is, will I get it done?"

"Indeed, that is the question," Jaco replied. "So I will ask it. Will you do this for me?"

"How important is it to you that you get the state to remove that restriction?"

"Very important. When I had the Wahite mine there, I found a new vein, but I couldn't tap into it because it was restricted. I need that restriction ended."

Underhill held out his hand to silence Jaco.

"I don't think you understood my question. Now, listen again, and listen very carefully. How important is it to you that you get the state to remove that restriction?"

The confused expression on Jaco's face was replaced by an understanding smile.

"Oh, I would say, twenty-five hundred dollars," Jaco ventured.

Underhill shook his head. "No, that doesn't sound important enough."

"Three thousand?"

"I would think something that important would be worth at least five thousand dollars."

Jaco sighed. "Five thousand dollars," he said. He was quiet for a moment. "All right, five thousand dollars, but not one penny will be paid until after the restriction has been lifted."

"It will be gone within two days, and you may make your plans accordingly."

"You can guarantee this?"

"I can. And as you said, I won't expect a penny until after you are able to move onto Mount St. John."

Jaco nodded his head in gratitude. "Thank you, Senator."

"However, Mr. Jaco, if I get this done for you, and you don't keep up your end of the bargain, be advised that I can, quite easily, bankrupt your operation."

"Don't worry, you will be paid."

"Oh, I'm not worried," Underhill said with a diabolical smile. "You must try the chardonnay here." Underhill poured a glass for Jaco. "It is really quite good."

Underhill had every confidence that he would be able to remove the restriction that was preventing Jaco from expanding. And why shouldn't he have confidence he could get the job done? After all, he was the one who had gotten the restriction put on in the first place.

The Red Cliff to Mitchell road

Frank Petro, following the directions given him by Harris, waited behind a butte that not only afforded him a good view of the road, it also kept him out of view. Harris had described his brother to Frank.

"It will be impossible for you to miss him. He's quite a large man, and he wears a beard that comes down to his chest."

Frank had not seen anyone on the road for the entire morning and he was glad. He wanted nobody around.

Frank wanted to smoke, but he was afraid that the smell of tobacco would give him away. So, to assuage his craving, he took a pinch of tobacco from his pouch and, even though it wasn't chewing tobacco, put some in his mouth. He had just done that when he took another look, and that was when he saw the approaching rider. A quick perusal let Frank know that there was nobody else in sight.

As Harris had said, Abe Harris was easy to identify. The man coming up the road was easily over two hundred pounds, and he had a long, black beard. He seemed to be almost dozing in the saddle, not looking around at his surroundings as would a regular rider, but merely slumping in his saddle, content that the horse knew where it was going.

Abe Harris continued his ride, completely indifferent to anything around him. For a moment, Frank was concerned as to whether or not he would actually be carrying the money as Abe's brother had said. Why would anyone who was carrying so much money, be so unaware of his environment?

"Well, I'll soon know whether or not you've got the money," Frank said very quietly. "'Cause if you ain't a-carryin' it, I'll be callin' on your brother again."

Frank waited until Abe Harris was no more than ten yards away, then he stepped out in front of him.

His sudden appearance in the road startled the horse and he reared up, causing the rider to have to struggle to get him under control.

"Mister, it looks to me like your horse is about to get away from you," Frank said with a little laugh.

"What the hell are you doin', standin' in the middle of the road like that?"

"I've got a message from your brother," Frank said.

"From my brother? He's with my pa today. Did somethin' happen to Pa?"

"It ain't about your pa."

"Then, what's it about?"

"Your brother wants you dead," Frank said, pulling his pistol and pointing it at the rider.

"What?" the rider shouted in fear.

When Frank squeezed the trigger, he could see the puff of dust from the shirt at the point of impact of the bullet. And even from here he could hear the rider grunt as he was hit. It looked as if he was trying to stay erect, but he was unable to, and he slid from the saddle and lay on his back on the ground.

Frank pulled the hammer back on his pistol and approached the downed man.

"You carryin' five hunnert dollars?" Frank asked.

"How . . . did . . . you know?" Abe gasped.

"Your brother told me."

"My brother?"

"Yeah, it's like I told you, he wants you dead."

"Why would my brother want me dead?"

"He prob'ly wants you dead 'cause he's a greedy son of a bitch," Frank said, pulling the trigger again. Abe Harris died with a look of hurt disbelief on his face.

Frank searched the man's pockets and found only thirty-seven dollars.

"What?" he said aloud. "You only have thirty-seven dollars?"

Frank was about to get very angry when he saw the money belt. The money belt had fifty ten-dollar bills.

"Yeah," he said with a smile. "This is the easiest five hunnert dollars I ever made."

Remounting, he rode back toward Red Cliff and was at least five miles beyond where his encounter with Abe Harris had taken place before he saw anyone else on the road. It was a man, woman, and two kids in a buckboard.

"Howdy!" Frank greeted with a broad smile and a tip of his hat. "Would Red Cliff be ahead of me?"

"Yes, sir, no more than five or six miles," the man replied.

"Thank you much. Nice-looking kids you have there."

"That was a nice gentleman," Frank heard the woman say as he rode on into town.

After returning to Red Cliff, Frank dismounted in front of the Turkey Neck Saloon, then went inside to order a beer. There would be no need to nurse the beer this time—he could afford it and as many more beers as he wanted.

After the beer was delivered, Frank turned his back to the bar to peruse all the women, to see which one he liked best. He could not only afford one now, he could also afford to be choosy.

"It's funny, but when you was in here before, I didn't think you had any money," the woman said half an hour later as she sat up in the bed and held the sheet up in an attempt to provide some modesty.

Frank laughed. "What are you a-coverin' your titties for? It ain't like I ain't seen 'em. Hell, I seen ever'thing a while ago."

"I was working then, honey. I ain't workin' now."

"You're funny," Frank said as he pulled on his boots.

"Now that you have some money, you can come back and see me again."

"Why should I do that? Now that I got money, I don't have to spend it all on one woman."

"Where did you get the money?"

Frank stepped over to the bed and slapped the woman, hard.

The woman screamed and put her hands to her face to ward off a second slap.

"It ain't none of your business where I got the money," Frank said in a low growl.

There was a knock on the door then, followed by a woman's voice. "Suzie, are you all right?"

Frank pointed his pistol toward the door and pulled the hammer back. "Tell her it ain't nothin', or I'll shoot through the door."

"Oh, Edna, it's nothing, dear, just part of my act," Suzie called, putting as much gaiety in her voice as she could.

"Well, for heaven's sake, you had me worried there for a moment," Edna said from the other side of the door.

Frank eased the hammer back down, then holstered his pistol. "You just saved your friend's life," he said.

Frank reached over and jerked the sheet down, exposing Suzie's nudity. She gasped, but didn't call out.

"I just wanted one last look, is all," he said with a chuckle. He left, just as Suzie clutched the sheet around her again.

Leaving the saloon, Frank walked down the street to the War Drum Restaurant. Over dinner, he thought about his situation. Having five hundred dollars wasn't bad, but he considered it only a start. Now he could afford to plan something much bigger.

What about the bank in Big Rock? he asked himself. The bank was still there, and the money hadn't been took, so it was still there as well.

Yeah, that seemed like a real good idea. But he would have to gather some men, because it wasn't anything he could do alone.

CHAPTER NINE

"We'll take the surrey in," Smoke said just after breakfast. "Monte wanted Cal and me to be present for the inquest, but I think it would be a good thing if all four of us showed up. Under the circumstances we could all contribute."

"Is this young man someone we can trust?" Sally asked. "After all, he did try and hold up a bank."

"Yes, ma'am, I guess he did," Cal said. "I mean, all he did was sit out front and hold the horses, and I guess you can say that's the same thing. But I talked to him, Miss Sally. And, yes, ma'am, I'd say that he is someone we can trust."

"All right, Cal, if you are satisfied that we can trust him, that's good enough for me. We must all do what we can to help him," Sally said.

Big Rock

The courthouse was at the corner of Sikes and Center Street. Unlike a trial that would require a jury and often draw a gallery of as many as one hundred interested citizens, this was an inquest, and it was held before a court that was nearly empty. There was no bailiff's announcement when the judge came in, but Smoke and everyone else present stood, anyway. The presiding judge, Marshall Craig, was tall and thin, with a pinched face and a full head of white hair. His eyebrows were heavy and also white. He expected to see Sheriff Carson and the prisoner, but he was surprised to Smoke, Sally, Pearlie, and Cal present in the courtroom. Joel Montgomery, the banker, was there as well.

"Sheriff, can you explain the presence of all these people? I can understand why Mr. Montgomery might be here, and perhaps even Smoke Jensen, since he took part in the capture. But why all the others?"

"Your Honor, I think they will all be able to make a contribution to help you with your decision," Monte said.

"My decision?"

"Yes, Your Honor, we are going to ask you for something."

"All right," Judge Craig said. "Prisoner, would you stand, please, state your name, age, and where you are from?"

At Monte's urging, the boy stood. "Your Honor, my name is Leo Beajuex, and I'm seventeen years old . . ."

"Wait a minute, are you telling me that you're only seventeen?"

"Yes, sir."

Judge Craig looked back toward Monte. "Sheriff, wouldn't this case better be heard by a juvenile court?"

"Your Honor, you have the authority to preempt the juvenile court and the prisoner has asked that you do so."

"You sure about that, Sheriff? Does he understand that he would be tried as an adult?"

"Yes, sir, he does."

Judge Craig nodded. "All right." The judge returned his attention to the young prisoner. "You've given your name and age. Where are you from?"

"For the last year or so, Your Honor, I've been movin' aroun' in such places as Texas, 'n New Mexico, 'n now here. But I started out in New Orleans."

"Thank you, you may be seated. Sheriff, I believe you said that you wanted to enter a petition?"

"Yes, I do. Your Honor, I don't know how much you know about my background, but for the last fifteen years or so, I think you would be willing to say that I have been a good sheriff, a good citizen, and I have made a positive contribution to society."

"Yes, I would agree to that," Judge Craig said. "Though I hasten to add, Sheriff, that I don't see how your admittedly glowing attributes are germane to the case I am to decide."

"Yes, sir, well, I'm about to tell you that. You see, Judge, the truth is I haven't always walked the straight and narrow. It was Smoke Jensen that gave me the break that turned my life around."

"Mr. Jensen, do you have anything to add to that?" Judge Craig asked.

"I do, Your Honor. I did give Sheriff Carson the opportunity, but he is the one who turned his own life around, just as Pearlie and Cal have done. And they were both young when they came to work for me, Cal about the same age as young Leo here."

"All right, Sheriff. I will accept that you have managed to salvage a productive life from a poor start."

"And now, I'd like to give that same break to the boy, here."

"You two were mentioned as well. Do you have anything to add?" Judge Craig asked, looking toward Pearlie and Cal.

"Only, that if it hadn't been for Smoke, I'd more'n likely be dead by now," Pearlie said. "Probably by being hung."

"Cal?"

"Me, Your Honor? Well, I tried to hold up Miss Sally. I pulled a gun on her. But even though I done that, she took me in 'n made me a good law-abiding citizen."

"Even though I *did* that," Sally corrected with a smile.

"Yes, ma'am, even though I did that," Cal said, smiling as well. "Miss Sally has taught me a lot of things, too, like going to school, even."

"Yes, sir, she's taught me, too," Pearlie said.

"Mr. Montgomery, you are the aggrieved party here. It was your bank the subject of this hearing tried to rob. How do you stand?"

"Your Honor, if Mrs. Jensen can forgive a boy for trying to rob her, I can forgive a boy for trying to rob me."

Judge Craig studied all those who had just testified on Leo's behalf for a moment before he spoke again.

"All right, Sheriff, it looks like now what happens to Leo Beajuex is up to you. Would you be willing to take full responsibility for the boy?"

"Yes, sir, I would."

"Leo Beajuex, come over here and stand in front of me," the judge ordered.

Leo did as he was directed.

"I want you to understand this. This inquiry was conducted in an adult court, which means, by law, you are now subject to the same penalties as an adult. That means you would not be sentenced to a juvenile detention center as you would have been by being tried as a minor, but you are subject to be sentenced to the state penitentiary for the crime of bank robbery. And for that crime, I hereby sentence you to twenty years in the state penitentiary."

Leo gasped. "Twenty years!"

"Your Honor!" Monte called out, but he was silenced by the judge's raised hand.

"Please, Sheriff, let me finish," Judge Craig said before turning his attention back to Leo.

"Your sentence is for twenty years in prison. However, due to the fact that these good citizens have testified on your behalf, I am going to put that sentence in abeyance. I am going to remand you to the sheriff's custody for two years."

"What does *abeyance* mean?" Leo asked.

"It means that because the sheriff and all these good people have gone out on a limb to speak for you, you won't have to go to prison. But I am telling you now, young man, that if you violate their trust, in any way, you will be taken to the state penitentiary to serve every year of your sentence, starting not from now, but from the moment of your incarceration. On the other hand, if you have honored that trust, I will add the codicil that two years from this date, if you have not gotten into any trouble, the remainder of your sentence will be vacated."

"Thank you, Your Honor," Monte said.

"Leo, do you understand the responsibility I have just put on your shoulders?" the judge asked.

"Yes, sir. Uh, Your Honor. And I promise that you won't be sorry for this. I'm goin' to make Sheriff Carson 'n all these other good folks just real proud of me."

"Young man, I certainly hope you are right," Judge Craig said. He slapped his gavel upon the table. "This hearing is adjourned."

First Monte, then Smoke, Cal, and Pearlie shook Leo's hand. Sally gave him a hug.

Smoke threw a celebratory dinner at Lambert's, and he, Sally, Pearlie, Cal, Monte, and Leo were sitting at a table in the middle of the restaurant. Occasionally one of them would reach up to snatch a roll that was flying through the air, that being the signature of Lambert's, a restaurant that advertised itself as "Home of the Throwed Roll."

"I want to thank you, all of you, for what you've done for me," Leo said. "I . . . I've never known anyone like you all. I mean, people that is good and decent."

"That *are* good and decent," Sally said as she spread butter on a roll that Smoke had just caught for her.

"Beg your pardon, ma'am?"

"You said, 'that *is* good 'n decent.' You were supposed to say, 'that *are* good and decent,'" Cal said with a little laugh. "You see, the thing you need to know is, Miss Sally used to be a teacher 'n she can't hardly get it out of her system."

"I still am a teacher," Sally said. "Though, apparently, I haven't done as good a job with you as I should have. Otherwise you would know better than to say 'can't hardly.' The word *hardly* is superfluous."

"Wow, I've never heard anyone who can talk like you do," Leo said, obviously impressed.

"Oh, Miss Sally can talk to beat all hell, yes, sirree, there ain't no gettin' around that, 'n that's for damn sure," Pearlie said. "I mean, if you just listen to her, why she can learn you lots of things."

Sally laughed out loud. "All right, Pearlie, you have put me in my proper place. I'll be quiet now and beg forgiveness for my intrusion."

"Ma'am, what do you mean Pearlie put you in place? I thought that was real good what he said about you," Leo said.

"Lord have mercy, my work is going to be cut out with you," Sally said, shaking her head but ameliorating the gesture with a friendly smile.

"Sheriff, now that you've got me out of jail 'n all, it seems to me like I'm goin' to have to find myself a job, and to tell the truth I'm not sure where to start," Leo said. "I mean, I just tried to hold up the bank in this town, so I'm not sure there will be that many people willin' to hire me."

"Monte, I'd be glad to take him on out at Sugarloaf," Smoke offered.

"I appreciate the offer, Smoke, but I think Leo will be working for me," Monte said.

"Workin' for you?" A broad smile spread across Leo's face. "You mean I'm goin' to get to wear a star?"

Monte chuckled. "Maybe someday," he agreed. "But for now I'll find other things for you to do. I'm sure I can keep you busy, and maybe you can learn a little bit about what goes on, on this side of the law."

"Yes, sir, I really would like that."

"If you don't mind, Leo, I'll drop in from time to time just to see how you are getting along," Cal offered.

"Thanks, I'd appreciate that. I ain't never really had no real friend before. And maybe you would bring some more cookies?"

Smoke glanced over at Sally, who cringed at Leo's comment but offered no correction.

"Oh, I think I can do better than that. I'll bring you some of Miss Sally's bear sign."

"What's that?"

"You've never eaten bear sign?" Pearlie asked.

"No, sir, I ain't."

"Haven't," Sally, Cal, Pearlie, and Smoke corrected, simultaneously.

Everyone, including Leo, laughed.

"Let's just say that they are about a hundred times better than cookies," Cal said.

"I'd sure like to taste them, then. I didn't think there was a thing in the world any better than cookies."

"Cal, you seem to be investing a lot of yourself into Leo," Sally said later that day after all had returned to the ranch.

"Yes, ma'am, I suppose I am," Cal agreed. "But I'll tell you the truth, Miss Sally, when I look at him, I see myself when I was just about his age. And I'm not fooling myself, if I had kept on going the way I was, I'm sure I would be dead by now, more'n likely by being shot while trying to pull off a robbery somewhere.

"The reason I'm still here is because someone gave me a second chance. And I'm just wanting to do that for Leo."

Sally smiled at Cal, then leaned over and kissed him on his forehead.

"Ha! Cal, some few years from now if this all works out, you're not goin' to lean over and kiss Leo on the forehead, are you?" Pearlie asked with a teasing laugh.

"Not unless you let me practice on you first," Cal said, starting toward him.

"Arrgh, no! Get away from me!" Pearlie shouted, running from Cal.

Smoke and Sally laughed out loud.

CHAPTER TEN

Denver

Albert Jaco stood just outside State Senator Rex Underhill's office, having told Senator Underhill's clerk, a moment earlier, that he was here to see the senator.

"The senator will see you now, Mr. Jaco," the clerk said, coming from the inner office.

"Mr. Jaco, come in, come in," Underhill invited. "Can I offer you something to drink? A cup of coffee, a glass of wine?"

"This isn't a social call, Senator. You sent word for me to come see you, and here I am. I hope you aren't going to tell me you couldn't get that restriction taken care of."

"On the contrary, my good man. Here it is," Underhill said, handing a document across the desk.

ACT *of*
RELIEF OF RESTRICTION

KNOW ALL MEN BY THESE PRESENTS that Mount St. John, heretofore set aside by covenant of the state of Colorado, has had such restriction lifted. Exclusive rights to prospect, develop, and mine any precious metals therein, are transferred to Albert Jaco. These rights are granted in perpetuity.

"Well, Mr. Jaco, you can't say that I don't deliver for you," Underhill said.

"Yeah," Jaco said. "Yeah, that's good, that's good."

"There is a codicil to the order."

"Codicil?"

"Yes, something you must sign in order for the act to take effect."

"What is it?"

"You must sign an agreement that all monies earned as a result of mining on Mount St. John will be assessed a thirty percent operational fee to be paid to the Colorado Department of Standards."

"What? I've never heard of such a thing."

"Legislation is a matter of negotiation. You must give something to someone else, and in order to get what you want, give and take," Underhill said. "Believe me, this was absolutely necessary to get this enactment passed."

"It's going to cost me thirty percent to get the silver out," Jaco complained. "Add that to the thirty percent you're asking for and it'll cost me sixty percent."

"You'll still have a profit of forty percent," Underhill pointed out. "And there are a lot of businesses that don't clear a forty percent profit."

Jaco nodded. "What is this Department of Standards, anyway?"

"It's a subcommittee that monitors all mineral extractions within the state."

"In other words, just another way for the state to get more money from the people," Jacob said bitterly.

Underhill chuckled. "Indeed that is so, Mr. Jaco. It would appear that you do have an understanding of how government works."

There was no state government entity called the Department of Standards. That was a shell created by Underhill as a means of collecting more money than the agreed-upon fee for getting the restriction lifted.

Sugarloaf Ranch

True to his word, Cal dropped in on Leo at least once a week for the next few months, then about six months after the court had remanded Leo into Monte's custody, when Sally learned that it was Leo's eighteenth birthday, she asked Cal if he would like to invite Leo out to spend the day with them.

"Yes, ma'am, thank you, I would like to do that," Cal replied. "It would be a good thing for Leo to have a home-cooked meal especially on his birthday, and especially one cooked by you."

"All right, why don't you ask him?"

"Cal, it turns out that I'm going to have to visit the blacksmith shop, so if you'd like, we can ride in together," Smoke invited.

"Yeah, I would like that," Cal said.

Big Rock

When Cal stepped into the sheriff's office later that morning, Leo was sitting at a table with a disassembled kerosene lantern spread out on a table in front of him.

"What in the world are you doing, Leo? You'll never get that thing put back together," Cal challenged.

"Tell 'im, Sheriff," Leo said.

Monte was leaning back in his chair, with his feet propped up on his desk, and when Leo spoke, he looked around from behind the newspaper he was reading.

"He's took apart three others and got them put back together," the sheriff said.

"Why are you doing that?"

"I'm cleanin' them," Leo said. "The burner, the wick spool, the chimney. If you get 'em all cleaned up, it makes 'em burn easier and brighter."

"How long will it take you to get that put back together? The reason I ask is Miss Sally said I should ask you to come out and spend your birthday with us for lunch and dinner."

"She's making a lunch for dinner?"

Cal chuckled. "No, what you 'n I have always called *dinner*, she calls *lunch*, and what we call *supper*, she calls *dinner*. It's kinda confusin' till you figure out what she means. Anyhow, if you can get that thing put back together in time, come on out to the ranch and have dinner and supper with us today."

"Ha! I'll have this thing put together in no time!" Leo promised. "Uh, I can go, can't I, Sheriff?"

"I have no problem with it. After all, it is your birthday. Oh, when you were sweeping out the cells, was Beemus awake yet?"

"No, sir, last time I looked in, Mr. Beemus was still sleepin' it off."

"Well, he had a pretty good drunk on last night, and I figured he'd be more comfortable in a jail cot than if I left him passed out in the alley." Monte pointed to the key hook. "Before you leave, how about going back there to let him out of jail? If he's still asleep, wake him up."

"Yes, sir," Leo said.

It took only a couple of minutes to reassemble the lantern, then, when Leo started toward the cell area, Cal went with him.

When they stepped back into the cell area, they saw a man with long white hair and a white beard, who was sitting on the edge of the cot.

"Good morning, Mr. Beemus," Cal said pleasantly.

"It's in the morning?" Beemus replied.

"Yes, sir."

"How many days have I been here?"

"You just come in last night."

"I was drunk when I come in, was I?"

"Yes, sir, you was drunk as a skunk," Leo said with a little chuckle.

"I need a drink. Was there any whiskey left in my bottle?"

"Yes, sir, there was 'bout half, maybe three quarters of a bottle left, but me 'n Cal here drunk ever' drop," Leo teased.

"You did what?" Beemus shouted, then he stopped and shook his head. "No, you're lyin' to me, boy, 'n the reason I know you're lyin' is 'cause there ain't no way I could get drunk on less'n a half a bottle, 'n more'n likely it took a whole bottle."

"You caught me, Mr. Beemus," Leo said with a smile. "When the sheriff brung you in last night, you didn't have a drop left."

"Good," Beemus said, nodding. "I'm sure glad I drunk all of it. I hate to see good whiskey go to waste."

"Good whiskey? The sheriff said it was the cheapest whiskey you could get at the Brown Dirt."

"Sonny, someday you'll learn that all whiskey is good whiskey," Beemus said. "Uh, listen, did I do anything while I was drunk? I mean, somethin' that's goin' to keep me in jail for a long time?"

"No, sir, the only thing you done was get drunk 'n start in a-peein' behind the saloon afore you finally passed out." Cal unlocked the cell door then pulled it open. "Fact is, Sheriff says you're free to go now."

"What, before dinner?"

"Yes, sir, Sheriff Carson told me to come back here and turn you out."

"The sheriff is turnin' me out before dinner," Beemus repeated, but this time it wasn't a question, it was a comment. "Damn, this town is gettin' cheap when they don' even feed their prisoners." Beemus grabbed his hat.

When the three men passed through the front office, Beemus looked over at Monte. "Hey, Sheriff, I thought you was supposed to feed your prisoners. How come it is that you're a-tellin' me I got to get out of jail afore I even get to eat my dinner?" he asked.

"We tried to feed breakfast to you, but we couldn't get you to wake, so we ate it," Monte said.

"What?"

"Here's a quarter. That'll get you the plate lunch special just around the corner at the City Pig," Monte said.

Beemus snorted what might have been a thank-you, then left.

"Cal, did Smoke happen to come into town with you this morning?" Monte asked.

"Yes, sir, he's just next door at the blacksmith shop. He's havin' Earl forge a couple of angle irons for him."

"Would you ask him to drop in and see me if he has a minute?"

"Sure will, Sheriff."

"Sheriff, is it all right if I go now?" Leo asked.

Monte made a little dismissive motion with his hand, and Cal and Leo left.

Because Earl's Blacksmith Shop was next door to the sheriff's office, it was less than a minute after Cal and Leo left that Smoke showed up.

Monte looked up as Smoke came in.

"Hello, Monte, what can I do for you this morning?" Smoke asked, using the question as a way of greeting.

"Have you read today's paper?" Monte asked.

"No, not yet." Smoke got a concerned look on his face. "Why do you ask, Monte? Has something happened that I should know about?"

"No, no, nothing like that," Monte said. "I'm sorry, I didn't mean to worry you. It's something else I'd like to talk to you about."

"All right, I'm listening."

"First, let me ask you this. Do you know Senator Chilcott?" Monte asked.

Smoke nodded. "I've met him a time or two. I haven't spoken to him since he agreed to take Senator Teller's place when Teller was appointed secretary of the interior. Why do you ask?"

"That's the newspaper article I was wantin' to talk to you about. I was reading in the *Big Rock Journal* that Phil thinks Chilcott isn't planning on going back to Washington when the new session is seated. Have you heard anything about that?"

"No, I haven't. But if that's what it says in the paper, it's probably true. Phil is really good about keeping up with such things. Of course, that's what makes him a good newspaperman, I guess."

"I reckon that's true. But reading that article got me to thinking. If Chilcott truly is going to leave at the end of this term, then that means that someone else is going to have to replace him, don't you think?" Monte asked.

"That's true," Smoke replied. "Monte, where is this discussion going? Are you getting a little ambitious, here? Are you telling me that you are thinking about standing for the U.S. Senate?"

"I don't know. I must confess that the idea does interest me, somewhat. But I can't help but wonder if I did decide to do something like that, how much support would I have? I mean, I'm just the sheriff in a small town and I wasn't even elected to this office. You started this town, Smoke, and you're the one who appointed me sheriff."

"I appointed you, yes, but, Monte, if we had to elect a sheriff today there is no doubt in my mind but that you would get the vote of every Big Rock citizen. That is, if anybody would be foolish enough to run against you in the first place."

"I appreciate that, and I think that's true but, like I said, this is just one small town. A senator would have to represent the entire state."

"Yes, but the citizens of the state don't vote for senators. If you decided to run, you would only have to win the approval of the members of the general assembly," Smoke said.

"That's true, but they will be influenced by their constituency, so the advantage would still lie with he, who is well known."

"Or with the person who can most effectively work the general assembly for votes he would need. And the truth is, Monte, that in that case someone who isn't well known would have about as good a chance as someone who is well known."

"Yes, I think you might be right about that. Smoke, if I decided to do such a thing, would I be able to count on your support?"

"You know you can, Monte."

Monte chuckled. "You know, Ina Claire tried to talk me into running for Congress back when we first became a state, and I did give it some thought but I passed on the idea. I think she was very disappointed that I didn't run. If I decide I'd like to try this, I know she would be looking down on me and giving me her approval."

"I'm sure she would."

"It's just that . . ."

Monte paused in midsentence.

"You're afraid that your past will catch up with you?"

"Yes."

"Monte, it took a special kind of person to come here and open up the West. Many of us did things that we aren't proud of; things that we needed to do to survive. You have not only survived, you have become, well, I'm not as good with words as Sally, but she would say something like, *You have become one of the stalwart members of our community.* And there is no doubt in my mind but that if you decide to make a try of the United States Senate that is exactly how everyone will think of you."

"Thanks for the words of encouragement, Smoke. It will give me something to think about while I consider whether I want to do this or not."

CHAPTER ELEVEN

Capitol Hill, Denver

Because the salary for a state senator was quite modest, only the wealthy could actually afford to take up the office and those who did become state representatives or senators did so for the prestige the office offered. However, there were some, men without scruples, who took the job in order to use the position to provide opportunities for personal enrichment. Rex Underhill was just such a person, and he had been able to turn his position as state senator into a most profitable occupation.

But if being a state senator was profitable, being a United States senator, he knew, would be much more profitable. And now with Chilcott's announcement that he did not intend to return to the United States Senate, the way was open for Underhill to try and gain the seat.

Underhill knew of at least three other state senators and four representatives in the state general assembly who augmented their salary in the same way that Underhill did, by selling their position, influence, and vote to the highest bidder. He and the others not only knew of one another, they often worked together, uniting to make their graft more powerful.

Where better to start, he asked himself, than with one of those solons whose vote would be for sale?

Senator Nathaniel Toone was one of the other corrupt senators, and he was the first one Underhill went to with his plan.

"And why should I help you become a United States senator?" Toone asked.

"Consider this, Nate. As a United States senator there will be many more opportunities to, let us say, convert service to profit. And I don't intend to keep those opportunities to myself. Look at it as a means of expanding your own opportunities as well, since I will be your conduit into new avenues of remuneration for us all."

Toone raised his finger. "I will support you," he said. "But if I find one example of you holding out, I'll ruin you."

"Now, why would I piss in my own pudding?" Underhill replied with an ingratiating smile. "Why, I expect most of my business will come from those of you who share this same shadow profession."

"Yes, you may have a point there. I can see where that might be so." Now Toone smiled as well. "All right, let's do it."

Sugarloaf Ranch

"Miss Sally, this is about the happiest birthday ever, and not only that, this was one of the best meals I've ever had," Leo said. "I thank you, ma'am, for invitin' me out."

"You're very welcome, young man," Sally replied.

"Leo, I see that you are wearing your pistol. Are you any good with it?" Cal asked.

"I don't know. Good enough, I guess."

Cal chuckled. "If you don't know, that means you aren't good enough. Come on outside with me, let's do some shooting."

"All right," Leo agreed.

"Don't shoot yourself in the foot, now," Pearlie teased as the two young men left.

Smoke waited until they were gone before he told of his visit with Sheriff Carson, adding that at this point, he had not yet decided whether to seek the upcoming vacant seat in the United States Senate or not.

"I didn't want to talk about it while Leo was in here, because if Monte wants him to know about it, I think he should have the right to tell him, himself."

"Well, I think Monte should make a try for it. I know that he would make a very good senator," Sally said. "And I don't believe he would ever lose contact with the people he represents, as so many others have."

"He is a little concerned about his past," Smoke said. "If you recall, he sold his gun for a while."

"Yes, but only to those parties who had a legitimate need for a hired gun. And if you remember, the very reason we met him was because he would not use his gun against us," Sally replied.

"That's true," Smoke agreed.

"And anyway, the most important thing is that, regardless of his past, he is a genuinely decent person," Sally insisted.

"Salt of the earth," Smoke added.

"So, do you think he'll run?" Pearlie asked. "Because if he does run, I'll sure vote for him."

Smoke chuckled. "Right now, your guess is as good as mine as to what he's going to decide. But if he does decide to try for it, you won't be able to vote for him."

"What do you mean I won't be able to vote for him? I voted for Frederick Pitkin for governor in the last election, didn't I?"

"You won't be able to vote for him because U.S. senators aren't elected by the people. They are appointed by the general assembly," Sally said.

"Really? I didn't know that. Somehow, it doesn't seem right that I'm a citizen, but I can't vote."

"Tell me about it," Sally said.

"Oh, oh, you have just hit on a sore spot with Sally," Smoke said with a little smile. "Women's suffrage."

"Women suffering?"

"Yes. We're suffering because we can't vote," Sally said without further explanation.

"You know, I've heard some folks saying that they don't think women should get the vote because they don't think women are smart enough to know what they're doing," Pearlie said. "Well, I don't know about all the other women, but, Miss Sally, I think you should be able to vote because, man or woman, I do believe you're the smartest person I've ever known."

"Nice try, Pearlie, but your piece of birthday cake won't be any bigger than anyone else's," Sally teased.

* * *

"Take a shot at that little branch for me," Cal said after he and Leo had walked a safe distance away from the house.

"You think I can't hit it?" Leo asked.

"I don't know. Can you?"

Leo raised the pistol to eye level and fired. His bullet snapped off a piece of the branch and with a smug expression on his face he turned toward Cal. "You didn't think I could do it, did you?"

"Proud of yourself, are you?"

"Well, yeah. You told me to shoot at that little branch. That's what I done, 'n I hit it."

"That's what you did, all right," Cal said. "But you aimed at it."

"Of course I aimed at it. That's what you told me to do, isn't it?"

"No, I told you to shoot it; I didn't say anything about aiming at it. Why did you aim at it?" Cal asked.

"Cal, you ain't makin' no sense at all."

"Why did you aim at it?" Cal asked again.

"Because I wanted to hit what I was shootin' at. That's why."

"Shoot at it again, but don't aim this time."

"What do you mean, 'don't aim'? I don't understand. Cal, you ain't, uh, well, it's like I said, you aren't making any sense. How am I going to hit it, if I don't aim? How could anyone hit that little limb there without aiming at it? I mean, even aiming at it, it's a hard shot."

"This is what I mean," Cal said, drawing and shooting in one smooth motion. Again a little piece of the branch flew off.

"Wow! How did you do that?" Leo asked. "You didn't even aim."

"I thought the bullet onto the target."

"I don't understand what that means. How can somebody think the bullet to the target?"

"Here's the thing," Cal said as he put his pistol back in the holster. "There's no sense in drawing really fast, if you have to stop and aim. You have to draw, aim, and shoot, all at the same time. And in order to do that, you have to think the bullet onto the target. Now, you try it."

Leo pulled the pistol and, automatically, started to raise it. He stopped himself, then held the gun out in front of his body and fired. He missed.

"You know why you missed?" Cal asked.

Leo chuckled. "Yeah, I missed 'cause I didn't hit the target."

"No, you missed because you thought you would miss. And I told you, the bullet goes where you think it will go."

Leo shook his head and chuckled. "Lord have mercy, Cal, you need to listen to what you're sayin'. Bullets don't know you are thinking about them, because . . . they're bullets. So how can you think a bullet to its target?"

"Let me show you what I mean when I say 'think a bullet to its target.'"

Again Cal made a quick, smooth draw, firing the instant the gun came up, and again a piece of the limb flew off.

"Like that," Cal said.

"How is it that you are able to shoot like that?"

"I learned from Smoke."

"And now you're learning me."

"No, I'm not learning you, I'm *teaching* you." Cal laughed. "That's good grammar, and that, I learned from Miss Sally. If you are around here enough, you'll learn that Miss Sally is pure dee hell on using the right words."

"I know what you mean. She's already learned me . . . I mean taught me a few things," Leo said. "But right now I'd rather be learning to shoot, so I don't reckon she would have anything to do with that."

"Hah, don't be getting the wrong idea about Miss Sally. Grammar isn't the only thing she's good at. She's as good a shot as I am. Pearlie, too, and she's nearly as good as Smoke."

"You're kidding me. There's no way a woman could do that."

"There have been a few bad guys who made that same mistake. It was the last mistake they ever made."

"Miss Sally must be some lady," Leo said.

"She sure is," Cal said. "Now, here, let me help you out. What you want to do is turn yourself at an angle so that you aren't facing the target." He put his hands on Leo's shoulders and repositioned him the way he wanted him to go. "Now, don't turn your body, but look at the target by turning your head back toward it."

"Why do I want to do that?"

"It makes you a smaller target. It doesn't matter now, because that tree isn't going to shoot back," Cal added with a chuckle. "But you may as well get yourself into the habit of standing this way."

Cal helped Leo reposition himself. "Now, do you have a feel for how you're standin'?"

Leo nodded in the affirmative.

"Bring the pistol up to eye level and aim at the target, just as you did the first time, but this time, don't pull the trigger," Cal said.

"I thought you said, don't do that."

"Forget about that for a moment. I want you to do it this time. But remember, don't pull the trigger."

Leo brought the pistol up to eye level and aimed it. "Bang," he said.

"Good. Now, close your eyes and lower your pistol so that it is pointing straight down. Aim at the target again, but this time with your eyes closed."

"What do you mean, aim at it again? How am I going to do that if my eyes are closed?"

"Just listen to me, Leo. Close your eyes, then with your eyes still closed, bring your arm back up, thinking about where the target is. When you think you have it lined up, tell me."

With his eyes still closed, Leo brought his arm up until he thought he was aligned with the target.

"Pull the trigger, but don't open your eyes."

Leo pulled the trigger.

"Now, open your eyes and look."

Leo opened his eyes and saw that his bullet had hit just below the small branch he had been shooting at. It was a miss, but it was a very close miss.

"Wow, look at that! I almost hit it!" he said excitedly.

"Yeah, well, almost is pretty good, but it's not good enough. Now, spread your feet apart about the width of your shoulders. Keep your legs straight, but not stiff. Think you can do that?"

Leo tried it a few times, then he nodded. "Yes, I can do it," he said.

"That's very good."

"Cal, what about my other hand?"

"What do you mean, what about your other hand?"

"Well, I was just thinkin'. It seems to me like if I had a gun in the other hand, I'd be twice as likely to hit the target. I mean, what with shootin' two guns instead of one."

"No, you would be only half as likely to hit your target."

"Why would you say that?"

"Which bullet would you be thinking about?"

"Why, I'd be thinkin' about both of 'em."

Call shook his head. "It's impossible to think about both bullets at the same time. It's not just the bullets, you can't think about any two things at the same time."

"That's not true."

"Miss Sally made you a chocolate birthday cake and we're going to have it for dessert tonight. I want you to think about a big ole piece of that cake."

Leo smiled as he contemplated the cake. "I can almost taste it."

"What's the sum of ten, five, and seven?"

"It's, uh . . ."

"Are you still thinking about that chocolate birthday cake?"

"No, I'm cipherin' . . . wait. You're right. You can't think of two things at the same time, can you?"

"No, and nobody can. The only reason you'd ever want two guns is in case you run out of bullets with your first one," Cal said.

"Yeah, I guess I see that now."

"All right, let's continue," Cal said, resuming his instruction. "Put your pistol back in the holster, then look at your target by turning your head and eyes slightly without moving from the neck down. When you know exactly where the target is, pull the pistol from the holster, but don't raise the gun to eye level. Shoot it as soon as your arm comes level."

"Should I try a quick draw?"

"No. That comes later. First learn to shoot, then you can learn to draw. The fastest draw in the world doesn't mean anything if you can't hit your target. Now, pull the gun and shoot it."

Leo pulled the pistol and fired as soon as it came level. He had no idea where the bullet went.

"Don't try and think your bullet to that little limb, right now. Just think it into the trunk of the tree."

Leo drew and fired again, just nipping the edge of the tree trunk.

"You know when I said, think about Miss Sally's chocolate cake? Would you believe me if I said that she makes the best cake in the world?" Cal asked.

"If she bakes as good as she cooks, yeah, I believe you."

"All right, then, what do you say we go have us a piece?"

"Yes!" Leo responded enthusiastically.

"But not now."

"What do you mean, 'not now'? When?"

"We'll go as soon as you can put three rounds in that tree, chest high and close enough together that I can cover all three bullets with the palm of my hand."

"Can you do that? I mean, put three bullets into the trunk of the tree and cover it with . . ."

Before Leo could finish his sentence Cal drew and fired, the three shots so close together that it sounded like one sustained roar.

"Ha! You only hit it once!" Leo said.

"Let's check it out."

The two walked toward the tree, but even before they got there, Leo could tell that there was more than one bullet there. There was one hole, but it was enlarged enough to accommodate all three bullets Cal had fired.

CHAPTER TWELVE

"I never thought I'd be able to do it," Leo said as he polished off a huge piece of chocolate cake. "It's a miracle."

"No, if you want to know what the real miracle is, it's that you are learning to shoot at all, considering the one that's teaching you. Cal can barely shoot himself," Pearlie teased.

"Oh?" Sally said. "Who was it that Cal beat at the Fourth of July celebration last summer? Oh, wait, it was you, wasn't it?"

"Ahh, Cal just got real lucky is all, and I was having an off day."

"And Miss Sally beat both of us," Cal said.

"Only it didn't count, because they didn't let women compete," Sally said.

"Well, you can see why, can't you, Sally? There's not a man in Big Rock that you can't outshoot, and they just don't want to be shown up, is all," Smoke said.

"You mean Miss Sally is a better shot than Sheriff Carson?" Leo asked.

"She is a better shot than any man in Big Rock," Smoke repeated.

"Smoke, you can't actually make a definitive statement about that," Sally said. "Monte and I have never competed against each other."

"No, and you aren't likely to, as long as that dumb rule is on that says you can't shoot in any shooting contest," Cal said. "But I bet you could beat him."

"I don't mean no offense or nothin', Miss Sally, but I never knowed no women that could shoot that good," Leo said.

"Uhnnuh!" Sally said, pressing her hands to the side of her head.

"I'm sorry, like I said, I don't mean that I don't believe you can't shoot."

Pearlie laughed. "It's not that you are challenging her, Leo, it's the way you are saying it."

"Good for you, Pearlie. Now you say it correctly, will you, please? I can't stand to have that sentence stuck in my brain."

"I mean no offense, Miss Sally, but I have never known any women who could shoot that well."

Sally smiled. "Very good, Pearlie. Now, young man, come with me. I plan to give you a demonstration, which I hope will prevent you from jumping to conclusions in the future."

Not only Leo, but everyone walked outside with Sally. Leo watched as she put two bottles on two fence posts, separated by about twenty yards. Then she moved away so that standing at the apex of the triangle, she was twenty yards from each of them.

"Is she going to draw and shoot without aiming, the way you did, Cal?"

"Oh, you just wait and see. It'll be much more than that," Cal replied.

After Sally was in position, she put a pie pan on the ground in front of her.

"What's the pie pan for?"

"Just hold your horses, Leo. You're about to see somethin' that if I just told you about it, you wouldn't believe me," Cal said.

Sally put a bullet in her hand, then held her hand out over the pie pan.

"Smoke?" Sally said.

"Now!" Smoke called.

Sally dropped the bullet, then pulled her pistol and fired twice, breaking both bottles before the clank of the bullet in the pie pan.

"Good Lord a'mighty!" Leo said, stunned by what he had just seen.

"Now, in addition to the birthday cake, I also made an apple pie. Does anyone have room enough to have a piece?" Sally asked calmly, as she put the pistol back in its holster and started toward the house.

Everyone but Leo began to follow Sally. Cal took several steps before he realized Leo wasn't with them.

"Leo? You coming?"

"Good Lord a'mighty," Leo said again.

Big Rock

"Oh yes, I am well aware of how good Mrs. Jensen is with a gun," Monte said after Leo told the sheriff about his visit to Sugarloaf Ranch. "She is a most unique woman, she is beautiful, a better shot than any man I know, courageous to a fault, and she is smart as a whip. Yes, sir, Smoke drew a royal flush when he met up with her."

"What was Mrs. Carson like? Could she shoot real good, like Miss Sally?"

Monte shook his head. "I don't know any woman who can shoot as well as Mrs. Jensen. This isn't to say that Ina Claire couldn't shoot pretty well herself. She was very good with a long gun, as good as most men, I would wager.

"I said that Smoke drew a royal flush when he met up with Mrs. Jensen, but I drew four aces with Ina Claire. She was also beautiful, courageous, and smart. But that wasn't the best thing about her."

"What was the best thing about her?"

Monte looked at Leo and smiled. "The best thing about her was that she took a low-life scoundrel like me, someone who had only taken from society, and she not only put up with me, she actually loved such a person. More than that, she made me into the man I am today, someone who gives to society, rather than takes from it."

"That's kind of like what you're doin' for me, Sheriff," Leo said.

"I'm certainly trying to," Monte agreed.

"Maybe someday I'll find a woman like that."

"Hold up your right hand," Monte said.

"What?"

"Do you want to be a deputy?"

"Yes! More than anything! But I thought you said I was too young."

"That was when you were seventeen. You had a birthday today and that means you are eighteen. Besides, there were a lot of brave soldiers who fought in the war who were even younger than you are. And, since you were old enough to be an outlaw, I don't see why you wouldn't be old enough to be on this side of the law now."

Monte opened the middle drawer of his desk and took out a star. "Now, hold up your right hand."

Leo did so.

"Do you, Leo Beajuex, swear that as deputy sheriff you will faithfully follow the orders given you by any superior law officer, that would be me, and that you will serve Eagle County and the state of Colorado, to the best of your ability?"

"Yeah, I will," Leo replied excitedly.

"No, the correct response is, *I, Leo Beajuex, so swear.*"

"Oh. I, Leo Beajuex, so swear."

"Then I, Monte Carson, as sheriff, do hereby appoint you my deputy."

Leo stood there, proudly, as Monte affixed the badge to his shirt.

"Now, how would you like to make the rounds for me?"

"Yes, oh yes!" Leo said.

"Son?" Monte called out to him as he started toward the door.

"Yes, sir?"

"Don't let that badge go to your head. Remember you are to serve the people, not try 'n lord it over 'em. I know that there are some lawmen who do that, but as far as I'm concerned, anyone who would do something like that is the scourge of the earth."

"Sheriff, I'm goin' to try 'n be as much like you as I can," Leo replied.

"That's a nice thing for you to say, son, and I appreciate it. But what I really want is for you to be your own man, that is, as long as being your own man also means you're abiding by the law."

"I'll do that, Sheriff, I promise you."

Leo threw a proud little wave toward Monte as he left to make the rounds for the very first time, on his own.

After Leo left, Monte stood in the window of his office and watched as his new, young deputy walked west on Front Street, touching his hat in greeting to every lady he met. Monte had called him "son." Maybe he was pushing it a bit, but he enjoyed thinking of Leo that way. If things had worked out differently, he and Ina Claire might have had a son of their own. Or perhaps he and Rosemary.

As it turned out, Ina Claire wasn't able to have children. And Rosemary didn't live long enough.

"Ina Claire and Rosemary," Monte said. "I reckon by now that the two of you have met, up there in heaven. And if you have, I know you have made friends with each other by now. Funny that I've been able to have the love of two women, but here I am, all alone again."

Monte sat back down at his desk and thought of the event that had so changed his life.

The Linus Carson farm
Jackson County, Missouri, 1863

Rosemary had just stepped out onto the back porch to draw a bucket of water from the pump when she saw the soldiers coming into the yard. They were Yankee soldiers, she could tell not only by their uniforms, but also because she recognized the Williams brothers, Reuben and Angus. Reuben was a captain, and the leader of the group. Angus was a lieutenant.

Setting the bucket down she walked out to the end of the porch to speak to them.

"Hello, Reuben," she said. It wasn't a particularly friendly greeting, but neither was it particularly hostile. Because the Williamses owned a nearby farm, she had known Reuben and Angus from the time they were children together. In fact, there had been a time in Rosemary's life when she had thought that she might, one day, marry Reuben. But, like many Missourians, her family and the Williams family had been divided by the war.

"It's *Captain Williams*," Reuben said stiffly.

"All right, Captain Williams, why are you here?"

"Where is Jerry Carson?" Captain Williams asked, referring to the man Rosemary did marry.

"I don't know. I haven't seen *Captain* Carson for several days," Rosemary emphasized the word *Captain*.

"He isn't a captain. He's a secesh traitor and a thief. Yesterday, he and his band of bushwhackers robbed a pay courier. Since he's your husband, I figure he more'n likely brought some of the money here."

"If he did rob a pay courier it was a part of the war, and any money he may have gotten would be used by the Confederacy. He certainly wouldn't have used the money to enrich himself," Rosemary said emphatically. "Anyway, I don't know where he is."

"I don't believe that you don't know where he is. I believe he might be hiding out right here, in this house."

"He isn't here. There is a war going on, and he

moves around," Rosemary said. "As a matter of fact, it has been almost a month since I saw him last."

"Yeah? Well, know this. When I find him, I'm going to hang him."

"Reuben, you wouldn't do that. Yes, I know that the war has divided you, but you, Angus, and Jerry have always been friends, good friends. Why, you have fished together, hunted together, surely you don't mean what you are saying."

"Oh, but I do mean it," Reuben said.

"What has happened to you, Reuben? You were never like this. You, you were sweet on me once, remember?"

"Yeah," Reuben said. "Only thing is, you chose the wrong man. And it's like you said, there is a war going on. And I'm afraid that I have no sympathies for traitors, like your husband."

"The men who have chosen to fight for the South aren't traitors—they are following their conscience, that's all. Just as you are following yours."

"You mean like your father-in-law, the colonel? I hear that he has left General Price's army. I suppose you are going to tell me that you haven't seen him, either?"

"No, he's here. He's in bed, sick."

"Bring him out."

"No, I can't do that. I told you, Colonel Carson is sick."

"Bring him out," Reuben repeated. "You're both going to have to leave this farm."

"Leave the farm? What do you mean, we're going to have to leave the farm? Why would we do that? This place belongs to my husband and his father. You've got no right to order us to leave."

"Yeah, I do," Reuben said. He reached down into his dispatch case and removed a piece of paper, then, holding it in front of him, he began to read.

"General Order Number 11.

"Headquarters District of the Border,

"Kansas City, August 25, 1863.

"1. All persons living in Jackson, Cass, and Bates counties, Missouri, and in that part of Vernon included in this district are hereby ordered to remove from their present places of residence within fifteen days from the date hereof. Officers commanding companies and detachments serving in the counties named will see that this paragraph is promptly obeyed.

"2. All grain and hay in the field or under shelter, in the districts from which inhabitants are required to remove, will be taken to such stations and turned over to the proper officers. All grain and hay not confiscated will be destroyed along with all houses and outhouses of the property thereon.

"By order of Brigadier General Ewing."

Reuben folded up the order and returned it to his dispatch case. "The time for voluntary removal has passed," he said. "All your crops, barns, grain storage sheds, and your residence will be burned."

"No!" Rosemary shouted. "You can't do that!"

"I've just provided you with General Ewing's orders that not only say I can, but that I must do that. I intend to follow those orders." Reuben looked back at the soldiers who were with him. "Light the torches," he ordered, and a dozen men lit torches, then spread out to start the fires. Rosemary could hear the shrieks of the terrified mules.

"No, Reuben, for God's sake, turn the animals out! They are mules, they aren't Confederates!"

The panic-driven screeches of the mules grew even more piteous.

"Please, Reuben! At least turn the mules out!"

"You would be better to concern yourself about your father-in-law, than a few dumb animals," Reuben said. "You have one minute to get him out before we set fire to the house. And that traitorous husband of yours as well. I know that he's in there."

Rosemary went into the house then returned, a moment later, holding a shotgun.

"You'll not burn this house!" she shouted angrily, raising the shotgun to her shoulder.

Before she could pull the trigger, Reuben shot her, and a little mist of blood exploded from the impact of the bullet that took out one of her eyes.

"Reuben, no! My God, you just shot Rosemary! Don't you realize what you did? Rosemary!" Angus shouted in horror.

"You saw what happened, Angus, she pointed that shotgun at us, I had no choice," Reuben said. Dismounting, he walked up to Rosemary and looked down at her. She was lying on her back and her eyes were still open, the expression on her face one of horror.

Reuben reached down and removed a gold chain and locket from around her neck.

"Now, burn the house," Reuben ordered.

"Reuben, no!" Angus said.

"You read the orders same as I did," Reuben replied.

"Can't we at least get the colonel out first?" Angus asked.

"We don't have time to be dragging any sick Confederates around with us. Now, Lieutenant, give the orders to burn the house." Reuben laughed, cynically. "I've got an idea we'll see Carson come runnin' out soon as the fire starts."

"You're my brother, and my commanding officer, but I can't give those orders," Angus said.

Reuben glared at his brother, then he looked at the two men who had been detailed to burn the house. They were holding burning torches.

"Butrum, Greer," Reuben said, his words little more than a growl.

One of the men tossed his torch in through the front window, the other tossed his torch onto the inflammable shakes of the roof. Within seconds both torches found purchase and the flames grew quickly in intensity.

"Rosemary! Rosemary!" a weak voice called out from within the house.

"Burn, secesh, burn!" Butrum called out, then he followed his shout with loud, maniacal peals of laughter.

As the troop of soldiers rode away half an hour later, columns of smoke roiled into the air behind them.

"Well, I guess Carson wasn't in there, but we've hurt him," Reuben said with a little chuckle. "And we've hurt him bad."

"We shouldn't have killed Rosemary," Angus said. "And we shouldn't have burned the house with Mr. Carson in it."

"Would you rather she have killed me?"

"I don't think she would have. I think she just wanted to stop you from burning the house. Reuben, we have known her, and Jerry, since we were very young children. And it's like Rosemary said, you were sweet on her at one time."

"Yeah, well, she made her choice, didn't she?" Reuben replied.

"We could have at least taken Mr. Carson out of the house before we set fire to it," Angus said. "For God's sake, Reuben, when you broke your arm while we were kids, it was Colonel Carson who put you in his wagon to take you into town to the doctor."

"I don't recognize ranks in the rebel army," Reuben said.

"His rank doesn't matter, he was a human being, someone we knew, someone who was a friend to us," Angus said.

"It was an act of war. If you are too lily-livered to fight, maybe you should try and get a job as some general's aide-de-camp. You can carry his hat and gloves around." Reuben laughed at his own mocking comment.

"You didn't kill her because she was a rebel, you killed her because she chose Jerry over you," Angus said. "And don't think Jerry isn't going to call all this in someday."

"Shut up, you've said enough."

Big Rock

Although it had been several years since all that had happened, as Jerry Carson, who now went by his first name, Monte, sat at his desk, recalling the moment, it was as if his wife and father had just been killed yesterday. No, they weren't killed, they were murdered. And it was that moment that the war became very personal for him, so personal that, for him, the war didn't end with the surrender at Appomattox.

Monte opened his desk drawer and pulled out a framed picture of Rosemary. The picture had been taken right after their marriage and Monte had paid an artist to tint the picture so that the photograph he was looking at now captured Rosemary in all her glory. Her eyes were blue, there was a pink tinge to her high cheekbones, and the barest suggestion of a smile on her red lips.

As he studied her picture the pain was as intense as it had been on the day he learned of her death. And now he carried in his heart the pain of loss of both Rosemary and Ina Claire.

Monte put Rosemary's picture back into the desk, then walked over to the small stove whereupon sat a coffeepot. He poured himself a cup of coffee, then tried to will the sad memories away.

CHAPTER THIRTEEN

The five hundred dollars that Frank Petro had earned by killing Abe Harris lasted about four months, then he robbed a small, remote store, killing the store owner and his wife, and that gave him enough money to keep him in food and liquor for a while longer. But the more he thought about it, the more appealing was the old idea of robbing the Bank of Big Rock.

And why not? It had been over six months since the last time anyone tried and those who made the attempt were killed without a dollar being taken. That meant that everyone was probably taking for granted the security of the bank. Besides, the money was still there, and as far as Frank was concerned, the bank owed him.

Frank had read the *Big Rock Journal* article about the attempted robbery and had even torn it from the paper so he could read it again. By now he had read it so many times that he almost knew it by memory. And one thing that stuck out in his mind, was what the sheriff had said.

"I just had a feeling," Sheriff Carson said. *"When I saw those four men riding into town, I just had a feeling."*

From that article, Frank deduced that what had given them away was the fact that four strangers had ridden into town together. In order to have a successful bank robbery all Frank had to do was make sure that he did nothing beforehand that gave the sheriff a "feeling."

At first, Frank was a little hesitant about returning to Big Rock. After all, his previous visit had been disastrous. But then, as he thought about it, he realized that he had not actually been a part of the robbery. In fact, he had not even gone into town. That meant nobody had seen him, so there was no reason why he couldn't go to Big Rock. There was only one person who could connect him with the bank robbery, and that was Leo Beajuex. He didn't have to worry about Leo, because by now he was pretty sure that Leo was in the state prison at Canon City.

Frank rode into town, touching the brim of his hat in a friendly greeting to the ladies who were going about their daily commercial activities as they walked up and down the boardwalk. He rode by the bank and gave it a cursory glance then turned right on Sikes Street and rode one block down to the Brown Dirt Cowboy Saloon. He didn't have to go that far to get to a saloon, since Longmont's was directly across the street from the bank. But he purposely avoided Longmont's Saloon because that was where Muley had been killed, and Frank had been there with him when it happened. Although some time had passed, he was concerned that there might be someone there who could remember him.

Tying his horse off at the hitching rail, he stepped inside.

"Hello, cowboy, would you like some company as you drink?"

It was difficult to tell how old the girl who greeted him was. She had blond hair, but Frank was sure it wasn't natural. She was wearing lip and cheek rouge, and her eyes were lined. The eyes were a bright blue, but there was a hardness to them that belied her age. Twenty-five? Forty-five? She could have been any-where in between.

Frank still had enough money to drink as much as he wanted, and with anyone he wanted.

"What's your name, honey?"

"The name is Delight," the young woman said with a practiced smile.

"All right, Delight, get me a beer, get yourself somethin', 'n join me." Frank picked out an empty table. "I'll be over there."

A nearby conversation caught his attention.

"Beajuex ain't really a deputy, though," some-one said.

"The hell he ain't. The sheriff give Leo a star, 'n he checks all the businesses at night to make sure they're locked up 'n all."

Leo Beajuex? They were talking about Leo Bea-juex being a deputy? No, it had to be someone else with the same name. The last time he saw Beajuex he was in jail. Surely, by now, he was doing time in the state penitentiary.

"Yeah, he does work for Sheriff Carson, but mostly what he does is just keep the office 'n the jail cleaned up, 'n he runs errands for him."

The second speaker laughed. "Well, hell, ain't that pretty much what a deputy is s'posed to do?"

The first speaker laughed. "Yeah, I guess you do have a point there."

"It just seems to me like he's too young to be a deputy."

"He's eighteen. I was with Benteen when Custer got hisself 'n all his men kilt. I was only eighteen then, 'n Custer's nephew, Autie, was kilt with 'em, 'n Autie warn't no older'n Beajuex is now, neither. So, don't be tellin' me he's too young."

"Who is it them two is talkin' about?" Frank asked the woman who had identified herself as Delight.

"Oh, they're talking about the young man Sheriff Carson's taken in," Delight said as she put the two drinks on the table. "Well, I say 'young man,' but he isn't much more than a boy, really." She laughed. "All the girls here are wantin' to be the first one to break him in."

"You said he was taken in by the sheriff. What do you mean by 'taken in'?"

"That's what's so fascinating about it. Why, do you know he tried to rob our bank? Well, he didn't exactly try to rob it, what he done is, he stayed out front and held the horses while the others went in to rob the bank, but they say that's near 'bout the same thing as robbin' it. Anyhow, what happened is the ones that went inside was all killed, and the boy, who was the only one left alive, gave himself up."

"And so now the sheriff has made Leo Beajuex his deputy?" Frank asked. "I wonder why he would do that? I mean, bein' as Beajuex was a bank robber 'n all."

"I told you, he didn't actually try and hold up the bank, he stayed outside. Besides which, he's just a real nice boy. Why, everyone in town likes him. He's the cutest thing, he's a deputy now, 'n he comes in here to have a look around, but he won't have nothin' to do with any of the girls, 'n the only thing he'll drink is sarsaparilla."

"Damn! It is him!"

"Oh, honey, do you know him?"

Frank hesitated for a moment before he answered. He shouldn't have said anything; he almost gave himself away.

"No, I don't know him. It's just that someone up in Red Cliff bet me that they was a boy deputy sheriff over here 'n I bet him they warn't. 'N now I'm goin' to have to give him the half-dollar I lost in the bet."

"Well, honey, you shoulda come over here 'n checked before you made the bet. Now you wound up losin' a half-dollar you coulda spent on me," Delight said.

"Don't you worry none about that, girl. I got myself another half-dollar," Frank promised.

When Frank left the Brown Dirt Cowboy Saloon he walked up to the corner of Lanning and Front Street from which he had a view of the sheriff's office. He was right in front of the City Pig Café so he went inside, ordered a piece of pie and a cup of coffee, then sat at a table by the window and continued to watch the sheriff's office. He was there for no more than five minutes when he saw the sheriff and Leo step out of the office. They talked for a minute or two, then the sheriff mounted his horse and rode off. Leo went back inside.

Frank finished his coffee, then walked across the street.

Leo had the two rifles and the shotgun lying on the desk in front of him, and he was cleaning the three weapons with an oily rag. When he first came to work for Sheriff Carson, this was the kind of thing he did all the time. Now the sheriff truly did regard him as a deputy, so while these menial tasks were no longer his principal occupation, he still did them without any reservations.

Leo wouldn't go so far as to say that he regarded Sheriff Carson as his father. In fact, he wasn't exactly sure how one related to a father, since his mother had no idea who his father was. But, if a sense of respect, admiration, appreciation, and belonging counted, then his relationship with the sheriff certainly filled that requirement.

"Son, no matter what you have done in your life, I have done worse," the sheriff told him once. "And as you can see, I've turned my life around. I have no doubt but that you can turn your life around as well."

It wasn't just the sheriff, it was Smoke Jensen,

Mrs. Jensen, and Pearlie and Cal who had come to Leo's aid.

Leo felt particularly close to Cal, because Cal had told him that he was his friend. Leo had never actually had a friend before. At one time he had thought that perhaps the men in the Petro gang were his friends, but that was before he knew what a real friend was.

All of his new friends had spoken to the judge for him, and there was no way Leo was going to let them down.

As Leo contemplated his newfound position in life, he continued to work on the task before him, using a ramrod to clean the barrel of the shotgun. He recalled his conversation with Sheriff Carson. What was significant about it was not only that the sheriff had shared with him the fact that he had a shady past, but the sheriff, with more and more frequency, called him "son." Leo knew that was just a figure of speech and not to be taken literally. But he also knew that the word was spoken in a caring way.

When the door opened, Leo looked up. "Did you forget som . . ." He stopped in midsentence when he saw that it wasn't the sheriff.

"Frank! What are you doing here?"

Frank's smile was somewhat mocking. "So it's true, what they say. You've gone over to the other side, have you, kid?"

"The other side?"

Frank pointed to the deputy's badge on Leo's vest. "You're a star packer now. You're the law."

Leo smiled, wanly. "Yeah, I guess I am."

"What about me, kid? Now that you are the law, are you going to arrest me? Are you going to turn me in to the sheriff for being one of the bank robbers?"

Leo shook his head. "Frank, you were less a part of that attempted bank robbery than I was. You didn't even come into town. You're not wanted here, and I've never even mentioned your name. The sheriff knows nothing about you."

Frank's smile broadened. "Good for you, kid! I knew you wouldn't turn against an old friend. And what you've done here is real smart."

"What do you mean, 'real smart'?"

"You got yourself made a deputy. That means you're on the inside. That's somethin' we can use."

"Use? How is this something we can use?"

"I'm not sure just how, yet, I'm goin' to have to think on it for a while. But, kid, what you done, I mean, not only keepin' yourself out of the pen, but gettin' yourself made a deputy, means that you was the smartest one of all of us."

"Frank, I'm not sure I know what you're talking about," Leo said, though he had an uncomfortable feeling that he knew exactly what Frank was talking about.

"I know, I know, I haven't quite figured it out myself, neither. But as soon as I do, I'll let you know."

"Frank, you're not goin' to cause any trouble while you're in town, are you?"

Frank held out his hand. "No, no, kid, that would be the last thing I want to do. You can take it from me, I'm goin' to be as good as a choirboy the whole time I'm in town." Frank laughed at the analogy.

"I'm not even sure what a choirboy does that's so good, but that's how good I'm goin' to be."

Despite himself, Leo chuckled. "Thanks," he said, relieved to hear it. Maybe his uneasy feeling wasn't justified.

As Frank Petro rode out of Big Rock, he thought about Leo as deputy sheriff. He knew that could be useful to him, he just had to have a plan that would take advantage of it. And the first part of his plan would be to put together a gang.

From the Denver, Colorado, *Journal:*

State Senator Rex Underhill
To Seek U. S. Seat

> While there have been rumors that Senator George Chilcott was contemplating giving up his seat in the United States Senate, they have been only rumors until now, but Senator Chilcott has recently substantiated those rumors. He will be leaving the Senate, and the first person to express interest in succeeding him is State Senator Rex Underhill.
>
> Senator Underhill is well known throughout the state for being able to get things done, his most recent accomplishment being to open up Mount St. John for the commercial acquisition of any valuable minerals therein contained.

State Senator Nathaniel Toone was the first to offer his public support for Senator Underhill's quest.

It has been suggested that Lieutenant Governor Horace Austin Warner ("Haw") Tabor may also be interested in seeking the seat being vacated by Senator Chilcott, but as of this writing, he has not declared.

The Gentleman's Club of Denver

"Well, it looks like you got a good send-off in the newspaper," Toone said.

"Not that good. Tabor got almost as much written about him, as was written about me," Underhill said.

"Well, hell, Rex, what do you expect? Haw Tabor owns the damn newspaper, after all."

"Do you think he will really make a try for the seat?" Underhill asked.

"He might, but he and the governor don't get along, so he's for sure not going to get Pitkin's support," Toone said.

"Have you forgotten that the governor and I don't get along, either?" Underhill asked.

"Yes, but it's like that joke about the preacher running from the bear. *Lord, maybe you ain't goin' to help me, but please don't help that bear.*"

Underhill chuckled. "I see what you mean. Even if the governor doesn't help us, we are ahead of the game as long as Tabor doesn't get the governor's endorsement, either."

"Exactly," Toone said with a big smile as he held his finger up.

"How many do you think I can count on?"

"We have six senators for sure, because we have done business with them," Toone said.

"Six, out of thirty-five," Underhill said.

"And eight representatives," Toone added.

"Out of sixty-five. So what you are saying is, I need fifty-one votes to win the seat, and so far I have fourteen. That's not very reassuring."

"Yes, but look at it like this. You have fourteen votes that are absolute. That means that anyone else who is going to try will have to overcome that fourteen before they can even begin to compete."

"Yes," Underhill said with a smile. "Yes, that is true, isn't it?"

CHAPTER FOURTEEN

Big Rock

"It is official now," Louis Longmont said. "Senator George Chilcott has let it be known that he isn't going to stand for reelection to the United States Senate."

"That's what I hear as well," Smoke said. "That's too bad, he's a good man. And because we are still a new state, we need good men to represent us."

"That's just what I said in an article I wrote for today's issue of the *Journal*," Phil Clinton said.

The three men were sharing a table in Longmont's Saloon, but it wasn't just any table, it was Louis Longmont's personal table.

"You wrote about the upcoming senate race?" Smoke asked.

"I did indeed. Here, have a look."

Selecting the Right Man for U. S. Senate

Senator George Chilcott has served the state of Colorado admirably, and should he desire to put his name before the Colorado General Assembly for the continuation of his term, this newspaper could endorse his candidacy with great enthusiasm. However, Senator Chilcott has made it known that he has no wish to return to Washington, and thus it is now incumbent upon us to find a new man to back for the U. S. Senate.

Accordingly, this newspaper will make a concerted search to locate someone whose background, intellect, honesty, and sense of service to others would justify an editorial support. To that end I am now requesting recommendations from our readers.

Whoever we select to support must be approved and appointed by our general assembly, thus we must conduct a vigorous campaign for our candidate in order that the legislators be well apprised of both the qualifications and the popular support of our candidate.

Smoke read the article and nodded in approval. "Very good article, Phil. I agree with everything you wrote."

"Thank you," Phil said. He thumped his fingers against the newspaper. "There was something I was going to put into the article, but I had second thoughts about it and left it out."

"What is that?" Louis asked.

"State Senator Rex Underhill has announced his candidacy. I should have stated my unalterable opposition to him. He is a man of such ill repute that I am at a loss to understand how he was ever elected to the state senate in the first place. And now, should he go to Washington to represent the state, that would be an unabashed disaster."

"Why didn't you mention it?" Smoke asked.

Phil shook his head. "Somehow I just didn't think it would be right to be against someone, unless I could show support for someone else. That's why I asked for recommendations from my readers, and now I'll be interested in seeing what the readers have to say, particularly with regard to whom they might support."

"I know just the person," Smoke said, recalling his earlier conversation with Monte Carson.

"Who?"

"I'd rather not say until I've had a chance to talk to him again."

"Again?" Louis said. "Smoke, do you mean to say that you have already spoken to someone about this very thing?"

"Yes," Smoke said.

"Has this person shown some interest?" Phil asked.

"He has," Smoke replied. "Now I'm going to see just how deep that interest is."

"And you think he would be a good senator?"

Smoke smiled. "I think he would be an outstanding senator."

"All right, as provisional chair of the Big Rock Senatorial Selection Committee, I hereby authorize you to approach your candidate on our behalf," Phil said.

"Who made you the provisional chairman?" Louis asked.

"Well, given the fact that, for the moment the Big Rock Senatorial Selection Committee exists only in my mind, and I am the only member of said committee, doesn't it stand to reason that I would also be its provisional chairman?"

Louis chuckled. "Indeed it does."

"I'll go have another meeting with the person I'm talking about, and see if I can get him to agree to make a try for the seat," Smoke said.

"Yes," Monte said in response to Smoke's question a few minutes later. "I read the article. I read both articles, the one that Phil wrote, and the one in the Denver newspaper. State Senator Rex Underhill has declared."

"Yes, that's what Phil Clinton said. Refresh my, mind, Monte, wasn't Underhill connected in some way to Lucien Garneau and Deekus Templeton when they tried to run roughshod over all the smaller ranchers here in Eagle County?"

"Yes. At least I always believed that Underhill put up some of the money for them, but there was never enough evidence to prove it."

"Yeah, well, as far as I'm concerned I don't have to prove it, all I have to do is believe it," Smoke said. "And believing it is enough for me to want to see almost anyone else but Underhill replace Chilcott."

"I agree with you," Monte said.

"So, what do you think?" Smoke asked. "Are you willing to give it a try?"

"Give me one more day to think about it."

"Monte, it's been almost a month since we talked about this. If you haven't made up your mind by now, how is one more day going to help?"

"How is one more day going to hurt?" Monte

replied. "Besides, the last time we talked it wasn't an absolute that Chilcott was going to leave the senate. Now that he has, I need to think very seriously about it."

"All right, like you said, one more day won't hurt. But I have to be honest with you, Monte, I can't see any reason in the world why you wouldn't run."

After Smoke left, Monte thought about his comment, "*I can't see any reason in the world why you wouldn't run.*"

"It's because you don't know the whole story," Monte said aloud. He opened the safe, took out a small box, then removed a gold chain and locket. The locket had belonged to Rosemary and when the locket was opened it contained Rosemary's picture, and the photograph of a much younger Monte Carson. Monte had kept this locket a secret from everyone, even from Ina Claire. He didn't want anyone to ask any questions about this locket, because it had a very dark past.

Jackson County, Missouri, 1866

Monte Carson didn't have the heart to rebuild the house and barn when he came back to his burned-out farm. Although the Williamses offered to buy the acreage from him, he refused to sell to them. His refusal to sell had nothing to do with them killing his wife and father, because at the time, he had no idea who had done that. He didn't sell to them simply because there was still bad blood between them as a result of them having chosen opposite sides during the war.

There were several veterans of the war who either,

like Monte, had nothing to come home to, or were just too unsettled to return to civilian life. Some of these men began a life outside the law, and though some of the outlaws were veterans from the Union army, most were Confederate veterans.

Monte was one of the latter, and he actually started an outlaw gang. The gang called themselves the Gray Brothers, taking the name from the color of the uniforms they had worn, and in the case of some of them, were still wearing.

Monte had insisted that they not kill any innocents.

"We can take their money," he told the four men who rode with him, "but we'll not take their lives. Right now there are a dozen or more outlaw gangs riding through Missouri and Kansas, and most of the other gangs are killing people. As long as we don't kill anyone, we'll never be the ones they are looking for the most."

The Gray Brothers were fairly successful in their operations, robbing stagecoaches, money couriers, and even an army paymaster. And they did it all without killing anyone.

Then, at about the same time Monte learned that Reuben Williams, his onetime neighbor and friend, had a gang of outlaws, he also learned that Reuben Williams was the man who had killed his wife and his father.

The moment Monte learned that, he changed the focus of his gang. He began looking for the Williams brothers. And because the outlaw gangs had an "underground telegraph," as the secret communications between them was called, Monte found them within less than a month.

He found them on Crooked River; Reuben and

Angus Williams, Luke Butrum and Arnold Greer. Butrum and Greer, Monte had learned, were the two men who had actually set fire to the house.

"No," he told the other members of the Gray Brothers when they offered to go with him. "This is something I must do by myself."

It was the middle of the night when he approached the Williams brothers' campsite, and the campfire had burned down, but there was enough of a golden gleam that he could see the four sleeping men.

"Wake up, you sons of bitches!" Monte said, shooting into the air.

All four men were startled awake.

"What is it?" Butrum asked. "What's goin' on?"

Monte started to respond to the question when he saw that Reuben Williams had been sleeping with his pistol, and he pointed it toward Monte. Monte shot before Reuben could, and Reuben fell back with a bullet hole in the middle of his forehead.

"It's Carson! Kill 'im, kill 'im!" Butrum shouted.

Butrum got a shot off but it went wide of its target. Monte returned fire and didn't miss. Greer had his gun in his hand, but like Reuben, Greer was unable to get a shot off and he went down with a hole in the middle of his chest.

"I'm not shooting! I don't have a gun and I'm not shooting!" Angus Williams shouted in panic. He had managed to get to his feet and now he was standing there with both hands up in the air. "Don't shoot, Jerry, don't shoot! We were friends once, remember? We were friends!"

In his rage, Monte pointed his pistol at Angus and pulled the hammer back.

"Please, Jerry, I was there, but I didn't have anything to do with it! I tried to talk Reuben out of it!"

When Monte first heard the story of the murder of his wife and father, he had not only been told who the principals were, he was also told that Angus had not personally participated, and indeed had protested it. Because of that he knew that Angus was telling the truth.

Monte lowered his pistol, and when he did he saw a flash of gold around Reuben's neck, and he recognized it at once. Bending over he removed the chain and locket. It was a locket that he had given Rosemary before he left for the war. When he had given it to her it had held two photographs, one of her and one of him.

He opened it and saw that only Rosemary's picture remained.

"Why, you son of a bitch!" he said angrily as he looked down at Reuben's body. "After what you did, how did you have the nerve to carry her likeness?"

"I'm sorry, Jerry. I'm so sorry," Angus said. "I told him not to do it. I don't know what got into him. It was as if he had gone mad, or something."

Monte stared at the trembling man in front of him, the man who had once been his best friend. Finally he sighed and holstered his pistol.

"Don't ever let me see you again, Angus."

Monte turned to leave.

"Wait!" Angus called out to him. "Jerry, you killed three men here. What am I supposed to do with them now?"

"That's your problem," Monte said as he disappeared in the dark.

* * *

Monte left the outlaw trail the very next day, returning to his burned-out farm. It had been confiscated by Order Number 11 during the war, but by now all such property was released back to the original owners.

Monte finished rebuilding his house and had started on his barn when six men came riding up. They were led by Angus Williams.

"What is this, Angus?" Monte asked, looking up from the board he was sawing.

"You are under arrest, Jerry," Angus said.

"Under arrest? Arrest for what?"

"For the murder of Luke Butrum, Arnold Greer, and my brother, Reuben."

Monte had no means of resistance. The six men were armed, and he wasn't.

Within two weeks after his arrest, Monte was tried for the murder of Reuben Williams. They didn't try him for the murder of the other two, the tactic being that if, somehow, he wasn't found guilty the first time, they could retry him two more times without violating the double-jeopardy clause.

They didn't need to retry him, because he was found guilty the first time, and sentenced to hang. On the night before he was to hang, he was visited in his cell by Dale Bohannon, a man who had served in his company during the war.

"Sergeant Bohannon? What are you doing here?"

"It's the Reverend Bohannon, sir, and I'm here to pray for your soul," Bohannon said in a very stentorian voice.

"How long are you going to need, preacher?" the jailor asked.

"Tomorrow morning this man is going to meet his Maker. I shall require at least thirty minutes, I would say. But I must ask you to leave, sir. The counseling between a preacher and his lamb is sacred and private."

The jailer nodded, then returned to the front of the office.

"Captain Carson, I have a key to your cell," Bohannon said quietly.

"What about the jailer?"

Bohannon smiled. "He's having a cup of coffee, but this coffee won't keep him awake."

Monte held up his hand. "Sergeant, I don't want . . ."

"Don't worry. I put only enough laudanum in his coffee to make him sleep."

"How long will it take to work?"

"I'll check. If he took a couple of drinks when he went back, he's out by now."

Bohannon left, then returned less than a minute later to unlock the cell door.

"He's sound asleep. There's a saddled horse tied off in front of Buckner's Mercantile. There's a rifle in the saddle sheath and twenty dollars in the saddle-bags."

"Dale, I don't know how to thank you, nor how to ever repay you."

"It wasn't just me, Captain. Everyone who ever rode for you put in a little money for you."

Monte left Missouri and rode into Kansas that very night.

Over the next year, Monte managed, for the most part, to avoid any direct conflicts with the law.

However, though he never looked for a fight, neither did he back away from one, be it with an outlaw or an overbearing peace officer. The very ferociousness with which he settled accounts had brought him a degree of notoriety.

Monte soon discovered that his skill with a pistol was a marketable commodity so he made a living selling his gun to the highest bidder. For a while, Monte Carson rode side by side with Big Jim Slaughter, one of the most feared men in Wyoming Territory. But when Monte decided to reform his ways and give back fifty thousand dollars in stolen army payroll, he made an enemy of everyone who was on the wrong side of the law and became a friend to Smoke Jensen.

CHAPTER FIFTEEN

Big Rock

Sheriff Monte Carson had a bottle of bourbon in his desk and he poured himself a glass as those past memories drifted away. He would have continued his path of walking the narrow line between law and outlaw, had it not been for Smoke, and, if he was being honest with himself, Ina Claire. Smoke provided him with the opportunity to settle down, and Ina Claire gave him the desire to do so.

And now he had the chance to take his life in a new direction. He held the as-yet-untouched glass of bourbon out and looked up.

"I know you're up there, lookin' down at me, Ina Claire. I can feel it. So you're the first to know, I'm goin' to give it a try."

When Smoke stepped into the sheriff's office the next day, Monte knew exactly why he was there.

"Yes," Monte said before Smoke could say anything.

"Yes?"

"I'll put myself up for the Senate."

"Good, good!" Smoke said.

Monte chuckled. "Here's the thing, though. I don't have any idea what to do next."

"Why don't you let your campaign manager handle that for you?"

"Do I need to get a campaign manager? I mean, this isn't an office you win by getting people to vote for you."

"Didn't you just say that you don't have any idea what you're supposed to do next?"

"Yes, I did say that."

"All right, then you need a campaign manager."

Monte smiled. "You wouldn't be hinting around that you would like the job, would you?"

"Maybe," Smoke said, returning the smile. "That is, if you'll have me."

"Yes! Yes, absolutely!"

"All right, I accept."

"So, Mr. Campaign Manager, what do we do next?"

"In two days there's going to be a meeting, not only of the town, but of several citizens from Eagle County and even some from a few of the surrounding counties. The purpose of the meeting is to discuss what input we can have in the appointment of the next senator. We'll put your name up then."

"Smoke, you haven't told anybody yet that I'm planning to run, have you?"

"No. We'll do that at the meeting."

Monte nodded.

"On the morning of the meeting, I'll stop by and we'll go together," Smoke offered.

* * *

"I think Monte would make a wonderful United States senator," Sally said that evening, "and I'm going to do all I can to help him."

"What can you do, Miss Sally? You're a woman, so you can't vote for him," Cal said.

"Neither can you," Sally replied with a smile. "The only people who can actually vote for Monte are members of the general assembly. So, the only way the average citizen can help is to do whatever we can do to influence the state representatives and state senators to vote for the candidate of our choice. And that means that in the case of sending a senator to Washington, women will have as much input as men."

"I hadn't thought about like that, I mean the women's influence angle, but you are right," Smoke said.

"Didn't you tell me that you are Monte's campaign manager?" Sally asked.

"Yes, I am."

Sally flashed a challenging smile. "Then you *should* have thought about it. Fortunately, the campaign manager's wife will come to the rescue."

"Good, I appreciate that," Smoke said. "Uh, what do you have in mind?"

"You just leave that to me," Sally said.

Big Rock

Sally was president of the Eagle County Betterment Association, an organization made up of the more affluent women of the area. She also belonged to the Big Rock Beautification Society, as well as the Children's Benefit Alliance. She arranged for all three groups to throw a joint "tea" for the ladies of the county.

The venue for the meeting was the ballroom of the Dunn Hotel, and today it was crowded with ladies from Big Rock and neighboring towns. A filled, silver punch bowl occupied the middle of a long table flanked by various cookies and pastries prepared by the ladies of the three clubs. For the first several minutes the ladies visited with one another and the room resonated with dozens of conversations and occasional trills of laughter. Then Sally tapped a spoon against an empty crystal glass to get everyone's attention.

"Ladies, today the gentlemen of our community will be meeting at the Cattlemen's Association Building to discuss who they are going to endorse for the next United States senator from Colorado. Now, while we do not yet have the vote, though I'm certain the date will come when women will be granted full citizenship rights, we do have something else. We have influence, and in the case of choosing a United States senator, influence is all anyone has.

"Sheriff Monte Carson has agreed to put his name forward, and I've no doubt but that in the men's meeting today, Monte will be selected as our nominee. And I'm here to ask each and every one of you to support this fine man."

Support for Sheriff Carson seemed to be universal among all the women, and for the next several minutes there were proposals and discussions on how best the ladies could support him.

"I have a proposal," Mary Beth Brubaker said. "I think we should organize a Ladies for Monte Carson for Senator group, and I suggest that Sally Jensen be chairwoman of the group."

"Excellent proposal, and I second it," Nancy Kinder said.

There was universal approval, not only of the formation of the group, but also of Sally as its head.

"Ladies, I accept this honor you have given me," Sally said. "And I will get busy on planning things we can do to help bring this about."

Sally had come into town ahead of Smoke, and as Smoke, Pearlie, and Cal rode into town they saw Sally's phaeton, as well as several other phaetons, surreys, buckboards, and even a couple of farm wagons parked on the street near, and in front of, the Dunn Hotel.

"It looks like Miss Sally has drawn quite a crowd," Pearlie said.

"I never had any doubt but that she would be able to," Smoke said. "And the good thing is, she'll have them eating out of her hand in no time."

"Oh, there's no doubt about that," Pearlie said.

"Smoke, if you don't mind, I'm goin' to ride on down to the sheriff's office and visit with Leo while the rest of you do all your politickin'," Cal said. "You won't need me in there anyway. You already know where I stand on this."

"Go ahead, Cal, we'll pick you up on the way back home," Smoke said.

The streets were crowded with horses and wheeled vehicles, and the boardwalks were filled with pedestrians. Smoke didn't think he had ever seen so many people in town and, thanks to Sally, there were about as many women as there were men.

There were so many horses in town that every

hitching rail all up and down Front Street was full. However, McKnight and Keaton Freight Company had opened up their corral so there was space for Smoke and Pearlie to tie their horses off there. The Cattlemen's Association Building was next door to McKnight and Keaton, so it was a short walk. When Smoke and Pearlie stepped inside a moment later, the meeting room was filled, not only with the cattlemen who made up the membership, but with men from every occupation and station.

Smoke exchanged pleasantries with several of the men, then drifted to the back of the room. There, on a table, was a big coffeepot sitting on a kerosene burner. Smoke turned the spigot and watched as an aromatic brown stream filled the cup. His coffee acquired, he turned toward the others who were gathered for the meeting.

In addition to Smoke and Pearlie, Louis Longmont was present. So were the lawyers Bob McCord and Dan Norton. The banker Joel Montgomery was there as well as Ed McKnight and Elmer Keaton. And of course, Phil Clinton of the *Big Rock Journal* was there, not just as a journalist, but as a participant.

By mutual agreement, Dan Norton was conducting the meeting.

"Gentlemen, we are gathered here to put forth our choice of the man we would like to submit to the general assembly as the next senator from the state of Colorado," Norton said.

"We've already got one man to worry about," Larry Martin said. Martin was the Eagle County land assessor.

"Are you talking about Rex Underhill?" Mike Bray asked. Bray owned a medium-sized ranch.

"Yeah," Martin said.

"I don't think he's goin' to be much of a problem. From all I've heard of him, he's as crooked as a snake."

"Yeah, well, sometimes being crooked seems to work to politicians' advantage," Martin said.

"Not if we get the word out about the son of a bitch. All we have to do is let enough people know what he's really like," Bray said.

"You forget, he's already a member of the state legislature. Do you think he's actually going to be turned down by his own? Hell, half the people in Denver are as crooked as he is."

"I hear that Horace Tabor is considering putting his name up as well," Elmer Keaton said.

"Yeah, and they don't call him the Silver King for nothing. His mine has made him over a million dollars," Norman Lambert said.

"Why would he want to be a senator?" Ed McKnight asked. "He's got more than a mine to run, he has other businesses, too. It seems to me like being a senator would just get in the way."

"Look, we can't be focusing only on the negatives here," Dan Norton said. "Yes, Underhill has submitted his name for the job, but our job is to find the person that we think is the best man to represent us in Washington, then do all we can to convince the general assembly that we have chosen wisely."

"The way I look at it we've got two excellent choices from among our own people," Bob McCord said. "I could be happy with either Smoke Jensen or Monte Carson."

"Hear! Hear! Excellent choices!" Joel Montgomery said.

"Gentlemen," Smoke said, holding up his hand and calling for recognition. "I would say that the fact you have put me in consideration to be a very high honor. But, perhaps I can say something that will make the decision easier. I would like to withdraw my name from consideration and put my personal support behind the candidacy of Monte Jerome Carson."

"Yes!" Phil Clinton shouted. "A good choice, and Sheriff Carson could ask for no one better to stand for him than Kirby Jensen."

"Hear! Hear!" several others said.

"I have no objection to the nomination of Sheriff Carson," Keaton said. "But I think our cause would be better served if we actually voted and had more than one choice."

"I concur," Norton said. "Of course, the floor is open to nominations, but before we proceed, I would like to submit the following resolution for approval. And if it is approved, I want the signature of every man here present to be affixed to the bottom of the document."

"Read the document, Dan," Lambert asked.

Norton picked up the document and held it pointedly in front of him with one hand on top of the sheet and the other hand on bottom, then began to read:

"Be it known that we, citizens of Eagle County, state of Colorado, United States of America, by these presents and our signatures hereto attached, hereby resolve to select as candidate of the United States Senate the best man that circumstances and capabilities allow. And be it further resolved that he who shall be selected shall enjoy, without reservation, the total support of this nominating body."

Putting the paper down he looked out over those who had come to the meeting.

"Does anyone object to this resolution?"

When no one objected Norton had everyone present sign, then the voting began, the two candidates being Sheriff Monte Jerome Carson and Robert A. McCord who, like Dan Norton, was a lawyer.

Smoke spoke on behalf of Sheriff Carson, keeping his address pithy.

"I can find only one reservation about sending this man to the United States Senate," Smoke concluded, pointing to Monte. "We would be losing the finest sheriff in the entire state."

Smoke's words were met with enthusiastic applause.

"Thank you, Smoke. Now, who will speak for Mr. McCord?"

"I will," Tim Murchison said. Tim owned the saddle and leather store.

Tim's talk lasted no longer than Smoke's nominating address had been, and he concluded with a reminder that Robert McCord provided, free of charge, his services to every charitable group in the county.

When the voting started, the outcome became obvious rather quickly until McCord stood up in the middle of the voting and asked to be able to say a few words.

"The floor is yours, Bob," Dan said.

McCord glanced over at Smoke.

"I agree with Smoke Jensen that, even being considered by my friends and fellow citizens is an honor almost beyond description. However, I think that in the interest of unity and comity I would like to withdraw my name from these proceedings and ask that we have a unanimous vote for Monte J. Carson."

"Hear! Hear!" someone shouted.

"I move that the vote be by acclamation," Phil Clinton said, and Louis Longmont seconded.

"Mr. McCord, this is just real good 'n I'm glad that Sheriff Carson is goin' to be our senator 'n all," Andy Brown said. "But I sure don't see nothin' funny about it."

"Funny?" McCord asked.

"Yeah, you said 'in the interest of comedy.' But it seems to me like we're doin' somethin' serious 'n important here. I don't see no comedy to it at all."

"You're right," McCord said with a condescending smile. "What we have done here is serious and important."

The next day the *Big Rock Journal* reported on the results:

Monte Carson Candidacy Put Forth

Yesterday nearly one hundred ranchers, ranch hands, businessmen, and professional people gathered in the Eagle County Cattlemen's Association Building to select a nominee for U.S. senator. Two names were contemplated, Sheriff Monte Carson and attorney Robert McCord; Kirby "Smoke" Jensen having earlier withdrawn his own name from consideration.

Each candidate had his champion speak for him, your editor extolling the virtues of our sheriff, and Tim Murcheson promoting Bob McCord's many and obvious qualities. As the election proceeded, however, it soon became apparent that Sheriff Carson was enjoying a significant lead. At that point lawyer McCord, showing the grace and savoir faire for which this attorney is so well known, withdrew his name from the nominating process and urged unanimous support for the candidacy of Sheriff Monte Carson. McCord's proposal was met with approval and Sheriff Carson was nominated without objection.

Smoke Jensen, who is arguably one of the best known and most highly regarded citizens of the state of Colorado, has agreed to direct Sheriff Carson's quest for the prestigious position.

Even as the gentlemen of the above-mentioned gathering were making known their choice for the next United States senator from Colorado, so, too, were the ladies of our fair city and county engaged. A joint meeting of three ladies' clubs, their numbers enlarged by nonaffiliated women, decided to a launch Ladies for Monte Carson for Senator and selected Mrs. Smoke Jensen to lead them in their expressed purpose.

By this declaration I am now going on record as being in absolute support of the candidacy of Monte Jerome Carson as the next man to go to Washington, D.C., there to represent Colorado in the United States Senate. This newspaper will do all it can to bring about this result.

CHAPTER SIXTEEN

Denver

"Did you see this article?" Underhill asked, holding out the current issue of the Denver newspaper. "Sheriff Monte Carson has announced his candidacy for U.S. Senate."

State Senator Toone glanced at the paper, then chuckled and tossed it aside. "A small-town sheriff from a county that doesn't have enough people to fill a train? I hardly see that as anything to be concerned about."

"Don't sell this sheriff short," Underhill said. "He has Smoke Jensen on his side. I'm sure you've heard of him."

"Of course I've heard of Smoke Jensen. Who in the state hasn't heard of him? But Rex, really, a small-town sheriff, compared to you, a sitting senator in the very legislature that will ultimately make the appointment? Believe me, you have nothing to worry about."

"Yeah, I guess you're right."

"On the other hand you, and I, for that matter, have made quite a few enemies in both the senate and the house, and I'm not sure we can count on them." Toone picked up the paper and looked at it again. "Also, it would be much better if Smoke Jensen wasn't involved. His endorsement of Monte Carson could be quite significant. Jensen is so well known and highly regarded in the entire state that I believe he could be elected governor if he actually wanted the position."

"Yeah, it would be better without Jensen," Underhill agreed.

Underhill returned to his office, read the article. Toone was right, Smoke Jensen could be a problem.

"You and I have clashed before, Mr. Jensen, you just don't know it," Underhill said aloud.

Underhill opened his desk drawer and pulled out a file folder. The file folder was marked *Eagle County Land Project.* The first thing he saw was a telegram. It had not been sent to him, but it had been pirated by someone who had been paid, by Underhill, to violate his trust with Western Union.

BY THIS MESSAGE MALCOLM PUDDLE TRANSFERS POA TO KIRBY JENSEN. POA LIMITED TO PAYING TAXES ON LONG TREK RANCH IN NAME OF MALCOLM PUDDLE. NOTARIZED POA TO FOLLOW. MALCOLM PUDDLE

Acquisition of the Long Trek Ranch was a major part of the plan he and Lucien Garneau had for amassing their holdings in Eagle County, and this would seem to prevent them from getting control of the Long Trek.

Underhill had given the telegrapher ten dollars and asked him to send a telegram. That telegram was the next item in the file folder.

TO ATTORNEY ROBERT DEMPSTER
MOVE QUICKLY TO PAY TAXES DUE
ON LONG TREK RANCH AND BY SO
DOING ACQUIRE PROPERTY FOR
LUCIEN GARNEAU.

Underhill figured that his message to Dempster would enable him to take advantage of the opportunity presented by the delinquent taxes. But that opportunity was thwarted by Smoke Jensen. Underhill learned what happened by a letter from Dempster himself. That letter was the next item in the file folder.

Dear Senator Underhill:

It is with the greatest of regret that I must report the failure of my effort to secure the transfer of Long Trek Ranch. And while I am using this letter to report upon my lack of success, I shall also use it to explain, and perhaps mitigate the circumstances which prevented me from fulfilling the task you had assigned.

I was already standing at the counter at the land clerk's office when Kirby Jensen, best known as Smoke Jensen, came in saying that he had the power of attorney to probate Humboldt Puddle's will, and that he wished to pay the taxes on Long Trek.

You may be aware that Smoke Jensen is a man of considerable renown, especially in regard to his skill with a pistol. Nevertheless, armed with

*the knowledge that I was there first, I offered the
information that it was my intention to make
the tax payment, telling him that once I did so,
ownership of the Long Trek would be transferred
to me.*

*I hasten to point out to you, sir, that the
ownership would have been temporary in nature
as I would have immediately taken the necessary
steps to place ownership of the property into the trust
that has been established between you and Lucien
Garneau. I also point out that the existence of the
trust, as well as the trustees, remains undisclosed
as a part of my confidentiality agreement.*

*I should not have told him that I hadn't made the
payment yet, because that gave him the opening he
needed to challenge me by saying that it wasn't too
late for him.*

*I assured him that it was too late as I had
arrived first; I had the necessary funds for the
transaction, and had only to complete the forms
before ownership would be transferred to me.*

*Jensen asked me how I intended to fill out the
forms, and thinking that an odd question, I asked
what he meant by that.*

*When I tell you what happened next, you will
understand, and perhaps forgive the failure. He
asked me, "How are you going to write with a
broken hand?" speaking in words that were as
cold as ice.*

*I demanded to know if he was threatening me,
and what happened next sent chills up my spine.
Jensen smiled at me, but believe me, Senator, there*

*was absolutely no humor in the man's smile. On
the contrary, it was absolutely diabolical.*

*"It is not a threat, it is a promise," Jensen replied
in that same cold, soulless tone of voice as before.*

*As you know, Senator, I am a lawyer, so I
threatened to bring charges against him and have
him put in jail, reminding him that Mr. Pratt, the
land office clerk, was my witness. But Pratt, in an
act of unbelievable cowardice and betrayal to his
oath of office, said that he had neither seen nor
heard anything.*

*I hope by the above story that you can
understand how, with the physical threat to my
person hanging over me, I had no choice but to
stand by impotently and watch as the two dollars
in back taxes were paid and ownership of the land
snatched from my very fingers.*

*I hope, also, that you can find it in your heart to
forgive my failure.*

> *Your obedient servant,*
> *Robert Dempster*

There were a few other items in the folder but
Underhill closed it before he examined any of them.

Smoke Jensen had thwarted his plans once
before, and now, because he was taking an active
role in Sheriff Carson's quest for the U.S. Senate,
Jensen was once again standing between Underhill
and his goal.

"Not this time, Jensen. Not this time," Underhill said.

Underhill chuckled. At the moment, he had a

great advantage in his dispute with Kirby Jensen. Jensen didn't even know that the two were personal enemies.

Big Rock

"Our next senator!" someone shouted when Monte Carson stepped into Longmont's Saloon.

The others in the saloon cheered.

"Hey, shouldn't the candidate buy a round of drinks?" someone asked.

Monte laughed and held up his hand. "Boys, I may be a candidate for the United States Senate, but I'm doing this on a sheriff's salary."

"All right, all right, just this one time, drinks are on the house," Louis said. "We'll call it a campaign donation," he added with a smile.

As everyone rushed to the bar, Monte looked around. "Has Smoke been in today?"

"No, I think he mentioned that he had some calves to deal with, so I'm sure you'll find him at Sugarloaf."

"Thanks."

"Good luck, Senator!" someone called as Monte left the saloon. Monte replied with a wave tossed over his shoulder.

When Monte stepped into the sheriff's office a few minutes later, he saw Leo and Cal drinking coffee and engaged in deep conversation.

"That ain't, I mean, that isn't true," Leo said with a little laugh. "That can't possibly be true. You're makin' that up."

Cal held up his hand. "I swear and hope to die, it's true," Cal said.

"What are you two boys talking about?" Monte asked.

"Cal said there's been some dime novels that was wrote about Smoke Jensen."

"No, I didn't. Don't misquote me, or Miss Sally will have my head," Cal said. "What I said was, there have been some dime novels that *were written* about Smoke Jensen."

"He's telling you the truth," Monte said. "Ned Buntline has written four books about Smoke, Edward Wheeler has written a few, so has Richard Ellis, and they aren't the only ones."

"Wow, Smoke must be real rich from those books," Leo suggested.

"Nope," Cal said. "That's the funny thing about it, don't you see? Smoke doesn't get any money at all from them."

"That's not right," Leo protested.

"No, it isn't, but that's how it is," Cal said.

"Cal, did Smoke come into town with you?" Monte asked.

Cal shook his head. "No, there are some calves that need castrating, and Smoke 'n Pearlie are sort of bossin' the ones that are doin' it."

"I need to ride out there and see him. Leo, keep an eye on the town while I'm gone."

"Yes, sir!" Leo said, responding proudly.

Smoke was watching the castrating operation, though his presence wasn't actually needed as Pearlie had the situation well in hand. He looked up just as he saw Sheriff Carson approaching. Smoke walked over to let himself out through the gate of the corral so he could meet him.

"Hello, Monte, what's up?"

"Smoke, I have a huge favor to ask of you."

"Oh?"

"The nominating committee has come up with a campaign fund of five thousand dollars so I'm going to be doing some traveling around the state. As you no doubt know, Mark Worley, who was my deputy, has been hired by Wheeler to be their city marshal. That means that Leo is the closest thing I have to a deputy right now and though he has been working out better than I thought he would, given his age, I don't think I should leave the protection of the town in his hands, alone. I wonder if I could count on you to fill in as sheriff while I'm gone."

"If I'm going to be your campaign manager, I'll be making most of the trips with you," Smoke replied. "What about using Pearlie? He's a good man and I trust him implicitly."

"Yes," Monte agreed. "Yes, that would be great. Do you think he would be willing to do it?"

"Let's ask him."

"Let's see," Pearlie said after Monte asked him the same thing he had asked Smoke. "Do I want to get my hands all bloody cutting the nuts off a dozen more calves, or would I rather walk around Big Rock like King of the Walk with a star on my shirt? Hmm, I choose the star on my shirt."

Smoke and Monte laughed.

"Can you start tomorrow?" Monte asked.

"Tomorrow would be fine," Smoke said. "We'll be finished with the cutting by then."

"Damn, I'm not gettin' out of it, am I?" Pearlie asked, taking in the castrating with a wave of his hand.

The smile on his face indicated that his complaint wasn't real.

"Afraid not," Smoke replied, matching Pearlie's smile.

"All right, Sheriff, I'll be there tomorrow, bright-eyed and bushy-tailed," Pearlie promised.

"Thank you, Pearlie, I appreciate that."

"Maybe when you're a big important senator, you can invite me to Washington and show me around," Pearlie suggested.

"I'm afraid someone will have to show me around first."

"Look there, riding up the road," Pearlie said. "I told you Cal wouldn't miss lunch."

"Speaking of that, now that you are out here, Monte, you may as well stay for lunch as well," Smoke offered.

Monte nodded. "Thank you, I believe I will." Monte walked over to greet Cal as he dismounted. "Is everything all right in town?" he asked.

Cal laughed. "Don't worry about that, Sheriff. Your deputy has everything well in hand."

"Everyone in the county is proud of you, Sheriff," Sally said as they sat around the table having lunch. "A United States senator? What an awesome responsibility."

"Yes, ma'am, I'm sure it will be," Monte said. "But let's not get the cart before the horse. I haven't been appointed yet."

Smoke chuckled. "I'll just bet that when you were a young man growing up on a little farm in Missouri that you never dreamed of being a United States senator someday, did you?"

"No, I never did," Monte said.

"So, you're from Missouri, too, are you?" Cal asked. "Just like Smoke."

"Yes, just like Smoke."

"The only difference is, Monte grew up not too far from the big city of Kansas City, while I was on a forty-acre farm on Shoal Creek in Stone County, a long way from anyplace big enough to be more than a wide place in the road," Smoke said.

"Missouri had about as many folks fightin' on one side durin' the war as the other side," Cal said. "Which side did you fight for?"

"Cal, that isn't something you want to ask just anyone," Pearlie said.

"He isn't just anyone. He's Sheriff Carson, he's a friend."

"Yes, I am a friend," Monte said. "And because I know all three of you, I don't mind telling you that I fought for the South under General Sterling Price."

"Ha! You know what, Miss Sally? That makes you the only Yankee here," Cal said with a laugh.

"I suppose it does," Sally said with an agreeable smile.

"Monte, I think our first trip should be to Denver, where I can introduce you to a few friends I have in the general assembly," Smoke offered.

A wide smile spread across Monte's face. "Thanks, Smoke, you don't know how much that means to me. I was trying to come up with some way to ask you if you would."

CHAPTER SEVENTEEN

The Spot Saloon, Denver

The Spot was a long way from the Gentleman's Club, not only because it was on the opposite side of town, but also because of the total ambience of the establishment. Whereas the Gentleman's Club was well lighted and spotlessly clean with lots of mahogany and leather, The Spot was dim and dingy, with a floor stained by expectorated tobacco.

Underhill felt uncomfortable in such a place and he dusted off the chair before he sat down. He didn't know any of the customers and he was sure that none of them knew him. And it was for that reason he had chosen this as the place to meet Ebenezer Priest. He didn't want anyone to know about the business he had come here to discuss with Priest.

"One thousand dollars?" Priest said, replying to a comment Underhill had just made. Priest was not a very large man, noticeable perhaps only because he had a nose that seemed too large for his face, thinning blond hair, and pale blue eyes.

"Yes, one thousand dollars," Underhill said. "One hundred now and the rest after the job is done."

Priest stroked his chin. It had been a long time since he had as much as one hundred dollars in his hand, and he had never had one thousand dollars at one time.

"Five hundred for Smoke Jensen, two hundred and fifty for the one they call Pearlie, and another two hundred and fifty for the one they call Cal."

"Smoke Jensen? He's the one that . . ."

"Killed your brother, Jeremiah, yes," Underhill said. Underhill smiled. "That ought to give you some added incentive."

"It ought to do what?"

"Give you another reason, in addition to the money, as to why you might want to kill Jensen and the others."

"I reckon so," Priest said. "But here's the thing. I've heard of all three of them people, 'n truth is, I'm not sure I'd want to go up agin any of 'em."

"I'm not asking you to make this a fair fight. I'm just asking you to kill them, any way you can."

"I want fifteen hunnert dollars, 'n I want five hunnert of it now," Priest demanded.

Underhill drummed his fingers on the table. He didn't think he would have any trouble getting more support than Carson if it just came down to him and Carson. But Carson's association with Smoke Jensen would make it much more difficult, so he needed Jensen gone. And from his experience with Garneau, he knew that Pearlie Fontaine and Cal Wood would also have to be included in any plan to eliminate Jensen.

"All right," he said. "Fifteen hundred dollars."

"And five hunnert now?"

"Five hundred now," Underhill agreed with a nod.

Smiling, Priest reached across the table to shake Underhill's hand. "They's goin' to be some funerals in Eagle County soon," he said.

Red Cliff

Ebenezer Priest was in the Turkey Neck Saloon in Red Cliff when he saw Pete Merck, an old friend. Actually, *old acquaintance* would be a better definition because people like Priest didn't actually have friends.

"You here to meet him, too?" Merck asked.

"Meet who?" Priest replied.

"A feller by the name of Frank Petro."

"No, I've never heard of him. Why would I want to meet him?"

"Money, that's why. This here Petro feller has an idee that could make us five or six thousand dollars apiece."

Five thousand dollars was considerably more than the fifteen hundred he had been offered by Underhill, and the figure got his attention. "Five thousand dollars? Doin' what?"

"I don't know, he ain't said yet. But it has somethin' to do with the town of Big Rock."

Big Rock? Priest thought. Big Rock was where he was told he could find Smoke Jensen. He wondered if there was some way he could take on both jobs.

"I ain't here in particular to meet him, but I

might be interested if he's willin' to let me join in," Priest said.

"I'm sure he will. Tyler said he was lookin' for some people, which is how come I'm here to meet 'im. I'll put in a good word for you."

Decatur, Colorado

One week later Frank Petro, with his gang all gathered—Isaiah Arias, Dave Tyler, Pete Merck, and Ebenezer Priest—were in the Full House Saloon in the town of Decatur. The *Decatur Mountain News* carried the story of Sheriff Carson being nominated as one of the candidates to be considered for the United States Senate. Frank showed the newspaper to the other four who shared his table.

"Did you boys see this?" Frank asked.

"Yeah, I seen it. What about it?" Arias asked.

"Don't you see?" Frank replied. "If the sheriff is going to be running all over the state trying to get people to support him for senator, that means there won't be nobody left back in town to guard the bank."

"That don't make no sense," Merck said. "You know he'll be leavin' a deputy behind."

"Yes, he will!" Frank said with a broad smile. "And that's the best part of it!"

"What are you talkin' about?"

"Do you know who is the deputy sheriff in Big Rock?" Frank asked.

The other four men looked at one another, their expressions making it obvious that they couldn't answer Frank's question.

Finally, Merck responded, "We don't have no idea."

"Why, it's Leo Beajuex, that's who it is," Frank said. And when the name didn't register with any of the others, he gave them a further explanation.

"Leo Beajuex is a good friend of mine."

"You mean you got a deputy sheriff as a friend?" Arias asked.

"What are you doin' makin' friends with the law?" Tyler wanted to know.

"He warn't always a-wearin' a star. Fact is, me 'n him has done some jobs together. 'N when he helps us rob the bank in Big Rock, why, that'll be the biggest one we've ever done." Frank didn't mention that he, Beajuex, and a few others had tried to rob this same bank with the result that three of them, including his brother, were killed.

"Wait, are you sayin' that the deputy that's goin' to be left behind is goin' to help us rob the bank?" Arias asked.

Frank smiled. "Yeah, that's exactly what I'm sayin'."

"There's somethin' you ain't thinkin' about, Petro," Priest said.

"What's that?"

"You ain't thinkin' about Smoke Jensen."

"What's Smoke Jensen got to do with it?" Tyler asked.

"Jensen lives there," Priest said. "Hell, from what I heard, he started the town. 'N you know damn well he's got lots of his own money in that bank. You think he's just goin' to sit there 'n let us come in 'n rob it?"

When Priest first mentioned Smoke Jensen, Frank was afraid that he knew about the previous bank attempt and how Smoke Jensen was partly the reason it had failed. He decided to find out just how much Priest did know.

"How is it that you know so much about Smoke Jensen?" Frank asked.

"I've heard plenty about the son of a bitch. Fact is, he's kilt my brother."

Frank felt a sense of relief that Priest was apparently unaware of the previous attempt at the Bank of Big Rock.

"I've heard tell of this Smoke Jensen feller, too," Tyler said. "Maybe before we make a try at the bank, we ought to make sure he ain't in town."

"How are we goin' to do that?" Arias asked.

"I'll go into town and check it out," Frank said.

"Didn't you say you knowed this deputy feller that's there?" Priest asked.

"The deputy's name is Leo Beajuex and yes, I know him. It's like I said, me 'n him's good friends."

"Then maybe you oughtn't not be the one to go," Priest suggested.

"Yeah, I think Priest is right. I'm thinkin' maybe you ought not to be the one to go into town," Arias said.

"Someone needs to go," Frank said. "We need to know whether or not Jensen is in town."

"I'll go," Priest offered, thinking this would give him the opportunity to accomplish his first job without compromising the second. "I'll find out iffen the son of a bitch is there or not."

"Yeah, it'll be good to make sure Jensen ain't there, but the most important thing we want to know is whether or not the sheriff is gone," Frank said. "On account of, if the sheriff is gone, well, then we can work our deal with Leo. So soon as the sheriff leaves, you come tell us."

Big Rock

True to his promise to introduce Sheriff Carson to some of his friends in the general assembly, Smoke had made arrangements to take Monte to Denver and speak with a few people he called the "movers and shakers" of Colorado state politics. Now, with the invitations issued and accepted, Smoke, Sally, and Cal were at the depot waiting with the sheriff for the train to Denver. Sally and Cal had come to see them off, but only Smoke would actually be making the trip with Monte.

"I'll introduce him around to a few people then we'll take the next train back," Smoke promised. "I won't be gone more than three days at the most."

As it turned out, Smoke, Sally, and Cal were off to one side by themselves, having been temporarily abandoned by Monte. That was because Monte was in the middle of the depot platform, surrounded by a dozen or more well-wishers.

"He seems to have caught on to the idea of how to mingle with his constituency," Sally said.

"Yes, ma'am, if what you said means shakin' hands 'n slappin' backs 'n all, why, he sure is doin' that," Cal suggested.

No more than twenty feet away from where Smoke and the others were standing, Monte reached out to take the hand offered him by Arnie Stone. Stone was a hostler for the stagecoach depot.

"You tell them folks in Denver that we need a

senator from the people, not some highfalutin bigwig from the city," Stone said.

"Ha! What if, after Monte becomes the senator, he turns into a highfalutin bigwig his ownself?" one of the others asked.

"Boys, if that happens, I'll come back here and put a target on the seat of my pants," Monte promised.

The others laughed.

Pearlie hadn't arrived yet because he was already attending to his duty as interim sheriff. He had promised, though, that he would be there before the train left, and at the moment he was less than a block away in Nancy's Sweet Shop.

"And what do you call that?" he asked, pointing.

"That's a cranberry scone," Nancy said. She sliced off a small piece and handed it to him. "Try it."

"Uhm, uhm, that is good," Pearlie said, smacking his lips in appreciation. "Bein' as I'm the acting sheriff now, I won't be able to eat any of Miss Sally's bear sign so I reckon I'll be stopping in here from time to time."

"Why not, that cute young deputy stops in here a lot, doesn't he, Nonnie?"

"Mama!" Nancy's daughter squealed in protest.

"Don't tell me you haven't noticed him."

"Mama, please!"

Nancy put her arm around Nonnie. "I'm sorry, sweetheart, I was just having a little fun, is all."

"Please don't say anything like that in front of Leo, it would embarrass me to death."

"I promise," Nancy said.

Pearlie was smiling at the interplay between mother and daughter when he heard the whistle of the approaching train and remembered that he had promised to see Smoke off. "I have to go now, but don't you ladies sell everything before I get back," he said, raising his finger as he started toward the door.

"If we do, we can always make some more," Nancy called out to him.

There was only one building between the depot and the sweetshop, and when Pearlie stepped out front, he met Leo, who was walking swiftly from the sheriff's office.

"Hurry up, I don't want to miss tellin' them good-bye," Leo said.

"We've got plenty of time. The train isn't even in the station yet," Pearlie said.

"Wow, look at this!" Leo said. "There sure are a lot of people here at the depot."

"Yeah, and a lot of them made signs," Pearlie said.

Pearlie was talking about the signs that several of the well-wishers were holding: OUR NEXT SENATOR, SHERIFF CARSON, MAN OF THE PEOPLE, and one sign which read: SHERIFF CARSON WILL PUT BIG ROCK ON THE MAP.

"What does he mean by that?" Leo asked pointing to the sign. "Pearlie, you mean Big Rock ain't already on the map? Why, how does anybody ever find us?"

"It's easy, they just follow the railroad track and, next thing you know, here we are," Pearlie teased.

"Yeah, I reckon that's so."

The whistle was very close now, and the train

could be seen coming around the final curve before reaching Big Rock.

"Here it comes!" someone shouted excitedly. "Here comes the Eagle Flyer!"

The Eagle Flyer was so named because it ran from Denver to Red Cliff and other towns in Eagle County, including Big Rock.

"Well, hell, Carter, we can all see that," another answered.

Pearlie loved to watch the trains arrive and depart. The locomotive would sweep by with wheels as tall as Pearlie, being driven by the long, thrusting drivers, steam escaping from the drive cylinders, glowing cylinders dropping from the firebox, and the rattle and clang of the slowing cars.

Even after the train stopped it was still alive with the measured puffs and wheezes of the relief valves venting the excess pressure, and the snap and pop of the cooling bearings and journals.

"Hey, Smoke, while you're in Denver, how 'bout pickin' up a new hat for me?" Pearlie asked.

"You just bought a new hat a couple of months ago," Smoke said.

"Yeah, but it wasn't the right color. I mean, being as I'm the sheriff now, seems to me like I ought to be wearing a white hat. And I've tried both at the Big Rock Mercantile and Murchison's Leather Goods and neither one of them has a white hat."

"Pearlie, you won't be able to see your silver band if it's on a white hat," Cal said.

"Oh," Pearlie replied. "Yeah, I hadn't thought about it. Yeah, you're right. Never mind, Smoke. I'm good with this one." Pearlie took off his hat, shaped it a bit, and repositioned the silver band.

Monte, who had been graciously accepting the good wishes of all the citizens there gathered, now came over to join Smoke. He glanced toward Pearlie and Leo.

"You two men take care of the town for me while I'm gone," he said.

"Don't give us a second thought," Pearlie said. "You just do what you have to do to get yourself elected senator. We'll take care of any bad guys that might pop up."

Monte chuckled. "I have no doubt but that you will."

Phil Clinton stepped up to Smoke and Monte then. He was carrying two copies of the *Big Rock Journal.*

"There's a story here, on the first page, that I think the two of you should read," Clinton said.

"You've given us an endorsement?" Smoke asked with a smile.

"I've already done that, and I will continue to do so by way of my editorials. But the story I want you to see is more along the lines of 'know your enemy,' or in this case, 'know your competition.'

"I have posted an article about State Senator Rex Underhill, who is also seeking the seat."

"Damn, he already has a one-vote advantage over me, doesn't he? I mean, seeing as he can vote for himself," Monte said with a little laugh.

"I hope you don't take this as an endorsement," Clinton said. "But as a newspaperman, I am honor bound to report the news, and this is news."

The conductor who stepped down from the train a moment earlier was studying his watch. He snapped the cover shut, then looked out over the crowd, rather surprised at the size of it.

"Board!" he called, importantly.

Smoke gave Sally a kiss, then shook hands with Pearlie, Cal, and Leo.

"Smoke, do what you can to make our sheriff the next senator!" McKnight called.

"I'll do my best," Smoke called back just as he stepped up onto the train car.

CHAPTER EIGHTEEN

Onboard the Eagle Flyer

Once the train got under way Monte lifted the window and stuck his arm out to wave at his well-wishers, doing so until the train was well out of town and only empty land lay adjacent to the tracks.

"That was a good turnout, wasn't it?" Monte said, now sitting in his seat across from Smoke.

"Well, what did you expect? I let everyone know that you had left orders with your deputy to shoot anyone who didn't show up to tell you good-bye," Smoke said.

"What?" Monte gasped, though he knew even before the smile broke out on Smoke's face that he was teasing.

"It's because the people like and support you, Monte. You have been a very good sheriff, and appointing you to the position is one of the smartest things I ever did," Smoke said.

Monte was quiet for a moment, thinking about all the strange twists and turns in his life that had gotten him to this point. He was quiet because he was so filled with emotion that he wasn't sure he could speak. Finally, the words came.

"Accepting your offer to be sheriff *is* the smartest thing I've ever done," Monte said.

"Tickets. Tickets, please," the conductor said as he came through the car. When he got to Smoke and Monte, he smiled.

"Sheriff Carson!" the conductor said with a wide smile of greeting.

"Hello, Beans," Monte replied.

"Is it true you are going to be our next senator?"

"I'm certainly going to try."

"Well, I will be writing both my representative and my senator to let them know, in no uncertain terms, where I stand," Beans said. He collected the tickets from both Smoke and Monte, then moved on through the car.

"What's in the newspaper Phil gave you?" Monte asked.

"I haven't read it yet, but he said it was an article about Rex Underhill trying for the Senate seat," Monte said.

"You know, Smoke, there's something about Rex Underhill that I never told you," Monte said.

"What's that?"

"Do you remember when that Frenchman, the one who passed himself off as a colonel, tried to take over most of the county by running out all the other ranchers?"

"Yeah, I remember. He said his name was Garneau, Lucien Garneau. Though as I recall, that wasn't his real name."

"Yes, that's the one I'm talking about."

"What does he have to do with Rex Underhill?"

"Joel told me about a money transfer between Garneau and Underhill. It was rather substantial so I remember being curious about it at the time. Then later, after the trial, and on the night before we hung him, I asked Garneau about the transfer of money and if he had any connection to Underhill."

"What did Garneau say?" Smoke asked.

Je peux en dire plus en disant moins.

"What?"

Monte chuckled. "I asked Louis what that meant and even when he translated it to English I still had no idea what he was talking about. In English, what Garneau said was, 'I can say more, by saying less.'"

"Well, now, that is what I believe Sally would call an *enigmatic statement*," Smoke said.

"If that means somethin' that you can't quite understand, I would agree with her."

"But it bothers you, doesn't it?" Smoke asked.

Monte nodded. "Yes. What did he mean by, 'I can say more, by saying less'? I've given it a lot of thought, and I think it means that Underhill was mixed up in the whole affair. In some twisted concept of honor, Garneau didn't think that he should come right out and say so, but his 'saying more by saying less' meant that. I'm sure of it, without any evidence to point to Underhill, all I had was suspicion." Monte laughed. "And it's damn hard to make a case out of suspicion."

"If it is any consolation to you, Monte, I agree with you. A large transfer of money between the two men, and the strange comment Garneau made, neither implicating nor exonerating, makes me equally suspicious."

"Let's see what Phil wrote about him."

Smoke unfolded the paper and saw the article on the front page.

Rex Underhill Announces
For the United States Senate

State Senator Rex Underhill has declared his intention to stand for the United States Senate.

"I am a man with an extensive background in business, and with legislative experience. I want to use that experience in service to the citizens of the state of Colorado," Senator Underhill said upon making his announcement.

State Senator Rex Underhill is a member of the very body from whom he must get support in order to win the appointment to the senate. His quickness to declare his candidacy, as well as his standing with the general assembly would seem, at this moment, to make Rex Underhill an almost prohibitive favorite to secure the position. However, he has not yet secured the appointment and while he may garner some support in some circles, he will not receive the endorsement of the publisher of the *Big Rock Journal.*

The official position of this publisher, and of this newspaper, is, and shall continue to be, the unremitting support

and promotion of Monte J. Carson for
United States senator from the state of
Colorado.

"Phil Clinton is a good man," Smoke said after
both he and Monte had read the article.

"Yes, he is," Monte agreed. "Still . . ." He let the
word hang.

"Still what?"

"With Rex Underhill's money and contacts in the
state government, he's going to be a hard man to
beat," Monte said.

"Yes, but don't forget, Underhill doesn't have that
good of a reputation," Smoke said. "I've heard things
about how Underhill bent a few laws here and there
to get rich. And that is even before you told me of his
possible connection with Garneau."

"Yeah, I've heard the same things about him. In
fact, I think it was those very things that made me
even more suspicious about him after Joel told
me about the money transfer. But don't forget,
Smoke, my own past isn't exactly Sunday-school
clean," Monte said.

"Who do we know who does have such a clean
history?" Smoke replied. "I'm not sure I would want
anyone taking that close a look at my own past."
Smoke chuckled. "I'll tell you what, Monte. The best
thing we can do is just play this game with the cards
we were dealt."

"I'll play with these cards," Monte said. He smiled.
"Especially since I have an ace in the hole."

"Oh? What ace is that?"

"I have no idea who is managing Underhill's

campaign, but I will bet it all on the prospect that my campaign manager is better. You, Smoke. You are my ace in the hole."

"I appreciate your confidence in me," Smoke said with a gracious smile.

Big Rock

Once the train left the station, those who had come to see Monte off began to drift away. One, who had been imbedded in the crowd so that he wouldn't be seen by either Smoke or Sheriff Carson was Ebenezer Priest. The fact that both Smoke Jensen and the sheriff would be gone would be good news for Frank and the others because it truly did open up the town for them, making it much easier to carry off the bank robbery.

But, as far as Priest was concerned, he wished Smoke Jensen would have stayed around for a while longer; just long enough for him to kill the son of a bitch.

Wait a minute. Frank said that his friend was going to be the deputy, but there were two men standing there wearing deputies' badges. Who was the second man?

Priest observed the two badge-wearing men without himself being seen.

Son of a bitch! One of them was the man who called himself Pearlie!

Priest smiled. This might work out well after all. Because he was getting fifteen hundred dollars to kill the three men, Pearlie was worth five hundred dollars. And killing him would also take care of the extra deputy so that only Frank's friend remained, the one who was going to help them rob the bank.

Priest was supposed to go back and tell the others just as soon as he learned that the sheriff was gone, but given this new development he decided it would be worthwhile to wait until he had taken care of Pearlie. He would do that tonight, and that would give him the rest of the day to find out as much useful information as he could.

He decided to begin his reconnoiter by checking out the bank.

When he stepped inside there was already someone standing at the teller's cage, which was good, as it gave him an opportunity to have a good look around. Between the front door and the teller's cage was a table with an inkwell and a pen on it. The teller stood behind a half wall, painted wood at the bottom and with glass on top. Through the glass and to his left, Priest could see a rather substantial-looking safe, sitting on the floor. To his right, and on front side of the half wall, was a desk with a man sitting behind it who was writing in a ledger book of some sort.

"Thank you very much, Mr. Wilkerson, and tell Mrs. Wilkerson I said hello," the bank teller said as the customer before Priest concluded his business.

"May I help you, sir?" the teller asked with a friendly smile. The teller's window had bars at the top, but it was open at the bottom so that money and bank drafts could be passed through.

"Yes," Priest said, stepping up to the window. He put a ten-dollar bill down on the counter. "I wonder if I could have ten one-dollar bills for this?"

"Certainly, sir."

After leaving the bank, Priest made a very thorough

perusal of the town. He checked the roads in and out of Big Rock, and all the balconies and upper-story windows that might provide a shooter easy access to a group of men who were trying to make an escape. He also checked the space in between the buildings as well as the alleyways behind them. By the time the sun sank behind the western range of mountains, Priest had gathered information on the bank and the town that he was sure would be very helpful to the others in making the final plans.

He decided to have a beer at the Brown Dirt Cowboy Saloon, because he was closer to the Brown Dirt than he was to Longmont's.

"Hello, honey," one of the bar girls said, greeting Priest as he stepped inside. "Would you like some drinking company?"

"Yeah, why not?"

"My name is Mollie, what's your name?"

"Priest," he replied as he walked with Mollie down to the far end of the bar. "Beer," he said to the bartender.

"You know mine, Paul," Mollie said with a smile toward the bartender.

Mollie might have been a pretty young woman at one time, but the dissipation of her trade had already had an effect on her. There was a hardness about her that even her practiced smile couldn't dismiss.

"Would you like to take a table?" Mollie asked. She liked to get her customers to a table for two reasons. One reason was that a sitting customer would be more inclined to buy her multiple drinks than a standing customer would be. Also a sitting customer was less likely to get too fresh with his hands. Not that she was opposed to her customers putting their hands on her, but, by the time their relationship had reached that stage, they were paying for the additional privilege.

"No, I'd as soon stand here," Priest said.

Paul put the drinks before them, beer for Priest, and what looked like whiskey, but was actually tea, in front of Mollie.

"Say, do you know a man that calls hisself Pearlie?"

"Pearlie? Yes, I know him. He's a really nice guy, anytime he's in here he treats all the girls like we, well, like we were just like anyone else."

"There's nothin' at all nice about the son of a bitch," Priest said in a low growl.

"Why would you say that?"

"Because he, 'n a man named Smoke Jensen, kilt my brother."

"Oh, honey, I'm sorry to hear about your brother."

"Yeah, well, I'll make it right, someday. I'll make it right."

Mollie found Priest's demeanor and words a little frightening so she tossed down the rest of her drink, then put the empty glass down on the bar.

"Thank you for the drink, honey. Now, you have a real nice time while you're in town, all right? Bye now."

Mollie walked away as Priest continued to stare down into his glass of beer.

CHAPTER NINETEEN

As Priest nursed his beer in the Brown Dirt Cowboy, Leo was following Pearlie while they were making the rounds. When they stepped into Longmont's Saloon it was quite busy, with some men standing at the bar. At least four of the tables were full, and some of the tables had women, not bar girls, but women from the town, as ladies who frequented Longmont's suffered no diminution in social standing.

There were several conversations ongoing, but they were quiet, interspersed occasionally by the laughs of men and women, though the laughter was never intrusive. The piano player was playing a tune that Leo didn't recognize, though he thought it was pretty.

"Pearlie, Leo, come join me," Louis called, inviting them back to his special table. "Sam," Louis called to his bartender. "Give our two gendarmes a beer on the house."

"I'd rather have a sarsaparilla," Leo said.

"What's a gendarme?"

"It's French for 'police,'" Leo said.

"*Avez-vous* speak *français*, Leo?" Louis asked.

"*Oui, ma mère était créole et parlait français*," Leo answered.

"Ah, so your mother was Creole, was she? I thought it might be something like that, your name being Beajuex. I must say, by the way, that I have known some beautiful Creole ladies," Louis said. He held the tips of his fingers together, then made the gesture of kissing them.

"My mother was a beautiful woman," Leo said, his reply touched with a bit of melancholy.

"Here are your drinks," Becky said, smiling as she brought them to the table.

"*Merci*," Leo said.

"*Le plaisir est pour moi*," Becky said.

"You speak French, too?" Leo asked.

"Oh, honey, you can't work for Mr. Longmont without learning some French," Becky said.

Pearlie held his beer out and he and Leo touched glasses.

"I take it that Smoke and Monte got away all right today," Louis said.

"Yes, we went down to the depot to watch them leave," Pearlie said. "Louis, you see a lot more people than I do. Do you think Monte has a chance of actually becoming our senator?"

"Oh, I think he has an excellent chance," Louis replied. "In fact, I would say that the odds are rather good that, within six months, he will be establishing his domicile in Washington, D.C."

"What does it mean to 'establish a domicile'?" Leo asked.

"It means he will be moving to Washington," Louis explained.

"Pearlie, how far off is Washington?"

"Oh, it's a long way off, nearly a week by train, if you count all the times you'll have to change trains. Why do you ask?"

"I was just wondering. I mean, if Sheriff Carson gets elected and has one of them domiciles in Washington, what will happen to me? The judge said I was going to have to stay with him for two years, or I'd wind up havin' to go to prison. I don't want to go to prison, but if he goes to Washington, I won't be able to be his deputy anymore. It's got me a little scared, to be honest."

"Leo, I promise you, you don't have a thing to worry about. If the sheriff is elected, if nothing else, we'll take you on out at Sugarloaf."

"You really think Mr. Jensen would do that?"

"I am absolutely positive he will do that."

"Thanks," Leo said, the expression on his face turning from one of worry to one of relief.

"All right, what do you say we go out and carry on the fight against crime and bad people?" Pearlie suggested. "Well, we'll carry the battle only against bad men. I like bad women," he added with a chuckle.

"They're not all bad," Leo said.

"Who isn't all bad?" Pearlie asked, confused by Leo's response.

"Whores. They aren't all bad." Leo was thinking of his mother and the other women of de Plaisir Maison. "Most of them are very nice."

Pearlie started to ask what someone as young as Leo knew about whores, but he checked his question. He didn't know about Leo's background, but he guessed that he must have had a personal reason for making such a comment, and that was enough for him.

"You're right, Leo. I've known some mighty fine soiled doves," Pearlie replied.

The two walked west on Front Street, turned south on Tanner, then east on Center Street. They didn't go all the way down to Malone Avenue, because there was nothing on Malone but private homes. Most of the businesses on Center Street were closed because, except for the hotel and the stagecoach depot, they were all professional buildings.

"I've noticed there doesn't hardly anything ever happen on this street," Leo said. "And I reckon that's because they're most always closed by this time of night, except for the Brown Dirt Cowboy."

The Brown Dirt Cowboy was on the other side of Sikes, but unlike the restrained conversations in Longmont's, Pearlie and Leo could hear the noise of the Brown Dirt from almost a block away. Loud voices and even louder guffaws of laughter rolled down the street from the saloon, mostly from men, but there were a few high-pitched cackles from the women. It wasn't until Pearlie and Leo were quite close that they could even hear the sound of a piano, because the music was drowned out by everything else.

Leo started to go in, but Pearlie reached out and pulled him back.

"Uh-uh, kid."

"What's wrong?" Leo asked. "Aren't we goin' to go in 'n check it out?"

"We're going to check it out, all right, but you don't just walk into a place like this. Has nobody ever taught you how to go into a saloon?"

"I don't reckon they have. What is there to going into a saloon? I mean, we just went into Longmont's a while ago 'n we didn't do nothin' special."

"The Brown Dirt is different."

"All right."

"Now, pay attention to me, Leo, and go in exactly as I do. *Exactly*, do you understand?"

"Yes, sir," Leo said, agreeing to follow Pearlie's suggestion, though it was obvious that he had no understanding as to what this was about.

Pearlie stepped in through the batwing doors, then moved quickly to one side, keeping his back pressed up against the wall. Leo entered the same way and stood beside him.

"When you've been around for a while, you make enemies," Pearlie said, quietly explaining to Leo why they were doing this. "By stepping through the door quickly, then putting your back against the wall, nobody can shoot you in the back. Now, we can look over the saloon and study everyone in here. Are there any strangers? Are they heeled? Do they look like they can use a gun? And what's even more important, is to look for someone who isn't a stranger, someone you might have made an enemy of at some time in the past.

"Then, and only then, when you have checked out the entire saloon, should you go on inside."

Ebenezer Priest saw the two men as soon as they came in. He didn't look directly at them, but he did watch them in the mirror. He saw the way they entered, just real careful, pretty much the same way he entered a saloon. A few of the bar girls greeted the two men.

"Hello, Pearlie. You the sheriff now?" Mollie asked.

"I'm just actin' as a deputy while Monte's gone. I'm helping Leo."

"Hello, Leo," Mollie said teasingly.

"Hello, ma'am."

"Leo, you are the cutest thing," Mollie said. "You two boys come on in.

"Anything you want, you just ask for it," she added, striking a seductive pose.

Priest thought there might be a possibility that Pearlie would take one of the whores upstairs. If that happened it would be easy to take care of him. He could go up the stairs without catching anyone's attention and find out which room they were in. After that all he would have to do would be wait for a few minutes, until Pearlie got "busy," so busy that he wouldn't be on the lookout for anyone who might come through the door. And he for sure wouldn't be wearing his gun. Priest could kill him and the whore with a knife, and nobody would be the wiser for it until after he was gone.

"Hello, Pearlie, Leo. Come have a drink with us," somebody called from one of the tables. The gregarious man was a cowboy from a neighboring ranch to Sugarloaf. Pearlie knew him only as Dusty.

"We'll join you for a few minutes, Dusty, but we better not drink, we're working," Pearlie said.

"Working? Oh yeah, someone told me you was

deputyin' for Sheriff Carson." Dusty laughed. "That bein' the case, you may not want to be seen with the likes of a common cowboy."

"Nonsense, common cowboys are the best kind," Pearlie replied.

"Pearlie, I know you said we ought not to drink no more, but I am a little thirsty. Do you think it would be all right if I was to have me another sarsaparilla?" Leo asked.

"Boy, don't you know if you keep drinkin' those things you're goin' to turn into a sassafras root?" Pearlie teased.

"I don't care, I like them."

"Yeah, go ahead, grab yourself a sody pop and come on over to the table with Dusty and me."

As Leo walked over to get his drink, Pearlie took a chair at the table, then looked back toward the far end of the bar. He had noticed the man standing there as soon as they had come in. There was something about him that caught Pearlie's attention, but he just couldn't put his finger on it, though he could almost swear the man was watching them in the mirror. No, not watching them, studying them.

He didn't want to cause a disturbance by confronting him right now. Besides, it was probably nothing more than idle curiosity on the man's part. Nevertheless, he decided that he would keep an eye on him. Pearlie reached down to loosen the pistol in his holster, though he did it unobtrusively.

Priest nursed his drink as he continued to study, by way of the mirror image, the two star packers who had come in. Because Pearlie had joined the man who had called out to them, it quickly became obvious that Pearlie had no plans to take a whore upstairs. That meant Priest would have to find some other way to take care of Pearlie. He finished his drink, then left the saloon.

Pearlie watched the man leave, still a little curious about him.

"Dusty, that man that's leaving now, do you have any idea who he is?"

"Nope," Dusty answered. "I ain't never seen 'im before. Why do you ask?"

"No particular reason, I suppose," Pearlie replied. "I was just curious, is all."

Leo came back then, carrying his sarsaparilla.

"Pearlie, if Sheriff Carson goes to the Senate, who do you think will be the new sheriff?" Dusty asked. "You?"

"Me?" Pearlie laughed. "No, thank you, I have no wish to have a job that would make me a target for anyone on the dodge who might happen to come through here."

"But you're wearing a badge now."

"Yeah, but I'm just doing Monte a favor. If he goes to the Senate we'll just have to get someone else, that's all. He may not be as good as Monte at first, but whoever we wind up with will come along, I'm sure."

"What about you, kid? Would you like to be the sheriff?" Dusty asked.

"I don't know," Leo answered. "I wouldn't be ready for it now, but maybe someday when I'm older I would think about it."

"Good answer," Pearlie said.

They visited for a few more minutes, then Pearlie saw Leo take the last swallow of his drink.

"I expect we had better go before my deputy here gets drunk," Pearlie teased.

"You can't get drunk on this, can you?" Leo asked seriously.

Pearlie laughed. "Not unless something's added to it. But Andy's a pretty sneaky kind of a guy, and I wouldn't put it past him to do something like that." Andy was the bartender.

"Come on, let's get back to the office, where I can beat you in a game of checkers," Pearlie suggested.

"Bet you can't. Checkers is one of the things that I'm just real good at," Leo said, accepting the challenge.

"Don't be so sure of it."

Priest was glad that he had made a thorough perusal of the town earlier today. Because he had done so, he now had a pretty good feel of the layout; he knew where all the alleys were, and he knew what buildings had space between them. When he left the saloon a moment earlier he walked up Sikes Street for a couple of buildings, then darted in between two of the buildings and stepped into the alley, then came back until he was behind the Brown Dirt. He walked up alongside the Brown Dirt, between it and Sikes' Hardware Store, then stood in the dark between the two buildings and waited.

CHAPTER TWENTY

Pearlie and Leo stepped out of the saloon and stood facing each other for a moment.

"Are we going straight back to the office, or are we going to walk around the block again?" Leo asked.

"Ha," Pearlie said. "You may wind up being a pretty good deputy after all if you put duty before pleasure. Or, is it that you are just afraid to face me across a checkerboard?" he teased.

"Afraid? I'll show you who's . . ."

Leo stopped in midsentence because that was when he saw someone move out from the side of the building with a gun leveled toward Pearlie's back. It was the same man who had been standing at the end of the bar.

"Pearlie!" Leo shouted, drawing his gun as he pushed Pearlie aside.

The man fired just as Leo shoved Pearlie and as a result he missed what should have been an easy shot.

Just a second after the man fired, Leo pulled the trigger and saw a little squirt of blood in the middle of the gunman's chest. He watched as the shooter dropped his gun and grabbed his chest.

"I thought you . . ." the gunman said with a strange, almost disbelieving expression on his face.

Whatever he thought, his comment was left incomplete as he pitched forward, facedown.

By now Pearlie had his own gun out, but it was not necessary that he take a shot, because the danger was over.

"I wonder what he was trying to say," Leo said.

"I don't know, it was kind of strange. Do you know him?" Pearlie asked.

Leo shook his head. "I ain't never seen him in my life."

"He was watching us when we were inside."

"I wonder why he wanted to kill you."

Pearlie shook his head. "It's like I said when we walked into the saloon a while ago, I've made more than a few enemies in my life. I expect this was one of them."

By that time the patrons of the Brown Dirt Cowboy, having heard the two gunshots, one on top of the other, hurried outside to see what was going on. They saw both Pearlie and Leo with pistols in hand, and a man who, but a few minutes earlier, had been standing at the bar, now lying facedown. Dusty went over to squat down beside the prostate figure and put his fingers to the man's neck.

"Is he . . . is he dead?" Leo asked.

"Yep. He's deader'n a mule-kicked bobcat," Dusty said.

"Dead," someone said.

"He was goin' to shoot Pearlie in the back," Leo said, believing it was necessary to defend himself. "I didn't have any choice. I had to shoot 'im."

"That's true," Pearlie said. "If it hadn't been for Leo, I'd be a dead duck by now."

"Well, kid, I reckon you've earned the right to wear that star," Dusty said. "No more thinkin' of you as just someone that keeps the jail swept out."

"I killed him," Leo said in a quiet and disbelieving voice.

"And saved Pearlie's life," one of the saloon patrons said.

"Why was he after you, Pearlie? Why would he want you dead enough, to shoot you in the back?" Dusty asked.

"I don't have any idea why he wanted to shoot me," Pearlie said. "Though, I did notice him standing at the bar when we were in there a while ago. And there was something about him that was making me a bit uneasy."

"Yeah, I remember you asking me about him."

"I know why he wanted to kill you," Mollie said. Mollie had come outside to join the others, which by now included just about every patron of the bar.

"Yeah, Mollie, I seen you talkin' to 'im earlier," Dusty said. "Did he tell you why?" Dusty asked, surprised by the girl's comment.

"Not exactly, but I know that he was mad at Pearlie, because of somethin' that either Pearlie or Mr. Jensen done to his brother. But I didn't think he'd actually do nothin' like this, 'cause if I had'a knowed it, I woulda warned you."

"I did something to his brother?"

"That's what he said."

"What's this man's name, does anyone know?"

"He said his name was Priest. But he didn't give me his first name."

"Jeremiah," Pearlie said resolutely.

"That was his first name? Jeremiah?"

"No, that was the name of his brother. Jeremiah Priest worked for Deekus Templeton and that Frenchman who called himself Colonel Garneau, if any of you remember. They came in here killing and stealing, and planning to take over the whole valley before we stopped him.

"It was actually Smoke who killed the son of a bitch, but it could just as easily have been Cal or me."

"Yeah," Dusty said. "Yeah, I think I do remember that little fracas."

"Is it all right if I send someone for Tom McBride?" Emmet Brown asked. "Leavin' him out here is bad for business."

Brown owned the Brown Dirt Cowboy Saloon.

"Yeah, go ahead," Pearlie said. "Leo, let's go play checkers."

A few minutes later Pearlie had the checkerboard all set up on the desk. Leo had said very little since they left the saloon and now he sat just staring at the board, deep in thought.

"Are you all right, Leo?" Pearlie asked.

"Yeah, I'm all right." The reply was quiet and obviously distressed.

"Is this the first man you ever killed?"

"Yeah."

"And it's bothering you?"

Leo made no audible response, but he did nod his head.

Pearlie reached out to put his hand on the young deputy's shoulder. "Leo, if you hadn't killed Priest, he would have killed me. You traded one life for another." Pearlie smiled. "And I like the trade. Look, I've killed quite a few men myself, so has Cal, so has Sally, even. And Smoke has killed more than any of us. But none of us have ever had a hard time sleeping at night, because in every case it was necessary. And the son of a bitch you killed today needed killin'." Pearlie looked at the checkerboard.

"Now, are you just going to sit there and mope, or are you going to play checkers?"

"I'm not only going to play, I'm going to beat your scruffy ass," Leo said as he made the first move.

"Ha! Is that any way to talk to your elders?" Pearlie replied as he made his own move.

In Denver, even as Pearlie and Leo were playing checkers, State Senator Bill Lewis was hosting a reception in the ballroom of the Crawford Hotel, which was located in Union Station. There were several other members of the general assembly present for the reception, as well as businessmen, miners, and cattlemen.

"Well, Smoke, it looks like we've got a good turnout for your friend," Senator Lewis said. Lewis had come to join Smoke, who was standing by the punch bowl with Representative Josh LaPlant. Monte was mixing with the others, introducing himself to those who didn't know him and conversing with those who did.

"Monte is going to have a hard row to hoe, seeing as Rex Underhill is trying for the same seat," LaPlant said. "And of course, everyone who can actually vote for him, and I'm talking everyone in the entire general assembly, knows Underhill personally. Monte doesn't know more than a handful, and many of those he met here, for the first time tonight."

"Tell me, Josh, how well do you know Rex Underhill?" Senator Lewis asked.

"I know him better than I ever wanted to know him," LaPlant replied.

"And are you going to vote for him?" Lewis asked.

"I'm here tonight, aren't I? I'm going to vote for Monte."

"Let me ask you this. If Monte wasn't running, would you vote for Underhill?" Lewis asked.

"Are you kidding? I would vote for a wild coyote before I voted for that son of a bitch," LaPlant replied.

Lewis chuckled. "Well, there you go, Josh. Sheriff Carson may have a problem in that not enough people know him, but I think Underhill's problem may be that too many people do know him. And I would say that gives Sheriff Carson an advantage."

LaPlant laughed. "You may have a point there, Bill."

"There is someone else who is thinking about entering the race, though, and he may actually give us a problem," Lewis said.

"You're talking about the lieutenant governor?" Smoke asked.

"Yes, and unlike Underhill, Tabor is a good man."

"He is a good man, but don't forget that Tabor got right in the middle of the Leadville miners' strike and the governor had to take over and settle it himself. A lot of people are going to remember that Tabor wasn't able to handle it," Josh said.

"Tabor was handling it just fine, though he was upsetting a lot of people. Actually, I think Governor Pitkin probably agreed with what Tabor was doing, but he also knew that it could be political suicide for both of them." Lewis chuckled. "Pitkin had the good sense to withdraw. Tabor had the courage to get involved in the first place."

"The problem with any politician is that being in public service puts your past right out in front of everyone so that you can be examined like a butterfly pinned on a board, and any little thing can cause people to turn on you," LaPlant said.

"If Tabor does put his name up, will you support him?" Smoke asked.

"No, I've made the commitment to support Monte Carson, and I intend to honor that commitment."

"Would you support Tabor if Monte wasn't running?" Smoke asked.

"Yes," Lewis replied. "If Monte wasn't seeking the office, I would support Tabor. Especially over Rex Underhill."

"Well, then, I'm doubly thankful for your help with Monte," Smoke said.

"Monte Carson's only public service has been as sheriff, and from all that I have been able to ascertain, it has been exemplary, such as that attempted bank robbery a few weeks ago. As the campaign goes on, I intend to make it my personal responsibility to make certain as many solons as possible know of Monte's sterling qualities, so they can compare him with Rex Underhill. Yes, sir, if I was a betting man, I would say that right now, Sheriff Monte Carson is the odds-on favorite to be Colorado's next United States senator," Lewis said.

LaPlant nodded. "I tend to agree with you, Bill. At any rate, I know I will certainly be supporting Carson and will do what I can to bring others over to support him as well."

A few minutes later Monte came over to talk to Smoke, and he shared with Monte what both Senator Lewis and Representative LaPlant had said about Monte being the odds-on favorite to win.

"Unless Tabor decides to run," Monte said. "Tabor is a good man. I'll be honest with you, Smoke, I don't know but what he wouldn't be a better senator than I would."

"Don't talk like that, Monte," Smoke said. "I've known you for a very long time, and you are as good a man as any I've known. You've never let me down."

"I've never actually been in this position before."

"Are you frightened of the responsibility?" Smoke asked.

Monte shook his head. "I'm not frightened of the responsibility, but I would feel awfully bad about letting down so many people who are supporting me now."

"Ahh, you worry too much," Smoke said.

"What's our next move?" Monte asked.

"I'm going to introduce you to the governor. I know the governor doesn't have a vote, but his support can't hurt," Smoke said.

The conversation between Smoke and Monte was interrupted by someone rapping loudly on a table. When they looked toward the sound, they saw that it was Bill Lewis trying to get everyone's attention.

"Folks, folks, can I have your attention, please?" Lewis called out.

All conversation ceased.

"Folks, we have ten of our thirty-five senators and seventeen of our sixty-five representatives here tonight. I know that this is going to put you on the spot but I'm going to ask now, for a public commitment from each of you here. Can we all agree that Monte Carson has our support?"

"Against Rex Underhill? Hell, yes!" someone said, and the others laughed.

Lewis went around to every state senator and state representative present and got a positive response from all of them.

"This obviously isn't enough to make up the majority of the general assembly, but it is over half of the numbers you need, and I would say that is a pretty good start," Lewis said. "It also means that if we are going to get our man into the U.S. Senate, we are going to have to work every one of our friends in the house and senate just as if we were trying to get a bill passed. Gentlemen, enjoy the rest of the evening, because tomorrow your work begins."

CHAPTER TWENTY-ONE

Smoke had no problem in getting an appointment with Governor Frederick Walker Pitkin the next morning. He knew the governor quite well—so well, in fact, that he held a state commission from the governor as a special law enforcement officer. The governor wore a long, somewhat unkempt beard.

"So this is your sheriff Monte Carson," the governor said.

"This is the man, Governor."

"Smoke speaks very highly of you, Sheriff, and anyone he puts that much faith in, deserves my attention," Governor Pitkin said, stretching his hand across his desk. "It's a pleasure meeting you."

"Believe me, Governor, I consider meeting you a most distinct honor," Monte replied.

"Well, he does know how to get on a man's good side, I'll give him that," the governor said with a little laugh. "And you would be the next senator from the great state of Colorado?"

"Yes, but only if I am lucky enough. I realize that I am going to have some stiff competition with Senator Underhill seeking the same office."

Governor Pitkin gave a scornful snort. "That may be so, but if State Senator Underhill becomes our next United States senator, he will certainly have to do so without my support."

"Governor, I know that you tried for the office yourself last year," Smoke said. "But I have also heard that you have no intention in making another try."

Pitkin chuckled. "Yes, I found it was easier to get thirty-five thousand votes from the population at large than it was to get fifty-one votes from the general assembly. I have no intention of making another try."

"What about the lieutenant governor?" Monte asked.

"What about him?"

"I've heard rumors that he might run."

"Horace Tabor is a good man," Pitkin said. "We've had our differences, but he is a good man. However, I don't think he's going to run, and even if he does make the decision to run, I've made my commitment to you. I don't go back on a commitment once it has been made."

Neither Smoke nor Monte replied to the governor's comment because they weren't sure what the correct response would be. The governor flashed a big smile at the two men.

"Do you mind if I call you Monte? After all, if you are going to be one of our senators, we should be on a first-name basis, don't you think?"

"Well, yes, sir, that is, assuming I become our next senator."

"I've been in politics for a long time, Monte, and if there is one thing I'm quite good at, it is reading the political winds. And I would say, right now, that you are the leading candidate, certainly with regard to Rex Underhill, and though it would be closer if Horace did decide to run, I believe there is a good chance that you would beat him as well. Why, I would support you, just based upon Smoke's recommendation alone."

"My having Smoke as a good friend has been one of the high points of my life. I'm pleased that he has spoken well of me, and I am both honored by and appreciative of your support."

"You do understand, though, that my support will be limited to vocal endorsement only. I'll have no vote in the legislative procedure that will actually select the next senator."

"Yes, sir, I understand."

Governor Pitkin shook his head. "I'll be honest with you, I don't know how practical this system is for selecting senators, and I'm not sure I appreciate it, but state legislative approval is how our founders decided to select United States senators. Already there is a movement to do away with legislative appointment and make senators subject to a direct election of the people of the state. And why not? If we have to run for election to be a governor, seems only right the senators should have to run. That way, they truly would be responsible to the people, and not to some political clique."

Governor Pitkin smiled. "Now, Smoke, Monte, if you want the advice of an old campaigner, you should go shake some hands and meet a few people. It has been my observation that the candidate who shakes the most hands, generally winds up with the most votes, whether you need thirty-five thousand or fifty-one."

After they left Governor Pitkin's office Smoke suggested that they visit the lieutenant governor.

"Do you know Horace Tabor? Are you friends with him?" Monte asked.

"I know him. I can't say that we are friends, but that's only because we have only a casual acquaintance, and there has never been anything happen between us that would prevent us from being friends."

Smoke wasn't certain that Lieutenant Governor Tabor would receive them but within less than a minute after the lieutenant governor's clerk stepped into the office to announce them, Tabor came out to meet them. Tabor was tall, thin, with a sweeping mustache and hair that had receded back to the top of his head.

"Mr. Jensen and Sheriff Carson," Tabor greeted. "Come in, please. John, some coffee for our guests?"

"Yes, sir," the clerk said.

Tabor's office had a sitting area, consisting of two facing sofas, with a low-lying table between them. Tabor sat on one of the sofas and indicated with a wave of his hand that Smoke and Monte should sit on the other.

"Sheriff, I hear you are seeking the office that Senator Chilcott is about to vacate," Tabor said.

"Yes, sir, I've decided to make a try for it."

"Do you have any previous political experience?"

"No, sir, other than being sheriff."

"And from all I have been able to ascertain, you have been a very good sheriff," Tabor said.

"Thank you, I appreciate the compliment."

Tabor smiled and held up his finger. "It is an observation, not a compliment, Sheriff. A compliment is a social amenity, often meaningless. An observation is a fact."

"Well stated, Lieutenant Governor," Smoke said.

"I suppose that the purpose of your visit is to solicit my support in your effort to become our next United States senator," Tabor said. "Am I correct in that supposition?"

"Before we get there, we have to ask you a question," Smoke said.

"You want to know if I intend to seek the office myself."

"Yes."

"I will tell you in all sincerity that I have given it a lot of thought. But to be honest with you, my consideration was based upon the fact that Rex Underhill had declared his candidacy. I think Underhill would be a terrible senator and I would run more to deny Underhill the office, than any wish to hold the seat myself. So," he said, interrupting his response with a smile, "if you have come to solicit my support, I will set aside any personal ambition to go to Washington and do what I can to help you. Underhill must not win."

"Thank you, sir," a grinning Monte Carson said as he reached out to take Tabor's hand. "Thank you very much."

"You've seen Pitkin, then?"

"Yes, we have."

Tabor nodded. "Fred and I have had our differences, and we don't often agree on anything, but we are both in absolute agreement that Underhill must not be the one who is selected to represent us."

"I can promise you, Lieutenant Governor, that we will do all that we can to prevent that from happening," Smoke said.

Frank's outlaw camp

Frank and his newly assembled gang were gathered in an abandoned line shack about halfway between Red Cliff and Big Rock. It was here that they were making their encampment as they waited to put their plan to rob the bank into operation.

"Where the hell do you think Priest is, 'n how come he ain't come back 'n told us nothin'?" Merck asked.

"I don't know, I been wonderin' 'bout that my ownself," Frank replied as he poured himself a cup of coffee.

"Maybe one of us should go into town 'n find out why he ain't come back yet," Tyler suggested.

"Yeah," Frank said. "That might not be a bad idea."

"You goin' in?" Tyler asked.

"I'd better not. I don't want to run into Beajuex just yet."

"Why not? Didn't you say he would help us?"

"Yes, I'm sure he will. But he don't need to know nothin' 'bout what we got planned till just before we do it. I don't know how good he would be at keepin' ever'thing a secret, I mean, what with him bein' so young 'n all."

"I'll go in," Arias said. "I wouldn't mind havin' a beer or two."

"All right, go on in 'n find Priest 'n then you 'n

him come on back here. More'n likely he's layin' up with a whore 'n forgot all about us, so you make sure you don't go off 'n do the same thing."

"Ha! Depends on how good-lookin' the whore is," Arias said.

"Get back here today, with or without 'im," Frank said. "Only you tell him if he ain't with us when we do the job, he don't get in on the split when we divide up the money."

"All right," Arias agreed.

Big Rock

A little over an hour later Arias rode into Big Rock. He figured that the best place to find Priest would be in a saloon but he didn't have to spend more than fifteen minutes in Longmont's Saloon to know that he wasn't there, and he was pretty sure that Priest hadn't been there. This was not the kind of saloon that would appeal to someone like Priest, or to Arias, for that matter.

After Arias left Longmont's to look for another saloon, he saw a coffin standing upright, with a handful of people satisfying their morbid curiosity. Even before he was close enough to see the body, he had a feeling in his gut. When he drew even with the coffin, he took a look.

The coffin contained the body of Ebenezer Priest.

"Can you imagine? This son of a bitch actually tried to shoot Pearlie in the back. In the back, mind you," one those looking at the body said.

"One of these days outlaws are goin' to learn that they ain't welcome in Big Rock. 'N if they do come into Big Rock 'n try 'n start somethin', why, they're goin' to wind up like this feller."

"Yeah, with people like Sheriff Carson, Smoke Jensen, Pearlie Fontaine, 'n Cal Wood, they ain't likely to get whatever evil thing they got planned done before they wind up out in Boot Hill," another said.

"Yeah, well, what if Sheriff Carson winds up goin' to the U.S. Senate, what will we do then?"

"Hell, Monte ain't in town now, him bein' in Denver like he is, 'n this feller was took care of."

Even though Arias had located Priest and now knew why he had not returned with his report, he decided to have one more beer before going back.

"Who's that dead feller you got standin' up back there?" Arias asked the bartender, figuring that by so asking, there wouldn't be anyone who would connect him with the body.

"He told Mollie his name was Priest, but that's all we know. We don't know his first name."

"Who kilt 'im?"

The bartender smiled. "Funny you would ask that, because that's somethin' that is real interestin'."

Frank's outlaw camp

"Well, I know why Ebenezer Priest ain't come back to give us no report on the bank or nothin'," Arias said when he returned to the line shack later that day.

"Well, why didn't he come back?" Frank asked.

"He didn't come back 'cause what he done is, he got hisself kilt."

"Damn!" Frank said. "I give him a simple job like

goin' into town to find out if the sheriff is actual gone or not, 'n he winds up dead. What did he do, get into a card game or something 'n get hisself kilt?"

Frank was thinking of Muley Dobbs, remembering how the two of them had gone into town on a scouting mission, only to have Dobbs wind up getting killed.

"Oh, he wasn't in no fight or nothin'," Arias said.

"Well, if he wasn't in no fight, then how did he get hisself kilt?"

"He was kilt by Leo Beajuex, the same deputy that you said was s'posed to be your friend."

"What? How? What happened?"

"Seems like Priest was about to shoot someone in the back 'n your friend Beajuex shot him."

"Beajuex shot 'im? Are you sure?"

"Oh yeah, I'm sure. The whole town is a-talkin' about it, braggin' on 'im somethin' fierce."

"Hey, Frank, what kind of friend is it that you got, iffen he winds up a-shootin' one o' us?" Tyler asked.

"He wouldn't'a knowed that Priest was one of us, on account of he ain't never met 'im before, 'n if he wants to get in good with the people as a deputy, well, then he wouldn't'a had no choice but to shoot 'im." Unexpectedly, Frank grinned. "Besides which, now we got one less person we'll have to divide up the money with."

CHAPTER TWENTY-TWO

Onboard the Eagle Flyer

As Frank was learning of Priest's fate, Smoke and Monte were sitting across the table from each other in the dining car of the train that was taking them back to Big Rock.

"It looks like we're off to a really good start," Smoke said.

"Thanks to you," Monte replied. "Smoke, I knew you were, well, I guess the best way to say it is, 'famous,' but I had no idea how many people in high places not only know you, but respect you."

Smoke chuckled. "Well, let's not get too carried away here. After all, the people I introduced you to are all my friends. It stands to reason that they are going to speak well of me."

"Yes, well, the trick is to get them to speak well of me, at least to others in the general assembly."

"I think we can count on support from the ones we met, but I suppose it remains to be seen how well they are able to sell you to the others."

The sound of the wheels on the tracks changed and they looked out the window to see that they were passing over a trestle. For just a moment the two men enjoyed a view of cascading water.

"I love riding in a train," Monte said.

"It's good that you do, because if you are successful, you'll be spending quite a bit of time on trains between here and Washington."

"Smoke, about Leo," Monte said.

"What about him?"

"I don't think I can take him to Washington with me. As a matter of fact, I think the provisions of his release say that he can't leave the state, at least for the first two years. And if I can't be here to be responsible for him, he may have to go to prison to serve out his time. If I thought that would be the result of my becoming a senator, I'm not sure I would want the job."

"You don't worry about that, Monte. If you wind up in the United States Senate, I will personally go see Judge Craig and get him to amend his order so that Leo is remanded into my care."

"How would Sally feel about that?"

"Are you kidding? Sally would be in seventh heaven. She thrives on taking in stray critters, whether they have four legs or two. If it comes to it, Leo will be in good hands."

A smile of relief spread across Monte's face. "Thanks, Smoke. I don't mind telling you, that has been bothering me."

Big Rock

Pearlie was standing on the depot platform when the train rolled into the station. He watched the passengers detrain, then walked out to meet Smoke and Monte.

"I brought Seven into town for you, Smoke," Pearlie said, speaking of Smoke's horse. "Miss Sally thought you might prefer that to her coming for you in a buckboard."

"Is that really what she thought? Or is she just being lazy?"

"Whoa, if you're ever goin' to call Miss Sally lazy to her face, I want you to let me know before you do it, so I can avoid the explosion," Pearlie said.

Smoke laughed. "You have a point, Pearlie, and if you understand that, then you know damn well that it's not something I would ever do."

"Where's Leo?" Monte asked.

"He's back in the office," Pearlie said. "I asked him to stay there because I thought it might be best if I met you alone."

"Oh? Why, is there a problem?" Monte asked, noticeably concerned about Pearlie's comment.

"No, no, nothing's wrong!" Pearlie said quickly when he noticed Monte's reaction. "It's just the opposite, in fact. Leo saved my life."

As Smoke and Monte gathered their luggage from the trip, Pearlie told them the story of the shooting incident.

"How did he take it?" Monte asked.

"I think he was a little upset with it at first, but he's all right with it now. I probably didn't have to meet you first; I just thought it might be a good idea to let you know about it before you saw him."

"Yes, thank you, it was a good idea."

* * *

"Hello, Sheriff, Mr. Jensen," Leo said a few minutes later when Smoke, Monte, and Pearlie stepped into the sheriff's office.

"Hello, Leo. I hear you've been busy," Monte said.

Leo glanced toward Pearlie.

"I told him," Pearlie said.

"So, you know," Leo said hesitantly. "I can't help but wonder what Judge Craig is going to think about me killin' someone."

"Judge Craig will think the same thing about it that I do," Monte said reassuringly. "You did well, son," Monte said. "As a matter of fact, I'd say that you've actually earned that star you're wearing, and I'll be pleased to have you wear it for as long as you want to."

A broad smile spread across Leo's face. "I'm not in any hurry to take it off, Sheriff."

"Good. From this day forward, you aren't just my deputy in training, you're my actual deputy."

"Pearlie, now that the sheriff is back in town, you may as well come out to the ranch with me," Smoke said.

"Of course I'm coming back with you. And I'm looking forward to Miss Sally's cooking, so I probably will double your food bill."

"Thanks for standing in for me, Pearlie," Monte said.

Pearlie shook his head. "Sheriff, if there is any thanks due, it's from me to Leo." Pearlie looked at Monte's young deputy. "I owe you my life, kid, and I won't forget it."

Leo flushed with pride.

"Come on, Pearlie, let's go have a beer with Louis before we go back. I imagine he and all the regulars at Longmont's will be wanting to know how our trip went."

"You don't have to ask me twice to have a beer," Pearlie said. "Especially since you're buying."

"Wait a minute, who said anything about me buying?"

"Smoke, you're going to tell Louis and the others that everyone is just lining up to vote for me, right?" Monte teased.

"That's what campaign managers do, isn't it?" Smoke quipped.

"I suppose so, but I wouldn't really know, seeing as I had never even heard of a campaign manager before you volunteered to be one," Monte said. "Listen, there's no way I would even try this, if I didn't have you supporting me. And I know I've said this a dozen times or more, but thank you for going to Denver with me and, especially, introducing me to the governor and all your friends."

"You know, Monte, when you are a United States senator you are going to owe me," Smoke said with a big smile.

"I agree," Monte said. He chuckled. "And the only reason I agree is because I know you would never ask me to do anything that is illegal, unethical, or even unfair."

"Smoke!" Louis greeted when he and Pearlie stepped into Longmont's a few minutes later. "How did it go in Denver?"

"It went very well," Smoke said, and at the urging of Louis and a few others, Smoke gave a detailed account of the visit. He answered several questions then finally held up his hand to stop the questions.

"I'll answer all your questions later," he said. "Right now, I need to get home."

At that very moment, Phil Clinton, editor and publisher of the *Big Rock Journal*, was just arriving at Sugarloaf Ranch. He had driven out in his phaeton, which was painted in shining black lacquer, with the name of his newspaper prominent in gold, red-outlined letters on the side.

"Hello, Mr. Clinton, what brings you out here?" Sally greeted.

"I'm just passing through on my way to Wolcott," Clinton said. "I know you heard about the shooting yesterday. I thought you might like to know who it was that tried to kill Pearlie."

"It was somebody named Priest, wasn't it?" Cal asked.

"Yes, his name was Ebenezer Priest. His brother, Jeremiah, was killed in that final confrontation with the man who passed himself off as Colonel the Marquis Lucien Garneau," Clinton said. "And although it was Smoke, and not Pearlie, who actually killed Jeremiah Priest, I think Priest decided that he didn't have to be that particular in seeking his revenge."

"Garneau, yeah, I remember that son of a bitch," Cal said. He put his hand over his mouth. "Excuse the language, Miss Sally."

"In this case, Cal, you are excused," Sally said. "So it would appear that Garneau, who turned out to be neither a marquis, nor a colonel, or even named

Garneau, has come back to haunt us. His real name was Mouchette."

"Sheriff Carson hung him," Cal said.

"He did indeed. I covered the event, and when I published the story it actually wound up being republished in France," Clinton said, displaying some pride in the reach of his story.

"Oh, here comes Smoke," Cal said. "Pearlie's with him."

"I'd better be getting on, then," Clinton said. "I need to pick up a couple of articles from my reporter in Wolcott. Since they don't have a paper, they are dependent upon the *Journal* for providing them with their local news."

Clinton slapped the reins against the back of the team, and the phaeton rolled away.

"What are you doing here, Pearlie? Did you get fired?" Cal teased as Smoke and Pearlie rode up.

"Nah, I just had to come back out here and make sure you were behaving yourself," Pearlie replied good-naturedly.

"How was your visit with the governor?" Sally asked Smoke.

Smoke nodded. "It was great. You know, Sally, I think Monte may very well be our next senator. Monte made a really good impression on everyone we met, including the governor. I think Pitkin is going to petition the general assembly for him."

"What about Lieutenant Governor Tabor?" Sally asked. "I've heard that he is thinking of running for the Senate seat."

"Ah, yes, and we met with that august gentleman as well," Smoke said. "It seems that he was considering it, but only as a means of stopping Rex Underhill.

But, after meeting Monte, Tabor has decided not to run but to support Monte instead."

"Oh, Smoke, that is wonderful!" Sally replied enthusiastically.

"Yes, it is. Bill Lewis packs a lot of weight in the state senate and Josh LaPlant in the house. And, besides those two, we now have the support of the governor and the lieutenant governor. I would say that things are looking very good for our friend."

"Smoke, you have to promise me that when Monte does become senator, you'll take me to Washington to visit him," Sally said.

"I can see us doing that," Smoke said. "By the way, was that Phil Clinton I saw driving away as we rode up?"

"Yes, he's on his way to Wolcott," Cal said. "He stopped by to tell us why Ebenezer Priest wanted to shoot Pearlie."

"Ebenezer Priest, huh? I didn't know his first name, but I do know why he wanted to shoot me," Pearlie said. "He told Mollie that he thought I was the one who shot his brother."

"Mollie?" Sally asked with a bemused expression on her face.

"She works at the Brown Dirt."

"I see. Well, so we have Leo to thank for you still being here with us," Sally said.

"Yes, ma'am, we sure do. But I owe thanks to Cal, too."

"To me?" Cal asked.

"Yes. He told me to tell you that he 'thought' the bullet to the target, and that you would know what he meant."

Cal chuckled. "Yes, I know exactly what he means."

"He's having sort of a hard time with it, though."

"Do you mean because he had to kill someone?" Sally asked.

"Yes, ma'am. It was the first time he ever had to do anything like that."

"But he is aware that it was you or Priest, isn't he?"

"Oh, he's aware, all right, and that's sort of helping him. But I don't think we're ever going to have to worry about him carving notches onto his gun handle and turning into some young gunhand."

"I never was worried about that," Sally said. "I've looked into his soul, and I like what I see."

"I'm glad you do," Smoke said. "I've told Monte that if he winds up going to Washington, we'll take Leo in. I hope that's all right with you."

"Of course it's all right with me."

"And, Sally, when I said we would take him in, I didn't mean as just another hired hand."

"Smoke Jensen, do you think Pearlie and Cal are *just* hired hands?" Sally asked pointedly.

Smoke looked over at Pearlie and Cal, who were following the conversation with apt expressions on their faces.

Smoke laughed.

"Pearlie and Cal, hired hands? No, if they were just hired hands, I would have fired them a long time ago. I'd say they are more like cockleburs under my saddle than hired hands. I'm totally convinced they were put on earth to drive me crazy."

"How are we doing so far?" Cal asked with a whimsical smile.

"Oh, I would say you are doing a damn good job of it," Smoke replied.

"Don't listen to him, Cal," Sally said. "Smoke feels about the two of you just as I do. You are family."

"The kind of family you make bear sign for when they come back home after being gone for a while," Pearlie said.

Sally laughed. "You can quit your hinting, Pearlie. As it so happens, since both you and Smoke were gone, I did make some."

CHAPTER TWENTY-THREE

Denver

"How good is Luke Shardeen?" Rex Underhill asked.

"He's the best," Al Jaco said. The two men were having a drink on Underhill's back porch, looking out toward the Front Range of mountains.

"Better than Smoke Jensen?"

"There isn't a deadlier gun in all of Colorado than Shardeen."

"If he's all that good, why haven't I ever heard of him?" Underhill asked.

"You haven't heard of him because he *is* that good."

Underhill shook his head. "Jaco, I swear, you aren't making a lick of sense. You say he's the best in the state and when I say I've never heard of him, you say that's because he is so good."

"Think about it, Underhill. He's killed fifteen men that I know of, and he's managed to keep his name out of the newspapers. It isn't good for someone who is in his business to be known beyond the very few who he can use to set up jobs for him. It is his anonymity that gives him a freedom of operation. If everyone in the state knew him, or even knew of him, he wouldn't be able to do his job."

"How do you know about him?"

"There are some who know about him, other gunmen, a few sheriffs."

"Is he fast?"

"What difference does it make whether or not he is fast? You aren't paying for fast. You are paying only to have Jensen taken care of."

"Killed," Underhill said.

"Yes, killed. And you don't have to be fast to kill someone, you just need to be willing to do it. And that's the difference between Shardeen and other hired guns. They like to make a reputation for themselves, so they'll goad their victims into a gunfight. Shardeen does no such thing. He just kills."

"And Sheriff Carson. Monte Carson is actually the one I'm going for, but I know that we won't be able to get to Carson without taking care of Jensen first," Underhill said.

"That's the way I see it, too."

"I've already been disappointed once, you know," Underhill said, thinking about Priest. "I hired someone who had the motivation and was supposed to have the skill to kill Jensen, but he wound up getting himself killed. When can I see Shardeen?"

"Are you willing to meet his price? No quibbling, you either pay him what he's askin' for, or he'll walk away."

"All right, five thousand dollars is an awful lot of money, but I'll pay it, however, I don't intend to pay it up front. I'll pay it when the job is done. Now, when I can I see him?"

Jaco smiled. "He's here now."

"What do you mean, 'He's here now'? You mean he's here, in my house?"

"Mr. Shardeen, come on over and meet Senator Underhill," Jaco said in a voice that was only slightly above conversational level.

To Underhill's total shock, a man stood up from behind a large potted plant that was at the edge of the porch. There was nothing remarkable about his appearance; he could have been a clerk in a store, or a lawyer, or a newspaperman. He was about five feet eight, with short and well-combed brown hair. His eyes did stand out, though, because they were an unusual shade of brown, which in certain light made them look almost yellow.

"Five thousand dollars," Shardeen said by way of greeting.

"Yes, that's for taking care of both Smoke Jensen and Sheriff Carson."

"You want me to kill them both."

"I want you to, uh, take care of them."

"You mean you want me to kill them."

"I, uh, don't really like to refer to it in those terms."

"You want me to kill them," Shardeen repeated. His voice was low, not only in volume but in register, and it came out almost like a hiss.

"Yes," Underhill said with a surrendering sigh. "I want you to kill both of them. And while I will meet your price without argument, I don't intend to pay you until after the job is done. You can trust me; I will not try and renege on you."

Shardeen's smile could best be described as diabolical.

"There is no need for me to trust you," Shardeen

said in the same low hiss. "After the job is done if you don't pay me what you owe me, I will kill you."

St. Elmo, Colorado

Shortly after they returned from Denver, Smoke and Monte went out again, this time to visit as many newspapers across the state as they could in the hope of getting their editorial support. So far their travels hadn't met with universal success, but Monte had gotten the endorsement of a little more than half of the newspapers he had visited. Sally came with them this time, and Smoke wasn't blind to the fact that her charm and her intelligent way of presenting the case were very helpful to their efforts.

"St. Elmo," the conductor said, walking down the aisle of the car. "We're coming into St. Elmo. Unless you're gettin' off here, I'd recommend you remain on the car 'cause we'll only be here for about five minutes."

"What's the name of the paper here?" Sally asked.

Smoke looked at the sheet of paper Phil Clinton had prepared for him. The publisher of the *Big Rock Journal* had listed every newspaper in the state for them, including the name of the publisher.

"*St. Elmo Defender*, Sherman Kyle's the publisher."

"Let's check into the hotel first," Sally suggested. "I want to freshen up a bit."

One hour later the three of them walked into the office of the *St. Elmo Defender*. They were met by a man who was wearing an ink-stained apron. He was bald except for a narrow band of hair just above his ears, and he was wearing rimless glasses.

"Would you be Mr. Kyle, the publisher?" Smoke asked.

"I'm the publisher, editor, reporter, ad salesman, typesetter, proofreader, printer, handyman, and janitor."

"Well, we don't need to talk to your whole staff, just one of you," Smoke teased.

Kyle laughed. "Good response. Which one of my staff do you wish to talk to?"

"The publisher."

"All right, I'll talk to you as publisher and give the rest of my staff a break."

"Mr. Kyle, this is my wife, Sally, I'm Smoke Jensen, and this gentleman is Sheriff Monte Carson."

"Monte Carson. You are the one seeking the Senate seat," Kyle said.

"Yes," Monte replied with a surprised smile. "You know about this?"

"I'm a newspaperman, Sheriff, I'm supposed to know about such things. Am I to take it that you have come seeking an endorsement?"

"Yes."

"I'm afraid I don't know very much about you, Sheriff, and I'm even more afraid that I know too much about your opponent. Tell me a little about yourself and why you want to be a United States senator."

For the next several minutes Monte, Smoke, and even Sally engaged in a spirited conversation with the newspaperman, answering his questions and offering up vignettes to provide Kyle with as much information as they could.

"All right, Sheriff, Mr. and Mrs. Jensen. You've sold me. I will give you my endorsement and if you'll come back later this afternoon I'll give you a galley sheet before I do the run."

"Thank you," Monte said, reaching out to shake Kyle's hand.

"Mr. Kyle, do you have a list of the women's clubs of the town, and who the ladies might be that are in charge?" Sally asked.

"I do indeed," Kyle replied. He smiled. "As a matter of fact, my wife, Virginia, is the president of the biggest ladies' club in town."

"It's almost lunchtime," Smoke said when they stepped out of the newspaper office. "What do you say we have lunch in the hotel dining room, then decide what to do this afternoon?"

The dining room was fairly crowded but they were able to get a table without having to wait.

"There are quite a few people in here," Smoke said.

"Yes, and it's perfect," Sally said. "Monte, we'll order for you. In the meantime, I think it would be good for you to go around to all the tables and introduce yourself."

"Why? They can't vote for me," Monte said.

"No, but their senator and their representative can," Sally said insistently.

Smoke laughed. "I'll bet you had no idea what a bossy woman Sally could be, did you?"

Monte chuckled, then started out on his assigned task.

* * *

One of those present in the dining room at the moment was Luke Shardeen. He was here because Al Jaco had told him that Sheriff Carson and Smoke Jensen would be here.

Jaco had been following the progress of Smoke Jensen and Monte Carson as they campaigned around the state. It was easy to do so, because many of the newspaper articles were shared by wire, and a few had even given their schedule. Jaco had let Shardeen know, by telegraph, when Carson and Jensen would be in St. Elmo.

Shardeen was sitting only three tables away from Smoke, Sally, and Monte. He recognized Smoke Jensen on sight. He and Jensen had never met before, but a few years earlier Shardeen had made a point to look Jensen up, not to meet him, but just to see what the man looked like. He was well aware of Jensen's reputation and he was certain that the time would come when the two men would meet in a confrontation that only one of them would walk away from. He believed that he had the advantage of Jensen since he could recognize him on sight, whereas Jensen had no idea who he was.

Because he recognized Jensen, he was sure that the man with him must be Sheriff Carson. But he had no idea who the woman was.

Then Shardeen saw Carson get up and begin moving around. After a couple of stops, he came to Shardeen's table.

"Good morning, sir, please allow me to identify myself. I'm Sheriff Monte Carson, and I am campaigning for the United States Senate. You can't vote for me, of course, but I would like to ask you to contact your state senator and state representative asking them to vote for me."

"Who's the pretty lady with you? Your wife?" Shardeen asked.

"No, sir, that would be Mrs. Jensen. She is the wife of Smoke Jensen, a very good friend of mine, and they are helping me with my campaign."

"Smoke Jensen," the man replied in a low, sibilant tone. "Yeah, I've heard of him."

Carson smiled. "Oh, I think most people in the state, indeed in the West, have heard of Smoke Jensen. He is quite well known, highly regarded, and I'm very honored to call him my friend. Do keep my name in mind, would you?"

"Oh yes, Sheriff Carson, I will keep your name in mind."

Monte continued making the rounds, returning to his own table just as the waiter was bringing the food.

"Well, now, that was very good timing, wouldn't you say?" Monte said. "I arrived at the same time as the food."

Monte looked at the food on his plate. "Fried squash," he said. He got a very strange look on his face and was silent for a long moment.

"I'm sorry, do you not like fried squash?" Sally asked.

"I like it fine," Monte said, pointing to his plate. "It's just that fried squash was absolutely Ina Claire's favorite and seeing this . . . I just couldn't help but . . . I'm sorry," he finally said. He smiled. "I'm fine. Please forgive me for the melancholy moment."

Sally reached across the table to put her hand on

Monte's arm. "Be melancholy all you want, Monte," she said tenderly. "You are with friends who also loved Ina Claire."

The sad moment passed and the conversation picked up as they enjoyed their meal. Finally, Sally addressed the schedule for the afternoon.

"This is what we're going to do," Sally said. "We're going to take Monte to meet the presidents of the various ladies' clubs, and then to arrange for the ladies to have a joint meeting so we can introduce him."

"Good, I think you should do that," Smoke said.

"By the way, you said, '*You* do that.' I get the distinct impression that you don't want to be with us," Sally said.

"It isn't that, Sally. Why, I would love to be with you," Smoke said, not very convincingly. "It's just that I would be in the way. You will relate to the ladies much better than I would. Monte will have to go with you, of course, because he is the purpose for your visits with them. Think about it, Sally. What purpose would I serve, other than to stand around looking like someone who doesn't know up from down?"

Sally laughed. "All right, you can stop your presentation, you've made your point, I won't ask you to go to the meeting with us. Why don't you go have a beer or something and we'll meet later in the afternoon?"

"Sally, would you mind if I had a beer with him before we do this?" Monte asked. "I think I'm going to need a little fortification before I meet with a bunch of women."

"I swear, you would think that I'm asking you men to step into a lion's den or something," Sally teased.

"A she-lion's den, and that's worse," Smoke teased.

"All right, Monte, go have your beer. I'll wait in my room."

"Room 212, isn't it? I'll knock on your door when I'm back," Monte said as he and Smoke left the table.

CHAPTER TWENTY-FOUR

"Room 212, isn't it? I'll knock on your door when I'm back."

Shardeen smiled as he heard the exchange. He had just been given the way to accomplish his task and earn five thousand dollars.

Shardeen watched the two men leave, then he saw the woman go upstairs. After waiting for a couple of minutes until he was sure that both Carson and Jensen were gone, he went up the stairs and walked down the hallway to Room 212.

Initially his plan was to kill her as soon as she opened the door, but as he thought about it, he changed his mind. He decided it would be better to keep her alive so that when Carson knocked on the door, she would be able to invite him in.

He looked up and down the hallway and seeing that it was empty, pulled his gun and knocked lightly on the door.

"Monte?"

Shardeen didn't answer, he just knocked on the door again, then it was opened.

"Come on . . ." the woman started to say, but she

stopped in midsentence when she saw a pistol pointed toward her.

With the pistol, Shardeen motioned her away from the door, then he stepped inside and closed the door behind him.

"Well, isn't this a surprise?" she said. "You aren't Monte. Who are you, if I may ask?"

Shardeen was totally shocked by the woman's response to seeing an armed stranger come into her room. He expected a scream, which he would have terminated immediately, or fear-stunned silence. He did not expect such a dispassionate conversational inquiry.

"It doesn't matter who I am," Shardeen said when he got over his surprise and was able to speak. "All that matters is that you do exactly what I tell you to do."

"And what is it that you are going to tell me to do?"

There wasn't even a hint of fear in the woman's voice, and her complete equanimity was beginning to make him nervous.

"When the man who wants to be senator knocks on the door a few minutes from now, you are going to call out for him to come in," Shardeen said.

"Oh, heavens, if you want him to come into the room, you'll never get him to come in that way."

"What do you mean, he won't come in?"

"He will expect me to open the door for him. If I just call out to him, which he knows is something that I would never do, I'm sure he would realize at once that something is wrong."

"All right, when he gets here, open the door for him. And if you do everything I tell you to do, exactly as I tell you to do it, you don't have to be afraid."

"Afraid?" The woman laughed. "And just what makes you think I'm afraid?"

"How can you laugh when I have a gun pointing at you. You're . . . you're acting crazy," Shardeen said.

"Now, that is funny. You come into my room, threatening me with a gun, and you say that *I'm* the one that's crazy?"

"I ain't never met no woman like you before."

"Not only do you begin your sentence with a double negative, and the word *ain't*, you compound it with another negative. What you should have said is, *I've never met any woman like you before.* Excuse the grammatical correction, but I was a teacher once, and I suppose I always will be. We may as well get acquainted while we are waiting for your rendezvous with Monte Carson. My name is Sally Jensen. And you are?"

"Luke Shardeen, but . . ." Shardeen stopped in midsentence, angry with himself for giving the woman his name. But he couldn't help it; the woman's unusual response to him was making him crazy. "It don't make no difference what my name is, we ain't exactly strikin' up a friendship here."

"No, I wouldn't think so, and to be honest, it would be very difficult for me to sustain any such friendship, given your abysmal use of grammar. And now that I know your name I suppose my own life is in jeopardy, isn't it? I mean, once you kill Monte, you can't very well leave a witness who actually knows your name."

"I . . . you talk too much."

Sally laughed again. "It's funny that you would say that. From time to time my husband has accused me of the same thing."

"Why are you acting like this? Why ain't you afraid?"

"Oh, should I be? I'm sorry, I thought you told me I had no reason to be afraid."

"Shut up, lady, just shut up! You're driving me crazy!" Shardeen put his free hand to the side of his head.

At that moment there was a knock on the door.

"That would be Monte," Sally said quietly.

"Go, open the door, then step aside so I can get a good shot at him. Otherwise, I'll be shooting you to get to him."

"You'd better stand over there," Sally said, pointing to one side of the room. "Otherwise, he'll see you as soon as I open the door."

"Oh yeah, good idea," Shardeen said.

Sally waited until Shardeen was in position, then she walked over to the door.

Shardeen either didn't realize it, or didn't think about it, but the door opened inward and that meant as it opened it would block Shardeen's view of Monte. In addition, Sally would have to take but one step and she would be out of sight as well. She opened the door.

"Hello, Sally, are you ready to . . ." Monte started but before he could finish his question, Sally jerked his pistol from his holster, shoved him to one side, then stepped back into the room.

"What the?" Shardeen yelled, shocked by the sudden appearance of Sally with a pistol in her hand. He raised his gun to shoot, but Sally shot first, her bullet hitting him in the middle of his chest. In a reflexive action Shardeen pulled the trigger of his own gun, but the bullet plunged harmlessly into the wall beside the door.

The entire "gunfight" was over in less time than it took a shocked Monte Carson to realize what was going on. Peering, cautiously, around the door, he saw Sally standing there, holding a smoking pistol.

"Is it over?" Monte asked.

"Yes," Sally said.

Monte stepped into the room and saw a man lying on his back, his eyes open, but unseeing, and still clutching the gun.

Sally turned the gun around and handed it butt-first back to Monte. "Thanks for the loan of your pistol."

"Oh, think nothing of it, I was glad to oblige."

"I expect there will be a slight delay in our meeting with the ladies' groups until after the sheriff gets here," Sally said.

"Let's go downstairs," Monte suggested. "We can notify the desk clerk to get the sheriff, and while we're waiting for him, I'll go get Smoke."

"Yes, I expect that is what we should do," Sally agreed.

When they stepped back out into the hallway, there was a rather portly man standing just in front of the open door of his own room.

"What . . . what just happened? I thought I heard a gunshot."

"You did," Sally said, closing and locking the door behind her. She offered no more information and the man stared at Monte and Sally as they went back down the stairs.

Less than ten minutes later Sally and Monte were back. Smoke was with them this time, and so was

Benjamin Denton, the sheriff of Chaffee County. Shardeen's body was lying where he fell, with the gun still in his hand.

"So this is Luke Shardeen, is it?" Sheriff Denton asked as he looked down at the body. "Well, I've heard of the son of a bitch, but I've never actually seen him before." Then realizing that Sally was standing there with them, he touched the brim of his hat and nodded. "I beg your pardon for the language, ma'am."

"Sheriff Denton, I'm the one who killed the son of a bitch, remember? I'm sure not going to take offense to you calling him what he is."

Denton chuckled. "No, ma'am, I reckon not."

Denton poked at the body with the toe of his boot, but he didn't turn him over.

"Have you ever run across this man before, Monte?" Sheriff Denton asked.

"No. Like you, Ben, I've heard of him, but neither have I ever seen him before."

"Well, if you don't know 'im, 'n you ain't actually never seen him before, why is it, do you reckon, he was a-wantin' to kill you?"

"I would say that it was more of an assassination attempt than a murder," Sally said.

"What makes you say that?"

"At one point he used the phrase 'the man who wants to be senator.' That gives the murder a political connotation, and to me, that suggests that he didn't want Monte to be a senator. And to that end, he was willing to kill him to keep it from happening. That makes it an assassination."

"I'll be damn," Denton said. "You have to wonder

why Shardeen would care one way or the other who the next senator might be."

"I don't think he did care," Smoke said. "Shardeen was a man who sold his gun for money. It was the man who hired Shardeen who doesn't want Monte to be a senator."

"So all we have to do is find out who most doesn't want Monte to be senator and we'll have . . ." Sally started, then she stopped in midsentence.

"Yes," Smoke said, agreeing with Sally's incomplete sentence.

"You're talkin' about Rex Underhill, aren't you?" Denton asked.

"I'm glad it's that obvious," Monte said.

"It might be obvious, but at this point, it is only supposition. We can't prove it," Sheriff Denton said.

"We don't need to prove it. We just need to know it," Smoke added cryptically. "Perhaps by knowing it, we can avoid any such thing in the future."

"Sheriff Carson, Mr. Jensen, Mrs. Jensen, what do you think about this article?" Sherman Kyle, the publisher of the *St. Elmo Defender*, asked.

Endorsement Given

> It is with great enthusiasm that the *St. Elmo Defender* endorses the candidacy of Monte Carson for U. S. senator. Mr. Carson has served as sheriff of Eagle County for some time now and in that position has won the acclaim from his constituents and the respect of his peers.

It is to be hoped that this newspaper, which enjoys a broad readership among the solons of our state, will have no little influence in effecting the appointment of Monte Carson to the United States Senate.

Smoke smiled, then struck the paper with the back of his hand. "Mr. Kyle, I would say that is an outstanding endorsement, and we thank you for it."

"Willingly given," Kyle said. "No, let me revise that statement. It is not just willingly given, it is given with great enthusiasm."

"What about the other, uh, news that we made by being here?" Monte asked.

"You're talking about the shooting incident in the hotel." It wasn't a question, it was a statement, as Kyle had been thoroughly apprised of the shooting and had interviewed both Sally and Monte.

"Yes."

"On any other day it would be my lead article," Kyle said. "But I don't want that story, as important as it is, to detract from my endorsement of Monte Carson. So I put it below the fold."

SHOOTING IN THE MORNING STAR HOTEL

The peace and tranquillity of the residents of the Morning Star Hotel was disrupted when at, lacking ten minutes of one o'clock, two shots rang out on the second floor.

The cause of the shooting was the failed attempt of one Luke Shardeen to assassinate Monte Carson, who is a candidate for the United States Senate. Why Shardeen felt constrained so to do, is a question without answer, as this newspaper has already gone on record to support this good man for that position.

It may be that Shardeen was of the belief that killing a candidate for the Senate would, in some way, elevate his own status. The result of his nefarious attempt at notoriety ended badly for him, and well for the general public. Shardeen was himself killed, and his remains are now with Porter Prufrock, our most capable mortician. There will be no public interment of this despicable individual as his remains will be deposited, without ceremony, in potter's field.

"I do hope, Mrs. Jensen, that you have taken notice of the fact that I did not use your name in the article," Kyle said.

"Yes, I did notice, and I appreciate that, Mr. Kyle. You are a good man," Sally said.

"I do try to be. And, Sheriff Carson, whom I very much hope to be able to address as 'Senator Carson' soon, I extend my best wishes to you on your effort to serve our state in such capacity."

"Thank you," Monte replied.

CHAPTER TWENTY-FIVE

Denver

"I thought you said he was good!" Underhill said. He was complaining angrily to Jaco about the failure of the man Jaco had said would be able to kill Carson and Jensen.

"I don't know what happened," Jaco said. "All I've been able to find out is that Shardeen was killed while he was trying to kill Carson."

"Am I never going to get rid of this man?"

"I've been giving this matter a lot of thought," Jaco said. "And I think I may have come up with an idea. But it will be expensive. Very expensive."

"So you think you have located another gunman who has an elevated sense of his own worth? So far two men who had reputations of being efficient killers have failed in their attempts to take out either Jensen or Carson. What makes you think another gunman would fare any better?"

"I'm not talking about another gunman," Jaco said.

"Then, what is it? And what do you mean by 'very expensive'?"

"I expect it's going to cost at least ten thousand dollars," Jaco said.

"What? Ten thousand dollars?" Underhill exploded. "Are you out of your mind?"

"Hear me out," Jaco said. "It's going to cost ten thousand dollars, yes, but I will pay half of it."

"You will pay half?"

"I will." Jaco smiled. "Underhill, you have been a valuable asset to me as a state senator."

Underhill bristled at not being addressed as "Senator" but he withheld comment, as he listened to the rest of Jaco's comment.

"As a United States senator, I expect your value to me will be many times greater. Because of that, it would be to my advantage to get you into that position, so I am willing to put up five thousand dollars of my own money in order to get this done."

"Who will we be paying the ten thousand dollars to?" Underhill asked.

"We aren't paying it to anyone. It is strictly expense money, to cover the cost of what I'm going to have to do."

"I don't understand, what is it you are going to do?"

"You'll know when it happens, and when it happens, we will have no more problem with Carson, or with Jensen."

"When are you going to do it? The reason I ask is, I fear that Carson is gaining ground. I already know several representatives and senators who have said they are going to support him."

"Soon," Jaco said. "I'm going to do it soon."

* * *

When the Eagle Flyer pulled into the depot at Big Rock, Smoke, Sally, and Monte were met by Pearlie, Cal, and Leo.

"So, tell me, Pearlie, how did things go in my absence?" Monte asked.

"Things went well, and I would like to congratulate my deputy. He did a fine job," Pearlie replied. "He found two unlocked doors on his rounds, and he got a drunken menace off the street."

"A drunken menace." Monte chuckled. "Did you keep Lloyd Beemus around long enough to feed him breakfast the next morning?"

"Eggs, bacon, fried taters, biscuits, and gravy," Leo said.

"And about half a gallon of coffee," Pearlie added.

"Beemus has never really given me any trouble," Monte said. "But every now and then he decides to get drunk, then he passes out in the street, and I wind up putting him in jail. I'm almost certain he does it just so we'll feed him a nice breakfast the next day."

Pearlie started to take off the star, but Monte held out his hand. "No, you keep it for a while. I'm sure I'll have to be making a few other trips and I'll be needing you again."

"That's fine," Pearlie said. "But in the meantime, I need to get back to the ranch." He looked over at Cal. "With Smoke, Miss Sally, and me gone, why, there's no telling what kind of a mess Cal has gotten it into."

"What ranch? I lost it in a card game," Cal teased.

"We read about your adventure in St. Elmo," Pearlie said as the four of them rode the buckboard back to the ranch. "Here, we send you off just to talk to a bunch of ladies, and someone tries to kill Monte."

"Thanks to Sally, he didn't," Smoke replied.

"You mean it was Sally that stopped him? Hmm, that part wasn't in the paper," Cal said.

"We didn't want it to be," Smoke said.

"You know, with Monte being a sheriff, you can sort of expect that someone might want to kill him," Pearlie said. "But I have to confess I don't know why anyone would want to kill a senator who isn't even a senator yet."

"Yes, but it is the very fact that he isn't a senator yet that is the whole point of it," Sally said.

"The whole point of it? You mean they wanted to kill him because he *isn't* a senator? I don't understand what you mean," Cal said.

"He isn't a senator yet, and someone doesn't want him to be. I think whoever that someone is, is willing to kill him to keep that from happening," Sally said.

"I'll bet that someone is Rex Underhill," Pearlie said. "He's also running for the senate and from some of the things I've heard, I wouldn't put it past him to try something like that."

"I would say that's a pretty good guess," Smoke said.

"If that's true, how come the sheriff hasn't put him in jail?" Cal asked.

"Because he's a bigwig in the government, that's why," Pearlie said, the expression on his face expressing his anger over the situation. "He's too big to go to jail."

"Nobody is too big to go to jail," Smoke said. "But Underhill's position does make it easier for him to cover up his part. But all that means is that it might be a little harder for us to prove he's trying to win the seat by killing his opponent."

"Perhaps so," Sally agreed. She smiled. "But *harder* doesn't mean *impossible.*"

Kansas City, Missouri
The law office of Morgan, Travathon and Williams

"Mr. Williams?"

Looking up from the newspaper he was reading, Angus Williams saw his secretary, Marilyn Grant.

"Yes, Miss Grant?"

"Judge Blanton asks if you need any more time in preparing the arbitration agreement between OFMCO and Potashnik Transportation?"

"I have two more days before it is due, don't I?"

"Yes, sir, I think His Honor is just offering you more time if you need it."

Angus shook his head. "I'll have it done by tomorrow."

"All right, I'll tell his law clerk."

"Thank you, Miss Grant."

Angus turned his attention back to the *Kansas City Journal of Commerce.* There was an article in the paper that caused a flood of memories to return, memories that weren't particularly pleasant.

After Angus's life had been spared by Monte Carson, Angus had an epiphany and left the outlaw trail. Then, upon learning that Governor Fletcher was offering clemency to any of the outlaws who would turn themselves in and forswear all future criminal activity, he decided to take advantage of the opportunity thus presented.

"Have you directly, or indirectly, ever participated

in a murder?" Robert Wingate asked. Wingate was the attorney general for the state of Missouri.

Angus knew that a prerequisite for clemency was the requirement that the candidate had never committed murder, and he hesitated for a long moment before he answered. There had been a lot of killing during the war, and he could justify all of it, except for the killing of Monte Carson's wife, Rosemary, and Carson's father, Linus. Angus couldn't help but believe those killings were nothing more than murder. He had thought so at the time, and he had spoken out in opposition.

But despite his misgivings he was there when it happened, and as far as he was concerned, that made him complicit.

"You are hesitating, Mr. Williams," Wingate said. "Perhaps I should rephrase the question. Have you directly, or indirectly, participated in the death of any citizen, since the end of the war?"

"I have not."

"Then, by authority of Thomas C. Fletcher, governor of the state of Missouri, you are hereby granted absolute clemency, to include the expungement of your record. You are free to go, Mr. Williams. I hope you take advantage of the opportunity the governor has so graciously granted."

"Thank you," Angus replied.

As a man no longer wanted by the law, Angus had participated in the hunt for Jerry Carson and, when they found him, he had been the one who actually made the arrest. Carson was tried, convicted, and sentenced to hang, but somehow managed to escape from jail on the night before the sentence was to be carried out.

After he escaped he totally disappeared, and after a few months of looking for him, Angus gave up the search. He read for the law, passed the bar, and was now a full partner in the legal firm of Morgan, Travathon and Williams. And, because the firm represented railroads and riverboat operations, his association with them had been quite profitable. Angus Williams was now a wealthy man.

His newfound success eventually caused him to forget about Jerry Carson, but the article in the newspaper brought it all back to him. Carson was lost, but now he was found.

Angus turned his attention back to the newspaper.

Candidate Announces for Senate from Colorado

BY TELEGRAPH—Senator George Chilcott having made it known that he has no wish to continue serving in the United States Senate means that his seat will be open for the next Congress.

It is expected that many Colorado citizens will seek the seat, and one of the first to throw his hat in the ring is Monte J. Carson. Mr. Carson is a sheriff in the town of Big Rock and has earned a most admirable reputation in that position. It is believed that Sheriff Carson's sterling background and his myriad of friends will do him well, and many believe that he may be the leading candidate for the seat.

Angus Williams read the article with great interest. "So," he said, speaking aloud his thoughts, though quietly enough that nobody could overhear him. "That's where you went."

It was strange how things work out, Angus thought. Now he and Jerry Carson were bitter enemies, but it had not always been that way.

He recalled the time when he, his brother Reuben, and Jerry had been kids, playing on the Missouri River.

Jackson County, twenty years earlier

"I don't know," Jerry Carson said, looking at the raft the three boys had built. "I'm not sure it's safe enough to try 'n take it all the way across the river."

"You're a coward if you don't try," Reuben said.

"I'm not a coward, you take that back!" Jerry demanded.

Reuben was the oldest, Jerry was a year younger than Reuben, and Angus was a year younger than Jerry.

"Sure, I'll take it back, when you get across the river."

"Don't do it, Jerry." Angus warned. "It don't look to me like them logs will hold together. 'N if they all come apart, then what?"

"I don't know," Jerry said.

"You don't know? Jerry, you're the one that built the thing. 'N now you're a fraidycat to try 'n cross the river with it."

Jerry studied the raft, which consisted of four logs held together with rope. The problem was that the logs were all irregular in circumference so that with some of them, the rope had little purchase.

"Don't do it, Jerry," Angus warned.

"You don't have to worry none about that. Jerry ain't goin' to try 'n cross the river, 'cause he's a coward."

"Oh yeah? Well, you just watch. I'll see you on the other side," Jerry said as he pushed the raft into the river.

The raft got no more than a quarter of the way across before it began to come apart.

"Help!" Jerry called. He was no longer sitting on the raft, because there was no raft to sit on. By now what had been a raft was little more than several individual pieces of wood, not one of which could provide enough buoyancy to keep him afloat.

"Swim ashore, dummy!" Reuben called, laughing at Jerry's plight.

"I . . . can't . . . swim!" Jerry shouted.

"Reuben, we've got to save him!"

"The rope!" Reuben said. "Here, Angus, hang on to this end of the rope!"

Tying the other end of the rope around his waist, Reuben jumped into the water, then swam quickly to catch up with Jerry. He barely got there in time because Jerry was already being swept downstream.

"Grab a-holt!" Reuben shouted, holding his hand out.

Jerry managed to grab Reuben's hand, then began fighting to stay afloat.

"Quit fighting, quit fighting!" Reuben said. "Just hang on 'n don't do nothin'! We'll get you out."

Back on the riverbank Angus saw that Reuben now had hold of Jerry, or, to be more accurate, Jerry had hold of Reuben.

"Now!" Reuben shouted, the words rolling out across the water.

Angus wrapped the tail end of the rope around his waist so he wouldn't drop it, then started up the bank, pulling his brother and Jerry out of the water.

"All right, all right, we're on the land," Reuben shouted. "You can quit pullin' now, you ain't doin' nothin' now but plowin' up the field with us."

Looking back toward the river Angus saw that both of them were out of the water and now lying wet and exhausted on the riverbank.

"What did you do that for if you can't swim?" Angus asked when he walked up to the two who were panting hard to get their breath.

"I didn't want to be called a coward," Jerry said.

The three were already friends, but they became even better friends after that, hunting together, fishing together, and when Jerry married Rosemary Woodward, Angus was his best man. Reuben, who had also been sweet on Rosemary, didn't show up for the wedding, and that was the beginning of the rift between the two.

Then came the war and, like families and friends all over the nation, they split up. Monte J. Carson went off to fight for the South, while Reuben and Angus wore the blue.

The present

As the memories of the distant past began to fade, Angus recalled how that, even though they were on opposite sides in the conflict they had, for the most part, managed to avoid coming into direct contact. That all changed, though, when Reuben applied Order Number 11. That incident left Rosemary and Mr. Carson dead, and it led, after the war, to Monte's vengeful visit in the middle of the night, when Jerry killed Reuben.

Was this Colorado sheriff, who would be senator, the man he had known as Jerry Carson? He remembered that Jerry went by his middle name, Jerome, and he knew that Jerry Carson's first name had been Monte. Nobody had heard a word from Jerry Carson since he escaped jail on the night before he was to be hanged but Angus was absolutely convinced that this was the same man.

There was really only one way to find out, and that would be to visit the town of Big Rock and meet the Monte Carson of this story, in person. And because he had been tried and convicted for the murder of Reuben Williams, Jerry Carson was still a fugitive from justice in Missouri.

Williams reread the article. "Mr. Monte Carson, if you are the Jerry Carson that I know, I can tell you right now, that you can disabuse yourself of any idea that you will be a United States senator. I guarantee you, I will stop it."

CHAPTER TWENTY-SIX

Frank's outlaw camp

Frank Petro stood just outside the line shack and watched the sun setting over Mount of the Holy Cross, so named because of the cross-shaped snow-field on its northeast face. In the line shack behind him, Arias, Tyler, and Merck were playing a three-hand game of poker, though the total pot consisted of no more than sixty cents or so.

Frank had been invited to take part in the card game, but he had declined.

"Sorry, boys, but I can't get worked up over a game played for pennies," he said.

"Yeah, but pretty soon, after we hit that bank in Big Rock, we'll be playing for big money," Arias suggested.

"You might be, but not with me. I'm goin' to California with my money, 'n I plan to buy myself an orange grove."

"Orange grove?" Tyler said with a little laugh. "What the hell do you want with an orange grove?"

"A man with a good orange grove can wind up

makin' more money than a rancher," Frank replied. "And you don't have to castrate, brand, or feed oranges. 'N you don't have to drive 'em to market. They're just waitin' right there on the trees for you, 'n all you have to do is pick 'em."

"Yeah, well, I ain't goin' to do nothin' like that," Merck said. "When I run out of money from this bank, I'll just find me another 'un to rob."

"Speakin' o' robbin' banks, when is it that we're a-plannin' on robbin' this one?" Arias asked.

"Very soon," Frank said. "I'll be goin' into town tomorrow to talk to Leo 'n get it all set up."

Big Rock

Monte had been back in town for two days that could almost be described as *whirlwind days,* due to all the activity he was involved with. First there was the meeting with the Eagle County Cattlemen's Association, then with the Denver and Pacific Railroad people, then with the school board. Every group wanted to offer their support in getting their favorite son into the Senate, and every group had their own idea of what they thought he could accomplish for the "folks back home."

This morning Monte was sitting at his desk looking at some of the more recent wanted posters. The office was filled with the scent of freshly made coffee, and he asked Leo to bring him a cup.

"Sheriff, don't you think some doughnuts would go good with your coffee this morning?" Leo asked as he put the cup in front of Monte.

"Well, a sinker would taste pretty good right now, but the thing is, Nancy's Sweet Shop is all the way down to the other end of the street, 'n I just don't feel like walkin' that far," Monte said.

"I'll go!" Leo offered enthusiastically.

"Ah, that's all right, you don't have to. I wouldn't feel right sending you down there just for a few sinkers. You can stay here and I'll go get 'em."

"No, really, I'll go, I don't mind."

Monte chuckled. "Tell me, Leo, are you really wantin' a doughnut? Or is it somethin' else you're hankerin' for? Like maybe Nancy's daughter?"

"Well, I'm doin' it for you, Sheriff."

"Really? For me?"

"Yes, sir. They're goin' to be havin' a dance Friday night to raise money for your campaign. 'N bein' as I'm deputyin' for you, why, it only seems right that I would go to the dance, don't you think? 'N if I go to the dance, well, I think it would be just real nice if Nonnie was there, too."

Monte gave Leo twenty cents. "All right, get ten of them. You can't have too many doughnuts around."

"Nonnie, here comes that young deputy," Nancy said as, through the window, she saw Leo approaching."

"Mama, maybe it would be better if you finished putting the cookie dough together. You do it a lot better than I do. I'll see what Leo . . . uh, Deputy Beajuex, wants."

Nancy chuckled. "If you're sure you don't mind waiting on him," she said.

"Oh, I don't mind," Nonnie said, self-consciously touching her hair as Leo pushed open the door.

Nonnie was an exceptionally pretty girl with hair

the color of golden wheat and eyes as blue as the sky. She had high cheekbones and dimples that appeared when she smiled, as they did now when she greeted Leo.

"Hello, Leo."

"Good morning, Nonnie," Leo said. "The sheriff sent me down here to see if ya'll had any doughnuts ready."

"Ya'll? How many is ya'll?" Nonnie teased.

"Makin' fun of my accent, are you?" Leo replied. It wasn't an antagonistic response as his grin indicated. "I told you I'm from New Orleans, and that's how we talk."

"Is New Orleans beautiful? I've always thought I'd like to go there someday."

"Yes," Leo said with more feeling for the city than he thought he would have. "It is a beautiful city." He wondered if he would ever be able to return.

"How many doughnuts do you want?"

Leo put two dimes on the counter. "Ten," he said.

"Deputy Beajuex, are you aware that there is a dance Friday night? It will be in the ballroom of the Big Rock Hotel," Nonnie said as she began putting the doughnuts into a paper bag. "Will you be going?"

"That all depends."

"Depends on what?" Nonnie asked with a concerned expression on her face.

"Why, on whether or not you'll be there."

Nonnie's somewhat anxious expression was replaced by a wide smile. "I'll be there," she said as she handed the bag of doughnuts over to Leo.

* * *

Frank had been passing by the depot when, just ahead, he saw Leo going into the bakery. Dismounting, Frank wrapped the reins around the hitching rail and stepped through the door. Now he was standing inside, his entrance not having been noticed by either Leo or the young woman behind the counter. It quickly became evident to Frank that Leo's presence here was more than a casual commercial activity.

"My word, Nonnie, are you just going to let that customer stand there?" Nancy asked, coming to the front of the store.

"Oh!" Nonnie gasped, putting her hand over her mouth in surprise at seeing the man standing there.

"Frank!" Leo said. His response was more than surprised, it was closer to shocked.

"Hello, kid," Frank said.

"You . . . you know him?" Nonnie asked. There was something about the man that the young girl found disquieting, but she couldn't put her finger on what it was.

"Yeah, I know him," Leo said without further clarification.

"How may I help you, sir?" Nancy asked with a professional smile.

"Oh, I reckon I'll have me a sinker," Frank said, getting out a couple of pennies.

"I, uh, had better get these back down to the sheriff's office," Leo said, holding up the sack.

"You'll be there Friday night?" Nonnie asked.

"I'll be there."

Leo's smile as he left the sweet shop was somewhat forced, not because he was making a commitment to be at the dance, but because of the unexpected appearance of Frank Petro. Leo started back up the street toward the office, hoping Frank wouldn't call out to him.

His hope was in vain.

"Hey, kid, wait for a moment, would you?"

Reluctantly, Leo stopped to wait for Frank to catch up with him.

"What do you want, Frank?" Leo asked.

"Here, now, is that any way to greet an old friend?"

"I thought we had agreed that it might be better for both of us, if you didn't come here anymore."

Frank shook his head. "No, kid, I don't remember sayin' anythin' like that."

"Why are you here?"

"Well, ain't comin' here to see my old friend reason enough?"

"That's just it, Frank. You're a friend but we're livin' in different worlds now. I'm a lawman, 'n if I was doin' what I was supposed to be doin', I'd be turnin' you in to the sheriff now."

"For what? I ain't done nothin' in this town."

"No, but you've done other things."

Frank chuckled. So have you, kid. 'N you can't very well start turnin' me in for things that you done, too."

"No, I guess not," Leo agreed.

"Let me ask you somethin'. Was you just bein' a lawman when you shot Ebenezer Priest?"

"You know about that?"

"Yeah, I know about it. Priest was my friend."

"I didn't have 'ny choice. He was about to shoot Pearlie in the back, 'n Pearlie is my friend."

"Who is Pearlie?"

"Like I said, Pearlie is my friend. And when the sheriff is gone, Pearlie takes over for him."

"Wait, are you tellin' me that when the sheriff is gone that this man Pearlie takes over for him? I thought you was the deputy."

"I am, and actually that's what Pearlie is, too. When the sheriff's gone we're both deputies."

"So, is the sheriff gone now?"

"No, he's back."

"When is he leavin' again?"

"Why are you askin' that?"

"Oh, no reason in particular. It's just it makes me feel good thinkin' about my good friend bein' a deputy 'n all."

"Well, I'm not sure exactly when he'll be leavin' again, but more'n likely it'll be soon, 'cause he's goin' to be just runnin' all over the place."

"Think he'll be here or gone next time I come here?"

"Actually, Frank, I think it would be better for both of us if you didn't come around anymore at all."

"You may be singin' a different tune, soon as I let you in on somethin' I got goin'."

"What do you mean, let me in on something? Frank, I ain't interested in anything you've got going."

"You will be, soon as you find out what it is."

"Now you're getting me worried, Frank. Just what do you have in mind?"

"I'll let you know when the time comes." Frank flashed a big smile. "In the meantime, you do the best job you can as deputy. I'm just real proud of you makin' good 'n all, 'n I wouldn't want to see you do anythin' that would cause you not to be deputyin' anymore."

Leo felt a sense of relief. "I'm glad to hear that you think that, Frank, 'cause I really do want to do the best I can in this job. Uh, would you like to meet the sheriff? I mean, he don't know nothin' about you, so it wouldn't be no problem."

They were just passing by Longmont's when Leo issued the invitation.

"No, you go ahead 'n take the doughnuts down to 'im. I think I'll just step in here 'n have me a couple of beers. That's why I come into town, you know, so's I could say hello to m' old friend 'n get me a couple of beers."

"Frank?"

"Yeah, kid?"

"You're not goin' to make 'ny trouble while you're in town, are you?"

"No, kid, I ain't goin' to make no trouble today," Frank promised.

"Good," Leo said. He didn't notice that Frank had limited his promise to make no trouble to *today*.

"Who was your friend?" Monte asked a moment later when Leo stepped into the sheriff's office.

"My friend?"

"The fella you were talking to as you came walking up."

"Oh, uh, he didn't give me his name." Leo forced a smile. "I think he was after a couple of the doughnuts."

"Ha! Well, I'm glad you kept them away from him."

"Let's have one now, Sheriff. I been smellin' 'em all the way here."

"Is she goin' to the dance?" Monte asked with a knowing smile.

"Yeah," Leo said, and the thought of Nonnie at the dance forced away any of the uneasiness he had felt from his meeting with Frank Petro.

"I just come walkin' up the street here with a young fella that was wearin' a deputy's badge," Frank said. "That ain't for real, is it? I mean, someone that young actual bein' a deputy 'n all?"

Frank was standing at the bar in Longmont's alongside two others who were having a morning beer.

"Oh, you must be talkin' about Leo Beajuex. Yeah, he's pretty young, but it's real, all right," one of the two men said.

"What kind of deputy would someone like that make?" Frank asked. "Hell, he don't look much like he's even dry behind the ears yet."

"Yeah? Well, it could be that a feller named Ebenezer Priest was thinkin' hisself the same thing," the other drinker said. "But he didn't think it long, 'cause when he challenged young Beajuex, why, Beajuex shot 'im down."

"To be honest, though, Adam, that Priest feller was shootin' at Pearlie, not at Beajuex."

"That may be true, Roy, but it don't mean that young Beajuex didn't handle hisself good," Adam said, "on account of if he hadn't, why, Pearlie woulda wound up deader'n a doornail."

"Yeah, you got that right," Roy said.

"Well, I'll say this about that young feller," Frank said. "He does have an eye for the ladies. I stopped into the bakery to get myself a sweet roll this mornin' and I seen this deputy, what did you say his name was? Beajuex?"

"Yeah, Leo Beajuex," Adam said.

"Well, anyhow, I seen Beajuex talkin' just real sweet with a pretty little girl that was workin' there, more'n likely no older'n Beajuex is his ownself."

Roy laughed. "Yeah, that would be Nonnie Kinder. She's Miz Nancy Kinder's daughter. She's a real sweet kid 'n she's been no trouble for Miz Nancy, which is a good thing, seein' as her father was a train engineer who got hisself kilt in a train wreck back when Nonnie was just a tyke."

"So she 'n Beajuex are keepin' company, are they?" Frank asked.

"I don't know as I can actual say that," Adam said. "I mean, it ain't like they're together all the time, or nothin' like that, seein' as they're both workin' but . . ." Adam paused then smiled. "But I'd say it's a pretty good bet that they like one another."

Frank nodded. This was good information to know, in case his planning didn't quite go as well as he wanted.

CHAPTER TWENTY-SEVEN

The dance was sponsored by the Big Rock Beautification Society for the purpose of raising money for Monte's senatorial campaign. A band was hired from Denver, and when the train arrived several were there to greet the musicians.

Leo was there to meet the band but in his case, he was there on official duty. Monte had given him the assignment of getting the band checked in to the Big Rock Hotel. For the rest of the day the residents of the hotel, as well as the people walking down Center Street, could hear the band practicing, from the high skirling of the fiddle to the strum of the guitar and the thump of the bass fiddle. A group of children were gathered in the space between the hotel and the Rocky Mountain Stagecoach Depot. Some were looking in through the side windows, but others were whirling and dancing to the music, laughing as they did so.

* * *

Out at Sugarloaf Ranch Smoke and Sally were having a conversation in the keeping room.

"Do you think Senator Underhill really was connected to Mouchette?" Sally asked.

"Monte thinks so."

"If that's true, maybe that's why Underhill is trying to have Monte killed," Sally suggested. "I mean, so the connection will never come out."

"Well, just being connected to him isn't really enough to get him into any trouble. I mean, there's nothing to connect Underhill to all the killing that went on."

"No, but if enough people in the legislature thought he was connected to a convicted felon, they might be hesitant about voting for him."

"Sally, Underhill has a bad enough reputation on his own, that I don't think any connection to Mouchette would matter one way or the other. I don't see any way that Underhill is going to get enough votes to beat Monte, and I don't think Underhill does, either. That means the only way he can win . . ."

". . . Is to get rid of Monte," Sally said, completing the sentence.

"Yes."

"And that means he's going to try again."

"Yes, but since we know that now, I think we can be ready for him."

There was the sound of clomping feet on the front door, then it was pushed open slightly, and they heard Pearlie call out to them.

"Smoke? Miss Sally?"

"We're in here, Pearlie," Sally called back.

A moment later Pearlie and Cal stepped into the room and presented themselves to Sally for inspection.

"What do you think, Miss Sally? Is this better with a vest, or without a vest?" Cal asked.

The two were wearing their newest shirts for the dance. Cal's shirt was a bright orange; Pearlie was wearing a subdued green.

"Oh, I think a vest would look quite nice," Sally said.

"Ha! I told you she would tell you to cover up that orange," Pearlie teased. "You look like a pumpkin."

"Yeah, well, better a pumpkin than a stalk of celery," Cal challenged.

"So you say," Pearlie retorted. He turned his attention to Smoke. "Smoke, I was thinkin', I mean, this being a highfalutin thing tonight to raise money for the campaign, 'n with ever'one dressed up to put on the dog, why don't we take the carriage? Cal 'n I will sit up front 'n drive, while you 'n Miss Sally sit in the back like a king 'n queen or somethin'."

"Oh, I think going in the carriage would be a lovely idea," Sally said.

Pearlie smiled. "That's good that you think that, 'cause I've already got the carriage ready to go. It's sittin' out front now."

"And I polished the lanterns up so that they are really shinin'," Cal added. "Wait till you see it."

Big Rock

A little over half an hour later the carriage, pulled by a matched team of grays and with the lanterns gleaming, rolled into town. It stopped in front of the hotel.

"You folks go on in, I'll park down at the livery," Pearlie said. The livery was only one block south of the hotel.

"I'll walk back with you," Cal offered.

Tim Murchison was sitting at a table just inside the door. A neatly printed sign on the table read:

TICKET *$1*
Proceeds for
CARSON FOR SENATE.

"Hello, Smoke, Miss Sally," Tim said.

Smoke gave Tim four dollars. "This is for Pearlie and Cal. They'll be along directly."

"Do you see how many people are here? We're raisin' a lot of money for the campaign, don't you think?"

"Oh yes, Mr. Murchison, I think everyone is doing a wonderful job," Sally said.

A moment later Pearlie and Cal came in and Tim waved them on out into the ballroom.

Louis Longmont had closed his saloon for the event, which freed up Becky and Julie, the girls who worked there. That was a good thing because it made a better balance since there were more men than women.

"Ladies and gents, choose your partners and form your squares!"

Pearlie and Cal were frequent visitors to Longmont's Saloon so they moved easily to Becky and Julie, who accepted their invitation without hesitation.

Nonnie smiled somewhat self-consciously at Leo, and he walked over to her and held out his hand.

"Shall we dance, Miss Kinder?"

"Miss Kinder?"

"I'm just being polite."

"I think it would be more polite if you called me Nonnie."

"Tout ce que vous voulez, madame, votre souhait est ma commande."

"What? What did you say?"

"I said, 'Whatever you want, my lady, your wish is my command.'" Leo laughed. "I just said it in French."

"Oh! I didn't know you could speak French. That is so . . . so elegant!" Nonnie said, her eyes flashing in excitement.

"My mama spoke French. A lot of people in New Orleans speak French, so I grew up speaking as much French as I did English." Leo remembered, but didn't say, that the French-speaking people of New Orleans were often ostracized.

Within a short time after the dance began, several of the dancers began to take notice of Leo and Nonnie, not just because Nonnie was an exceptionally pretty young woman, but also because of the way they were dancing. Actually, it was the way Leo was dancing. Few had seen anyone with as much poise and graceful movements as Leo's, and with his lead, Nonnie was able to keep up with him.

"Oh my, you are such a marvelous dancer, young man," Sally said when the band was taking a short break. "Wherever did you learn to dance so well?"

For just a moment Leo had a mental flashback to the de Plaisir Maison in New Orleans, and all the dancing he did with the women who worked there. He was the pet of all of them, and they had begun dancing with him almost as soon as he could walk.

"My mama and her friends taught me," Leo said,

without being specific as to what kind of friends they were. Actually, as he thought back on it now, he realized they were good friends—they had never treated him any way except with kindness and affection. He was ashamed of himself for having ever been ashamed of his mother and the others.

"They certainly taught you well," Sally said.

"Uh, would you like to dance with me?" Leo asked.

Sally laughed. "You mean, you are all right dancing with an older woman?"

"Miss Sally, I was dancing with all my mama's friends from the time I was five years old, so I'm used to dancing with older women."

A broad smile spread across Sally's face, and Leo suddenly realized that he might have just committed a faux pas. He moved quickly to recover.

"Besides, you are so beautiful I sure don't think of you as an older woman."

Smoke, who had been listening to the exchange, laughed out loud.

"I mean . . ."

"Kid, you'd better stop there while you're ahead," Smoke suggested.

"Yes, sir, I reckon so."

Shortly after the break ended and the dance resumed, Frank Petro, Isaiah Arias, Dave Tyler, and Pete Merck arrived. All four were armed when they stepped up to the table to buy their tickets.

"Gentlemen, if you are going to come in here, you are going to have to leave your guns outside," Tim Murchison said.

"I don't take my gun off for anyone," Arias said, the words little more than a growl.

"That's fine, sir. If you want to keep your gun, you

certainly may do so," the owner of the leather goods store said politely. "But you'll have to stay outside to do it. You can't come in here with it."

As it so happened Sally was dancing with Leo at that moment, and Smoke was over at the refreshment table, trying to decide on the pastry he wanted to try. He was close enough to the entrance to hear what was going on, so he walked over to stand by his friend.

"Any trouble, Tim?" Smoke asked, walking over to the table when he overheard the conversation.

"These gentlemen don't seem to want to check their guns," Tim replied.

"Perhaps you missed the sign out front," Smoke said. "It clearly says that no guns are allowed inside."

"Are you tryin' to tell me that there ain't nobody in here that's wearin' a gun?" Arias asked.

"What is your name, sir?" Smoke asked.

"Arias."

"Mr. Arias, if you would look around the room, you would be able to see, quite clearly, that nobody is armed. That means you don't have to be afraid."

"Afraid?" Arias shot back at him. "What makes you think I'm afraid? I ain't afraid of nobody!"

"Well, then, there's no need for you to be wearing your gun, is there?" Smoke asked with a disarming grin.

"Let's see how afraid you are!" Arias said, suddenly going for his gun. As he started to raise his gun he was shocked when Smoke, in a move so fast that Arias couldn't even follow it, reached out and snatched the gun cleanly from Arias's hand. In the same move, he brought the gun down on Arias's head, dropping him to the floor.

That move not only shocked the men who had come in with Arias, but aroused the attention of many who were already inside.

"Oh dear," Sally said, stopping right in the middle of the dance.

"What is it?" Leo asked, concerned that he might have done something.

"There seems to be some sort of trouble at the sign-in table," Sally said.

Looking toward the table Leo saw that Smoke was holding a pistol on four men. One of the men, apparently injured in some way, was being supported between two other men. But it was the fourth man, Frank Petro, that made Leo gasp.

"Frank!" he said, speaking the name before he could hold back.

"Who?"

"Uh, nothing, I was just wondering what was going on, is all."

Sally had clearly heard Leo call out a name, but she didn't question him about it. Instead, she walked over to stand near Smoke.

"I tell you what, boys, I want you to all drop your pistols in this bag," Smoke said, handing over a cloth sack that had been used to carry in some of the decorations. "If you don't give us any more trouble tonight, you'll all be able to pick up your guns from the sheriff's office tomorrow."

"We'll keep our guns," one of the men said. "We'll leave, but we'll be leavin' with our guns."

Smoke shook his head. "No," he said. "I don't think you will. Now, be gentlemen and drop your guns in this bag."

"Do what he says," Frank said, drawing his own pistol with a thumb and forefinger.

Within a moment, all had complied.

"Well, good for you," Smoke said. "And now, just to show you there are no hard feelings, you four men are welcome to attend our dance, and I'll even pay the entrance fee for you."

It had not been Leo's intention to get too close but curiosity got the better of him and he drifted toward the front. That was when he saw Frank looking right at him.

Damn, Leo thought.

The two men exchanged long looks, then Frank broke off the eye contact and spoke to Smoke.

"I saw that Longmont's was closed. Is the Brown Dirt open tonight?"

"Yes, I believe it is," Louis said, having also come to the front. "Emmet and I spoke about it, and we thought it would be important to keep at least one of the saloons open."

"Come on," Frank growled, speaking to the others with him.

By now Arias had recovered from the grogginess of the blow to his head, and he glared at Smoke as he held up his finger. "I'm going to remember you, mister. Yes, sir, I am going to remember you."

"Well, it is nice to be remembered," Smoke quipped.

"What? Look here . . ."

"Arias, come with us now, or stay here and get yourself into even more trouble," Frank ordered.

Arias held his glare for a moment longer, then turned and left with the others.

"The excitement is over, folks!" Louis said, holding up his arms. "Let's get back to dancing."

The music began again, and the dancers moved back onto the floor.

"Leo? I do believe you owe me the rest of this dance," Sally said with an easy smile.

"Yes, ma'am, I reckon I do," Leo replied, thankful that Frank Petro had left without any personal interaction.

CHAPTER TWENTY-EIGHT

"Leo, I'm going over to the City Pig for breakfast," Monte said the next morning, after the dance. "I imagine those men who tried to get into the dance while armed last night will be coming in here this morning to pick up their guns. Go ahead and give them to them. We've got no reason to hold them."

"Uh, wouldn't it be better if you did that?" Leo replied. "I mean, you bein' the sheriff 'n all."

"No need for me to do it. There's nothing to it. When they come around this morning, just let them have their guns."

"Yes, sir," Leo said, his response little more than a mumble.

"Leo, are you all right?"

"Yes, sir, I'm fine."

"I'll be back in a little while, then you can go over to the City Pig for your own breakfast," Monte said. He smiled. "Unless you'd rather go down to Nancy's Sweet Shop and have a doughnut with Miss Nonnie."

The worried expression on Leo's face was replaced with a smile and just the touch of a blush. "She is pretty, isn't she?"

Monte laughed out loud. "That's what's wrong with you. I should have seen it sooner. You've been bit by the love bug."

"Go get your breakfast, Sheriff," Leo said.

"Ah, so you're givin' the orders now, are you? All right, I'm going."

Frank Petro and the three men with him were standing behind the Big Rock Theater, which was just across the street from the sheriff's office. Frank had been keeping an eye on the office and he saw Sheriff Carson step out of the office, then turn to his left and start toward Lanning Street. Frank kept an eye on the sheriff until he went into the City Pig Café.

"All right, boys, let's go get our guns," Frank said.

The three men crossed the street, then the gang followed Frank in through the front door. Leo was sitting at the sheriff's desk, drinking a cup of coffee, and he looked up without any show of surprise.

"I guess you men have come for your guns," he said.

"Well, now, Leo, is that any way to treat your old friend?"

"Hello, Frank," Leo said.

"There now, that's better. I want you to meet some more of my friends. These here boys is Isaiah Arias, Dave Tyler, and Pete Merck."

Leo nodded but he didn't speak.

"I don't know how much of a friend we can be, seein' as you kilt my friend," Merck said.

"Priest was your friend?"

"Yeah."

"Well, I didn't really have much of a choice, seein' as how he was fixin' to kill one o' my friends," Leo said.

"Here, now, fellers, we ain't got no need to be a-arguin' twixt ourselves," Frank said.

"What did you come into town for, Frank? I thought me 'n you had a deal," Leo said.

"Well, that's just what I've come to talk to you about. You 'n me makin' a deal, I mean."

"We already have a deal, which is the only deal I want with you, and that's for you to stay out of town. Why did you all try 'n come into the dance with your guns for? Didn't you see the sign? It said 'no guns.'"

"Ahh, there didn't nothin' come of it," Frank said with a dismissive wave of his hand. "But you're right, we was dumb to do somethin' like that which would get folks to lookin' at us. 'Cause, with what I've got planned, the fewer people there is in town that notices us, the better it is."

"What are you talkin' about? What do you have planned?"

"I'll tell you soon enough," Frank said. "You're goin' to liken the deal, trust me on this. It's goin' to put more money in your hands than you ever even seen before."

"Why are you tellin' me this, Frank? I don't want no part of nothin' you've got planned. I'm a deputy sheriff now."

"Yeah, well, that's exactly why I *am* tellin' you this. I figure you bein' the deputy, most especial when the real sheriff is gone what with him wantin' to be a senator 'n all, why, it's goin' to work out just real good."

"No, it's not," Leo said. "I told you, I'm the deputy sheriff now. Do you think I won't tell the sheriff if you've got 'ny plans to break the law in town?"

"What about that little ole girl that works down at the bakery? What's her name? Nonnie?"

"What?" Leo asked, feeling a charge of fear.

"She's just a real purty thing, now, ain't she? It would pure dee be a shame iffen anything was to happen to her."

"Frank, don't you dare touch her!"

"Oh, don't worry none, kid, I don't have no intention of hurtin' her or anythin'. I mean, as long as you don't go shootin' off your mouth to the sheriff or nothin'."

Leo and Frank glared at each other for a long moment, before the sheriff came in.

"I just thought I'd bring me 'n you both some biscuits 'n bacon back so we could have our breakfast here," Monte said as he stepped inside, carrying a sack. "Oh, hello, boys. You come to pick up your guns, did you?"

"Yes, Sheriff."

"There's no trouble, is there, Leo?"

Frank looked back at Leo with a crafty smile.

"No, Sheriff, there's no trouble."

Monte set the breakfast sack on the table, then picked up the cloth bag containing the pistols that had been confiscated the night before.

"Sorry 'bout that little problem last night, boys," Monte said, holding out the pistols one at a time to let them claim their own. "But we learned a long time ago that we would have fewer problems when we had these town dances, if we didn't let anybody come in with a gun. And we did have a sign posted."

"Yes, sir, you did, Sheriff," Frank said as he took his own pistol and shoved it into his holster. "That was all our fault last night 'n it won't happen again, I can promise you that."

"Well, no harm done. You boys enjoy your visit to our town," Monte said as he handed out the last pistol.

"I'm glad to see everything turned out all right with them," Monte said after the group left. "I guess they're a group of cowhands but they must be new, because I don't believe I've met them before. The one that was their leader seemed nice enough." Monte chuckled. "It's not like I've never raised a little ruckus in town before. These things happen and most of the time it never amounts to anything if you don't let it get out of hand."

"Yes, sir, I reckon that's so," Leo said.

"You sure you're all right, son? You seem awful quiet."

"Yes, sir, I'm all right," Leo promised.

Jefferson City, Missouri

"Governor Crittenden will see you now, Mr. Williams," the governor's secretary said.

"Thank you."

Governor Thomas Theodore Crittenden's white hair was long enough to be combed over his ears. He didn't wear a beard, but he did have a full mustache. He was also a rather large man and because standing was somewhat difficult for him he remained seated in his leather chair when Williams stepped into his office. Governor Crittenden had recently come under fire from some people for authorizing and paying the five-thousand-dollar reward to Bob Ford for killing Jesse James.

"What can I do for you, Mr. Williams?"

"I have found him, Governor."

"You have found who?"

"I have found Jerry Carson."

Williams showed the governor the article in the newspaper telling about Monte Carson seeking the Senate seat from Colorado. The governor stroked his chin as he read the article, then he looked up at Williams. "This says his name is Monte Carson."

"Yes, Monte is his first name, but growing up we all knew him as Jerry," Williams said. "Monte J. Carson. The *J* stands for Jerome, and it stands to reason that a man, wanted for murder, wouldn't use the same name, once he escaped the gallows. I know Jerry Carson, Governor. If this is the same man, and I'm sure it is, I will recognize him the moment I see him."

"What do you need from me, Mr. Williams?"

"I know that as a lawyer I'm an officer of the court and don't need to be deputized, but I would like an appointment as a special deputy for the state of Missouri. I would also like a warrant for his arrest and a request for extradition from you to the governor of Colorado."

"I'll provide you with a warrant, but extraditions are a little more difficult. Apparently, according to this article, this man has been doing a very good job as sheriff. Governors are always hesitant to grant the extradition of one of their citizens without almost having a trial there before they will release anyone."

"He murdered three men, Governor, and he was convicted and sentenced," Angus said. "My primary interest is in seeing justice done. As I said, he was tried, he was convicted, and he was sentenced to hang. Somehow he managed to escape on the very night before the sentence was to have been carried out."

"Very well, Mr. Williams, I will supply you with a deputy's commission, a warrant, and a request for extradition. This is very personal for you, isn't it?"

"Because of my brother, yes, sir, it is. But also I hate seeing that there is a possibility that he could actually become a United States senator. I would hate to think that a murderer would be rewarded with a seat in the United States Senate."

Sugarloaf Ranch

"Smoke, those men who came to the dance last night, wearing their guns," Sally said. "Did you know any of them?"

"No, I don't think so. At least, I didn't recognize anyone," Smoke said as he buttered a breakfast biscuit. "Why do you ask?"

"The reason I ask is because Leo knew one of them."

"Leo told you that he knew them?"

"Not in so many words," Sally said. "And I'm not sure that he knew all of them, but I think he might have known one of them."

"What do you mean, 'not in so many words'?"

Sally told how Leo had uttered the word *Frank* and how Leo and "Frank" had stared at each other.

"Friends?"

Sally shook her head. "No, I wouldn't describe the expressions on their faces as friendly."

"Hmm, that's interesting. I wonder if this Frank person was someone Leo might have known when he was on the owlhoot trail."

"I'm sure that's it," Sally said as, without being

asked, she refilled Smoke's coffee cup. "Smoke, I've been thinking."

"You want me to ask Leo about Frank?"

"No," Sally said with a dismissive wave of her hand. "I was just a little curious, is all. But what I'm thinking about has nothing to do with Leo."

"All right, what do you have in mind?"

"I was thinking that I might go to Greeley. They have a couple of very active women's groups there and I would like to get them involved in Monte's campaign. That is, if you don't mind."

"No, I don't mind at all. I think it would be a real good idea," Smoke agreed. He smiled. "And I think it is a particularly good idea that you didn't include me in your visit to the women's groups."

Sally chuckled. "I thought you might appreciate that. But if you don't mind, I think I'll take Cal with me."

"Yes, by all means, take Cal. He'll be good company for you."

"How would you like to take a train trip?" Monte asked Leo later that same morning.

"A train trip? Yes, yes, I would like it very much! Where are we going?"

"*We* aren't going anywhere. *You* are. You're going to Greeley."

"Tired of me already, Sheriff?" Leo asked with a smile.

"Well, yeah," Monte answered with a chuckle. "But that's not why I want you to take a train trip. Joel Montgomery is getting a transfer of forty thousand dollars from the bank in Greeley, and it's coming by train. I thought it might be good for you to ride along with the money. You don't have to be in the express car, but I promised Joel I would guard the transfer."

"When do you want me to go?"

"You'll go tomorrow. I'll give you enough money to eat and spend a couple of nights in a hotel room while you're in Greeley, then you can come back on Thursday."

"I've never been in a hotel room," Leo said.

"Well, then, you have an adventure before you, don't you?"

"Yes, sir, I suppose I do."

"I think I'll go down to the depot and get your ticket," Monte said.

Leo watched Monte leave, then he had another cup of coffee and began thinking about the events of this morning. Frank Petro had threatened to hurt Nonnie, and Leo knew that he was just the kind of man who would carry out his threat. It could be, however, that Sheriff Carson had just given him the means by which he could save Nonnie.

He wasn't sure what Frank had in mind, but he believed Frank was talking about holding up the bank. And if he did hold up the bank, Leo had no doubt but that some innocent people would be killed. He couldn't warn Monte, or even Pearlie, about it, because he had no idea when they were going to do it, and if Frank got wind of the fact that he had warned someone it would put Nonnie in danger.

Leo could prevent all that if he could present Frank with a better plan. The question was, Where was Frank, and how could he get in touch with him?

If Frank and the others were still in town, Leo was almost certain he knew where they would be. And because the Brown Dirt Cowboy was but one block down Sikes Street, it would be easy enough to check out.

As soon as Leo stepped inside, using the method of entering a saloon that Pearlie had taught him, he saw Frank and the others sitting at a table in the far corner. When he caught Frank's eye he made a motion with his head, summoning Frank to him.

"Take a walk with me, Frank," Leo invited when Frank came outside.

"What have you got on your mind, kid?"

"If I told you an easy way for you to get your hands on forty thousand dollars, would you promise never to hurt Nonnie and to not ever come back to town again?"

"Kid, you can believe me when I say that once we rob the bank, we won't ever be coming back to this town."

Leo shook his head. "No, the money won't be in a bank, the money will be on the way to the bank."

"What do you mean, 'on the way to the bank'?"

"It's coming by train, and I am the one who will be guarding it."

A broad smile spread across Frank's face.

"You? You are guarding it?"

"Yes."

"How big of a cut do you want?" Frank asked.

"I don't want any of it. I just want your promise not to bother Nonnie and to never come back to Big Rock again."

"That sounds fair to me. When is this supposed to happen?"

"On Thursday. The money will be on the nine o'clock train coming out of Greeley."

"And you will be guarding it?"

"Yes."

Frank laughed again. "I knew damn well this friendship with you was going to pay off."

CHAPTER TWENTY-NINE

Smoke had found an empty building he could use for the campaign headquarters. It was just around the corner from the sheriff's office, next door to the dentist's office. The building actually belonged to Dr. Chiddister, who had made it available free of charge as his "contribution to Monte's run." A large sign was nailed up in front of the building.

CAMPAIGN HEADQUARTERS
MONTE J. CARSON
for U. S. Senate

Smoke was in the campaign headquarters when Monte stepped in, holding an envelope.

"Smoke, what do you think of this?" Monte asked, handing him the envelope. "I picked it up with the mail this morning."

Dear Sheriff Carson,
I have read many articles about you in the newspapers that are carrying the account of your attempt to become a United States senator. However,

State Senator Rex Underhill is also running for the U. S. Senate, and there are many articles about him as well.

Senator Underhill already has a background in legislative service, and indeed, he has shown himself to be a friend of the miners of Colorado, having recently removed the restrictions on mining on Mount St. John. Because of his support I am considering endorsing the candidacy of Senator Underhill, and, as I have a very good relationship with many in the general assembly, I believe my support would be of significant benefit to him.

However, I do not intend to give this support to Senator Underhill until I have satisfied myself that he is actually the better candidate. To this end, I am inviting you to come take a tour of the Silver Prince mine, located on Mount St. John. Perhaps if you would visit the mine and speak to some of my miners, you would get an idea of how your time in the U. S. Senate could be of some significant benefit to one of Colorado's most important industries, in which case I would support you.

> *Your obedient servant,*
> *Albert Jaco*

"That's quite a letter," Smoke said.

"Well, what do you think? Should I go?"

"Monte, do you know anything about this man, Jaco?"

"Not too much," Monte replied. "About the only thing I know is that he has made a lot of money mining silver. Do you know anything about him?"

"Not much more than you do, I'm afraid."

"The only thing I've ever heard about him is that he is a very wealthy man and there are some who suggest that it is impossible to be wealthy without leaving a shadow on one's trail."

"What do you think about that?" Smoke asked.

Monte laughed nervously. "Smoke, as it so happens, you are a very wealthy man. You are also my very good friend. You have made a lot of friends and a lot of enemies in your life, and I've no doubt but that some of those enemies may have said a few untrue things about you. So until I see for myself, I'll consider any suggestions about Jaco's past to be just that, suggestions."

Smoke nodded. "I think that's a wise decision. I also think we should take Jaco up on his invitation."

"Yes, I think so as well. When do you think we should go?"

"Sally is about to leave for Greeley to talk to some ladies' groups there, on your behalf. I don't want to leave until Sally gets back, but I think as soon as she returns, we should send word to Jaco that we accept his invitation."

"That sounds like a workable plan to me," Monte said. "Now, what do you say we have lunch?"

Smoke smiled and nodded. "Yes, lunch. That sounds like an even more workable plan."

Onboard the train to Greeley, Colorado

Leo had left Big Rock at four o'clock in the morning for the 180-mile trip to Greeley. So far he had been under way for six hours, counting the one hour layover in Denver, where he had changed trains. The train began slowing and the conductor came through to announce the stop.

"Sterling," he called. "We're comin' into Sterling. If this isn't your destination, don't leave the train, we'll only be here for a few minutes."

The depot was built of wood; a step-down building with two stories in front while the back half was only one story. Leo was surprised to see that the single passenger waiting to board the train was Frank Petro.

"Hello, kid," Frank said, sitting in the seat beside him.

"You shouldn't be here," Leo said, speaking barely above a whisper.

"Why not?"

"I just don't think we should be seen together, is all. I mean, seeing as I'm goin' to be helpin' you out."

"Yeah, well, that's the point, don't you see? The other boys 'n me just wanted to make sure that ever'thing is still goin' good, just the way you said it would be."

"You don't plan to be on the train with me all the way to Greeley, do you?"

"No, I'll be gettin' off at the next stop. That's where the others are, 'n that's where the horses are. I just thought we ought to make some plans, is all."

"What kind of plans?" Leo asked, looking around nervously.

"Plans about how we're goin' to handle this. You got 'ny ideas?"

Leo shook his head. "I was just goin' to wait 'n see what happens."

"All right, then, I'll make the plans. I've already looked at the railroad maps, 'n I know where ever' water tank is. One of 'em is at Pawnee Buttes. When the train stops there, we'll hold it there, while you hand the money pouch to us."

"I won't have the money pouch—that'll be the messenger. I'm just along as the guard."

"Well, then, you take the pouch from the messenger so you can give it to us."

"No, now, wait," Leo said, holding up his hand and shaking his head. "That wasn't in the plan."

"What do you mean? You said you was goin' to help us, didn't you?"

"Yes, but I didn't say nothin' 'bout me actually takin' the money from the messenger. I figured that me tellin' you when the money would be on the train, 'n me not doin' anything to try 'n stop you, would be all that I would have to do."

"Uh-uh, kid, it don't work like that. Once you cross the line to help us, there ain't no turnin' back. You're goin' to be as guilty as the rest of us, so you may as well take the money from the messenger. You do that, 'n there won't no harm come to the girl, 'n I promise you, I won't never come back to Big Rock again."

"You don't understand, Frank. If I do that, I won't ever be able to go back to Big Rock, either."

Frank chuckled. "No, I reckon not."

"So that means I'm going to want my share," Leo said.

"What?"

"I told you where the money would be, and I told you that even though I'm supposed to be the guard, I won't actually do anything to try and stop you. But that's not enough for you, now you are saying that I have to actually get the money and hand it to you. If

I do that, that makes me one of the robbers, and that will mean that I can't ever go back to Big Rock because I'm going to have to start over somewhere else.

"Also, if I don't go back, the judge said I would have to go to prison. This changes everything, Frank. I'm going to need some money, so I want a share."

"How much of a share?"

"Well, there's five of us, and there's forty thousand dollars, so I want eight thousand."

Frank shook his head. "I'm not sure the others will go along with you gettin' a full share, I mean, you not actual doin' the robbin' or nothin'."

"What do you mean I'm not doing the robbing? I'm the only one who actually is doing the robbing. All you and the others will be doing is taking the money I stole. I want a full share and I want to ride away with you."

"We only got four horses."

"I'll ride double with you and I'll buy a horse and tack in the very next town."

Frank stroked the stubble on his beard for a moment while he contemplated Leo's proposal.

"All right," he said. "All right, you got yourself a deal."

Again, the train began to slow, and Frank leaned over to look out the window.

"This here is Dent," he said. "This is my stop."

Greeley

When Cal and Sally boarded the train in Big Rock, they were unaware that Leo had left for the same destination the day before. Cal and Sally left on the eight o'clock train that morning, and after a full day of travel, including a train change in Denver, they reached Greeley just before seven o'clock that evening. After leaving the train, Cal retrieved the luggage as Sally secured transportation for them, the vehicle being a trap with driver.

"Where to, ma'am and sir?" the driver asked as he placed the two pieces of luggage in the back of the two-seat carriage, open all around, though it did have a top.

"The Oasis Hotel," Sally said.

"Yes, ma'am, our newest and finest. You will be very comfortable there."

Situated on a corner, the Oasis Hotel was a large, three-story brick building with a wraparound porch on the ground floor and a deck on the second floor. Both porch and deck were furnished with chairs and benches so that the residents could see the passing traffic on the intersecting streets, which were Main Street and Apple Avenue.

"We have hot and cold running water in every room," Robert Olnvey, the proprietor, said proudly. "And a fine dining facility right here in the hotel. I think you will find our accommodations quite satisfying."

"I'm sure we will," Sally said as she and Cal signed the register.

"If you don't mind, Cal, I think I would like to take a bath before dinner to freshen up from the train ride."

"No, ma'am, I don't mind at all. As a matter of fact it sounds like a pretty good idea to me, too."

Once Cal was in the room, he took a long look at the amenities the room offered. The lights overhead were gas, and because there was a constant pilot light, all he had to do to illuminate the entire room was turn a small valve on the wall by the door. That fed gas to the lanterns, and the crystal prisms cast a bright light to fill every corner of the room.

In addition to the convenience of instant light, there was a smaller room that had a footed, cast-iron bathtub and a flush toilet.

"I've never seen anything like it," Cal said over dinner in the hotel dining room that evening. "We ought to have somethin' like that back at Sugarloaf."

"Running water would be nice," Sally agreed. Then, putting aside the wonder of indoor plumbing, they made plans for the following day. It would be filled with activity.

Unbeknownst to either Cal or Sally, was the fact that Leo Beajuex was already in town, having arrived the day before. Shortly after his arrival he presented himself to the president of the Union Bank.

"Mr. Ward, I'm Deputy Beajuex from Big Rock. I believe you asked for a guard to go along with the money you'll be sending to Mr. Montgomery at the Bank of Big Rock?"

"My word," Ward said, staring at Leo with gray eyes that were set under heavy eyebrows. "You are the deputy?"

"Yes, sir, here is a letter from Sheriff Carson."

"You seem awfully young."

"That's true, sir, but I'm afraid there's nothing I can do about that except wait until I'm not awfully young anymore."

Ward stared at Leo for a moment, then he laughed out loud. "I suppose that's true," he said. "All right, Deputy, I'll be glad to have you escort the money transfer. The shipment will be put on board the train Thursday morning. In the meantime, enjoy our fair city."

"Thank you, I shall."

When Leo tired of walking around, he went into the Dime and Dollar Saloon, entering the way Pearlie had taught him, then he stepped up to the bar and ordered a sarsaparilla.

"Here you go, young man," the bartender said, putting the glass before him with a smile. "So, has Sheriff Ferrell hired hisself a new deputy?"

"I'm not Sheriff Ferrell's deputy."

"Then why is it you're a-wearin' that badge?"

"I'm Sheriff Monte Carson's deputy. He sent me over here to do a job for him."

"Monte Carson? Say, ain't he wantin' to be a senator or somethin'?"

"Yes, sir, he is, 'n he would be a good one, too."

"Hey, Reynolds!" one of the other customers called. "You goin' to stand down there babblin' all day, or are you goin' to come down here 'n get my whiskey?"

"I'll be right there," the bartender replied.

CHAPTER THIRTY

Sally and Cal got their day started the next morning by visiting the *Greeley Tribune*. There, they gave the publisher a letter they had been given just for that purpose by Phil Clinton of the *Big Rock Journal*.

"Yes, I know Phil, and a fine, fine journalist he is," the publisher said. "He has asked for my cooperation, and so I shall."

"Thank you, Mr. McCauley, for your courtesy," Sally said.

"What, exactly, would you like me to do?"

"Well, the thing I would like most would be your endorsement for Monte Carson. But if you don't wish to make that big of a commitment yet, I can understand it. At the minimum, though, I would like for you to publish an article telling about my appearances before the ladies' groups today. I have already made arrangements to speak, and here are some of my notes if you would like to have an idea of what I'll be saying."

"I'll be glad to write something about it, Mrs. Jensen," McCauley promised with a wide, unforced smile.

Before she spoke to any of the ladies' groups, Sally

visited several of the businesses in town, introducing herself and pitching Monte's candidacy.

"You know what I'm thinking, Miss Sally," Cal said between a couple of their stops. "I can't help but think what a good thing it would be if Mrs. Carson was still alive so she could campaign for the sheriff with you."

"Yes," Sally agreed solemnly. "That would have been a wonderful thing. She was a wonderful lady, a great help to Monte, and a very close and personal friend."

"Oh, I've made you sad," Cal said. "I'm sorry."

"Don't be silly, Cal. It's never sad to think of dear, departed friends. Whenever we remember them, they are alive for those memories."

"Yes, ma'am," Cal said. "I like to think that's the way it is." Cal had lost a true love a few years earlier.

They stopped at a couple more businesses, then Cal pulled out his pocket watch and checked the time.

"It's about time for your first ladies' thing, isn't it?" Cal asked, the words carrying little enthusiasm.

"Not just the first group, but I'll be speaking to the largest ladies' group in Greeley, and one of the largest in the entire state."

"That's quite an honor," Cal said, showing no more enthusiasm now than he had with his first observation.

"You are welcome to come to the meeting with me, Cal. You could sit in the back."

"I, uh, do I have to . . . uh, that is, do you really think I should come?"

Sally chuckled, amused by Cal's discomfort at the idea. "Why, Cal, are you suggesting that you would rather not come?"

"If it's all the same to you, Miss Sally, I believe I'd rather poke a railroad spike up my nose."

Sally laughed. "All right, have fun poking a railroad spike up your nose. I'll meet you at McKenzie's Restaurant for dinner at six this evening."

"Yes, ma'am," Cal said.

Sally watched a happy Cal walk away, then she stepped into the Greeley Baptist Church to speak to her first group of women.

Her theme, as she spoke with the ladies' group here, and in those places where she had spoken earlier, was always the same.

"In this endeavor we carry as much weight as the men," Sally would say. "For the only input man or woman can have in the selection of our United States senator is the weapon of influence."

Sally would pause for a moment and then, with a sly grin, continue. "And one of the very first things we learned as little girls was the art of influence. Am I right, ladies?"

That observation would always elicit a laugh and an agreement.

By his third day Leo had examined the town pretty closely. He found the cheapest place to eat, and he found a park where he could just sit and pass the time in a very pleasant location.

There were several saloons in town, but Leo settled upon the Dime and Dollar, not only because it was the cleanest one, but also because by now he was able to order as many sarsaparillas as he wanted to, without having to answer a lot of questions. The bartender recognized him, and even some of the regulars, so he was able to stand at the bar and enjoy his drink of choice without feeling intimidated.

"You were here yesterday, weren't you, honey?" one of the bar girls asked. Leo was certain that she was a percentage girl, and nothing else.

"Yes, ma'am, I was," Leo replied.

"Oh, honey!" the girl said with a lilting laugh. "You don't have to call me ma'am. My name is Sadie. What is your name?"

"Leo."

"Leo, would you like to spend some time with me?"

"Yes, ma'am, I s'pose I could, as long as you know."

"As long as I know what?"

"As long as you know that I have a girlfriend."

Sadie laughed, then reached out to lay her fingers on Leo's cheek. "Oh, honey, you are the sweetest thing. But don't you worry, we aren't going to do anything that might make your girlfriend jealous."

For the next few minutes Leo and Sadie talked, and Leo couldn't help but feel transported across space and time until, once again, he was with his mother and her friends at the de Plaisir Maison back in New Orleans.

"You sweet thing, I wish I could do it for you, but I see that I can't," Sadie said after a few minutes. She reached up to touch him on the cheek, and for some reason that Leo couldn't understand, his cheek flamed at the touch.

"Your girlfriend is a very lucky lady. But I'm going to have to spend some time with some of the other customers, because I do have to make a living."

Leo watched Sadie walk away, then he stood there for a while, staring down into his glass of sarsaparilla. He had told Sadie that he had a girlfriend. But he knew that, after this trip, he would no longer be able to think of Nonnie as his girlfriend. With what he had planned, there was a very strong possibility that he wouldn't be going back.

Finally, feeling the need for a visit to the privy he stepped out back. When he came back in, he was shocked by who he saw standing at the bar. He had to look twice to confirm that it was who he thought it was.

Yes, it *was* Cal, but what was he doing here?

This could cause all sorts of problems. If Cal knew of the plans Leo had concerning Frank Petro and the transfer of funds from the Union Bank of Greeley to the Bank of Big Rock, he would try and stop him.

Leo found himself between a rock and a hard place. If Cal tried to stop him, someone was going to be hurt. And if Cal did stop him, Nonnie could be hurt.

It would be best if Cal didn't even know he was here.

Leo stepped back out into the alley so that he wouldn't be seen. He hurried up through the gap between the Dime and Dollar Saloon and Rafferty's Grocery Store, which was right beside it.

A few minutes later Leo was standing on the bank of the Cache la Poudre River. He couldn't help but chuckle every time he heard someone refer to these little streams as *rivers*.

"You want to see a real river, take a look at the Mississippi River in New Orleans," he said, speaking aloud.

He wondered where Frank and the others were right now, and more than that, he wondered what would happen tomorrow when the train would be hit on its way back to Big Rock.

Was he making a mistake? Maybe he shouldn't be doing this, but he couldn't take a chance on Frank hurting Nonnie. And he knew Frank well enough to know that he would carry out his threat.

Back in the Dime and Dollar Saloon, Cal was unaware that he had just missed seeing Leo, unaware even that Leo was in town. At the moment he was just killing time while Sally spoke to the women's groups. Standing at the end of the bar, nursing his drink, he looked around to take the measure of the place. The Dime and Dollar Saloon wasn't quite as nice as Longmont's, but it was considerably nicer than most of the saloons he had been in. And he should know saloons, since he was practically raised in one.

Leo had shared with him that his mother had been a prostitute and that he had been raised in a whorehouse in New Orleans. Cal could relate very strongly to that, because his own past was not that dissimilar, though he not yet shared that bit of information with Monte's young ward. He had asked Sally what she thought about him telling Leo about his own past.

"I think you should hold that in abeyance for a while," Sally had told him. "There may come a time when Leo needs to know that his background isn't all that unique. He may need a boost to feel good about himself, and you can provide him with that boost by sharing your story with him."

Now, as Cal stood here drinking a beer, his recalling that conversation with Sally caused him to think about his past. He had lived in the town of Eagle Tail, Kansas, and though he was only twelve years old, he was able to earn a little money by sweeping the floor of the Beer Barrel Saloon, the saloon where his mother worked. His past certainly hadn't been typical of other boys his age, but there was little in his early life that was typical.

"Your mama is a whore. You know that, don't you, boy? You do know that your mama is a whore, I mean, she ain't tried to keep it a secret or nothin', has she?"

The man who was talking was one of the cowboys who frequented the Beer Barrel Saloon. "Your mama is a whore and you don't even know who your pappy is, do you? Hell, for all I know, I might be your pappy. I've sure bedded your mama often enough."

Cal's face burned as the two men who were at the table with the cowboy laughed.

"How does it feel to be a whore's kid?"

Cal didn't answer.

"For crying out loud, Bill, let the boy be," the bartender said. "He's a good boy, and he comes here every day after school and works hard. He's never given me no trouble."

"I'm just funnin' him," Bill said.

"I doubt that he's havin' much fun from it."

Cal had been able to put all that behind him. He hoped Leo could do the same.

CHAPTER THIRTY-ONE

"Would you like another beer, friend?" the bartender asked, interrupting Cal's musing.

"No, I think I'll have a sarsaparilla instead," Cal said, thinking about the free soda pop Fitzgerald had provided for him, not just for the week, but for the rest of the time he had worked there.

"That's funny," the bartender said.

"You think there's something funny about drinking a sarsaparilla?" Cal challenged.

"No, sir, there ain't, I mean, there ain't nothin' particularly funny about it, 'n I don't mean nothin' by what I said. But the reason I said it was funny is 'cause I don't get more'n one or two people ask for a sarsaparilla a month, 'n here you're the second one in just the last two days. And the other fella, he come in here yesterday and today, and sarsaparilla is all he will drink. He's a real young feller, 'n he's wearin' a deputy sheriff's badge."

Cal thought immediately of Leo.

"Is he still in here?"

"He sure is. He's right down . . ." The bartender pointed to the other end of the bar then paused and pulled his hand back. He got a puzzled look on his face. "That's funny, he was there just a couple o' minutes ago 'n I didn't see 'im leave."

Cal shrugged. He was sure it wasn't Leo. If it had been, Leo would have come over to talk to him. Besides, he had no idea what Leo would be doing in Greeley, anyway.

After leaving the Dime and Dollar Saloon, Leo wandered around Greeley for a while until he wound up in the Frog City Saloon. Frog City was to the Brown Dirt Cowboy, as the Dime and Dollar was to Longmont's. It was stark and utilitarian.

He hadn't expected to see Cal in Greeley, but as he thought about it, he realized it probably had something to do with Sheriff Carson's campaign for senator. If Cal was here, Smoke might be as well. Under the circumstances, Smoke Jensen was the last person he wanted to see.

"What'll it be, gent?" the bartender asked as he wiped a spill from the bar in front of Cal.

"I'll have a sarsa . . ." Cal started, then he stopped in midsentence. "I'll have a whiskey," he said.

"Comin' right up."

Leo had never drunk whiskey before. But he had never been involved in a train holdup before, either.

When the drink was put before him, he stared at the glass for a long time.

"It's good whiskey, mister. As good as they serve over at that fancy Dime and Dollar," the bartender said.

Leo nodded, then picked up the glass. He didn't know whether he should sip it or toss the whole glass down. He had seen drinkers doing it both ways. He decided it might be best to toss it all down with one gulp.

Leo regretted his choice almost immediately. His throat was on fire, and the burning reached all the way down to his stomach. He closed his eyes tightly and put his hands to each side of his head.

"I told you it was good whiskey," the bartender said with a little chuckle. "You want another one?"

Leo started to order another whiskey, but decided against it. For one thing, he didn't want to be drunk and hungover for what he had to do tomorrow. And another and more immediate reason he didn't want the whiskey was because the first drink had set his insides on fire.

"I'll take a sarsaparilla."

"So, how did your meeting with all the ladies go?" Cal asked Sally over the dinner table that evening.

"It went very well," Sally replied brightly. "I'm happy to report that here, in Greeley, the support for Monte is quite enthusiastic. And how did it go with you? Did you actually enjoy poking a railroad spike up your nose?" she teased.

"Oh, now, you're going to hold that against me, are you, Miss Sally? I mean, you wouldn't have really wanted me at that meeting with you. You know I would have just gotten in the way."

"You are forgiven," she said.

"All right, then I confess that I didn't really poke a railroad spike up my nose."

Sally laughed. "I'm glad you didn't." She took a swallow of her wine before she spoke again.

"You know, the strangest thing," she added with a sudden change of subject. "I can't be sure, of course, and there was no way I could follow up on it, but I could almost swear that I saw Leo Beajuex."

"That is strange," Cal said.

Sally chuckled. "I know, I was just seeing things but it . . ."

"No, I mean it's strange that you think you saw him, because of what happened to me in the bar this afternoon."

"What do you mean? Did you see him, too?"

"No, I didn't see him, but something the bartender said certainly made me think about him."

Cal told Sally of his conversation with the bartender about someone who was young, wearing a badge, and drinking only sarsaparilla.

Sally laughed, then shook her head.

"We're both imagining things," she said. "What in the world would Leo Beajuex be doing in Greeley?"

"Yes, ma'am, that's just what I was thinking," Cal said.

"Oh, I got a telegram from Smoke today."

"A telegram? Is everything all right?"

"Everything is fine. Here, read it for yourself."

Cal took the telegram from Sally and examined the words printed on the paper by the telegrapher in the bold, all-capital letters.

HOPE YOU ARE HAVING SUCCESS WITH YOUR TRIP MONTE AND I HAVE BEEN INVITED TO TOUR THE SILVER PRINCE MINE. WILL DO SO WHEN YOU RETURN. LOVE SMOKE

"Speaking of when we return, we are still going back tomorrow, aren't we?" Cal asked.

"Yes," Sally said. "I think we did some good here, and I really believe we were able to help Monte in his campaign. But I don't mind telling you, I'm looking forward to getting back home."

The next morning Leo met Sheriff Ferrell at the sheriff's office, then at the sheriff's invitation, walked down to the bank with him.

"We'll have the packet ready in just a minute, Sheriff," Bill Waltrip said. Waltrip was the banker. "David Crader will take it down to the depot and hand it over to the express messenger."

"We're in no hurry," Sheriff Ferrell replied.

"David, you make certain you get a receipt from the messenger."

"Yes, sir, I will."

A few minutes later the three men were walking from the bank toward the depot. David was carrying a leather-and-canvas satchel, held closed at the top by a small padlock.

"David, do you ever wonder if we are here to keep anyone from stealing the bag from you, or to keep you from just grabbing the bag yourself and running off?" Sheriff Ferrell asked.

David chuckled. "That's a good point, Sheriff. I suppose you could look at it either way."

"Of course, I suppose that Leo and I could grab it and run off ourselves, when you think about it," Sheriff Ferrell said with another chuckle.

Leo laughed with him, but it was a forced laugh.

The door to the express car was open as they approached. The express messenger, who was a small man with a closely cropped mustache under a nose that seemed disproportionately large for his face, stepped up to the door and looked down at the three men. He was bald, and the rimless glasses made his blue eyes look oversized.

"I was told to expect a delivery," he said. He dropped a ladder down. "Come aboard, and we'll take care of it."

Leo and the sheriff stood by and let Crader climb aboard first, then they followed him up. Leo watched as the messenger opened the safe.

"I'll need you to sign the receipt," Crader said.

"As soon as I count the money," the messenger replied.

A short time later the money was counted, put back into the bag, then into the safe. The safe door was slammed shut.

Leo stared at the safe for a moment. There seemed such a finality to it. How would he ever be able to take the money from the safe if the door was closed and locked?

"Barry, this is Deputy Leo Beajuex," Sheriff Ferrell said. "He'll be making the trip back to Big Rock with the money."

"Oh? And will you be riding in here with me, Deputy Beajuex?" Barry asked.

"No, I'll be back in the cars."

Barry laughed. "Good choice. This car doesn't ride well, and as you can see"—he took in the car with a wave of his hand—"there is no place but the floor, on which to sit."

"Well, I'd better get back to the office," Sheriff Ferrell said. "Leo, you give my best to Sheriff Carson and tell him I've already sent letters to my representative and my state senator telling them that I wanted them to vote for Sheriff Carson."

"I will, Sheriff, and I know he will appreciate it."

By now Leo, Sheriff Ferrell, and Crader had left the express car and they were standing alongside it when Sally and Cal arrived. Leo didn't see them, but Sally saw him.

"My goodness, Cal, I wasn't losing my mind after all," Sally said. "I did see Leo yesterday. There he is with Sheriff Ferrell."

"Why, it sure is him," Cal said. "I'll go talk to him as soon as I get our luggage taken care of."

"He must be here on some official business, which means he is traveling as cheaply as he can. Please invite him to join us; I'll take care of the difference in the cost of his ticket."

"Yes, ma'am," Cal said.

"Hello, Leo, imagine seeing you here!" Cal greeted effusively a few minutes later.

Leo turned toward him.

For just a moment, Cal was puzzled by the expression on his friend's face. Instead of the happy smile he expected, Leo looked confused, almost as if he was displeased to see him. Then, as if realizing the expression he was projecting, Leo smiled and extended his hand.

"Cal, what are you doing in Greeley?"

"Why, I'm campaigning for your boss, of course. Miss Sally spoke at some ladies' groups yesterday. What are you doing here?"

"Sheriff Carson asked me to come. The bank here is transferring some money to the bank in Big Rock."

Cal chuckled. "Yeah, banks do that all the time, though I don't have any idea why. Oh, Miss Sally wants you to come ride with us. We're traveling first class," he added with a smile. "I'd just be willing to bet that you've never traveled first class before."

"Are you kidding? I've never traveled any kind of class before. When I come here, it was the first time I had ever even been on a train. But the only kind of ticket I got is what the conductor said was a day coach ticket."

"You don't have to worry any about that. Miss Sally is going to take care of paying off the difference."

"Still, what I'm supposed to do is keep an eye on the money that's being sent. So I expect I should stay where I'm supposed to be."

"Oh, don't be silly, Leo. You're in the day coach, which is way back toward the rear of the train. The parlor car is at the front. If you ride with Miss Sally and me, you'll be that much closer to the money."

"Yes," Leo said. "Yes, that's right, isn't it? All right, I'll ride with you and Miss Sally."

CHAPTER THIRTY-TWO

Four men were camped out near the Pawnee Buttes, about ten miles southwest of Greeley. Three of them were eating the rabbit they had earlier cooked over an open fire. The fourth stood up and began taking a leak.

"What the hell, Merck? You got no more sense than to piss where we're tryin' to eat our breakfast?" Arias asked.

"Hell, I ain't pissin' on nobody's food," Merck said. "Move away."

"I can't move now. If I do, I'll piss on my pants."

"If you don't move now, I'll put a bullet in your ass!"

"Damn, you got a mean temper, Arias, you know that?" Merck said as he moved away.

"Let's get back to what it was we was talkin' about," Tyler said. "Frank, you're sure Beaujex is goin' to help us?"

"Yeah, I'm sure," Frank answered as he pulled a piece of meat from the bone then stuck it in his mouth. "He ain't got no choice but to help us, on account of he knows what will happen to that little ole girl he's sweet on iffen he don't."

"What's his share of the money?" Merck asked after he finished relieving himself and returned to the others. He reached for the rabbit, and Arias slapped his hand away.

"That hand's been on your pecker, don't you be usin' it to touch the rabbit we're eatin'. I'll tear some of the meat off for you."

"He said he wants a full share, but he ain't goin' to get it," Frank said.

"What do you mean, 'he ain't goin' to get it'? You think just tellin' 'im we ain't goin' to hurt that little ole girl of hisn will be enough to keep 'im from wantin' any of the money?" Merck asked.

Frank flashed an evil smile. "It don't matter what he wants, 'cause I aim for us to kill 'im, soon as he helps us rob the train."

"I thought you said he was your friend."

"Yeah, he was, but I don't believe in lettin' friendship get in the way of doin' business," Frank replied with a diabolical grin.

"When is it that the train is s'posed to get here?" Arias asked.

"I looked at the schedule real good, 'n from what I can figure, it'll get here 'bout eleven o'clock this morning," Frank said. He pointed to the water tower that was within sight of where they had spent the night. "'N we won't even have to stop it, on account of it'll have to stop its ownself so's it can take on water."

"And you're sure robbin' the train is better'n holdin' up the bank?" Tyler asked. "I mean, if the sheriff is out campaignin' 'n all, and Beaujex is the deputy, seems to me like robbin' a bank woulda been easier'n holdin' up a train."

"Think about it," Frank said. "The bank is right in the middle of town. After we rob it, we still have to get out of town, 'n with all the people there it wouldn't take no time at all for 'em to get 'em up a posse to come after us. But we can hold up a train right out in the middle of nowhere, 'n they sure as hell can't make up a posse with the passengers that's on the train. 'N even if they could, how would they follow us? They won't have no horses."

"Yeah," Tyler said. "Yeah, that makes sense when you think about it."

"The only thing I want to think about is the ten thousand dollars that's goin' to be my share," Arias said.

It had been a successful trip to Greeley, and Sally had been gratified by the number of people who had promised to give their support to Monte Carson in his quest for the Senate seat. Almost all had agreed to write to representatives and senators in the general assembly and to hold receptions to get others to do the same thing.

Although the trip had been successful, it was also tiring, and Sally was glad to be coming home. She smiled as she thought of the report she would give Smoke. She knew that he would be proud of what she had accomplished during her trip, and it would give him something to think about while he and Monte were touring the mine.

She wondered if she should go to the mine with him. It might be interesting, touring an actual working mine. But she knew, also, that it would be tiring, and she was already tired. She smiled. *Smoke, you're on your own for this one*, she thought.

Leo had accepted the invitation to move up to the first-class car with them, and her thoughts were interrupted when he stood up.

"Where are you going?" Sally asked.

"I, uh, I'm just goin' to step out onto the vestibule 'n get a little fresh air," Leo said.

"What are you talking about? The air's better in here," Cal said. "The window's up so we're getting a breeze. If you go out there, all you're going to do is wind up breathin' a lot of smoke."

"Yeah, I, uh, I think I'll go anyway," Leo said.

Sally and Cal watched him walk toward the front, but not until he left the car did Sally speak.

"Cal, has Leo said anything to you?"

"Said anything about what?"

"I don't know, it's just that there is something very peculiar about his behavior. He has barely spoken a word, and he keeps looking out the window as if he is looking for something."

"Well, yes, ma'am, but don't you think that maybe Sheriff Carson sending him to guard the money shipment might cause him to act like that?"

"I suppose," Sally replied, though the tone of her voice indicated that she wasn't entirely convinced. "If that is what's bothering him, I suppose he'll be his old self once we get back home."

"I think I'll step out onto the vestibule with him. Maybe I can find out if anything is bothering him."

"Would you? I'd feel a lot better about it if I knew it was just nervousness over his responsibility."

When Cal stepped out between the cars he saw

Leo standing on the bottom step, holding on to the assist rail and leaning out so he could look forward.

"Hold on there, Leo, that's not a very smart thing for you to be doing!" Cal shouted. "Get back up here!"

Leo came back up onto the platform.

"What were you doing down there like that?"

"Cal, you 'n Miss Sally ought not to be on this train," Leo said.

"What do you mean we ought not to be here? Miss Sally did what she was supposed to do in Greeley, now it's time for us to go back home."

"You don't understand," Leo said. "This train is going to be robbed, and you 'n Miss Sally will just be in the way."

"How do you know the train is going to be robbed? And why are you saying that we'll be in the way?"

"I know that it's going to be robbed because I set it up," Leo said. "I told Frank Petro that there would be forty thousand dollars on this train."

"What? Leo, why would you do such a thing? I mean, after all that everyone has done for you. Why, you would be in the state prison right now if not for Sheriff Carson and Smoke. And yes, even me. But you'd double-cross us like that?"

Leo shook his head. "It's not like that, not like the way you're sayin'."

"Then you tell me how it is."

"Nonnie Kinder."

"What does Nonnie have to do with it? Good Lord, Leo, you aren't saying that you want to steal money so you and Nonnie can run off together, are you? She's a good girl. What makes you think she would run off with someone who would rob a train?"

"That's not it. Frank said that if I didn't help him, he would hurt Nonnie, maybe even kill her."

"Don't you think that if you told the sheriff about this, or Smoke, or even Pearlie or me, that we would protect her?"

"You don't know Frank. He's real mean, he would find a way to hurt her, I know he would."

"Frank?"

"Yeah, he's someone that I knew from . . . from before, when I was an outlaw."

"If you're plannin' on robbin' this train, you're still an outlaw as far as I'm concerned. "And I'm tellin' you right now, Leo, you won't be robbing this train, because I'm not going to let you do it. Who is this man, Frank?"

"You know Myron Petro, the man that planned the bank robbery? He was Frank's brother. Frank was part of the holdup, too, only his job was to stand lookout just outside of town for when we went ridin' out after we got the money. But we never got the money and Frank didn't have nothin' to do with the actual robbery, so he just rode away."

"You've never mentioned him, have you?" Cal challenged.

Leo shook his head. "No, I never mentioned him. I wasn't sure he'd done anything wrong. Besides which, I hoped he would go his way and I would go mine, and I'd never see him again."

"But it didn't work out like that, did it?"

"No, it didn't. He come to see me to tell me that if I didn't help him, he would hurt Nonnie."

"So that's why you're going to help him rob the train," Cal said. It was a statement, not a question.

Leo smiled, for the first time in their conversation.

"No, 'n that's the part you don't understand. You see, I'm not going to help him, I never was actually goin' to help him, he just thinks I am. It has been my plan, all along, to stop him. Cal, I set all this up as a trap. When he and the others with him try and rob the train, I'm going to stop them."

"How do you plan to stop them?"

"I'm going to shoot them. It'll be easy, they won't be expecting it, so I'll have the advantage. I figure I can get at least two of 'em before they get me."

"How many are there?"

"Four, all told."

"Then that leaves two left," Cal said, pointing out the obvious.

"Yes, but I'll make sure that Frank is the first one I shoot. If I kill him and at least one more, I think the other two will leave."

"Or they'll kill you," Cal suggested.

"They might. But at least Nonnie will be safe."

"Leo, that is one of the dumbest plans I've ever heard of. You're going to get yourself killed."

"Maybe, but there's no need for you 'n Miss Sally to be killed. Cal, please, go back into the car and look out for her."

"What, and miss all the fun? No, my young friend, I intend to be right here with you."

A relieved smile spread across Leo's face. "Good, good, thank you, Cal."

"What is your plan?" Cal asked.

"Plan? I don't have a plan."

"I thought you said you had a plan to stop them. Well, just what were you going to do?"

"I don't know, I was just sort of going to wait and see what happens."

"Are they already aboard the train?" Cal asked.

"What? No, I don't think so. Frank told me they would come aboard at one of the times when the train stopped for water. At a place called Pawnee Buttes."

"Then let's go find out where that place is, so we can be ready for them," Cal suggested.

"How are we going to do that?"

"The engineer and fireman will know."

When Cal and Leo dropped down into the engine cab from the coal tender, the fireman and engineer were shocked and frightened at the unexpected intrusion.

"Here, here, no need to be frightened," Cal said quickly, holding out his hand. "We're here to help you."

"Help us how?" the engineer said.

"I'm Deputy Wood, this is Deputy Beajuex. We're escorting the money transfer from Greeley to Big Rock."

"What money?" the fireman asked. "We aren't carryin' any money."

The engineer nodded his head. "No, no, they're right about that, Doodle, we are carryin' money, I just forgot to tell you about it." The engineer looked back toward Cal and Leo.

"But what are you two boys doin' up here in the cab? If you're guardin' the money, shouldn't you be back in the express car?"

"No, we're goin' to stop it before it gets that far," Cal said. "Is there a water tank at Pawnee Buttes?"

"Yeah," the fireman said.

Cal nodded. "That's where they plan to hit us."

"So, you want us to stop before we get there or somethin'?" the engineer asked.

"No, we'll make the stop there," Cal said. He smiled. "But we'll have a few surprises in store for them when we get there."

CHAPTER THIRTY-THREE

"All right, here it comes," Frank said. "Arias, as soon as the train stops, you climb up onto the engine cab 'n shoot the engineer and fireman. With both of them dead, there won't be nobody left to drive the train, 'n that means it'll be a long time afore anyone finds out about the robbery. 'N when they do find out, we'll be long gone from here."

"What about Beajuex?" Merck asked.

"Accordin' to what we got worked out, he's goin' to tell the express car messenger that he had better keep a-holt of the money. Then we're supposed to point our guns at 'im and force him to turn it over. That way, nobody will know that he's helpin' us," Frank said. He flashed an evil smile. "Onliest thing is, we ain't just goin' to point our guns at 'im, we're goin' to actual shoot him dead."

"What about the express messenger?"

"Kill 'im, too. That way there won't be nobody left alive to tell who done it."

"What about the passengers?"

"They ain't goin' to be able to get much of a look at us, seein' as they'll be in the cars 'n all. But if any of 'em is dumb enough to climb down out o' one o' them cars, why, we'll shoot them, too. Now, get out of sight 'n don't show yourselves till the train comes to a complete stop."

Merck chuckled. "Damn, you got this thing figured out slick as a whistle."

"I told you boys when you all agreed to come with me that I had some ideas that would make us all rich. 'N this is just the first one. I figure we could do four or five jobs like this before anyone would ever figure out who's doin' it, 'n by that time we'll be long gone from Colorado 'n I'll be raisin' oranges in California."

"Rich," Arias said with a broad smile. "Son of a bitch, we're goin' to be rich."

"It's this red lever, here on the left," the engineer said, pointing out the brake to Cal. "I'll divert the steam and start slowing down, then when we get to the water tank, move it all the way down, and that'll bring the train to a complete stop."

"All right," Cal said. "We'll take it from here."

As the train slowed for the stop at the water tank, the fireman and the engineer hopped down then ran alongside the track, keeping pace with the engine, and on the opposite side of the train from the water tower. Cal and Leo remained in the cab.

"There's nobody there," Leo said.

"If nobody shows up here, we'll do it again at the next water stop," Cal said. He pulled the brake lever and the train came to a complete stop.

"There they are!" Leo said.

"Step back a little so they can't see you through the window," Cal suggested. "If they're expecting you to be in the express car, they don't need to see you here."

One of the four men used the mounting step and climbed up onto the engine platform with his gun in hand.

"Drop the gun," Cal said.

"The hell I will!"

Arias fired first, but in his excitement, he missed. Cal returned fire and didn't miss.

After the exchange of gunfire, both Cal and Leo hopped down from the cab.

"Drop your gun, Frank!" Leo called out.

"The son of a bitch has double-crossed us!" Frank shouted, and what resulted from the challenge was the explosive sound of the exchange of gunfire. When the shooting was over, all four of the would-be train robbers were down.

So was Leo Beajuex.

Big Rock

"Where's Sally?" Smoke asked. Smoke had come to the depot to meet the train, and was confused to see Cal get off by himself.

"She stayed in Denver to look after Leo."

"Leo?" Monte asked.

"He was shot during the train holdup."

"What?"

"Oh, don't worry, the money is safe, it's in the express car."

"Never mind that, how is Leo?" Monte asked, the expression on his face registering his concern.

"The doc says he'll be all right and can probably

come home in another few days. That's why Miss Sally stayed in Denver, so she can come home with him."

"It's all my fault," Monte said. "I shouldn't have sent him to guard the money shipment. He's too young."

Cal shook his head. "No, sir, he isn't too young. You should have seen him. There were four of them, and Leo didn't flinch. When the shooting was over, all four of the outlaws were dead. You should be proud of him, Sheriff."

Monte nodded. "Yes," he said. He smiled. "Yes, I am proud of him, and I'm going to let him know how proud I am, as soon as he gets back. In the meantime, let's get the money down to the bank."

Within the hour the story of Leo's heroics was being extolled in the saloons, spoken of in all the stores, and talked about on the streets of the town. In the meantime, Smoke, Monte, Pearlie, and Cal were back at the sheriff's office. Smoke and Monte were making preparations to visit the Silver Prince Mine.

"Sheriff, if you would like, I can stay here and deputy for Pearlie while you're gone," Cal offered. "I mean, seeing as Leo is going to be laid up for a while."

"Yes, thank you, Cal, I would appreciate that," Monte replied.

At that moment a young woman stepped into the sheriff's office. "Is it true?" she asked in a voice that was filled with concern. "Was Leo shot?"

"Yes," Cal replied. "But don't worry, Nonnie, he's with the doctor now, and he's going to be all right."

"You aren't just telling me that to make me feel better, are you?"

"No, I'm telling you the truth, he will be all right. He'll be back here in just a few more days," Cal said.

"Will you . . . will you tell me when he gets back?"

"Oh, I promise you, you'll know when he gets back. You were the last person he mentioned before I left him in Denver."

"Thank you, oh, thank you," Nonnie said, smiling through her tears, before she turned and left the office.

Cal thought about how it had been the threat to her life that got Leo into the shooting circumstance in the first place. But he had also come to the conclusion that whether or not that information should be shared, should be left for Leo to decide.

The discussion returned to making plans as to when, and how, to visit the Silver Prince Mine.

Denver General Hospital

Leo had been shot twice, once in the side and once in his shoulder. Fortunately none of his vital organs had been hit, and it was just a matter of extracting the bullets and giving him liquids to help him recover from the blood loss.

He had been told that he would be released today and now he was lying in bed, anxious for the doctor to come in and give him the final word, when there was a light knock at the door.

"Yes, come in!" he called, thinking it was the doctor.

"Hello, Leo," Sally said, stepping into his room.

"Oh, Miss Sally. I thought it was the doctor, come to let me go."

"He'll be here shortly. I just talked to him. But there is someone else here to see you."

"Cal? Sure, tell him to come on in."

"Not Cal," Sally said mysteriously.

Sally turned toward the door and crooked her finger.

"Nonnie!" Leo said, shocked to see his unexpected visitor.

"I brought you some cookies from our shop," Nonnie said. "I hope you don't mind that I came to visit."

"Mind? Nonnie, your visiting me is the greatest thing that could have happened to me! I'm very, very happy that you came. But, how did you know?"

"Everybody knows," Nonnie said with a sweet smile.

"Everybody?"

"Yes, everybody. You're a hero, Leo. Didn't you know that?" Nonnie asked.

"Wow," Leo replied. "I didn't know that. I ain't never . . ." Leo paused, then glanced over at Sally. "I mean, I haven't ever been a hero before."

Across town from Denver General Hospital, Angus Williams was in Governor Pitkin's office. Williams had just given Governor Pitkin the letter from Governor Crittenden of Missouri.

Governor Pitkin read the letter, then leaned back in his chair and put his hand to his forehead.

"I also have the extradition request with me," Williams said.

"How do you know, for sure, that Sheriff Carson is the same man mentioned in this letter?" Governor Pitkin asked. "I must know half a dozen men named Carson. It's quite a common name, you know."

"If I see Sheriff Carson, I will know immediately if it is Jerry Carson."

"Jerry?"

"He went by the name Jerry, until he escaped jail."

"And you know him?"

"Yes, Governor, I know him quite well." Williams handed the governor the request for extradition.

"This is all very disconcerting, Mr. Williams. I'm sure you are aware that Sheriff Carson is seeking a seat in the United States Senate. And now you tell me that he is an escaped, convicted, and condemned murderer."

"I am telling you that, yes, Governor."

"You can understand, I hope, that this is all very difficult for me to believe. Sheriff Carson's service as a lawman has been exemplary. And the support for his campaign for Senate has reached a degree to where I think it is inevitable that he will be voted on, favorably, by our general assembly."

"Look at it this way, Governor. If indeed your senatorial candidate, your Sheriff Carson, is the man I'm seeking, then I am helping Colorado avoid the extreme embarrassment of making a convicted murderer a member of the most exalted deliberative body in the entire world, the United States Senate."

Governor Pitkin nodded, barely making enough motion with his head to be noticed. He put his hand on the extradition request and slid it back across the table.

"You hang on to this," the governor said.

"Governor Pitkin!" Williams said, shocked to see the governor dismiss the document out of hand.

Governor Pitkin held up his hand to stop Williams's reply in midprotest.

"Hear me out," Pitkin said. "I want you to go see Sheriff Carson. If he is the same Carson you are looking for, then place him under arrest and notify me by telegram. I will grant the extradition at that time."

"Thank you, Governor."

"You may have some difficulty in locating him, because he is campaigning and there is no way of telling where he might be on any given day. But you might start your search in . . ."

"Big Rock," Williams said, completing the governor's sentence for him.

CHAPTER THIRTY-FOUR

Onboard the train to Big Rock

Sally bought tickets for Leo and herself on the Wagner parlor car and upgraded Nonnie's ticket so that she, too, could ride back to Big Rock with them. The parlor car had large, individual chairs that were comfortably stuffed and could swivel and lean back.

The furnishings of the car resembled the furnishing of the finest living room, with mahogany panels, shining brass plates and fittings, and hanging crystal chandeliers, though as the trip would be made during the time of daylight, their purpose for the moment was decorative only.

Because of Leo's injury he, Sally, and Nonnie were allowed to board early. They found their seats and were deep in conversation when the other passengers boarded. They took no particular notice of the impeccably dressed man who was carrying a small, leather satchel.

As Angus Williams took his seat in the parlor car, he paid no attention to the two women and one young man who were aboard, except to notice that both of the women were very attractive, and the young man had apparently been injured in some way.

Pearlie and Cal met the train when it arrived in Big Rock.

"Well, now, Nonnie is with them. Isn't that a surprise?" Pearlie said.

"Are you really surprised?" Cal asked.

Pearlie chuckled. "No, now that you mention it, I don't suppose I'm that surprised after all."

Pearlie and Cal walked over to the three of them, immediately expressing their concern over Leo's wounds. And though they included Nonnie in their initial greetings, they made no further notice of her. It was Leo who stated the obvious.

"Guess what? Nonnie came all the way to Denver, just to visit me."

"Now, why in the world would she want to do that?" Cal teased.

Cal's teasing made Nonnie blush, and she spoke quickly to cover her embarrassment. "I'd better go see Mama. I left on the very early train this morning and didn't tell her I would be gone."

Sally said, "Oh, heavens, child, you shouldn't have left without letting her know. Perhaps you had better let me go with you. I'll do what I can to ease her concern."

"Come on, Leo, I'll help you back to the office," Cal offered.

With the departure of Sally, Nonnie, Cal, and Leo, Pearlie was left alone. He studied the others who were milling around on the depot platform, those who had just arrived, those who were departing, and the others who had just come to meet the train.

He saw someone coming toward him, taking notice of him because of the way he was dressed. He was wearing a three-piece suit, tie, and bowler hat. As the man approached, he touched the brim of his hat.

"I see by your badge, sir, that you are a deputy. Would this position be in service to Sheriff Jerry Carson?"

"You mean Monte Carson?"

"Monte Carson, yes," the man said.

"Yes, I'm a deputy for Sheriff Carson. But I'm not his real deputy, I'm just sort of filling in for him, because he's running for the United States Senate."

"So I have heard. My name is Angus Williams. Jerry and I are old, childhood friends from Missouri."

Pearlie smiled. "Missouri, yes. That's where Monte is from, all right. But why are you calling him Jerry?"

"I'm sorry. His name is Monte Jerome Carson, but when we were growing up together, everyone called him Jerry. Where might I find him, if I may ask?"

"Well, you just missed him, Mr. Williams. Not more'n ten minutes ago he 'n Smoke left to visit with some folks at the Silver Prince Mine."

"Where is this mine?"

"It's about twelve miles north of here."

"Is there a place where I can rent a horse?"

"Yes, sir, down at the livery," Pearlie said, pointing.

Silver Prince Mine office
Mount St. John, Colorado

Rex Underhill stood at the window looking out over Frying Pan River and the work area of the mine.

There was a great deal of activity as miners were bringing cars loaded with rock and ore up from one of the three tunnels.

"How are you going to get them down into the tunnel?" Underhill asked.

"They're coming to tour the mine, so I'm going to have Moe Morris take them down into the Number One Tunnel," Jaco answered. "It's all played out anyway, and the way I have it set up, the charge will collapse the tunnel."

"Trapping Carson in the tunnel?"

"And Jensen," Jaco added with a satisfied smile.

"All I can say is, it had better work this time. I've tried two times before with people who guaranteed they could get the job done. Priest was killed by a deputy who wasn't much more than a boy, and Shardeen was killed by a woman. It seems like no matter what I try, I have been thwarted at every turn."

"Yes, well, let's see how they deal with one hundred tons of rock," Jaco said with a little chuckle.

"What about your man, Moe Morris? How will he get away from the others without arousing their suspicion?"

"He won't."

"What do you mean, 'he won't'?"

"Look, we can't just send them down in there, then blow up the tunnel. How could we explain that? It has to look like an accident. The charge will be a routine charge, to take down some ore from the Number Two Tunnel. But the way I have it set, that same charge will collapse the Number One with Carson, Jensen, and Morris in it. With one of my own men in there, it will reinforce the idea that the explosion is an accident. And Morris is expendable."

Underhill grinned. "I take it you picked Morris for a reason?"

"Yeah, the son of a bitch has been talking to some of the others about organizing."

"Here they come," Underhill said. "I had better not be seen."

"Step out back and go into the equipment shed," Jaco suggested. "I'll go out to meet them."

"This is a busy place," Monte said, and he and Smoke dismounted.

The mining complex consisted of several various-sized buildings of unpainted wood. Narrow-gauge tracks emerged from the mouth of three tunnel openings, and at least a dozen men were at work, moving carts on the tracks from the mine openings to a group of men who were using sledgehammers to break the large rocks into smaller rocks, then to the crusher, where a puffing steam engine was making the rocks even smaller. The smelter was also at work as smoke from the fire drifted over the area.

A big, bald-headed man emerged from one of the buildings and approached Smoke and Monte.

"Sheriff Carson?"

"I'm Monte Carson."

"Al Jaco," the man said, extending his hand. "And you must be Smoke Jensen."

"I am."

"Welcome to the Silver Prince Mine. I've arranged for one of my men to take you down into Tunnel Number One. We aren't working it today, so none of the miners will get in your way."

Smoke chuckled. "And more importantly, we won't get in their way, right?"

Jaco smiled and nodded. "I'm afraid you caught me there. But as I'm sure you can understand, we are a working mine and it would be very costly to shut down the operation, even for a few hours."

"Believe me, we do understand," Monte said. "And I very much appreciate the invitation."

"All right, as soon as I get you set up with miner's lamps so you can see where you are going, I'll have my man, Morris, take you down into the tunnel."

A couple of minutes later a short, bandy-legged man with a short scraggly beard and a scar, like a purple lightning bolt from the side of his eye down to his chin, came toward them carrying a couple of strap-mounted lanterns.

"My name is Moe Morris, 'n I'll be takin' you fellers into the mine. Put these around your head," he said. "When we get down into the tunnel we'll light 'em up so's we can see where we're a-goin', on account of without 'em, it's dark as a tomb."

Smoke and Monte fitted the lanterns, then followed Morris into the tunnel opening.

Just as Smoke and Monte were following Morris into the tunnel, Angus Williams arrived. The three-piece suit he was wearing drew the attention of several of the working miners. The one nearest Williams approached him.

"Mister, are you sure you are in the right place?" the miner asked, leaning on the sledgehammer he had been using.

"I believe that I am," Williams said. "Is this the Silver Prince Mine?"

"Yeah, it is."

"I was told that Jer . . . that is, Sheriff Monte Carson was here. Is that so?"

"Yeah, he's here. You just missed him, he went into Number One."

"Number One?"

"Number One Tunnel, that one," the miner said, pointing.

Williams started toward the tunnel.

"Mister, you ain't goin' to be able to see nothin' by the time you're a hunnert feet into the mine, it'll be too dark."

"Rusty, the way this feller is dressed, he could carry a low light," one of the men suggested.

"Come on, Clyde, you know damn well there ain't none o' the supervisors goin' to give him a low light," Rusty replied.

Low light, in miner's parlance, referred to the fact that the supervisors didn't wear a lantern on their head, because they didn't need to keep their hands free for manual labor. When they went down into the mine on an inspection tour, they carried a lantern, giving indication to the miners that a "low light" was coming, and thus everyone should look busy.

"Tell you what, mister. If you hurry, you'll more'n likely be able to see the lights of them that's just gone in," one of the other miners suggested.

"Thank you," Williams said. "That's just what I'll do."

"Hey, Rusty, oughtn't he better check in with the office afore he goes in there?" Clyde asked.

"That ain't our problem," he said as he picked up a sledgehammer and started breaking up some of the rocks preparatory to introducing them to the crusher.

"Ha! You got that right," Clyde said. He put his hand on the back of one of the ore carts holding some of the rock already reduced, and started it toward the crusher mill.

Jaco had stepped back to the equipment shed as soon as he saw Morris lead the two men into the tunnel.

"They're here, and they've gone down inside," Jaco called out to Underhill. "Come on back into the office, we can watch through the window."

"Will we be able to tell when it has happened?" Underhill asked as he abandoned the equipment shed for the headquarters' office.

"Yes, we'll hear the explosion, that's for sure."

"Will we see the smoke?"

"Maybe a little smoke from Tunnel Number Two," Jaco replied. "But about the only thing we really want to see from Number One is dust as it collapses."

Underhill nodded. "Good for you, Al, you're going to get this done. It's going to cost me five thousand dollars, but it will be worth it." Underhill smiled. "Hell, I'll be able to make that up from the railroads, within my first month in the office."

"How about a drink to celebrate?" Jaco suggested.

"We'll celebrate after we hear the explosion and know that we have them trapped," Underhill said. "But a cup of coffee will be fine while we're waiting."

Jaco poured two cups of coffee and brought one over to Underhill, just as there was a knock on the door.

"Yeah, come in!" Jaco shouted.

Rusty Cope stepped inside.

"Yes, Cope, what is it?"

"I just thought I'd tell you about that feller that went down into the mine."

"Yes, we know about them, that's why I sent Morris along to guide them," Jaco said.

"No, sir, I ain't talkin' about them. I'm talkin' about that real fancy-dressed feller that went down into the mine after 'em, 'cause he wanted to talk to Sheriff Carson."

Jaco and Underhill looked at each other.

"What do you think we should do?" Underhill asked.

"Nothing," Jaco replied. "It's too late now."

CHAPTER THIRTY-FIVE

"You men wait for me!"

The shout had an echo to it, and Smoke turned to look back into the darkness behind them.

"That's funny," Morris said. "Whoever that is that's a-comin', ain't got 'im no light, high or low."

The three men waited until a figure appeared from the darkness. Monte gasped.

"Angus?" he questioned.

"Hello, Jerry," Williams replied.

"What are you doing here?"

"I'm sure you know what I'm doing here. You are an escaped prisoner."

Monte shook his head. "Are you insane? You've come to take me back? You aren't even armed."

"I don't have to take you back," Williams said. "I've already served extradition papers and shown a Missouri warrant for your arrest to Governor Pitkin. Now that I've found you, all I have to do is identify you to the governor, and he will make the arrangements for you to go back."

"Monte, do you know this man?" Smoke asked.

"Yeah," Monte said in a quiet, almost resigned voice. "I know him. His name is Angus Williams."

"Tell him how you know me, Jerry. Tell him how you murdered my brother, someone who had been your friend for your entire life."

"How much of a friend could he have been when he killed my wife and my father?"

"That was war, and terrible things happen during the war," Williams replied. "There was no war going when you murdered my brother. That's why you were tried, convicted, and sentenced to hang. And I intend to see that the sentence is carried out."

"Mr. Williams, Monte Carson is my friend," Smoke said. "Do you really think I'm going to let you just come in here and take him back to Missouri?"

"It's as I told Jerry, Mr. Jensen. I have served the warrant and the extradition papers to Governor Pitkin. He will see to it that Monte J. Carson is returned to Missouri."

Back in the mine office, Underhill had just finished his coffee when he heard, and felt, a loud, stomach-shaking rumble. Smoke poured from Tunnel Number Two, while dust and a fine stone powder residue gushed from the mouth of Tunnel Number One.

"The explosion went off as planned," Jaco said with a broad smile. "We've got them trapped, and there is no way out."

"Now, Mr. Jaco, we can have that celebration drink," Underhill said, returning the smile.

Jaco had just poured drinks for them when there was a knock on the door and a shout from outside.

"Mr. Jaco! Mr. Jaco!"

Jaco walked unhurriedly to the door.

"Yes, Mr. Cope?"

"There's been an explosion and a mine collapse!" Rusty said.

"What are you talking about? You know we were going to bring down the south facade of Number Two. We've been making preparations for two days now. That's what you heard."

"Yes, sir, that may be, but me 'n some of the others seen a lot of dust 'n powder comin' out of One, 'n you know as well as we do, that means there was a collapse in One."

"Well, what if there was? We aren't working Number One anymore."

"But them men that went in! They're trapped in there!" Rusty said.

"Oh my God, you're right!" Jaco said, feigning concern. "Form a rescue team, quickly! We must see what we can do about getting them out of there!"

"Yes, sir, I'll get right on it," Rusty said, leaving the office to gather the others.

"You're planning to rescue them?" Underhill asked incredulously.

Jaco shook his head. "You needn't worry, there's a hundred tons of rock between the opening and where they are. Any rescue effort will never get to them."

"How do you know? Men can perform some unbelievable feats when they are sufficiently motivated, such as in a rescue effort."

"Trust me, they won't get through to Carson and Jensen, and in another minute or so, they won't even try."

By now the whistle was blowing a warning of the cave-in, and the miners were beginning to gather outside the mouth of Number One.

"Come with me, you'll see what I'm talking about," Jaco invited.

Afraid that yet another attempt to rid himself of Monte Carson was about to fail, Underhill followed Jaco outside. They joined the group of men who were gathered near the opening of Tunnel One, and Jaco held up his arms to get their attention.

"Men, there are three men trapped down inside and . . ."

"Four, Mr. Jaco," Clyde pointed out.

"Four? You mean another of our men, besides Morris, was with them?"

"No, sir, it warn't none o' our men. Who it was is, there was some real fancy-dressed feller that went down into the tunnel after Moe took them two in with him."

"All right, four. That's all the more reason . . ."

Jaco's exhortation to the others was suddenly interrupted by a low rumble, then more dust billowing from the tunnel opening.

"Boys," someone said. "That tunnel's still collapsin' 'n I ain't a-goin' into it," someone said.

"Me, neither," another added.

"But you heard what Mr. Jaco said. They's four men trapped down there," Rusty said.

"That may be so, but they's only one of 'em that's ourn, 'n I ain't goin' to go down there 'n get trapped my ownself."

"I'm afraid Collins is right, men," Jaco said. "I can't risk a dozen men for four men. It's just not worth it. I'm calling off any rescue attempt."

"You mean you're just goin' to leave 'em in there? They'll die if we don't go in there 'n get 'em," Rusty said.

"With this last collapse, who is to say that you would be able to get through to them anyway? And who is to say they were killed by the cave-in, anyway?" Jaco asked. "People die in mining accidents all the time. But I don't intend to have anyone else die in what is probably an impossible task. Just go on back to work now and . . . no, I tell you what. Out of respect for the men who were just trapped and more than likely killed, I'm going to close down the mine for today. Take the rest of the day off and just think about how lucky you are that none of you were trapped inside."

A few minutes later Underhill and Jaco were on their second celebratory drink.

"Do you see now what the ten thousand dollars was for?" Jaco asked. "This blast did as much damage to Tunnel Two as it did to Tunnel One, and it's going to cost me that much to clean it out and open it up again."

"As far as I'm concerned, Al, that was money well spent," Underhill said, holding up his drink in salute.

CHAPTER THIRTY-SIX

The thunder came from deep within the mountain, rolling frighteningly from the distant runs of the tunnel before stilling into an ominous quiet as dust and powder lifted by the concussion drifted through the tunnel.

"What the hell was that?" Williams asked, his voice reflecting his fear.

"Damn! We've had a mine collapse!" Morris said, the tone of his voice just as frightened as had been Williams's. "Come on, we've got to get out of here."

Morris started leading them back toward the mine opening when yet another rumble came echoing up through the canyon.

"Hold it, we can't go that way," Morris called. "Some of the tunnel is still fallin' in!"

"Are they blasting in here, Morris?" Smoke asked.

"No, sir," Morris replied. "Leastwise, they ain't supposed to be."

"Then why do I smell powder?"

"I don't know, but you're right, I can smell it, too," Monte said.

"I don't understand," Morris said. "I don't know

why anyone would set off a blast in here. We ain't minin' this tunnel, it's most all played out. There would be no reason to use the big powder in here."

"Unless someone wanted to trap us in here," Smoke said.

"My word, are you suggesting that someone might purposely want to trap us in here?" Williams asked.

"Think about it, Mr. Williams," Smoke said. "We were invited here to visit a working mine, but we were sent into a tunnel that isn't being worked. And even though it isn't being worked, someone set off an explosion. There can be only one reason for that. Someone wanted to kill us."

"Who would want to do something like that?"

"It's because of me, Angus," Monte said quietly. "This isn't the first attempt on my life since I declared for the Senate."

"So what you're sayin' is, somebody is willin' to kill all of us, just to kill you?" Morris asked.

"I've made a few enemies myself," Smoke said. "I guess someone figured they were getting a bargain, two for one."

"Yeah, only it's four for one, ain't it? I mean, with you 'n Sheriff Carson bein' the only real ones they was tryin' to get. Me 'n this here Williams feller just sort of got caught up in it."

"Are you sure you are just an innocent bystander?" Smoke asked.

"What do you mean?"

"Have you done anything to be on anyone's enemy list? If this was a planned explosion, whoever planned it had to know that our guide would be trapped as well. That being the case, I would think the guide ultimately chosen would be one whose getting killed would be a welcome aside."

"Damn, you're right," Morris said. "I have been trying to organize the men."

"I don't imagine Jaco was very pleased with you doing that, was he?" Smoke said.

"No, he wasn't, he got really . . . wait a minute! You're saying Jaco is doing this?"

"Actually, I expect Rex Underhill is doing this," Monte said. "Or, he is having it done. Jaco said in the letter he sent me, that he was supporting Rex Underhill. He said he just wanted to meet me, but now it looks as if his real motive was to get me here where it'd be easy for him to kill me."

"So then we are all targets."

"Except for Angus," Monte said. "Angus, old friend, it looks like you just showed up at the wrong place and at the wrong time."

"So it would appear," Williams said.

"Morris, how well do you know this shaft?" Smoke asked.

"Not all that well," Morris replied. "This was part of the old Trailback Mine, 'n it was closed whenever the state stopped all the minin' on Mount St. John. Then, when Mr. Jaco got it so's we could mine on the mountain again we didn't go back into this shaft, 'cause it was already played out."

"Monte, would you like to place a bet on who got the mountain opened for mining again?" Smoke asked.

"Not unless I can bet on Underhill."

"So now we have the motive," Smoke said. "Mr. Morris, is there any connection between this shaft and either of the two shafts that are still being worked?" Smoke asked.

"A crosscut, yeah!" Morris said. "There ain't none between this one 'n Number Two but they is one ahead, I seen it when I was lookin' around in here to see if there was any reason to start workin' this tunnel again. I ain't never really looked that close at it, but more'n likely it'll go to another old Trailback shaft, but if it does, I don't have no idea where it'll come out."

"It seems to me like we have no choice but to explore it and see where it will take us," Smoke suggested.

"How long will the light on these lanterns last?" Monte asked.

"We prob'ly got 'bout an hour 'n a half, maybe two hours, left on 'em," Morris said.

"What if it takes us longer than that?" Williams asked.

"All right, this is what we'll do," Smoke said. "Morris, you lead the way, with your lamp. Sheriff Carson and I will extinguish our lamps to save fuel. When your lamp goes dark, we'll give you one of ours."

"Yes, good idea," Monte said.

As Morris led the way, light from his head lantern cast a dim, golden glow on the hewn rock walls of the tunnel. Morris's lamp did nothing to illuminate the footing, though, and as they picked their way along the ore-car rails, they were always but one step away from stumbling.

After several minutes, Morris called out.

"Here it is! Here's the crosscut!"

There were no rails in the crosscut, because its only function was to provide a connection between parallel shafts. It was very narrow and considerably lower, so low that Smoke, who was the tallest of the four men, often had to duck his head.

After about an hour, the light sputtered, then went out, and suddenly everyone was plunged into a darkness that was so deep that when Smoke lifted his hand and held it so close that he could feel the heat of it, he still could not see it.

"Monte, give him your lantern," Smoke suggested.

A few seconds later a match was struck and the new lamp again lit the way.

Shortly after they got under way again, Williams cried out as he tripped and fell.

"Hold it!" Monte said as he knelt beside Williams. "Morris, shine your light down here."

Williams was in great pain as Monte and Smoke examined him.

"Where does it hurt?" Smoke asked.

"Here," Williams said, putting his hand down to his shin.

There was blood on the place Williams pointed out.

"That's funny," Monte said. "There's blood there, but there's no tear in the trouser leg. How'd he get cut?"

"This is goin' to hurt a bit," Smoke said. "But I need to pull your pants leg up to take a look."

"Go ahead," Williams said, his voice strained.

As carefully as he could, Smoke lifted the pants leg. He saw a bleeding wound and, beneath the wound, a prominent lump. He felt the lump, and Williams gasped.

"He's got a broken leg," Smoke said. "And the bone came through the skin."

"I don't see any bone," Monte said, looking at the wound by way of the lantern.

"It pulled back in, but believe me, it did penetrate the skin."

"We can't stay here 'n burn out our lantern. We're goin' to have to leave 'im," Morris said. "After we get out we can maybe come back with a stretcher or somethin'."

"No, please! Don't leave me alone in the dark!" Williams pleaded.

"Smoke, you and Morris go on. I'll stay here with him until you come back."

"No need for that," Smoke said. "We'll take him with us."

"How are you going to do that, when he can't walk?" Morris asked.

"I know how," Monte said. "Angus, do you remember when we were kids and used to carry each other piggyback?"

"I weigh a lot more now," Williams replied.

"That's all right, I'm a lot stronger."

With Smoke helping, Williams was able to get on Monte's back, though when he tried to position his legs, he cried out in pain.

They continued through the cross shaft for about half an hour until they reached a pile of rocks.

"This is the end of it," Williams said with resignation.

"No," Morris said. "This cross shaft wouldn't even be here if didn't connect to a tunnel on the other side. There's just been a rock slide, is all, 'n it don't even look all that solid. I think we can dig our way through without too much trouble."

Morris, Smoke, and Monte began moving the rocks. Even Williams was able to help, taking the rocks from them and tossing them behind.

"Feel that?" Smoke asked. "There's air coming through. That means the tunnel on the other side is open."

"Yes!" Monte said excitedly, and the three men redoubled their efforts. Finally, after an hour of digging, they were able to open a space that was just big enough for them to slither through, one at a time.

"Angus, you go through after Smoke. He can help you on that side, and I'll help on this side," Monte said.

"Why are you doing this?" Angus asked. "Why are you helping me? You know why I came."

"When we were kids, you were my best friend," Monte said. "Right now I'm just remembering that."

Because of his leg it was very painful for Williams to be half pulled and half shoved through the opening, but he made it through. Then, when they were in the other tunnel shaft, their luck changed for the better.

"Look over there," Morris said. "There's an old

ore car! We can put Williams in it 'n push him back to the surface!"

The sun was very low in the western horizon by the time the four men emerged from the opening of the abandoned mine tunnel.

"How far is it back to the Silver Prince?" Smoke asked.

Morris took a look around. "We're on Wahite Mountain. I'd say it's no more'n six miles or so back to the Silver Prince."

"There's no way I can go six miles, and I don't think you can carry me that far," Williams said.

"I could get a buckboard and come back," Smoke suggested.

"Yeah, well, I'll be goin' with you," Morris said. "I've got a few words I need to say to Jaco."

"I'll stay here with Angus," Monte offered.

Because Jaco had closed down operations for the day, there were very few workers still at the mining complex, most of them having gone to the small settlement of St. Johns at the foot of the mountain. Rusty Cope and Clyde Barnes were among the few who had remained and it was Clyde who pointed out the two men who were approaching on foot.

"Hey, Rusty! Ain't that Moe Morris?" Clyde said, calling attention to the two men.

"Yes, it is!" Rusty replied. "Where the hell did he come from? How did he get out of the mine?"

"I don't know, but there he is."

By now the others who were still at the mine had seen the two men and hurried out to greet them.

"Moe, damn! We thought you was kilt!"

"It sure is a happy thing to see you!"

"Yeah, well, it's happy to be out of there," Moe replied. "They's two more of 'em back at the old Trailback tunnel." He made a motion with his hand. "One of 'em's hurt 'n Jensen, here, will be needin' a wagon so's he can go back 'n get 'em."

"What do you mean, they are alive?" Jaco asked when Rusty brought him the news.

"They clumb out through the old Trailback tunnel," Rusty said. "Ain't that great?"

"They're still alive?" Underhill asked, repeating Jaco's earlier question.

"Yes, sir, they sure are, 'n Jensen 'n Moe is here, but Sheriff Carson 'n that feller that come to see 'em, is both of 'em back on Wahite Mountain at the Trailback tunnel entrance. They stayed back there on account of the fancy-dressed feller is hurt. Jensen wants to go back after 'em with a wagon. Clyde's fixin' 'im up with one now. That's all right, ain't it?"

"What?" Jaco asked, still stunned by the news.

"I asked if it's all right that Clyde gives Jensen a wagon so's he can go back 'n get Sheriff Carson 'n that injured feller 'n bring 'em back."

"Yes, that will be fine," Jaco said distractedly.

"All right, I'll go tell 'im to fix Jensen up."

"I can't believe they are still alive," Jaco said a moment later, after Rusty left the office.

"You said this was sure to take care of 'em," Underhill said.

Jaco pinched the bridge of his nose and shook his head. "Who would have thought they would be able to get out of there?"

"Am I never to get rid of Carson?" Underhill asked, his voice laced with frustration.

"There is an old saying that when you want something done right, do it yourself," Jaco said.

"What? What are you talking about?"

"I'm talking about us, you and me. We're going to take care of Jensen and Carson ourselves. And the man who is with them, whoever he is."

"Al, if you think I'm going to stand up against either Jensen or Carson in a gunfight, you are crazy. And you are even crazier if you do it yourself."

"Who said anything about standing up to them? I know this mountain like the back of my hand. The Trailback tunnel entrance is five thousand feet up the side of Wahite Mountain and the road from there to here is barely wide enough for a wagon. There are some turns that if you aren't careful you'll go right over the edge, and whoever is driving that wagon when they come back, is going to have their hands full, just trying to stay on the road."

"And that's your plan? To hope that they go over the edge of the road?" Underhill asked.

"No. My plan is to make *certain* that they go over the edge of the road."

* * *

"I'm not going to do it, Jerry," Williams said. The two men sat in the fading light as they waited near the mouth of the tunnel for Smoke to return.

"You aren't going to do what?" Monte asked.

Williams leaned forward and made a slight adjustment of the splint Monte had put on his leg. The splint consisted of pieces of wood Monte had been able to take from the bracing of the mine. He had used his and Williams's belts to hold it in place, and because the splint somewhat stabilized the break, Williams got some relief from the pain.

"I'm not going to take you back to Missouri to hang."

Monte chuckled. "Well, I'll tell you, Angus. That's just real nice to know."

"The truth is, you should never have been convicted in the first place. Reuben and the others shot at you before you shot at them. It was, clearly, self-defense."

"Yeah, well, you could have saved me a lot of trouble if you had said that during my trial."

"That was a long time ago, Jerry. I was young and angry. But I have a totally different perspective now."

"Because I saved your life?" Monte asked with an easy smile.

Williams laughed out loud. "Well, I admit, that does help tip the scales in your favor."

"Here comes Smoke," Monte said, noticing the wagon that was just now coming around the curve.

Monte stood to greet his friend as he arrived.

"I see you had no trouble getting the wagon."

"No trouble getting it, but it was hard getting it here. Only someone with a really good imagination would call this . . . footpath . . . a road. That's why I got a team of mules, I figured it will be easier for them to take us back than it would be for horses."

"You're probably right," Monte said. "But it's coming on full nighttime now. Are we going to try it in the dark?"

Smoke shook his head. "No, that would be foolish. We can spend the night comfortably here. I brought food and blankets for us. I also brought wrapping and some whiskey for Mr. Williams's leg."

"Whiskey for his leg?"

"To help clean the wound and to keep it from putrefying."

"Are you going to use the whole bottle, just for his leg?"

"Oh, I think there'll be some left for us. We'll start back at first light tomorrow morning."

CHAPTER THIRTY-SEVEN

Underhill and Jaco had come to Wahite Mountain, to a place Jaco identified only as the "Hairpin." They arrived just before sunrise and now the first light of morning illuminated the really sharp and very tight turn that gave this part of the road its name.

Jaco and Underhill were positioned about twenty feet above the road, hidden behind a granite finger that protruded from the side of the mountain. On the other side of the road there was a precipitate drop of several hundred feet, then the steep side of the mountain, which reached almost a mile farther down to the floor of the valley.

"Why don't we just shoot them and be done with it?" Underhill asked. "We've both got rifles; they won't even be able to see us from the road."

"Think about it, Underhill," Jaco said. "Bodies with bullet holes cause people to get suspicious. Bodies that wind up in a wrecked wagon that has tumbled a mile down the side of a mountain just mean that the driver was careless."

"Yeah," Underhill said. "Yeah, I see what you mean. So what are we going to do, shoot the team?"

"No, bullet holes in the mules would be the same thing, so when we start shooting, don't shoot to hit the mules, just shoot close by to scare them. I know those mules, we use them to draw up the ore cars, so they're used to being closed in. Out here in the open, they're going to be real skittish. They'll start running as soon as we start shooting, and Jensen or Carson, whoever is driving, won't be able to keep the wagon on the road."

"You're right," Underhill said. "If you want to get something done right, do it yourself."

"How are you doing back there, Mr. Williams?" Smoke asked. Smoke was driving, Monte was sitting beside him, and Williams was sitting up in the back of the wagon with his leg stretched out. The leg was now totally wrapped in bandages.

"I'll do fine as long as I don't have to get out and push."

Smoke laughed. "Wait a minute, Monte, you mean you didn't tell him about Gulliver's Hill?"

"I didn't want to worry him," Monte said, going along with the joke.

"I'll get out and push, as long as you're carrying me piggyback," Williams suggested.

"There it is, just ahead, that really tight turn I told you about," Smoke said. "This is the worst spot on the entire road, so if we get through this turn with no problem, we'll be just fine for the rest of the trip down."

"I've got an idea. Why don't I get out, walk in front of the team and just lead the mules around?" Monte suggested.

"You ought not to have any trouble doing that," Williams said from the back of the wagon. "As I recall, you had to do that with Rhoda half the time," he added with laugh.

"Rhoda?" Smoke asked.

"She was one of my pa's mules, and a more cantankerous critter was never born."

"You've got that right," Williams said.

"I'm surprised you remember her," Monte said.

"She kicked me in the side once. How am I going to forget her?"

"I guess you've got a point there," Monte replied as he climbed down from the wagon to grab the off mule by its harness.

"Come on, boy, let's walk around this curve very carefully."

Smoke was holding the reins loosely as he let Monte take full control of the team. Monte began walking them ahead.

"What the hell!" Underhill swore. "The son of a bitch isn't driving them, he's leading them!" Underhill stood up, raised the rifle to his shoulder, and aimed.

Smoke had no idea what caused him to look up. It may have been that when Underhill stood he cast an unexpected shadow. Or it may have been that the years Smoke had spent living on the edge of danger had provided him with an almost extrasensory peripheral vision.

"Monte!" Smoke shouted, shooting just a split second before Underhill did.

Underhill pitched forward. He dropped his rifle, then tumbled some twenty feet down the side of the mountain and onto the road, where his momentum carried him over the edge of the road for a long, long fall to the valley far below.

The mules tried to rear up and Monte had to fight them to keep them under control.

Almost immediately after those two shots there was another shot from behind the protruding granite finger, though from his position on the wagon seat Smoke couldn't see where the shot came from. He knew, however, that the shot had not been aimed at him or at Monte. By now, Monte had gotten the team back under control.

"Mr. Jensen!" someone called. Smoke recognized the voice as belonging to Moe Morris, the man who had led them out of the mine. "It's all right now, there won't be no more shootin'!"

"Monte, hold the team, I'm going to see what this is about," Smoke said. Hopping down from the wagon he started toward the granite wall.

When Smoke climbed up he saw Jaco lying dead and Moe Morris standing over him. Morris was still holding his gun.

"I overheard 'em talkin' 'bout this last night," Morris said. "I heard 'em plannin' on tryin' to make you go over the side of the road so I come up here 'n I waited on 'em. He's dead, 'tain't he?"

It didn't take much of an examination for Smoke to confirm Morris's observation.

"Yes, he's dead."

"I didn't plan on killin' 'im," Morris said. "What I

was goin' to do was just keep the two of 'em covered then give you a warnin'. But Mr. Underhill commenced a-shootin' 'n next thing you know I had to shoot Mr. Jaco to keep him from shootin' one o' you.

"You don't think this is goin' to get me in trouble, do you?"

"Mr. Morris, you just saved three lives. How is that going to get you in trouble?"

Sugarloaf Ranch, Christmas Day

The house was festooned with greenery and big red and gold ribbons. A large tree, which had been cut and decorated, now stood in the keeping room. A warm fire in the fireplace created a cozy atmosphere for those who had come to Sugarloaf to celebrate.

Monte Carson was there with his deputy, Leo Beajuex. Also present were Louis Longmont, Phil Clinton, as well as Nancy Kinder and her daughter, Nonnie. Nancy had brought pies and cakes to augment the roast beef dinner Sally had prepared.

"Where are Pearlie and Cal?" Phil asked. "I can't imagine them missing a Christmas dinner."

"They drove into town to pick up a guest who is arriving by train," Smoke said.

"It's beginning to snow, I hope it doesn't delay them for dinner," Louis said. "Or if it does, I hope we start without them," he added.

The others laughed.

"Monte, did you see Friday's newspaper?" Phil asked.

"You mean the one that said Tabor will be sworn in as senator on the twenty-seventh of January?"

"Yes. That could have been you, you know, if you hadn't gone to the capital and withdrawn your name."

"Monte not only withdrew his name, he is the one who asked Tabor to put his name in," Smoke said.

"Why didn't you stay in the race, Monte?"

"I am a convicted felon," Monte replied.

"Yes, but the request for extradition was withdrawn. You know nothing would have ever come from that. And there are very few people in the state who know that, anyway."

"It doesn't matter how many people know about it. I know about it," Monte said. "And I knew it when I first announced. I was living a lie, and I was cheating all those who were supporting me." He shook his head. "I don't want to live the lie anymore."

"Look at it on the bright side," Sally said. "We'll get to keep Monte with us, which means we'll still have the best sheriff in the entire state of Colorado."

"Hear! Hear!" Louis said, clapping his hands.

"Oh, here's Cal and the others," Leo said, looking through the window.

A moment later Pearlie, Cal, and Angus Williams came into the house. They stood just inside the door for a moment, brushing off the snow, then moved to the fireplace and stood there warming themselves.

"Hello, Angus. I'm glad you could come spend Christmas with us," Monte said.

"How's your leg, Mr. Williams?" Smoke asked.

"It's doing fine, thank you, no sign of a limp."

"Well, that's a good Christmas present," Sally said.

"Yes, ma'am, it is. And speaking of Christmas

presents, I have one of my own, and this seems as good a time as any to present it."

"Did you leave it in the carriage?" Leo asked. "If you did, I'll go out in the snow and get it for you."

"No, it's right here," Williams said. He reached into his jacket pocket, pulled out an envelope, then removed the paper inside. "If you don't mind, I'll read it to you."

Williams unfolded the page, then, holding it at the top and bottom, cleared his throat and began to read.

"I, Thomas Theodore Crittenden, governor of the state of Missouri, do hereby grant, by this pardon, full executive clemency to Monte Jerome Carson, absolving him of any and all crimes he may have previously committed within the borders of the state of Missouri."

"Angus! A full pardon?" Monte asked excitedly.

"You may not know this, my old friend," Angus said, "but I'm a pretty good lawyer."

"Thank you! You have no idea what a burden that has lifted!"

The others applauded.

Dinner was a happy affair, given not only the season, and the pardon, but also the fellowship of good friends.

"I have a present, too," Nonnie said, sharing her secret with Leo.

"Yes, a belt, and I'm already wearing it, see?" Leo said, displaying it proudly.

"No, I mean another present."

"Oh, Nonnie, no, I only got you a hairbrush, I didn't get you anything else."

"That's all right. We can give each other this present at the same time."

"I don't understand, how can we give each other a present at the same time?"

Nonnie flashed a big smile. "Come over here to the mistletoe, and I'll show you."

**Keep reading for a special excerpt of
the latest Western epic from
William W. and J. A. Johnstone!**

A JENSEN FAMILY CHRISTMAS

*The legendary members of the Jensen family gather together at
the Sugarloaf Ranch for one Christmas homecoming they'll
never forget—if they live through it . . .*

SMOKE JENSEN looks forward to spending a quiet
holiday with the family. But an unexpected arrival from
south of the border has him reaching for his guns,
defending his land—and risking everything he loves . . .

SALLY JENSEN strikes up a friendship with a lovely
Mexican woman—who turns out to be married to the
mysterious stranger plotting to steal her ranch . . .

ACE and CHANCE prepare to fight a gang of outlaws
trying to kill the man who raised them—but they're
going to need the help of the father they never knew . . .

LUKE JENSEN rescues three young children orphaned
in a shoot-out—and heads home for a surprise
reunion with children of his own . . .

PREACHER catches the eye of a beautiful and beguiling
widow—but he can't decide if she wants to
marry him, kill him, or both . . .

*Every Christmas season, the Jensens pray for peace on earth.
But then, for the Jensen family, danger is just
another holiday tradition.*

**Look for A JENSEN FAMILY CHRISTMAS,
on sale now wherever books are sold.**

The Sugarloaf Ranch, Colorado, 1902

Nobody thought about Christmas on the hottest day of the year.

Denise Nicole Jensen wore a man's butternut shirt with the sleeves rolled up over tanned, smoothly muscled forearms. After reining her horse to a halt, she lifted her left hand and removed the brown Stetson she wore. Thick, curly blond hair that had been tucked up inside the hat tumbled free around her shoulders.

With her right arm, she sleeved beads of sweat from her face and said, "Well, hell."

If Sally Jensen had been here, she would have reminded her daughter that ladies didn't curse, but Denny's mother was miles away, at the headquarters of the vast Sugarloaf Ranch. And Denny was disgusted at the sight that met her eyes when she topped the rise, so she believed a little cussin' was justified.

She might do even more of it before she was finished here.

She suspected the calf had wandered into the

mudhole first and had got stuck, and then the mama cow had responded to her baby's bawls for help, had waded out there, and had got bogged down, too.

The calf was in the most danger of being sucked under, so Denny knew she needed to go after it first. She gathered up her hair with her right hand and stuffed it back under the hat. Then she unhooked the coil of rope from her saddle and started shaking out a loop as she nudged her mount down the slope.

Her mother wasn't particularly fond of Denny dressing like a man, riding the range, and working like one of the Sugarloaf's regular cowboys, either, but Denny had an argument in her favor that was hard for Sally to dispute: Sally had done much the same thing when she and her husband, Smoke, Denny's father, had established the ranch here in Colorado's high country a quarter of a century earlier.

Denny rode to the edge of the mudhole, which was about thirty feet across. Both the cow and the calf were still struggling and bawling. Those pathetic cries were what had attracted Denny's attention in the first place.

She swung the loop over her head a couple of times and then cast the rope at the calf. Over the years, Denny had spent a lot of time practicing with a lasso, even when she was staying with relatives in Europe. The loop sailed out and settled flawlessly over the calf's head.

Denny jerked it closed with a flick of her wrist, then took a dally around the saddle horn and started backing her horse. She couldn't pull too hard, because she didn't want to choke the calf. The extra support from the taut rope allowed the calf to get better footing and make some progress toward the edge of the mudhole. Denny continued backing her horse to keep any slack out of the rope.

A few minutes later, with a sucking sound, the calf broke free of the mud. The thick brown gunk coated the critter's legs, belly, and chest.

Denny dismounted and went over to take the rope off the calf's neck. She rubbed its nose and said, "There you go. Now I'll get your mama out of—"

Free again, the calf turned and lunged right back toward the mudhole, obviously intent on reaching its mother.

Denny's eyes widened in surprise. She exclaimed, "You little bast—" as she threw herself toward the calf and grabbed it around the neck to try to stop it from getting right back into trouble.

The calf was strong and jerked Denny off her feet. She managed to hang on for several seconds before her hands and arms slipped on the mud-slick hide. The calf had pulled her into the mudhole, so when she lost her grip and fell, she landed face-first in the smelly stuff.

Gagging and gasping, she pushed herself up before the mud filled her nose and mouth, although it covered her face and the front of her body. She wasn't far into the mudhole, so she was able to turn herself around, crawl out, and flop down on the grass next to it.

Meanwhile, the calf promptly got bogged down again and started complaining.

Denny lay there for several minutes, too disgusted by this turn of events even to move. Then she sat up, pawed mud away from her eyes, and started blistering the air with a blue streak of curses that would have shocked any of her father's ranch hands but made them proud of her inventiveness.

The sound of delighted laughter from the top of the rise behind her made her fall silent.

Denny remained seated on the grass but half turned so she could look up the slope. The sight of her mud-masked face drew renewed gales of laughter from the three men on horseback who sat there looking at her.

"What the hell's so funny?" she demanded.

Her twin brother, Louis Arthur Jensen, wiped tears from his eyes and grinned as he said, "I was . . . I was just thinking that if all those dukes and counts who tried to romance you over in Europe could see you now, they wouldn't be so quick to try to seduce you!"

"You just shut up, Louis."

The two men with Louis were also twins, although the resemblance between them wasn't nearly as pronounced as it was between the younger siblings. William "Ace" Jensen was dark haired and broad shouldered, while Benjamin "Chance" Jensen was slender and had sandy hair. They were forty years old, almost two decades older than their cousins.

Ace studied the scene briefly with keen eyes and said, "What happened, Denny? You pulled that calf out, and then it ran right back in and pulled you with it?"

"That's right," Denny said. She struggled to her feet, a filthy, bedraggled figure now. "Maybe I'll just shoot both brutes and be done with it."

"No you won't," Louis said. "You'd never harm a defenseless animal, and you know it."

Denny's eyes narrowed as she said, "Maybe I'll just shoot me a laughing hyena instead."

Ace heeled his horse into motion. "Come on, Chance," he said. "Let's drag those cows out of there."

Chance said, "Do I look like a cowboy to you?"

It was true. In his brown suit, white shirt, string tie, and cream-colored Stetson, he wasn't dressed for range work. Chance's natural habitat was saloons, where he excelled as a poker player. From time to time, he and Ace took jobs—usually something that involved guns and trouble—but it was mostly Chance's skill with the pasteboards that supported their drifting ways.

"All right, I'll take care of it," Ace said.

While Louis and Chance rode down and dismounted to stand with Denny on the mudhole's bank, Ace shook out a loop and dabbed it on the calf first. When he had pulled the calf to safety, he snubbed the rope shorter and dismounted, leaving his horse to stand and prevent the calf from returning to the mudhole.

Then he swung up into the saddle of Denny's mount and used her lasso, which was still wrapped around the saddle horn, to catch the mama cow's horns and gradually work her out of the mudhole. Ace could have been a top hand if he'd wanted to be, so it didn't really take him long to rescue the two animals.

He turned them loose and sent them trotting off, then started coiling the ropes.

"Don't feel bad, Denny," he told his young cousin. "You would have gotten them out."

"Sooner or later," Louis added, earning himself another glare from his sister. "You know, I believe there's almost as much mud on you as there is in that bog."

Chance picked up Denny's Stetson, which had fallen on the grass when the calf jerked her off her feet.

"Your hat's all right," he said. "I suppose that's something to be thankful for, anyway."

Denny snatched it away from him and hung it on her saddle horn.

"There's a swimming hole in the creek about half a mile from here," she said. "I'm going to go wash this mud off." The hot sun would dry her clothes and hair quickly enough, she thought. "Mother doesn't have to know about this . . . debacle."

"We'll come with you," Ace said.

"You most certainly will not!" Denny's face flushed warmly.

"We'll keep our backs turned," Louis said. "Nobody's interested in peeking at a scrawny little thing like you, anyway."

"We'll sort of stand guard while you clean up, in case some other riders come along," Ace said. "Just cousins helping each other out."

"All right. I suppose." Denny took hold of her horse's reins but didn't mount. She didn't want to get mud all over the saddle. Instead, she began walking, leading the horse.

Her brother and cousins came with her, leading their mounts, as well.

Rocks in the creek had formed a partial dam, creating a natural swimming hole. Trees on the bank shaded it, giving it a cool, appealing look even on a blistering hot day like this one. Louis, Ace, and Chance sat on a fallen log, with their backs to the swimming hole, as Denny waded into it and then dived under the surface. When she came up, she began taking off the soaked, muddy garments so she could wash them out.

"As filthy as Denny was, it may take a while for her to get clean," Louis said. "We'll have to pass the time somehow. Have the two of you had any new adventures since you last visited the Sugarloaf?"

"Adventures? Us?" Chance scoffed. "You know things are always peaceful wherever we go."

Ace said, "Actually, we haven't run into any trouble for a while. Life's been downright tranquil."

"That's hard to believe," Louis said. "Trouble always seems to follow anyone named Jensen."

"We got that idea, even before we knew we were part of this family," Ace said.

Denny could hear them from where she was in the swimming hole, so as she scrubbed mud out of her shirt, she said, "That's right. The first few times you got mixed up with our father and Uncle Luke, you didn't know yet that you were related, did you?"

"No idea," Chance said. "We just thought we had the same last name."

"We started to get a mite suspicious, though," Ace said, "when Luke mentioned he'd known a woman with the same first name as our mother. And it wasn't a common name, either. Lettie."

Chance said, "I figured Ace was just thinking too much. He's got a habit of doing that. Of course, in this case, it turned out he was right. Your uncle Luke really *was* our father."

"How did you finally find out?" Louis asked. "I don't think I've ever heard that story."

"Neither have I," Denny said. "I'd like to know."

"It's a long story," Ace warned. "It'll take a while to tell."

"We have the time," Louis said, "and nothing else to do while Denny tries to get all that mud off."

"I'm working on it!" Denny said defensively from the swimming hole behind them.

Ace thumbed back his black hat and said, "Well, this was more than fifteen years ago when it all got started, and the weather sure wasn't as hot as it is right now. In fact, Christmas was coming on, which means it was mighty cold here in this part of Colorado . . ."

CHAPTER ONE

Big Rock, Colorado

The blue sky was so clear, it almost glittered, but the sunshine didn't pack much warmth as a cold breeze swept along the streets of Big Rock, Colorado. Smoke Jensen's wife, Sally, had insisted on pulling the thick lap robe over his legs, too, as they rode in the buggy to town, and if Smoke was being honest about it, he didn't really mind. The robe felt good.

She had said that he ought to wear his gloves, too, but he wasn't willing to go that far. A man couldn't draw and fire a gun as quickly when he had a glove on. Even though Smoke wasn't expecting any trouble in the settlement, he knew better than to run unnecessary risks.

Being careless wasn't how he had survived all the dangers that had come his way during more than three eventful decades of living on the frontier.

"You must be about frozen," he said to Sally as he drove toward the general store.

"Actually, I'm quite comfortable," she replied. She wore a fur hat with flaps that came down over her ears. A scarf was wound around her throat, leather gloves were on her hands, and the bulky fleece-lined coat she wore completely concealed the supple lines of her figure.

Despite all that, Smoke thought she was beautiful. He would always think she was the most beautiful woman he had ever seen.

"I still say Pearlie or Cal could have brought the buckboard in for those supplies you wanted."

"They have work to do," Sally said.

"And I don't?" Smoke asked with a snort. "I own the dang spread, after all. Well, we do."

"I'm glad you corrected yourself." Her voice was tart, but the smile she gave him took any sting out of it. "Anyway, I don't *know* exactly what I want. I have to think about it while I'm shopping to actually figure everything out. I need the makings for Christmas dinner, and even though we have decorations, we can always use more."

"I'm sure whatever you decide will be perfect."

"You're just saying that because you don't want to go shopping with me."

"No, I just have complete confidence in you," Smoke said with a smile.

Sally laughed and shook her head. She was still smiling when Smoke brought the buggy to a halt in front of Goldstein's Mercantile, where she would shop before visiting Foster and Matthews Grocery. He took the lap robe off of them, folded it, and placed it behind the seat. Then he jumped lithely to the ground and turned back to help her climb down from the vehicle.

Once Sally was on the ground, Smoke moved to tie the horse's reins to the hitchrack in front of the store. The horse was well trained and wouldn't bolt except in extreme conditions, but again, there was never any point in being careless.

"I'm going to say hello to Louis," Smoke told Sally, "but I should be back by the time you're finished at the grocery store. If I'm not, send somebody to find me."

Everyone in Big Rock knew Smoke Jensen. Although he would never get a swelled head about such a thing, he was the most famous citizen of the valley where the town and the Sugarloaf Ranch were located.

His fame extended well beyond those environs, too. Up in Idaho, for example, people still talked in awe about how he had killed more than two dozen gun-wolves in a bloody war against the men responsible for the deaths of his father, his first wife, and his unborn child.

There were plenty of other places where folks still remembered the man known variously as Kirby Jensen (his real name); Buck West, the wanted outlaw; and Smoke Jensen (the name most knew him by). For a short period of time after he and Sally had founded the Sugarloaf and settled down there, he had attempted to live anonymously, in the hope that he could put his reputation as maybe the fastest gun in the West behind him for good.

That hadn't worked, of course. Few men could deny their true nature for very long, and Smoke's nature was to battle against evil wherever he found it. So he hadn't tried to keep who he was a secret any longer, but he *had* made a determined effort to live his life as a peaceful, happily married rancher.

Sometimes that had worked. Sometimes it hadn't.

And despite his best intentions, the legend of Smoke Jensen had grown.

The town itself was part of that legend. It had been founded as a result of Smoke's clash with a power-hungry man determined to rule this part of the state by blood and gun smoke and any other means necessary. But that man had long since gone under, Smoke was still here, and Big Rock was thriving.

So it was no surprise that folks nodded and smiled at him as he left Sally at the store and walked along the street. Men shook his hand and slapped him on the back. Smoke had a grin and a friendly word for all of them.

At first glance, especially in the sheepskin coat he wore, he didn't seem that impressive a figure. He was just a man in the prime of life, with a face a little too rugged to be considered classically handsome, and ash blond hair under a brown Stetson.

A second look, though, revealed how wide his shoulders were, and when you watched him move, you could see the leashed power and easy grace of the man. He was like one of the big cats that could be found in the high mountains. He never seemed to rush, but he could be blindingly fast and deadly when he needed to be.

Today he was just bound for Longmont's, a combination saloon, restaurant, and gambling house run by his old friend Louis Longmont, where he intended to have a cup of coffee and invite Louis to come out to the Sugarloaf for Christmas the next week.

Louis stood at the bar in Longmont's, talking to the only bartender who was on duty. No customers were bellied up to the hardwood, drinking, but a number of the cloth-covered tables were occupied by diners enjoying a belated breakfast from the kitchen.

"Good morning, Smoke," the dapper, dark-haired gambler and gunman greeted his old friend. "What brings you to Big Rock this morning?"

"Sally needed some things from the store," Smoke said.

"Ah, the best reason of all, making sure your beautiful wife is happy."

"I notice that you're not married," Smoke pointed out.

"Well . . . what's best for one man may not be for another." Louis changed the subject. "Would you like a drink?"

"No, but I'd take a cup of hot coffee. I could use a little warming up after the buggy ride into town."

The temperature was comfortable inside Longmont's, with fires burning in two potbellied stoves tucked into opposite corners, not to mention the heat that filtered out into the main room from the ovens in the kitchen. Despite that, Smoke was still a little chilled inside, but he knew the coffee would take care of that.

"I'll get it, boss," the bartender offered.

"Thanks, Wiley," Louis said. To Smoke, he went on, "Shall we sit down?"

"I've been sitting on the ride in. Feels good to stand for a while." Smoke paused. "You have any plans for celebrating Christmas?"

"I assume I'll be here. People who don't have families need somewhere to go on Christmas, so they won't be alone."

"Well, you *have* a family . . . Sally and me, and

Pearlie and Cal and all the other folks on the Sugar-loaf. You have folks working for you who can keep the place going just fine, so why don't you ride out and spend Christmas Day with us?"

"Why, Smoke, I'm touched," Louis said. "I wouldn't want to intrude—"

"I just told you, we consider you a member of the family."

Louis smiled and said, "In that case, I'd be glad to—"

The bartender, who was carrying the cup of coffee from the kitchen door to the bar, stopped short as he looked out the front window. He said, "What in blazes?"

That caught the attention of Smoke and Louis, who followed the bartender's gaze and saw several fancy carriages and a number of riders moving past in the street outside.

"Is it a parade?" Louis murmured.

"More like a caravan of some sort," Smoke said. He stepped over to the bartender and took the cup from the man, nodding his thanks, then said to Louis, "Let's go take a look."

He strode to the door and opened it, letting cold air gust in for a moment. He stepped out onto the boardwalk, and Louis followed quickly, closing the door behind him.

Because of the chilly day, steam curled thickly from the coffee as Smoke lifted the cup to his lips and sipped from it. The hot liquid was strong and bracing. He had unbuttoned his coat when he went into Longmont's, and he didn't bother fastening it again just yet.

Louis stuck his hands in his trouser pockets to keep

them warm and said, "They appear to be strangers to Big Rock."

"I've never seen 'em before, that's for sure," Smoke said.

Four good-sized black carriages decorated with silver and brass trim were passing Longmont's. Each carriage was pulled by a team of four fine black horses. Their harnesses were also adorned with silver fittings. The drivers were Mexican and wore flat-crowned hats instead of the tall sombreros common below the border. As Smoke and Louis watched, the last carriage in line pulled out of the procession and stopped in front of Goldstein's Mercantile, where Smoke had left Sally a short time earlier.

Smoke made a quick count and determined that twenty men on horseback accompanied the carriages. They were about evenly divided between Mexicans and Americans, but they all had a couple of things in common.

They were heavily armed, and their weapons and their hardplaned faces marked them as hired gunmen, a breed with which Smoke was all too familiar.

"To quote my bartender," Louis muttered as he stood beside Smoke on the boardwalk, "what in blazes?"

Several of the riders cast flinty glances toward the two men on the boardwalk as they rode past. Not looking for trouble, exactly, but checking to see if any signs of it were brewing. Smoke returned the looks steadily.

"Looks like they're headed for the sheriff's office," he commented.

It was true. The first carriage pulled up in front of

the stone and log building that housed Sheriff Monte Carson's office as well as Big Rock's jail. The driver hopped down from the box and hurried to open the door on the side of the carriage next to the boardwalk.

A man in a thick fur coat and flat-crowned black hat stepped out of the vehicle. Just as his right foot touched the ground, the team lurched forward a step for some reason. That made the carriage jerk, and the man getting out of it lost his balance and almost fell. He would have if the driver hadn't reacted quickly and caught hold of his arm to steady him.

Despite that bit of assistance, the man in the fur coat yanked his arm free and pushed the driver back a step. The driver had a braided leather quirt dangling from its strap around his left wrist. The man in the fur coat ripped it away from him, strode forward, and started slashing at the horses in the team. One of the riders who had dismounted caught hold of the leaders' harness so the team wouldn't bolt as the man in the fur coat continued striking them with the quirt. Clouds of steam from the animals' hot breath filled the air around them as they whinnied in pain.

"Oh, no," Louis said softly as he looked over at Smoke.

"If you don't mind, Louis," Smoke said tightly as he thrust the cup toward his friend, "hold my coffee for a minute."

Connect with

Visit us online at
KensingtonBooks.com
to read more from your favorite authors, see books
by series, view reading group guides, and more.

Join us on social media

for sneak peeks, chances to win books and prize packs,
and to share your thoughts with other readers.

facebook.com/kensingtonpublishing
twitter.com/kensingtonbooks

Tell us what you think!

To share your thoughts, submit a review,
or sign up for our eNewsletters, please visit:
KensingtonBooks.com/TellUs.